SELKIE DREAMS

SELKIE DREAMS

KRISTIN GLEESON

KNOX ROBINSON
PUBLISHING
LONDON • New York

KNOX ROBINSON
PUBLISHING

1205 London Road
London SW16 4UY
&
244 5th Avenue, Suite 1861
New York, NY 10001

Knox Robinson Publishing is a specialist, independent publisher of
historical fiction, historical romance and medieval fantasy.

A CIP catalogue record for this book is available from the British Library.

ISBN 978-1-908483-27-0

Manufactured in the United States of America, Australia and the United
Kingdom.

Visit our website to download free historical fiction, historical romance and
medieval fantasy eBooks by our authors. While there, purchase our novels
directly and earn loyalty points. Sign up for our newsletter and our free
books giveaway. Join our community to discuss history, romance and fantasy
with fans of each genre.

www.knoxrobinsonpublishing.com

To Dave,
for his continued faith in me

ACKNOWLEDGMENTS

This novel would not have been possible without the help and support of various people who include Carlo Gebler, Frances Kay, Karen Charlton, Karen Rile at the University of Pennsylvania, Kate, Jean, Eibhlín, Anne, Moon, Sandra and all the members of the Yarburgh Writer's Group and Gerry MacBride. Also various members of the authonomy website including Bradley, Simon, Julia and Ross deserve thanks too. I am especially indebted to Rosemary Carlton, formerly of the Sheldon Jackson Museum in Sitka, who unearthed obscure details for me and read the manuscript with a keen eye for historical accuracy. Any mistakes in that regard are my own.

THE SELKIE OF SULE SKERRIE

An earthly nurse sits and sings,
And aye she sings by lily wean
And little ken I my bairn's father,
Far less the land where he dwells in.
Then in steps he to her bed feet
And a grumbly guest I'm sure was he
Saying here am I they bairn's father
Although I be not comely.
I am a man upon the land
I am a selkie on the sea
And when I'm far and far frae land
My home it is in Sule Skerrie.
It was no ill for a maiden fair
It was no ill indeed quote she
That the great Selkie of Sule Skerrie
Should have come and brought a bairn to mek.
And he had ta'en a purse of gold
And he had placed i' upon her knee
Saying give to me my little young son
And take thee up thy nurse's fee.
And it shall come to pass on a summer's day
When the sun shines bright on every stone
I'll come and fetch my little young son
And teach him how to swim the foam.
And ye shall marry a proud gunner
And a right fine gunner I'm sure he'll be
And the very first shot that e'er he shoots
Will kill both my young son and me.

Alas, alas the maiden cried
This weary fate that's laiden me
And when she sobbed and when she sighed
Her tender heart did break in three.

THE MYTH

Mam was a selkie.

The words roll over and over in my mind, relentless like the waves that crash against the rugged shoreline telling their own story outside my window. Their story is part of my story. A story that begins and ends with Mam.

Mam was a selkie. She would wrap me in her arms, the smell of the wind fresh in her hair and the sea on her breath and skin. Cook would tell me the story, her ample chest constrained in her wide apron, down in the heat-soaked kitchen that was more hearth and home than any other part of our large house. As Cook spoke these magical phrases I would close my eyes, press the medallion Mam gave me to my cheek and conjure her. Her dark hair, full mouth and slight frame took form from her remembered scent and touch, while the medallion seared my fingers from the heat of the conjuring.

The medallion was so ancient no-one knew its origins. Mam placed it softly in my bedclothes, while I lay sleeping, all pink-cheeked and milky in my cot. I see her now, fingering the worn contours of the metal, tucking it beside my curled little fist, then kissing me lightly on my forehead. It was not a kiss goodbye; it was a promise to return. She rose from my side and headed out to the shore past the jutting rocks that broke the water. Her feet were bare and her nightdress was light and filmy. She returned to the sea, the water enveloping her like her very own seal skin, taking her home.

Cook evoked these selkie images whenever I sat with her in the kitchen; the smells of her crusty sweet breads and thick rich puddings cuddling me like the arms of my own mother.

'Tell me the story again, Cook,' I would ask. 'Please, oh please.'

Cook would smile and hand me a bit of bread or cake, her sturdy fingers dusted in flour, and tilt her head, just so for the telling. Behind her, Polly the kitchen maid, her round face red from chopping or slicing vegetables, halted with her knife poised in mid-air, keen to hear the tale. Dark-haired Annie, the parlour maid, slipped out an 'oh lah' and downed her tea tray. She would never miss a telling, no.

Audience assembled, Cook would begin. Her voice was at first a hum, feeling for the rhythms of the sea, while I sat, a boat on the waves of her tale.

'Ah, the selkie, they are rare creatures, so they are, Máire. Rare and wonderful, as anyone will tell you who has seen them on the moonlit midsummer's night when they come ashore.'

'Why do they come ashore?' I wanted no part omitted.

'It's the midsummer moon. It takes them, strong and powerful-like and fills them with such joy, such wonder at life. It's a joy they must dance, while the moon pushes them on so.

'But such joy brings danger too. The only way the selkie can dance their joy is to shed their skins. And shed them they do, for who can pass up such a chance to dance on two feet to the rhythm of all the world? It catches them up so, blood afire, spinning their limbs while they dance on. The night wanes and still they dance, their breath ragged, their voices hoarse from their shouts and cries.'

I could feel my seal blood then, it was like music moving and pulsing through my arms, down into feet that swayed and twirled me round and round.

'But at the first sign of morning light they must go. They must take up their skins once again and return to the sea, or be doomed for seven years upon the shore.'

'Was that what happened to my mam?'

'Aye, it was so. She loved to dance, did your mam. She came alive when she danced. Her feet were quick and lighter than air, like a fairy so. It was no wonder then she couldn't break away from the dance one midsummer's night. And her seal skin no good to her then, once the dawn came. Seven long years she must wait before she leaves.'

'Seven, why seven?' I would ask.

'Why, seven is the number that always is, Máire. It's the magic number, the right number.'

'What happened on the shore when the morning came?'

'It was a gentleman found her, after she'd tucked her skin away in a rock crevice. He saw her there, a naked child, wailing in sorrow, the loss so heavy upon her. He took her and made her his ward, a child of his own, him a widower with only grown babbies living far from his home.'

'Did she look like me, my mam, did she?'

'Your mam was a rare beauty, she was. And don't you look just like her. You all dark, slender and fey-like, loving the sea as she did. And your father, well he was taken away with her, like everyone else.' It was then I would visualize my mam; picture her round face with her large eyes, so deep and mysterious.

'Was she like the other ladies?'

'Ah no, Finuola was different, quiet, full of thoughts you could see in her eyes. He was fooled by that quietness, took it for shy and meek so. And he was in her spell.' Cook would shake her head. Polly, with cap askew over coarse red hair, would sigh and call me 'poor wee thing' and pat my head or stroke my arm with her dimpled hand. Annie, now seated, honoured the tale with her silence and only nodded. And then Cook would continue, explain the sealskin that drew her back, back to the sea and to her home.

'Your mam left because she had no choice. She went back to her seal folk. The seven years was gone, and the pull from the sea came over her, strong and forceful like. It's her true folk, the selkies, they called her home. But where was her skin? The skin that kept her warm, that took her dashing through the water, smooth like lightning. She searched the rock up and down the shore, but the moon would not wait, nor would her folk. So off she went, walking into the sea, deeper and deeper, 'til her folk came and took her away.'

I am a lass upon the land, but I'm a selkie on the sea.

Cook sang the words, her voice so heavy with tears.

Though I knew the tale well and would mouth it sometimes along with Cook, it was Cook who had to tell it, because she told it best. She'd been there.

I knew little more of my mam than those fragments and stories wrapped in Cook's layered words, spoken and sung in a lilting cadence so different from the clipped tones my father and his class used. I threaded my own wishes and thoughts around and through Cook's tales and songs and they brought comfort during my childhood, serving as my mother's arms, her sweet voice, and the affection of the sisters and brothers I never had. I pulled these thoughts close to me as I tried to listen for the seal blood that flowed in my body, to feel it course through my veins, as surely as I was marked out among the people who moved in my world of home and church; the seal blood that set me apart from the other children and pushed me to tell them about my mam. I knew they half believed me. Perhaps it was my tilted eyes, coloured velvet brown and long-lashed. Or my straight black hair, all thick and silken, refusing any ribbons, pins or combs.

I lived in the kitchen then, basking in Cook's presence while she stirred some pot for my father's business dinners or giggled with Polly and Annie while keeping out of sight of my stern father. Always Father, never Papa or Daddy, for he was a genteel Presbyterian. A true Ulsterman. A good businessman. He never spoke of my mother; it was a subject he avoided with studious care, my existence the only reminder of a brief moment of folly. Periodically he would peer closely at me, correct my grammar and pull my vowels away from common Irish to the modulated tones that befit a daughter of the empire.

In the summer I would comb the rocks, searching all the crevices for her sealskin, hands red raw and bleeding from the fierce desperation of my desires. I never found it.

By the time I reached womanhood and donned the corsets, shoes and bustle-laden petticoats befitting a good Protestant girl of prosperous Belfast, the tale had settled in me, become part of my story to myself, showed me who I was and who I was not.

Part I

CHAPTER ONE

Ireland, Autumn 1889

It was the minister's request that found Máire seated in a carriage next to his wife, Mrs Engelton, rattling her way to the homes of the mill workers, along brick-paved streets, past large houses with precisely measured gardens enclosed by wrought iron fences. This was the third time she'd made these visits with Mrs Engelton as part of the Ladies' Missionary Society and Mrs Engelton, like her husband, never seemed to tire of explaining the need.

'It's a particularly poor lot that we visit today, my dear. And prone to backsliding. We must help them in any way we can.'

Máire nodded, only half-listening. Outside, the light began to dim as the buildings rose higher and loomed closer.

'Some have come from the country and bring all their silly notions and backwards ideas with them. They've no idea of basic cleanliness.' Overcome for a moment at the thought of such depravity she fanned herself with her handkerchief. 'But we'll teach them. They'll be quick to learn, they're Protestants.'

The carriage halted. They could go no further through the rambling streets that crowded together like pilchards in a tin. With her baskets in tow Máire alighted from the carriage and followed Mrs Engelton up the narrow alley to the cluster of homes. Like Mrs Engelton she held her skirt at a height that allowed for the sewage-stained ground but maintained her dignity. They climbed various stairs, keeping away from the wet walls to knock on assorted scarred and battered doors. To each family, crammed along a dingy bed or bench in their dark and airless homes, Mrs Engelton explained their duty with great patience.

'A clean home is evidence of a clean heart. And God loves a clean heart.' With a flick of her handkerchief she emphasized her point. 'Before we give thanks to God and break bread we must clean our hands and faces, like so.' The handkerchief glided over her cheek and nose, then her hands, an ethereal linen wonder, delicate with scent.

Standing above them, Mrs Engelton continued to speak to the numb and speechless faces while Máire held the basket filled with promises and hope. Eyes watering, noses running, the families awaited this bounty, like they awaited everything in their lives of limited food, limited schooling, limited work, limited room, lives that created a sum of endless limitations.

The speeches made, the mission ladies' hand-stitched handkerchiefs distributed with the loaf of bread and jug of broth, Máire and Mrs Engelton departed.

It was after leaving one of the homes, as they walked back down the alley to the street that Máire heard the sound of a fiddle coming from a waste ground that contained the broken bits and rubbish from the homes around them. She stopped and stared at the group of people gathered round a small open fire. Shouting and clapping rang out, beating a rhythm to the tune that a man with wild black hair bowed out on his fiddle in lively abandon.

'Tinkers. They must have come for the fair. They have no place here.' Mrs Engelton tugged on Máire's arm. 'Come my dear. Those people are beyond redemption of any sort.'

Máire turned to go but the wild-haired man looked up and held her eyes for a moment, a moment filled with a song that took her to the sea, its spray salting her lips. She licked them slowly, as the rhythm of the music wended its way through her feet and up along her body, vibrating against her chest. She lifted her arm to reach out, but Mrs Engelton tugged it away, breaking the link and propelling her forward, to the next alley, to the next home on the list of those deserving bounty.

The music remained with Máire throughout that day. In the evening it followed her to the dinner table, filled the room, possessed her feet and seized her fingertips. Tap, tapping. It was only when her father frowned that her hand stilled. She murmured an apology.

'I hear good things about you from Mrs Engelton,' said Mr Compton, their sole dinner guest. He was her father's business partner who dined with them often. Too often, of late.

'Good things?'

'About your work with those indolent wretches near the factories.' He poked one of his potatoes with his fork, directing it towards the meat sauce. 'Such a fine example to the rest of us.' He fixed her with a rheumy look.

She sighed inwardly and shaped a smile. She could see his watch chain stretching across his prosperous waist, a single tiny key the only ornament that hung from its links. Not an ornament, she told herself, a tool. An item of use. There was little difference between him and her father, bar their size.

'You are too kind, Mr Compton,' she said with forced effort.

He patted his bulbous mouth with his napkin in one efficient motion. His carefully trimmed beard was devoid of all evidence of the cigars he so enjoyed. A preparation applied? She smiled at the thought and examined his thinning hair but was disappointed there was no trace of even that kind of weakness.

Mr Compton cleared his throat. 'My daughter could use a fine example such as you,' he said. 'She's become ungovernable since her mother died.'

She fought to suppress a surge of irritation. 'But she's only ten and motherless.' Why was she defending a child that past encounters had revealed to be mean-spirited? But she knew it was the loss of her mother. Nothing could make up for that.

'You've seen the matter to its core,' Mr Compton said. 'She does need someone to take her mother's place. Someone to take her in hand.'

'Yes, yes she does,' Máire said hastily. 'A good governess could easily solve the problem, or perhaps a different school.' She lowered her head in the hope that she could avoid further notice, but not before she saw the looks exchanged between Mr Compton and her father. She searched the men's faces in panic, hoping for some further clue that might tell her how this shift had occurred, when Mr Compton had formed these thoughts that she would never willingly place there herself. But there was nothing, and the music had fled; not even an echo remained of its beauty. Above the sideboard the mirror showed only three seated figures and the nearly finished meal on the table.

There could be no outburst, no excess of feeling. In a rush she excused herself and rose from the table, gathered her skirts with a practiced lift and left the gentlemen to their port before any unseemly emotion overtook her. With a quick step, she made her way to the drawing room, the room that ruled her evenings at home; a room whose windows gave no view to the world outside and little light to the world inside. It was a place of mourning, dead and drear of any emotion save those that could be gleaned from the books on religion, history and botany that lined the heavy old bookcase behind the door.

Máire sank into her customary chair by the tea tray and poured herself a cup. She let the steam fill her nose and bathe her face as she tried to still her emotions. Just a few words and glances and yet so much meaning. Too much meaning to shrug off, and truth be told, it wasn't the first time such glances and innuendos had been given. The time had come. Gone were the days when she could linger for hours on the shore of her mam's old summerhouse, the sound of the sea thundering in her ears, imagining her father's first sighting of her mother as she waded the spumey surf, her hair filled with sea spray, her dress salt-stung and damp. The house was shuttered, as it seemed was her fate. Must she face what was so and abandon her dreams of what might be?

SELKIE DREAMS

She leaned over in her chair, ignoring the creak of her corset, and pulled the little volume of Shelley hidden in its place in her embroidery basket. Her mam's book, saved from her father's purging by Cook. The book found its familiar page with ease. A place of dreams.

The chain is loosed, the sails are spread,
The living breath is fresh behind,
As with dews and sunrise fed
Comes the laughing morning wind.

The words poured into her, seeking out the thirsty cracks of the persistent drought of her Belfast life. It was grace of a different sort than that found in a Sunday sermon and one she only glimpsed in her sojourns by the sea.

By the time her father and Mr Compton entered she had her sewing in hand and her book tucked away and she was able to meet them with calm. The men eased themselves into their chairs by the coal fire with satisfied sighs.

'Máire, why don't you read something to us. Something uplifting.' It was his custom and gave him great contentment to have her read of an evening. She rose and selected one of the volumes of sermons from the bookcase and sat down. After turning up the lamp she opened to the tract *Righteous Living* and attempted to keep her mind focused on the page in front of her. *Men must live in such a way that God alone is exalted. Salvation therefore is through faith in the righteousness of Christ, but before anyone can believe, he must be emptied of all pride and self righteousness.* The words became only meaningless sounds replaced in her mind, as was her habit, by the lyrical verses of another page in the volume in her basket.

Tonight her reverie was short-lived. Máire could tell her father was not soothed by the words. Tonight he fidgeted in his chair, until finally, he interrupted her. 'No, I don't think that's what's called for now. Find something else, if you please. I have in my mind to hear something on the benefits of marriage.'

Máire stiffened momentarily, then skimmed through the volume in an attempt to follow his directions. She was in no doubt of her father's mind at that moment and she could not pretend it didn't bother her. She tried to suppress the resurgence of panic and looked over at her father. 'I'm sorry,' she said. 'I find my head aches quite badly. Would you mind if I retire?' She waited for the assent she hoped he would give, despite his impatience with headaches and the weakness of will they indicated.

After a deep frown her father nodded. Both men rose as she stood and Mr Compton made his way over to her and took her hand. She tried not to wince at his ham-fisted clasp that barely allowed her blood to circulate, or to imagine his hands in more intimate contact with her.

He ran his tongue along his lips and a small drop of spittle fell onto his beard. 'My dear, you must restore your health to its full,' he said. 'I would see you exert your fine hostess skills for many more years to come.'

Máire could only nod before making good her escape after giving her father a peck on the cheek.

Upstairs, in the sanctity of her room, she collapsed into the window seat and looked out, breathing rapidly. Except for the narrow cracks of light that escaped through curtained windows, darkness cloaked the houses, their shapes barely discernible to the eye. At the end of the road a lone street lamp shone feebly on the pavement, creating a small shadow of itself at the base. As a child this single light had given birth to a nightly ritual in which Máire asked its blessing and care over Mam. She could almost feel her mother's presence then, whispering the prayer along with her. As she fingered the medallion that hung between her breasts the words came to her and she sent them out into the night. A moment of silence, then an echo in her head. *The chain is loosed, the sails are spread.*

CHAPTER TWO

A shaft of light awoke Máire and she opened her eyes and watched the tiny particles of dust circling to the floor. She had forgotten to close her drapes the night before and the room's unaccustomed morning light played havoc with the mustard-coloured walls and heavy furniture. Annie would only pretend to sniff and warn about the threat to the ugly Turkish carpet and the heavy velvet bed hanging.

But the shaft of light, with its dancing dust particles, reminded her of another rhythmical magic. The tinkers' music at the waste ground. She smiled at the memory and let the music it brought fill her body again and lighten her spirit. And later, as she sat unmoving under Annie's patient ministrations to her hair, the meaning of the shaft of light and the particles became clear. Mam had answered her prayers. Her breathing quickened and she fought for calm while Annie's fingers slowly weaved her hair around her head.

'Now, Miss, you must stay still,' Annie said. Her girlish voice held a hint of impatience.

Stillness, quiet, calm, she told herself. Annie was right. She must take each step with care. The step she considered was life-changing. She looked at Annie in the mirror, her bottom lip protruding with concentration. Would Annie mind? Máire smiled fondly at her. She remembered the day Annie came, ten years before, a thin stick of a girl with a thick country speech Máire could barely understand. Her early years of service had been punctuated by bouts of tears and apologies that Cook had eventually coached away. She had never minded Annie's blunders; they had only made her like Annie more. Made her feel that she wasn't the

15

only one who could easily earn her father's disapproval.

Later that morning, after her father left for the mills, Máire visited Cook in her warm domain to explain her needs for the afternoon and the arrangements for the evening meal. The breakfast dishes cleared and the grates cleaned, Annie sat at the table drinking tea. Polly stood at the sink scouring the pots, her sleeves rolled high around her ample elbows. A familiar and ordinary scene, yet Máire's throat tightened momentarily.

Máire explained her father's request for a light meal that evening since there were to be no guests and he would be working late. This was nothing unusual and she was glad for it, since it made her plans all the more easy. But Cook had her own ideas and she frowned.

'It does no good to be cheating the body of its rightful nourishment.' She cast a glance at Máire's own slight frame. But while Máire's build was no more than what her mother bequeathed her, her father's thin body seemed more a symbol of his temperament.

'It's his stomach, Cook,' she said. 'You know it causes problems.'

Cook folded her arms across her massive bosom. ''Tis more than a poor stomach the master suffers from.'

'Too busy for himself.' Annie glanced at Máire. 'And his child.'

Cook pounded the dough in front of her, a small 'tush' her only words of reprimand for Annie's comment. After a moment she looked up to study Máire, her eyes sweeping over her face, her dress. She frowned. 'Now so. I can see something's troubling you.' She patted the little stool beside the large table. Máire's old stool. 'Is it your father, now? He's got something up his sleeve. He's asked me if we have enough crystal in the house for a celebration.'

'What? When would he ever celebrate?' Polly said. She wiped her reddened nose with her sleeve, the button at its wrist pulling loose a strand of red hair from her cap. Annie giggled and Cook threw her a stern glance. Máire could sympathize with Annie's need to giggle at Polly's joke, for her father's idea of celebration was a cigar to seal a business agreement, but the words still made her flinch.

Máire looked down at the offered stool, worn smooth by years of pushing her skirt over the top of it, and passed her hand over it. How could she tell them anything, for to say one word would be to say them all? Cook would know what she planned, and would not approve, no matter the cause. Máire remained standing.

''Tis nothing, Cook,' she reassured her. 'Just a bad mood is all. I'll be fine.' Máire placed a bright smile on her face and asked Cook about the play the barrow man, Eddie, had promised to take her to. Cook eyed her briefly but allowed Máire to take her in another direction and began a description of the lighthearted play. Eddie had long admired Cook and her kitchen skills. It was these same impeccable and efficient culinary skills that made her father's associates envy him, enabled her father to overcome Cook's papist background and allowed Máire her closest bond.

With Polly and Annie sitting in rapt attention Cook relived every detail of the play, enacting scenes, changing voices, her eyes never leaving Máire's face. Máire knew she made this effort especially for her. It had always been so. Plays were something she could only dream about in her father's house, but Cook brought them alive; she was a keen observer of worlds both make-believe and real.

Máire listened to her description this time with new appreciation of Cook's efforts to bring excitement into her narrow life, and suddenly felt unworthy of such love and care, as well as shame that her forthcoming actions might indicate ingratitude. It was not so, she was grateful, and for a moment she almost gave into the urge to tell her all. Quickly suppressing such weakness, she excused herself and planted a quick kiss on Cook's cheek, an action that only startled her and provoked puzzled glances from Annie and Polly. Máire could feel Cook's eyes on her as she retreated up the stairs.

Later, after the noonday meal, Máire left the house with her basket in hand, its bulk heavy with the items she'd tucked inside. Items that carried much weight in her hand seemed light in the balance of the life they represented. Her life. A life that was summed up only by a handful of ribbons, a book of poems and her mother's medallion. She'd tucked them around a change of underclothing, something she didn't count as part of her life so much as a buffer between her and her present world.

Máire made her way on foot, the roads slick with wet leaves and a fine mist of rain. She walked by the stately homes, past the soaked, leafless trees in the Botanic Gardens and the drenched buildings of Queen's University. These sedate areas gave way to the busy roads of commerce; banks in the pristine white of Portland stone, shops selling beribboned hats and finely wrought clocks, and glass-fronted offices conducting the city's business. She looked over at the road to St. Malachy's, the large Catholic church with the ornate vaulted ceiling. Once, Máire had dared to cross the church's threshold, briefly peering inside to the spectacle within. She felt sure everyone would know she was an intruder, someone who didn't belong in such a richly decorated building. But no-one stopped her, and she stood there for some time, admiring the ceiling, the altar and looking out for the chapel that Cook told her was set aside for Mary, Our Lady. When she found it she thought it foreign and exotic and also beautiful.

Máire moved beyond the refined shops to the markets that resounded with hawkers shouting their wares in a language foreign to her ears. The smoky odour of chestnuts roasting swirled round cabbages of purple and green that kept company alongside pallets of fish, their eyes peering at women toting baskets stuffed with the ingredients of the day's meal. The stalls ended where the road narrowed, and the gutters ran wet with market refuse and the dirt and rubble of the soot-stained houses. These houses were less than stately, the crumbling edifices seeping water like tears, crying at the fate of their own decay and those who had to live there. These were the homes of the Less Fortunate, homes more like hovels and their very sight started Máire's heart pounding. Her steps quickened and her throat tightened. She hastened to the waste ground, the place with the broken bits and rubbish, where the music had kindled something deep inside her.

She heard the music first, the lilting tones of a fine old jig, and then the shouts and claps of the people. Her steps quickened until she reached the edge of the waste ground and saw him, his black hair still wild about his face, the fiddle at his chin, legs and arms beating their tune. The fire burned brighter this day, and the people were livelier. A concertina and another fiddle increased the music's reach and invited all to dance. The invitation leapt out at her, pulled her closer to this circle of joy, a circle filled with dancing figures with unfettered hair and bare limbs whirling wild in the air. Máire edged closer and her movement caught the attention of the fiddler, the man with his black hair flying all loose about him.

He gave his fiddle to another and moved over towards Máire with strides that kept to the rhythms around him. He took up her hand and with strength and firmness pulled it to the circle. After a moment's hesitation (was it only a moment?), she followed her hand, dropping her basket on the ground, her corset and dress objecting so, and found herself twirled and spun in rhythms that reached deep inside. Her head fell back and she laughed a wild shrieking laugh. A hand caught her hair, the snood and pins fell, the braid came undone and the black strands flew out like a spider's web. She whirled faster, spinning her hair around her body, feeling the rhythms of the dance that beat inside her. The fiddler caught her before she fell and led her to the edge of the circle, his laughter ringing sweetly in her ears.

'Ah girleen,' he said. His breath came in deep pants on her face. 'Yeh've the music in yeh for sure.' He brushed the hair from her eyes, eyes all velvet brown and long-lashed. His fingers stilled, his eyes took in hers.

'Ye're passing strange y'are,' he whispered. His face took on that faraway look, that look that held her eyes before and carried her to the sea.

'My mam was a selkie,' she whispered, unthinking. 'But she's gone now—gone back to the sea, to her home.'

He tilted his head to one side. 'Aye, I can well imagine so,' he replied softly. 'It's a hard life for a selkie on land, especially here, with no sea to comfort yeh and no life to call yer own.'

She nodded slowly, staring into his eyes, inky and dark in the shadow of his face. 'It was hard for her, this life here in the city. Away from the sea, away from her kin, her true kin that knew her for what she was.'

'But she left yeh.'

'Oh, she had no choice, you see. I was too young to go with her, too young for that life.'

His eyes flickered and darkened and he took up her hand, squeezed it, and then turned the palm outward. With his index finger he traced the lines embedded in her skin, the motion so slow and sensual she caught her breath. She sucked her lip.

'Your palm tells me yeh'll travel far,' he said. A smile played at his mouth. He raised her hand to his lips, kissing it so slowly and deliberately she could feel the heat from his breath on her palm. She shivered.

The moment stretched. Closing her eyes, she allowed her hand to remain captured by his, held up against his mouth. His words settled inside her and created a warm place in her heart. Emboldened by this feeling, these words that gave voice to her hopes and plans, Máire opened her eyes.

'Take me with you.' Her voice was filled with soft pleading. 'I would travel and see the places you see, feel the wind and sea in my hair and taste it on my lips. Please.' She could hear the desperate edge in her voice.

He stared down at her hand, the smile gone from his mouth. Then he raised his hand, brushing aside her hair and fingered the tightly woven fabric and finely stitched edges of her jacket.

'Yeh cannot come along with us. 'Tis no life for yer kind.'

'I can pay you,' she said. She willed the tears away from her eyes. 'I have a little money. I'll do anything to help.'

'Now what can yeh be doing to help? Can yeh milk the goats? Can yeh mend the pots? Can yeh cook on a fire?' He shook his head, his eyes pitying. 'I'm sorry, girleen, 'tis no good. I'd be doing yeh no favors to take yeh with us. It's a life I'm born to and sure, what else would I do? Ye're born ta somethin' different.'

Máire shrugged off his hand, fighting the sob that choked her throat and breath. Lowering her head she clutched her hands, nodded slowly then, catching up her basket, took herself away.

CHAPTER THREE

Máire walked quickly, her breath coming in rapid bursts, her hair wild and loose around her, flailing her mouth and eyes. She had no idea where she was headed. The skies darkened and sent a heavy rain that drenched the streets and pavements and her clothes. Máire tasted salt in the water that ran down her face and realized she was crying. Softly, she called for her mother, murmuring her name over and over. She hoped for a sign, some indication of what she might do. Gradually, the rain penetrated her clothes to her skin, forming damp patches up and down her back and along her shoulders. With a sense of resignation Máire realized she was near her own church and made her way there to find a dry refuge for at least a short while, some place where she might gather herself to consider her next step.

Inside the church Máire selected a pew just by the door and sat down. When she leaned over to place the basket at her feet, her hair spilled out in front of her to rest on her lap, a tangled mess, like her hopes. Slowly Máire tried to smooth out the worst knots and braid its wet mass, tying it off with one of her ribbons plucked from her basket. She sat back and closed her eyes.

'Miss McNair, you're early.'

Máire's eyes flew open and saw Mrs Engelton standing in front of her, inspecting her closely. Early? With a sinking heart Máire remembered the Ladies' Missionary Society Meeting.

'How fortunate,' Mrs Engelton said. 'You'll be able to assist us in preparing the tea things. But first perhaps you should find a cloth and dry off.'

Máire found herself ushered into the kitchen where other lady members busily unpacked plates of sandwiches and other foodstuffs for the afternoon meeting. She set her basket down on a table, conscious of her lack of gloves and hat and her plain gown.

Mrs Engelton pointed to her basket. 'Have you brought some cakes or buns for the meeting? If so Mrs Carlton will take them.'

Máire quickly shook her head uttered a few words about errands while she desperately scanned the basket for any tell-tale signs of its true purpose. There were none.

Mrs Engelton only nodded briefly before she swept the basket underneath the table and handed Máire a cloth to dry her face and hair. She insisted Máire remove her jacket, clucking and tsking while Máire struggled out of its damp confines, then handed Máire her shawl and insisted she go by the stove until the meeting started.

Too disheartened to argue, Máire found a chair and placed it near enough to the stove to gain some warmth from it. There she watched the other women in charge of refreshments set to work preparing the tea, cakes and little sandwiches that would constitute the offerings at the close of the meeting. Though the glances from the women were many and curious, they spoke only about commonplace things with Máire.

When the meeting finally began, Máire sat in the back of the room beside the ample form of Mrs MacArthur who kept vigil near the refreshment table. From this niche Máire could let her mind drift until the reports and presentations had finished and the sewing and knitting circles formed. Máire tried not to think of the tinker's words, but to recapture the rhythm of the dancing and the joy of the music he'd played instead. It had stirred something in her, emotions strong and deep that she had only ever felt when watching a roaring sea. Máire could feel it now, an aching rising up and out along her limbs. Her heart began to race and her breath became quick and ragged. She put her hand to her mouth to stop herself from crying out and focused on the speaker, Mrs Beaton. It was then she heard the name for the first time. Alaska.

'Alaska is a vast, vast land filled with snow and ice. But its lower regions contain islands covered in great leafed plants and ferns, both delicate and large, fruit, flowers and vines on all sides. We live along their edges, by the sea, where the seals, otters and myriad sea life swim, and behind us the mountains rise, snow-capped and majestic. And it is here, amid this beauty, that there is a need. A great need for those willing to serve.'

The words sent chills up Máire's skin and she fought a racing heart yet again. Afraid to draw breath lest she miss one word, Máire leaned forward to give her full attention to the letter Mrs Beaton read from her cousin, a missionary in Alaska. A land, in the view of Mrs Beaton's cousin, that needed more helpers for this work; teachers and ministers to go among the native peoples and lift them up out of their heathen lives. A land bounded by the sea, with snow-capped mountains and moss-covered trees.

There were private sponsors, women of great means and high repute in the Presbyterian Church in America, who would help any woman willing to teach these ignorant and heathen children. Mrs Beaton concluded the letter and added her personal appeal for those who would offer themselves up for such work. Questions and statements of support kept the excitement and interest of the group at a high level, but Máire grew impatient for the session to finish. She was anxious to take the next step, to begin her future, for she had no doubt that this was her true course. Her mother had been there, sending the rain, directing her here. She was certain of it.

When all the questions were answered and all the statements were finished, Máire made her way to the table where sheets of paper lay clean and white against the dark wood. Taking a sheet she sat at the table, picked up the pen, dipped it lightly in the inkwell and formed the words of her intent and commitment.

'This is a big decision, Máire,' Mrs Engelton said, looking over her shoulder. Her eyes were shining and her evident joy gave loose to the use of Máire's Christian name. 'You must of course discuss this with your father. But his dedication to the church is such that I can't help but think he would approve of such a noble act.'

Máire nodded absently, folded the sheet of paper carefully and presented it to Mrs Beaton who promised to forward it directly with two others to the Women's Board in America as soon as Máire consulted with her father.

'How long?' Máire asked Mrs Beaton, the tinker's music singing in her ears, lilting along her arms down to her feet. 'How long before we hear word?'

She smiled kindly. 'My dear, these things take time. I'm sure they will make as much haste as they can, for their need is pressing and the funds are in place.' She patted Máire's arm. 'The important thing to remember is you have offered yourself to serve. The Lord will provide the right path for you.'

The lure and promise of the sea carried Máire home. Her feet light and nimble among imaginary waves, she felt buoyed by the music that poured into her blood, blending with its heat and firing her soul. These visions and sounds swirled around Máire's bedroom as she changed for dinner, feeling happier than she had done for years.

She descended the stairs to the drawing room to greet her father before going into dinner, wrapped in her own images of the future, while the music inside her lifted her feet. Glancing up from his newspaper, her father rose and received her kiss casually, gave her a close look and narrowed his eyes.

'Your colour is unusually high, my dear,' he said. 'Are you ailing?'

Máire's hand rushed to her face in an attempt to hide the offending colour. 'No. No, Father. I've not long returned from my meeting and the air was fresh.'

Satisfied, her father nodded and returned to scanning the paper. After taking the seat across from him Máire cleared her throat slightly and reviewed the words she knew he must hear.

'Father, I've something of importance to share with you from the meeting this afternoon.'

Her father looked up again, his face full of polite interest.

She steeled herself, choosing her words carefully. She told him of Mrs Beaton's letter and the important mission work among desperate people crying out for good Christian values. Work that Máire professed to admire.

'Such efforts are of course critical for the advancement of society,' her father said. He folded his paper and removed his spectacles. 'It's the duty of all good Christians to assist others to understand and learn the importance of such values.'

'I knew you'd think so, Father. When I heard how much they needed help in this great task, I felt it deeply. Mrs Beaton stressed how important it was for us to take up the burden to lift people up and bring the word of God to them so they can better themselves.'

Her father nodded again, caught up in the notion presented to him, a topic that appealed to his ideas about spreading Christian values to support a good moral commerce to all ports far and near. Ports that would bring him the raw materials for his linen mills and support the businesses of his associates to create a demand for his own finished goods.

'Mrs Beaton is right,' he said. He took a deep breath and explained the situation to Máire, like he would any of his junior clerks who might not understand the grand plan behind his business. The God who determined all by the sweat of one's brow and the harvest it reaped. A harvest dedicated to His Glory. Máire nodded her way cautiously through this great wave of words, rode along their rise and fall, until they spent themselves. When he finished, he smiled, obviously pleased with his own eloquence.

'I'm sure that's so,' Máire told him. 'And it's to those tasks I feel a growing commitment. Mrs Beaton described one particular place that required our assistance. People who need our instruction, who desire to rise out of the darkness. Their need is so great that sponsors have put up the necessary funds to send people who are willing to serve.' Máire moved over to kneel beside him, taking his hand.

'Oh Father, I wish so much to serve,' she pleaded. 'I feel the call deep inside me and I can do nothing but answer it. To help these people.'

Her father stared down at her; his eyes dilated, his face grew pale.

'I know it wouldn't be easy for us to bear, to be separated at such great distance,' Máire said. 'But with your deep understanding of the importance of such work you'll appreciate this burning desire I have.'

'Máire, I'm sure you felt Mrs Beaton's words deeply,' he said, the colour returning slowly to his face. 'But I think perhaps you responded more from emotion born of whim, than a deep calling from God.' He gave her hand a gentle pat. 'A call to mission work is not something to be taken lightly, to follow on the spur of the moment. It's something that you must examine carefully, to understand that it's God's words you are hearing and not your own misplaced desires.'

Máire took a deep breath to still the protests that sounded inside her. The words he heard now must be words of his mind, not hers.

She kept her tone earnest. 'Father, I've held this in my heart for a long time, long enough that I cannot remember when it entered there,. I've heard the call and I tried to fill this call in the past by assisting Mrs Engelton and the church in the all the ways that I can. But I always felt it wasn't enough. Today, as I heard Mrs Beaton make her request, I knew this was the best path for me.'

Máire blushed at her cunning, but the conviction that this was the true path for her gave her strength. She did feel called by all who lived in the sea and in the mountains and the trees. And surely if God gave life to those creatures, should she not heed their call too?

'My dear,' her father said. 'I can see you feel this deeply now, with Mrs Beaton's words still fresh in your mind. They are indeed uplifting notions, inspiring noble thoughts and actions.' He took Máire's hands and pressed them firmly. 'You are my daughter and I must do what's best for you. It's my duty as your father.' After a moment he released her hands, patting one sharply, as if to awaken some better sense within her. 'Let's not be hasty over this decision. We must give it some time.' He smiled, more confident. 'Yes, given more time to consider this step I'm certain you'll know where your true commitments lie.'

Máire suppressed a sigh, knowing she would get no further with him at that moment. She would not give up though, no matter what manner of argument he might present. She was determined to succeed, despite his objections and the few qualms she had over a journey so far away to an unfamiliar people. She would be leaving her family, her father, Cook, Annie and Polly for a place she'd never seen. But, she assured herself, she did know what it was like, and that knowledge was enough to prove that it was a place she belonged.

In the end, Máire felt some sense of relief that she had at least convinced her father enough of her intent to defer any discussion on his own plans for her future. She was allowed to retire to her room where sitting at the window she gave herself over to thoughts of mission work in Alaska. It would be a place where she would find her home by the sea. She could visualize the trees, mountains and shoreline where she would be able to walk, to cast her eyes outwards to the sea and to feel the kinship of all its inhabitants.

CHAPTER FOUR

In the weeks that followed, Máire's father invited Mr Compton to dinner on many evenings, where he took great pains to include Máire in their conversations that pointed out Mr Compton's sterling financial attributes and strong moral character. Máire countered each conversation with her own growing understanding of foreign mission work and the lives of famous missionaries. She searched the accounts of their experiences for words she could use to reinforce her own expressions of commitment that slowly waged war on her father's concerns, all the while suppressing the anxiety over her own fitness that such accounts evoked. She assured herself that it was where she belonged, as she placed her Bible beside the tea service, ready to hand when she sat with her father in the evenings.

It was there, Bible on her lap, reading aloud to her father, that Mrs Engelton and Mrs Beaton found them one Sunday afternoon when they called to formally discuss Máire's prospects as a missionary. After the tea was brought, the women spent only a few minutes on the niceties before they broached the subject of their visit.

'I'm sure your daughter has made you aware of her chosen commitment to do God's work,' said Mrs Engelton. She smiled in Máire's direction as she replaced her cup carefully on its saucer. 'We are so very proud of her desire to become a missionary.'

'Yes, God's call to become one of his soldiers in Christ is not to be dismissed lightly.' Mrs Beaton nodded her head firmly, both chins in accord.

'My daughter has explained how your words moved her so much she felt she must take up the mission call.' Mr McNair waved a hand in

Máire's direction. 'However, I would not be doing my duty as a father if I did not insist she take some time to consider this. After all,' he smiled widely, 'You fair ladies sometimes are given to whims.'

Máire swallowed. She knew this was her best opportunity and she must somehow use the words of Mrs Beaton and Mrs Engelton to give her cause weight. 'Father, I know you have my best interests at heart, but I can assure you that I've thought about this long and hard, and it's not a whim. I do wish to serve as a missionary teacher to natives who need us so desperately.'

'Mr McNair, I've known your daughter for a long time,' Mrs Engelton said. 'Since she was a small child. And I can honestly say that I have not seen her so strongly committed to anything before this. I can see it is in her heart to go.'

'You cannot argue with the call of God,' Mrs Beaton said.

'Yes,' Máire told him. 'It is a call. And I must answer it.' There was truth in the words. She felt the call, had heard it so loudly inside her she felt others heard it too. Who or what it was that was calling her she was unsure, but her thoughts were of her mother.

Mrs Engelton and Mrs Beaton left a little while later after extracting a promise from Mr McNair that he would support Máire's mission work unless some other pressing concern arose. Máire felt a small sense of relief, but she knew he was still not fully convinced.

It was only a few moments after the ladies' departure that he pressed her further.

'Máire, I don't know how to make it more clear to you that I have a responsibility for your welfare. There are alternatives to mission work that are just as noble and suitable for a woman, such as marriage and motherhood.' He looked at Máire directly, his eyes holding hers. 'He's a good man. Well-established and able to provide for you. It would be a very suitable match.'

Máire tried to keep her gaze even. 'I know Mr Compton is a good man, worthy of a good woman to become his wife and mother to his children. I'm better called to mission work. Please understand.' Though Máire was of age, she knew there were many other ways he could make things difficult for her. She needed his consent.

Her father sighed. 'I think you could come to feel differently about marriage. Given time.'

'Possibly, given time,' she said. 'Perhaps if I served as a missionary first I might eventually feel I had sufficiently answered the call and I would consider marriage at the end of it.'

Mr McNair remained silent. 'Perhaps,' he said eventually.

Máire seemed to find it most difficult explaining to Cook her desire to become a missionary. Possibly it was because Cook knew her best that she understood the least. None of the reasons Máire had posed to her father weighed convincingly against Cook's piercing, doubting eyes. Nothing about Máire's compulsion to dedicate herself to help these people in need, or her desire to bring them nearer to God rang true with her.

'Now why would you be wanting to go to a strange, outlandish place, among foreigners who have unknown habits and God help us'—Cook rolled her eyes heavenwards and crossed herself quickly—'may be no better than animals!'

Máire looked down at her lap, her fingers twined in the folds of her dress. There was no inspiration there. The aroma of the baking bread that wafted from the oven across the room suddenly threatened to smother her. Máire swallowed deeply and looked up at her. 'It is not a strange and outlandish place to me, Cook. Don't you see? It's like home.' Máire paused and added quietly, 'Or it could be.' Her voice grew soft, pleading. 'There are mountains, trees and wide stretches of sea. I'll be able to see all that.' Máire's voice was a whisper. 'It's no longer possible here.'

Cook's eyes widened and she opened her mouth briefly before taking Máire up in her arms. 'Oh *mo chroí*,' she said, 'you precious wee thing. Why didn't you say so before?' She hugged Máire tightly and then pulled back. 'But why go to such ends, just to get away from marrying that old *bastún*? Surely your father would not mind if you told him you've no wish to marry?'

Máire looked at her through a veil of tears and shook her head slowly. 'You know yourself that isn't true. He would never understand and he would make it impossible for me to refuse, in the end.'

Cook sighed and loosed her hands from Máire's shoulders. 'You may be right. But I can't see that you need go to the ends of the earth.'

'I'm not, truly. I do feel called to go there, please believe me. It's a call that comes from Mam, I'm sure of it.' Máire looked deep into Cook's eyes and willed Cook to understand. Máire needed her understanding, because of what Cook meant to her and all she had done.

Cook's eyes showed only concern. 'Ah Máire, I can see you believe it's the place for you to go. I only hope you're right, so I do.' She squeezed Máire's arm.

With deep resignation, Máire saw that her father needed more than the word of Mrs Engelton and Mrs Beaton and her own promises to convince him to let her go. There was no other choice. She must go to the minister.

Lest she lose her nerve, Máire called on the minister the next day, rehearsing carefully in her mind the words she would say while she awaited him in his study. He opened the door moments later, bringing even more chilled air into a cold room heated only by a few feeble bits of coal in the fireplace.

'Ah, Miss McNair, I'm glad you called.' he said. 'I needed to speak with you.' He went over to his desk and sat down, his spare frame barely filling the high-backed chair, and fixed upon her eyes that had read thousands of sermons. Máire shifted her gaze and mumbled a response, her carefully assembled words thrown into chaos as her mind threw up a range of alarming reasons for his remark.

'I trust you and your father are well.'

While she made her brief assurances, the minister sifted through some papers on his desk, finally withdrawing a sheet. 'My wife has passed on to me a letter from the mission board in America. It seems they require that all missionaries complete a statement of faith.' He lowered the sheet. 'You are still committed to this path, Miss McNair?'

She managed to raise her eyes to his angular jaw. 'Yes, yes, Mr Engelton. I'm still committed to this.' A statement of faith. The words lodged inside her like a stone. 'A statement of faith?' she said in a weak voice.

'A statement of faith.' The words were firm, the purpose so clear Máire could not doubt the intent. He would find her out through this trick of words and most likely had done so already. Had her father spoken to him and persuaded him of her fraudulent attempt to serve God? She had thought herself so close to winning her way through, but now she realized she had never been close.

'Miss McNair, you hesitate. Come, come. I'm sure you can manage this.'

Máire tried to collect herself. 'I hesitate because I'm not certain exactly how to approach this request.'

The minister laid down the sheet, folded his hands and considered her. The room's dim light cast sulky shadows across his face and darkened his eyes. 'Of course. I can see your dilemma,' he said finally. 'Perhaps if you sketched out your religious life, the instruction you've had, the charitable work you've done with Mrs Engelton and then conclude with a description of your moment of conversion.'

'My moment of conversion?' The tightness that had filled her body had eased with his explanation until he reached the end. Conversion. A word she had both dreaded and loved in the days of her childhood when her wayward behaviour seemed such a trial to her father.

'Yes, Miss McNair. Your conversion. The moment you knew and trusted that the Lord died for your sins and the sins of Eve. The moment you knew God, could feel his grace filling your heart and your mind.' The words were said with precision and force, echoing the years of church and instruction, to hang over her now with menace.

He pushed a piece of paper, pen and inkwell towards Máire. 'I would have you write it here, if you please. The statement needs to be sent off as soon as possible if the arrangements are to go forward in good time.' He rose and began to button his black frock coat. 'You may have my chair if you like. I must go across to the church for a while. I shall be no more than an hour, though.'

After the door closed Máire remained in her chair, staring at the blank paper on the desk. She could think only of the dryness of her mouth, the rough edge of her back teeth and the faint musty odour arising from the chair that settled in her throat, causing her to retch slightly. She gazed around the room hoping for some comfort, fighting against the fragments of memories that awoke. Wicked, wicked child. A child that could not feel God's presence. A child that God did not feel worthy enough to convert. Sore knees and bruised arms through hours of praying and pinching the wickedness out of herself. Night upon night without sleep, reading Bible passages of punishment and sin. Bread and water, bread and water, until Cook put a stop to it. God hadn't heard her. There was no sign. Only silence. Silence from her father who made no remark on her covered arms, her drawn face and red-rimmed eyes. Silence from the minister who looked at her when a church elder bore testimony to his faith at the pulpit. Still, she sat through every Sunday service and willed and hoped for some change.

And then she knew why. Finally, at fourteen, just before she stood up to confirm herself as a member of the church, she realized the reason for His silence. It was because of her mother. She was a selkie, after all. Selkies have no soul so they could not enjoy God's grace. Máire's selkie blood prevented her from feeling God's presence. It was then, after this realization, she began her bleeding, Eve's curse.

How could she write then about something that had not happened? Something upon which the minister's whole life was based? A moment of the miraculous. But surely Máire knew about the miraculous. The miracle of her mother's love for her. A miracle that had become real for her at the moment of her greatest need. Would she be able to write of that? Máire took up the pen and dipped it into the inkwell.

A week later the minister came to see Máire's father. He was so convinced of her passionate commitment to God he wanted Mr McNair to add words of support to the ones he had written at the bottom of her statement. Under such pressure her father could only give his reluctant consent, but he added a condition that Máire serve no longer than three years, a promise he thought would keep his plans in place. Máire gave it, feeling such a promise held no more weight than the empty words of praise he gave her as they sat in the drawing room with the ladies of the church.

It didn't take long for the confirmation of Máire's acceptance as a missionary to come, only a matter of weeks. It was then, when all seemed settled, that Máire encountered her biggest hurdle, a hurdle that could not be overcome through reason or cunning. It was only by accident she encountered it, halted in her path on the kitchen stairs at the mention of her name in tones filled with strong emotion. And who but Cook would fill her name with so much emotion? Though it was to Eddie, her gentleman friend, that she spoke and it froze Máire in her steps.

'Tis myself I blame for it all,' Cook said.

'Woosht,' Eddie said. 'Now why would you do such a great daft thing?'

'Ah, Máire. She was such a lost wee thing as a girl. Those big eyes, so full of questions. I thought it would help, so I did. Telling her those tales of her mam.'

'And why not so? If it helped her.'

'It proved me own ruin in the end, don't you see? After all those tales she wants to go away so some far-off heathen place where anything might happen. And here I be, sent off when Finoula's child is no longer here to love and nurture as she wished.'

'Why would the master let you go?' Eddie said. 'And you the best cook in all of Belfast.'

'Because he hates me and my Catholic ways. I'm here only for Finoula, my own dear one. She left a note that night, a note I still have that said I was to look after the wee babe, no-one else. No nurse or nanny, just her loving Cook. And I was to stay until she married, when I would go with her, wherever that would be. He had to honour that note, as much as he hated to. He wouldn't be seen to do anything else. But with her gone, and more than likely never to return, what am I to do?'

'You'll marry me for sure.' Eddie said. Máire caught a glimpse of him putting his arm around Cook.

'Ah, go away with you.' Cook laughed and pushed him away. Sobering, she sighed heavily. 'No, there will be no good reference from him, so. He'd sooner see me on the streets.'

It was only when Cook shut the back door on Eddie some time later that Máire was prompted to escape from her stunned trance to her room upstairs. Confronted by the gaping trunk and folded clothes, she sat on her bed and stared numbly at the wall. Tears gathered in her eyes. Tears for what she'd heard and not heard, tears of perception and misperception. What had Cook kept from her all these years? Was there a letter? All her memories and conversations flooded her mind, now becoming a different view, an idea of herself somehow shifted. She thought through each new piece of information and applied it where she could, threading through the memories and the exchanges, to make sense of these new meanings, these new understandings.

What promise was made? Máire touched her chest where the medallion lay nestled in her breasts.

Her hand remained at her breasts while her heart slowly beat the passing time, the light fading from the room just as the images and memories retreated, the tide of her mind ebbing out to sea, leaving a vast emptiness. It was only at dusk, when the darkening room allowed her to see nothing but vague shapes around her that Máire found she could stir herself and summon Annie to help her change. Later, as Annie's deft hands held garments, fastened hooks and arranged hair ornaments she understood that though everything had changed, nothing had changed. She would still go to Alaska.

Part II

CHAPTER FIVE

Alaska, Summer 1890

Máire paused after she boarded the ship, removing her glove to put her hand to her cheek. She savoured the moist coolness on her face after the dusty train ride west. Below, on shore, stevedores shouted orders to men carrying crates and sacks up the plank and creaking pulleys lowered bigger cargo into the holds.

Though she would welcome a quick tidying to wash away the dirt of her journey, she dreaded going to her cabin where she knew Mrs Paxson awaited. Mrs Paxson was not only her escort to Alaska; she was also her future companion in mission work, a fact Máire had learned from the mission board during her brief stopover in New York. No official status for Mrs Paxson whose husband ran the trading post at the mission, but a great support nonetheless, they said. It was the manner in which the statement was expressed, and what remained unsaid that now gave cause to Máire's anxiety.

Finally, when she could put it off no longer, Máire descended the stairs to her quarters. The spare singles beds and small dresser to the wall under the port window were nearly obscured by the trunks and boxes that piled the bed and stood on the floor. An angular yet busty woman in black bombazine scanned the room with a frown.

Máire entered and placed her valise on the floor and introduced herself. 'I presume you're Mrs Paxson. The Women's Board told me you would be here. I'm Máire McNair.'

Mrs Paxson ignored her hand, setting herself instead to a close examination of her new companion. Máire shifted uncomfortably under the full weight of Mrs Paxson's penetrating gaze. She folded her arms across her chest, a small defense against the assault.

'You seem excessively thin for the task before you,' Mrs Paxson said finally.

With great effort Máire resisted the impulse to alter her posture, expand her chest, or make any movement to give bulk to her frame. 'I'm sure I'll do my best,' Máire replied.

'Well, there's nothing to be done about your size, but we can do something about your name. It's unsuitable. We'll call you Martha.'

Máire's mouth opened to form a protest. She could think of nothing to say that would convince Mrs Paxson that Máire's name was her own and no other would do. And so the moment passed.

Mrs Paxson left her soon after this exchange to attend to some business with the captain. Máire was grateful for the release and tried to use the time to settle her things and her thoughts. Her earlier optimism and hope had faded under Mrs Paxson's need for control. A need that even extended to her name.

Listlessly Máire picked up a small pamphlet from her trunk. On the cover was a young girl who had been under threat of torture by a local witch doctor for being possessed by a bad spirit. With the help of mission funds she had been rescued and now attended the mission school in Ft. Wrangell. Máire looked at the sweetly smiling girl, her dark hair pulled back from her face with eyes slanted like a Chinaman's, and imagined how terrified the girl must have felt during her torture. How could anyone do such a thing to a child? Máire opened up the pamphlet and found a brief list of the evil aspects of Tlingit culture that only help from missionaries could erase. 'Tlingits believe in idols, they give away all their possessions in wasteful ceremonies. Tlingits tattoo their skin, pierce their noses and deface other parts of their bodies in barbaric ways.'

She read on and found they were also 'quarrelsome, taking offence at the smallest slight', yet they were also 'welcoming and biddable in learning the hymns and scripture'. The information seemed too confusing and gave her little help to understand what the people might be like. Máire turned back to the image of the child where there seemed some reassurance. A child like that Máire knew she could help.

There was only just enough room for the servers to manoeuvre between the dining chairs and table of the officers' mess. Máire eyed the dubious meal dished onto her plate, but she knew that the fare on a military ship wasn't going to be high dining. She shouldn't complain; the passage to the mission was at their courtesy. The brass around the porthole windows and other fittings was shined to high polish though, and it sparkled in the glow of the candles that graced the table in an attempt at elegance.

Around her the conversation flowed. Captain Gordon, portly and agreeable, discussed politics with Mrs Paxson who sat on his right. Next to Mrs Paxson was Lieutenant Bissell, a man who despite his stocky stature wore his uniform with a casual elegance. It was her own companion who sat opposite Lieutenant Bissell that intrigued her. His name was Lieutenant Green, an unassuming name that gave no clue as to any of the elements of his character, nor explained the appearance that intrigued her so. No, they told her nothing about his mournful amber eyes, his threadbare but immaculate uniform.

Captain Gordon turned to her. 'So Miss McNair, you're going to go teach those natives a thing or two, eh.'

'Grace?' Mrs Paxson asked. 'Before we can begin any discussion we must thank the Lord for what will be laid before us.'

There was only the slightest hesitation before he nodded. 'Of course, Mrs Paxson.' He intoned a few simple phrases of thanks, his head bowed and his voice a deeper register. He nodded to Máire.

'Are you looking forward to your mission work?'

Máire smiled politely. She'd taken heart from the grace episode. 'Yes, Captain. Alaska sounds like such a beautiful place.'

'Well, it's no easy task, and many wouldn't take it on,' he said.

'We use any assistance that's available, Captain,' Mrs Paxson cut in. 'We owe much thanks to Mr Jackson and the Women's Board for sending another missionary. The help is desperately needed. There's much to do.'

'It's been a few years since we've been in these waters; does the work progress, Mrs Paxson?' Captain Gordon asked.

He reached for the wine carafe, carefully removed the glass stopper and offered it to fill Mrs Paxson's glass. She frowned and refused on her behalf and Máire's.

'Since its creation ten years ago the mission has come far. We now have a church, a school, a trading post and a manse for the minister, though he and his wife are currently recovering from an illness in Sitka.' She pursed her lips.

'How do you manage without them? Don't you need a minister?' Lieutenant Green asked.

'We manage,' Mrs Paxson said. 'I've been conducting the Sunday school among the Chilkat, some of the services and helping out with the sick ones. And Mr Paxson does what he can.'

Lieutenant Green nodded. 'I'm sure you both do more than your share, Mrs Paxson.'

Máire eyed Lieutenant Green. Had she detected an insincere tone? 'Who are the Chilkat?' she asked.

'The Chilkat are the Indians at the mission, dear girl,' said Mrs Paxson. 'They're part of the Tlingit tribe.'

Máire suppressed her irritation. She knew little enough about the people she was to work among. Her questions would wait for a later time. A later time that left her no wiser about the people themselves, but in little doubt of Mrs Paxson's involvement and commitment to the mission work of teaching the natives the civilized ways of the whites.

'I'm sure it must all seem confusing to you at the moment,' Lieutenant Green said in a low voice. 'And it's a brave thing to leave your country to live among strangers with very different customs.'

Máire looked at him quizzically. His words were so sympathetic, so knowledgeable she wondered at his background. She sought clues to his own experience, but his expression was guarded, belying the sentiments he had just uttered. And his eyes gave no clue.

'I imagine your life in the navy has taken you to many foreign places, yet you must miss your family.'

A shadow crossed Lieutenant Green's face as he looked at Máire. 'Yes, I do miss my family.'

Had she struck a chord there? 'I don't suppose you get to see them very often.'

'No, not often. We've been assigned to different areas of the western coast for several years now and my family live on the eastern coast.'

'Oh? Where? I was just in New York. It's an impressive city.'

Lieutenant Green gave a wry smile. 'My home is somewhat south of there, in a port city called Baltimore.'

'I suppose that's where your interest in the sea arose.'

'In part. My father was a merchant, an importer. Besides goods from foreign countries he also brought back exotic tales. Too much for any lad to resist.' He stared into his wine glass, swirling the liquid as if answers were held in its depths. 'Where is your own home, then?' he asked finally.

Máire told him of Belfast and her father. He quizzed her briefly about her father's business and showed some understanding of his attempts to modernize the factories. Still, Lieutenant Green did not seem to condone the endless hours her father spent attending to his business. 'A family can suffer when a father is seldom home.'

'I feel your own experience has taught you that,' Máire said. 'Your mother must have felt your father's absences keenly.'

'My mother died when I was a very young lad.'

Máire's breath caught. 'I'm so sorry.' On an impulse she briefly laid a hand on his arm. 'I too know what it is to grow up without a mother.'

Lieutenant Green looked down where her hand had been before raising his startling eyes to hers, his expression closed. 'Yes. It was difficult.'

All words of sympathy and sharing fled Máire's mind in the face of his shuttered eyes. She cast about frantically for a change in subject.

'But still, your career has now taken you to such interesting places, including Alaska. Perhaps you could help my own ignorance about the place.'

'What would you like to know?'

'I guess something of the nature of the people there.' She thought of the pamphlet. 'Do they really give away all their possessions?'

He frowned down at her. 'I'm not sure what I can tell you about them. From what I know they're a quarrelsome lot and most of them live in ignorance and filth.' His tone was offhand, dismissive. 'The land contains many exotic plant specimens, though. You'll find that interesting. And the waters teem with life.' He smiled at her. 'Whales. Have you ever seen a whale, Miss McNair?'

'No, Lieutenant. Never.'

He continued, describing the various kinds of whales and their habits. Máire followed his words, curious that he could show such interest and animation about the wildlife and give no attention to the Alaskan people.

'My dear, I think you must be tired. In fact it's been a long day for both of us,' Mrs Paxson said. She nodded to the captain. 'We'll leave you gentlemen to your affairs now and bid you goodnight.'

Máire could only follow Mrs Paxson's cue and mumble her excuses as she rose and followed Mrs Paxson to their quarters. It was only much later, in the privacy of her small bed, that she was able to review her conversation with Lieutenant Green. He was such a strange reserved man but with so much worldly experience that enabled him to perceive some things accurately. Or so it appeared. But what of his views of the Tlingit? Surely they were extreme. She sighed.

CHAPTER SIX

Máire leaned over the ship's rail to inhale the sea's fragrance. In the distance, a fine mist cloaked the view. Máire longed to be able to reach down and run her hand through the water and feel it slide over her fingers, silky and smooth. Instead she lifted her face to the tangy breeze that teased her hair like a tinker's bow. The music surrounded her now, filling her with such a desire to twirl around, her arms raised above her, she was hard pressed to remain still. During these moments Máire felt a tangible sense of release, a loosening of binds no less strong for their invisibility. This must be her home, it could be nowhere else, despite Cook's words, and what words could compete with this that stirred her so deeply? Máire held tight to this certainty. From this she fashioned a small bit of hope.

'Miss McNair. Martha.'

Máire suppressed a flinch as she turned to greet Lieutenant Green. William. He had asked that she call him by his Christian name in the evening that followed their initial acquaintance, a request made in an awkwardly formal manner. But though the manner was awkward there was an underlying hint of a plea that Máire couldn't help but relent. For, as he put it, she did hope they would become well acquainted. So at that moment it was not William's presence then that caused her to flinch, but the use of a name that wasn't truly hers. She had yet to summon the courage to correct him.

'Martha,' he repeated.

He came up beside her by the rail. 'I thought to find you here.' Máire looked up at him and noticed again the striking eyes that seemed so much like the colour of topaz. His sun-bronzed skin had reddened slightly under the sting of the wind, giving it a healthy glow. Unconsciously, Máire bit her own lips to bring colour to them, in the hope that her looks might be enhanced as well.

William leaned into the rail and propped his foot on the bottom ledge, his leg brushing her skirts in the process. She caught her breath and dared to look into his eyes and found no more clues there. What did he truly think of her? At times she had read barely concealed hostility, while other times she found a deep connection, an unspoken feeling that they shared some common ground and emotion.

'I was taking in the view,' Máire told him.

She gave a guilty glance at the mist. But then the words became truth, for the mist cleared under the sun's strength, revealing a scene that left her breathless. Mountains rose among tall fir trees to a sky clear and endless. The scene, mirrored in the water they now moved through, seemed to stretch out towards them, nearly touching the ship. It moved her so much that she could only remark on her inability to describe what lay before her. She laid her gloved hand impulsively on William's arm.

He covered her hand with his own. 'Yes, it's a view to be admired,' he replied.

He looked at Máire for a long moment that confused her anew and sent her hand to the rail and her glance back to the sea. Without any change in countenance, William calmly began to point out some landmarks for Máire, impressing her with his knowledge.

'It's a vast area, but you will eventually come to recognize places,' he said when he had finished.

'I hope so. It's all so new to me. I've much to learn.' Máire smiled up at him. 'Have you been to Alaska often?'

'I've been a few times, and as I mentioned before I've found the natives are nothing like us. Many of their customs are barbaric. On the whole they seem a very low sort of people and occasionally even dangerous. Frankly I don't know how much improvement you and other missionaries will achieve in these types.' William remained silent, his words hanging in the air between them.

'I can only hope that you're wrong, Lieutenant,' Máire managed to say finally. 'Surely teaching them and showing them the best way of living can bring them the culture and refinement you say they lack. Don't you support the mission work?'

William gave her a bitter look. 'My mother was a Coptic Christian, the oldest form of the faith, but missionaries would have them as heathen.'

'Coptic? I've not heard of that particular denomination.'

'No, well it's of no matter,' he said hastily and put a smile on his face. 'But if anyone can make a difference with mission work, you can.'

'I'm certain that if anyone can make a difference it will be someone like you,' he said.

His compliment filled her with more pleasure than anxiety this time, though she was unaccustomed to such flattery from a young man and had no idea how to reply to it. She smiled and decided to pick up an earlier conversational the thread.

'It must be wonderful to be able to visit so many different places. Have you been to other ports or countries?'

'Oh, many. Besides the ports here in the north, I've had the opportunity to visit places in South America, Mexico and Panama. And the ports of the east coast.' He recounted a few amusing tales that gave his face such ease Máire found herself laughing just to see him smile.

'You must enjoy the navy, then,' Máire said eventually. 'Despite some of the hardships and dangers.'

All the ease in William's face vanished. He shrugged. 'It has its moments. Having travelled at sea on occasion with my father, it seemed to him a good choice.'

'A good choice to your father only?'

William cocked his head slightly, his eyes focused on the horizon. 'Choice. I don't know if I really would use that word. Would you call it choice when it's something we're compelled to do because any other course of action would mean unthinkable hardship for all those you love?' His words, so heavy with bitterness, hung in the air.

Máire stared at him in confusion. 'I'm sorry. I don't understand.'

William turned to face Máire, his eyes narrowing. 'No. You don't understand, do you?'

The words were expressed with a sneering undertone that made Máire flinch, but then a small rush of anger filled her. 'How would I understand? I've not been long acquainted with you and there is much about you I don't know. I am sorry if I've caused offence, but I assure you it was unwitting.'

With a visible effort William gave her a weak smile. 'Yes. Yes. You're right on all counts and I've behaved inexcusably. Can you ever forgive me?'

His face, all rueful grin and contrite eyes, did much to loosen the little knot of emotion but left her no wiser about his regard for her. Her lack of experience with men's attentions was very evident. Would she be able to puzzle him out, given time and more knowledge of him and his background? She looked down at his hand, the tiny dark hairs that curled on the back of his fingers now golden brown from the sun. Fingers and nails finely wrought, almost delicate in their creation that suggested nothing of the hearty sailor. There she read some truth of him.

She looked up into his face then and smiled tentatively. 'William, my given name is Máire, not Martha.'

'Máire?' He spoke the name slowly, flattening the first syllable into a nasal that sounded so strange to her ears. He frowned. 'But why?'

Máire repeated her name again, slowly coaxing it along. 'I'm sorry. It was Mrs Paxson. She thought my own name too difficult and felt obliged to give me another one for the mission work. I confess I find it hard to accept. I would wish you to know my real name.'

William remained silent for some moments, the frown deepening on his face. 'No. I see what Mrs Paxson was about. And though I understand your reluctance to comply, you must. You don't understand what's at stake.'

Máire bristled slightly, so surprised and stung at his words she initially felt unable to reply. She moved away from him. 'No. I don't understand. What is at stake?'

William closed the space between them again. 'I'm sorry if I upset you, but I say this to help you, not to hurt you. There is so much of this world you are now in that may puzzle you and cause distress. You've come from a home and background that's sheltered and you won't be familiar with things like the importance of acceptance from those who support you and those you must work among. Without it there is little you can accomplish. Without it you can become less than nothing, seen by no-one, heard by no-one. It's not a life at all.'

'What gave you the idea that I would not be familiar with all that you have just spoken of? My own world was full of just such things. But though you may think it, I'm not like those of my world.' Tears pricked at her eyes. 'My mother died when I was barely a year. She gave me the name and there is precious little else I have of hers. Do you now see why it is so important to me?'

William studied her carefully, his eyes fixed on hers, searching deeply, slowly. 'Yes. Yes, I can see you mean what you say. But for all your words I must tell you that spirits stronger than yours have been crushed under the weight of what this world demands.' His tone took on a note of pleading. 'Please be guided by Mrs Paxson. Though she may have her faults, she is right in this case. She does it not to hurt you, but because it's for the best.'

Máire's resolve faltered under the weight of his explanation. Was it truly for the best? Would she be able to relinquish her name when that was who she was, her mother's daughter? She took a deep breath. 'I thank you for your concern. I'll think about what you've said.'

'Please do that. Máire.' He said her name slowly, his intonation improving on the last effort. 'If it helps and you will allow me, I will call you Máire in private, when there is only the two of us present.'

'Thank you, I would appreciate that.' Máire attempted a smile of encouragement. The result was poor but William wasn't deterred. He took her gloved hand and raised it to his lips. Máire didn't resist.

In the days to follow Máire found herself much in William's company as she tried to work her way through the conflicting ideas and perceptions of her new life. Must it be all that William intimated? As she spent more time with him, she came to understand that the deep undercurrents of his own life and experiences had influenced his perceptions and ideas. Though she was no more enlightened about what might have caused such dark views, she became more certain that it was not a truth for her life.

Mrs Paxson noticed the time Máire spent in William's company and made her disapproval known. Perhaps her disapproval stemmed from her concern that Máire's friendship with William would distract from her mission work. Whatever the cause, Mrs Paxson found as many opportunities as possible to waylay her when she conversed with William and direct Máire towards some little errand or discussion over mission work.

During dinner Mrs Paxson made her best efforts to ensure she was ensconced firmly between Máire and William, or at the very least to control the conversation in such a manner that it would discourage any private discourse. Captain Gordon welcomed such gregariousness, though at times both he and Mrs Paxson might struggle to make their opinions heard over the other. This seemed to happen most frequently when they discussed issues touching the mission work or the natives. Over one particular meal they exchanged strong views about one of the groups of Indians who, led by their clan chief, Kowklux, had moved from their old village into the mission so they could attend religious services more often.

'It's a vast improvement,' said Mrs Paxson. 'They're more directly under our influence and so I expect they'll progress more quickly, now. It's always been two steps forward and then one step back. It may continue so with the other clans in the area but we'll at least have better results with Kowklux's group.'

'But my dear Mrs Paxson, having such groups so close at hand draws in other, more unseemly elements.'

'What do you mean, Captain?' Mrs Paxson set down her fork.

'The latest government reports state that there's an increasing number of miners showing up in your area. They trade and mix with the Indians, share liquor and other things with them in return for food and local knowledge of the land.'

'They have no respect for the law, Ma'am,' William said quietly.

'What exactly do you mean, Lieutenant?' said Mrs Paxson. 'Pray make yourself clear.'

'I mean the miners don't seem to appreciate that it's for everyone's safety that the government banned the sale of alcohol to natives. The miners sell it to the natives anyway and when the natives get liquored up they dream up a war for no good reason and then it requires a firm hand to get them under control again. The navy has been called to action on more than one occasion.'

'Surely the Tlingits can't be that unruly,' Máire said. 'Perhaps they don't fully understand the situation.'

'Don't think us too harsh,' William said. 'These methods have been established through hard-won experience. And it is, after all, for their own good.'

'They're like children, Miss McNair,' Lieutenant Bissell said with a lazy smile. 'You must be firm to teach them the ways of the world, otherwise they become spoiled and disrespectful.'

Mrs Paxson nodded, her views in agreement in this case at least. 'You'll understand in time, Martha.'

Máire grimaced at the name, and hoped that she would never understand that kind of treatment.

On the last day of the journey Máire took her place at the rail, anxious to catch the first sight of her new home. She could not tear herself away and found little in her cabin to tempt her to remain while Mrs Paxson sat writing letters, reading or knitting. Máire confessed to herself some disappointment she was not allowed even the small triumph of finding Mrs Paxson succumbing to seasickness while she remained unscathed. Mrs Paxson ate heartily and passed the time as she might have done on any train.

William joined her at the rail just as they passed into Portage Bay. All around her glacier-covered mountains brushed the sky to fall in dramatic slopes to the tree-covered areas below. The water was thick with fish teeming in all directions. An eagle glided along a coastline with practiced ease, then seemed to hang suspended in the air, an unmoving still life as it caught the wind's currents. Drawn by this evidence of the wildlife, Máire questioned William closely about the sea inhabitants.

'I want to know everything, William,' she said with breathless exuberance. William smiled down at her. 'Well there's some you will already know from your own home, I think. Salmon, otters, ravens and eagles are wildlife found in your own land. Oh and seals, too.'

Her heart leapt at the mention of seals. 'You say seals? I've heard they're here, but I know little more than that.'

'These creatures are commonplace hereabouts,' William told her. He searched the horizon and pointed. 'See, there's some over there, towards that shoreline.'

Full of excitement, she looked over in the direction he pointed and recognized the seals playing among the jutting rocks. She watched them glide in and out of the water, their smooth skin glistening silver in the light. A moment later she heard a bark and smiled to think that greeting might be for her. She took heart from that cry of welcome, a sign of what was to come.

'Martha, you should go below to check your belongings now,' Mrs Paxson said as she came up behind Máire. She gave William an appraising look. 'There will be plenty of time to take in the views once we've reached shore.' The faded brown ribbons from Mrs Paxson's bonnet fluttered in the wind like tiny banners announcing triumph.

CHAPTER SEVEN

Máire tried to still her excitement as she made her way to the deck and watched the crew lower the boats that would take them ashore. Mrs Paxson and Máire would go in the first boat and the cargo and baggage would follow in the second.

She arrived safely in the first boat and turned to the approaching shore. Several buildings clustered together on the one side with the telltale church steeple in the middle and some oddly carved poles at the far end. Tiny figures gathered in front and further along the shore's edge. Máire's glance skimmed over these figures and the buildings to the view behind. A powerful and majestic mountain scraped the sky, its snow-capped edges smoking tiny curls of mist. Máire sighed.

A babble of shouts and riotous colour drew her attention from the view above to the shore in front. Unfamiliar words and sounds accosted her ears, as did pungent odours of smoke and fish. Women dressed in bright calico colours, bare feet visible from beneath their skirts, and scarves atop their heads, shuffled small children out of the way in readiness for their landing. Nearby, turbaned men with hair cut rough below their ears began to wade into the water, their dun-coloured trousers rolled to their knees. It wasn't all wild colour and excitement; among these rainbow clothes a few stood out in their darker browns and blacks of merino wool and thick cotton trousers, and the lighter whites and beiges of linen shirts.

Just before the boat could go no further a man from the group moved towards them, parting the fish that thronged the water. He wore none of the bright cottons or dark wools. His chest was bare and he glided through the water with a rhythm so graceful Máire wondered what the water might conceal beneath his hips. He was truly a creature of the sea with his dark tilted eyes and coal-black hair that hung long and loose about his shoulders, and a body that moved through the current like liquid.

He arrived at the boat and reached up for her. Wolf tattoos rippled on the back of his hands as he gestured her to come. Máire gasped at sight of such primal markings. The Indian noted her reaction but made no remark, only raised his brow a fraction and gestured once again for her to come.

'Daniel.' Mrs Paxson addressed this black-haired man with some surprise. 'We don't usually see you at the mission.' She nodded to a short wiry man wading through the water in Daniel's wake. 'Oh good, George, you're here. You can take me ashore. Daniel is taking Miss McNair, the schoolteacher.'

George nodded, his grizzled beard glistening in the sun, then turned back to his wife. 'It was only luck that Daniel was here at hand when the ship pulled into sight. Joseph is visiting his family and most of the other young ones are up at the summer camps.'

Daniel waited silently during this exchange, before reaching up once again for Máire. She shifted her weight to lean into his shoulders, feeling the rise and fall of his chest against hers, and for a moment she recalled another black-haired man with fluid rhythm and flashing eyes. She felt his body shift as he moved forward through water that flowed and pooled around thighs and then calves to bear witness to his human qualities. Surely the limbs were only temporary illusions. The silky smoothness of his chest and shoulders, the oily smell of his hair next to her cheek revealed his true origins.

He deposited her on the bank and, without a word, headed to the forest above that quickly swallowed him whole. Where was his home, if not here by the sea? How much claim on him had that forest that absorbed him so completely it was as though he were part of it? What was he, if not of the sea?

'Don't just stand there gawking, girl,' said Mrs Paxson. 'Get yourself up to the trading post and help Mr Paxson unpack the stores. I'll be along in a short while.' She turned back to the men surrounding her and continued to issue orders about the cargo.

Suppressing her annoyance Máire nodded, groped for her skirts and made her way towards the cluster of vertically planked buildings. When she reached the building most likely to be the trading post, she realized she had acquired a group of followers who now crowded behind her. Máire turned around and smiled feebly at them. Faces, very young and very old, male and female, stared expectantly at her. A young girl dressed in bright red calico pressed forward.

'Are you the school teacher?'

'Yes, yes.' Máire nodded vigorously. 'I am the school teacher.' She said it slowly and loudly, hoping they would understand her words. 'School teacher,' she repeated, pointing to her chest. 'Miss McNair.'

They all giggled. Had she said something wrong? Just as she desperately searched their faces for a clue to the misunderstanding, a door opened behind her.

'I thought I heard voices,' said Mr Paxson. He stepped down beside Máire, facing the group. 'I see you've found yourself a welcoming committee.' He spoke to the group using another language, a language full of air and sea. Their language. When Mr Paxson finished the group nodded and murmured, then turned to go. He watched them leave, a smile on his face.

'Rebecca,' he said. The young girl in red calico turned around. 'Tell your brother that I appreciate his help today. He disappeared before I could thank him.' The girl nodded then walked on.

'She speaks English well,' Máire said.

'Yep, she does, and her sister Sarah. They learned it from their brother Daniel,' said Mr Paxson. 'As for the rest, well, it depends. Some do, some don't and some speak a little. Their schooling depends on the comings and goings of the season. Mostly goings.' He smiled at Máire. 'Still, maybe now there's a regular school teacher here, there'll be more comings.'

Máire had barely heard the last few sentences, her mind still on his earlier words. 'You mean Daniel speaks English too?' She was surprised. He hadn't said a word to her, and his manner and dress—well, she could only think he wasn't from the common world. Was it the pamphlet that made her think so or was it something deeper? Something that made him have no need for words. But her common sense told her that Mrs Paxson had spoken to him in English, though Mrs Paxson more than anyone would seem to assume no-one would fail to understand the meaning of her words.

'Sure, Daniel speaks English.' He chuckled as if sharing some private joke.

Máire flushed, embarrassed at her unguarded words and searched for a change of subject. 'Why were they giggling at my words earlier? Did I say something amiss?' Máire described the situation to him and the words she spoke. Mr Paxson smiled slightly and shrugged his shoulders.

'Couldn't rightly tell you on that one,' he said. 'The Chilkat like a good joke though, 'specially puns. When all Tlingit say who they are, usually they say what house, kwaan and clan they're from. They might've thought you were saying you were from the school teacher clan.'

Máire flushed again, feeling the stupidity of her mistake, until the humour of the remark settled in. Then she laughed, a little too long and perhaps too loud. 'Are clans important to them, then?' she asked eventually.

'Oh yeah,' said Mr Paxson. 'Clan is everything.'

Maire thought of the Molloys and Kellys and the other relations that made up the families of Cook, Polly and Annie. They were sometimes called clans. Their stories and connections were complex and so intertwined Máire had long since given up trying to understand them fully. Were clans here as complex? Máire's thoughts drifted to Daniel as she wondered what his clan might be and how it might fit in with the others here at the mission.

CHAPTER EIGHT

Inside the trading post Máire found she could be of some use to Mr Paxson, a willing pair of hands that unloaded some of the crates and barrels the crew and native men brought in stages. She removed her hat, gloves and jacket and set about working in the store, an area the size of her parlour back home, fashioned of bare plank walls that boasted a window on either side of the front door. This room adjoined a back kitchen and the stairs to two small rooms above. Though she was in need of some refreshment, she didn't feel she could ask, especially if Mrs Paxson still worked tirelessly down by the riverbank. She smoothed her hair back from her face and took a quick look around as she waited for Mr Paxson to open the next crate of supplies.

Rough boards propped up by barrels acted as the service counter, and shelves lined the walls. It was here Máire worked, lining up tins and jars of goods. Mr Paxson dealt with the heavier items like the sacks of flour, sugar and coffee beans that cast strong earthy aromas around the room. There was little enough space for all these items, though it seemed a small amount of stores for a whole community. Perhaps there was an abundance of homegrown goods.

Mr Paxson caught Máire looking around the room and suggested they stop for a break. He apologized for not thinking of it sooner and offered her a cold drink. His manner was easy and Máire quickly warmed to him.

'Oh, I'm not overly tired, Mr Paxson. And I would think your wife is working twice as hard as I am. But I'd like a cold drink, please.'

'You sit down and rest a minute. Don't compare yourself to Mrs Paxson. She didn't come as far as you, Martha,' said Mr Paxson lifting an eyebrow. 'Besides, Mrs Paxson don't tire easy.'

Máire stiffened a bit at the use of the name that was becoming horrid to her. She muttered her own name to herself as she sank gratefully on the nearest crate, while Mr Paxson disappeared into the back room. She still felt uneasy enough over William's words that she had refrained from any sort of correction. She wasn't certain how much she had lost from this lack of action and she knew soon it would be too late to make a correction without appearing completely foolish.

Mr Paxson appeared with two tin mugs, one of which he presented to Máire. 'There, it looks like it'll have to be water,' he said. 'We haven't anything better until we get our own stores unpacked.' He sat down on the crate opposite her and took a deep drink from the mug. 'Now, Martha girl, tell me something,' he said. 'Whatever brought you way out here? And you being a foreigner to boot.'

Máire was somewhat taken aback by his frank questioning, but his earnest tone and friendly face took away any impertinence she might have read into it. Shifting uncomfortably she took a deep drink from her own tin mug before she tried to answer.

'Well, Mr Paxson, I- I wanted to help.' She stared down at her mug, fiddling with the handle. 'I heard about Mr Jackson's great need for teachers here in Alaska, and I thought it might be an opportunity to make a difference. To be among people who need me, that want my assistance.'

Mr Paxson raised an eyebrow and smiled slightly. 'Don't you have any poor folk in your own country?'

Máire tightened her grip on her mug and looked directly at him. 'Yes, Mr Paxson, we have the poor in Ireland. There are many societies and organizations that minister to the poor. My own church society does a particularly fine job of hemming handkerchiefs for the poor.'

Mr Paxson rubbed his chin with his hand and broke into a large grin. 'I see. Well, I think you'll find there's more to do here than hem hankies.'

Máire smiled wanly and decided to abandon her poor attempt at humour. She asked him about his own origins and what brought him to Alaska. Mrs Paxson had said little except she was from back east, somewhere near Philadelphia.

'I come from a small place in Iowa. Farm country,' he told Máire. Though she had no idea where Iowa was, it seemed far from Mrs Paxson city life. 'I ran the general store in town and knew Mrs Paxson's cousin. Mrs Paxson, Florence Baxter as she was then, visited those cousins. She wanted to be a China missionary, but they liked married couples. So we talked about going together. The adventure sounded fine to me. Turned out we were too old, though. Then, some years back, this chance came up to run the trading post and we took it.'

Máire nodded, trying to imagine the two of them courting in the farming country she had passed through on her travels here. She could not easily place Mrs Paxson beside him. Her lack of faith in their courtship provoked her next remark. 'You've made great progress here.'

Mr Paxson reflected a moment. 'You could say we've made progress,' he said. 'Mrs Paxson sure works hard to do what she sees is fit. No matter that she isn't official. Reverend Carter and his wife seem to be grateful for her help.'

'Will they be returning soon?'

He shrugged. 'Don't rightly know. The Reverend might be along shortly. It was a hard winter for those two. They aren't used to it and we ran short on provisions, had to make do. And Mrs Carter, well she'd just had a little 'un and came right on down with scarlet fever soon after. She needed some time to recover from all that. Reverend Carter didn't want to leave her when she was sick.'

'I'll be staying up at their home, though,' Máire said.

'Well, now—'

The front door opened then and Mrs Paxson entered. Mr Paxson rose and nodded to his wife.

'Ah, there you are, George.' She removed her hat and gloves and placed them on the counter. She eyed both of them and gave a little sniff. 'Everything seems to be in order now. The officers are up at the manse where we'll join them for dinner. Betty is seeing to them, but I'll have to go up later to supervise the cooking. She still needs some guidance with anything that is beyond boiling two eggs.'

'If the officers are up at the minister's house, where will I stay?' Máire asked. The answer, already hanging in the air, was one Máire could not bring herself to acknowledge, though once articulated it seemed worse.

'Here, of course,' said Mrs Paxson. 'Where else?'

'Of course,' Máire murmured.

'You'll stay with us while you're here,' said Mrs Paxson. 'You may not understand the finer points of proper behaviour in this country, but I certainly do. You can't stay at the minister's house alone. Once Reverend Carter is back it's out of the question. And we don't know when Mrs Carter will return. If she returns.' She pursed her lips. 'It makes sense if you just stay here. We have a room upstairs for you to use.'

Máire remained silent, uncertain how to respond but already beginning to accept the inevitable.

'Why don't you go up and tidy yourself? You do look as if you need it,' Mrs Paxson said. 'Your room is upstairs on the left. There's a washbowl on the table there. You can fill it with the water bucket in the kitchen.' She nodded in Máire's direction, a clear dismissal.

Máire looked down at her skirt and shirtwaist, the dust and smudges from her recent efforts marking erratic patterns across her front. Her hands were grimy; dirt lined the nails and creases of her fingers. Her face would certainly be little better. With a few murmured words, Máire gathered up her jacket, hat and gloves that she had placed over a barrel when she entered and made her way to the kitchen. It was a cramped place with barely room for a table and a wood stove that supported a battered old kettle and pot. Nailed to the wall above the table was a wooden cupboard, its scarred and weathered shelves containing a few pieces of crockery. Tucked against the wall was a small folding bed, a cloth draped neatly over it. Though the surfaces of the floor and table showed similar signs of a hard life, they were spotless, with no stray ash or windblown dust present.

Máire found the water bucket on the floor opposite an outside door. She took up her hat, now smaller and flatter than its original feeble shape, and pinned it back on her head, then donned her grey woollen jacket to leave her hands free for the bucket. Using her gloves as padding against the metal handle she lifted the bucket up from the floor and made her way to the stairs. The stairs were next to the kitchen door in a little area between the main room and the kitchen. She took hold of the wood rail worn smooth and climbed the narrow steps. The grey unpainted boards creaked under her slight weight. At the top of the stairs Máire took hold of the knob of the ill-fitting door on her left and turned it.

The room was nothing more than she expected. A far cry from the physical comforts she'd known in Belfast, it was spare of furniture and adornment, but nevertheless provided the basic needs. After setting the bucket on the floor Máire moved over to the small wooden bed covered in a patchwork quilt, its once lively colours now faded through seasons of service. She caught a hint of lavender fragrance when she ran her hand along the soft fabric that was still held fast by tiny stitches.

Beside the bed, the room was bare of any other furniture except a little table, the washbowl and a chair by the window. Automatically she moved towards the window and opened it, curious and hopeful of a view of the water. Beyond the houses and along the clearing stretched the water of the inlet, water that rose and fell with the tides, like the breath and rhythm of the ocean waves. She stood there, the view holding her locked and timeless, thinking of Mam. She closed her eyes. Despite the room's lack of frills and decorations and its almost cheerless furnishings, she could feel and smell the light and life from outside spilling into the room, to penetrate the remote corners and all the seams of the boarded ceiling above her until the room was flooded with it. Under its force the bones of each hand and foot melted slowly into one, as her skin became smooth and taut, glistening as sleek as a pearl. A distant cry sounded and an answer rose up from the deepest part inside her.

CHAPTER NINE

Sometime later, perhaps even two hours afterwards, Máire found herself lying across the bed as she stirred at the sound of Mr Paxson's voice. It seemed impossible that it might be time to depart for the manse. She hastily splashed water on her face and tucked stray hairs in her snood. There would be no question of dressing for dinner, something Mrs Paxson had already made clear aboard ship, making Máire feel shamed for even thinking to ask it.

In a light still bright enough for midday, Máire walked up to the manse with Mr Paxson, wearing the same grey woollen skirt and jacket, brushed as clean as her fingers could manage. Mrs Paxson had gone earlier, ensuring all the arrangements for dinner were in place. At the manse, a comparatively large building with a parlour, kitchen and dining area and two rooms upstairs, they joined Captain Gordon, William and Lieutenant Bissell. Before Máire and the rest were seated Mrs Paxson introduced her housekeeping assistant, Betty, a heavyset Tlingit girl who eyed them all suspiciously from the kitchen area while Mrs Paxson sang her praises.

Betty's subsequent performance led Máire to wonder at Mrs Paxson's own abilities and Betty's real value. The bread was doughy and the chicken, cut in pieces, was burnt to the pan. Máire watched her scrape it on to the platter noisily, then feared for the plate and chicken as she dropped it on the plank table in front of Mrs Paxson, endangering the gravy that sloshed vigorously in front of Máire.

'Have you been with Mrs Paxson long?' Máire asked when Betty shoved a bowl of vegetables at her end of the table. Máire frowned over their indeterminate colour that she could only suppose was a mixture of carrots and greens.

'Long enough,' Betty replied. She gave Máire a wary look before she lumbered to her seat at the other end of the table.

After Captain Gordon had said a brief grace they began their meal, a process that involved more toying and picking than eating. Mrs Paxson and Captain Gordon updated Mr Paxson on the events outside of the mission, things he might not have heard about from the traders and miners who passed through on their way up north. After a while the discussion turned to the mission news and Mr Paxson relayed the latest incidents. Though Máire was mildly aware of the discussion up to this point, when Mr Paxson spoke of the mission she listened intently. He told them that Chief Kowklux's nephew Tinneh-tark had insulted another powerful Chilkat man named Big Tom. In retaliation Big Tom had threatened to kill Tinneh-tark.

'So Tinneh-tark offers to make peace,' Mr Paxson explained. 'Then Big Tom comes down to the trading post to get some of our kind of food and calls Tinneh-tark to a feast of peace and blanket-giving, to make amends for his threat against Tinneh-tark. Tinneh-tark, for some reason, decided not to accept his offer and so Big Tom threatened him again.' Mr Paxson shook his head and took a drink from his cup. 'I thought it couldn't get any worse—there was gonna be war for sure. But then worse does happen when Tinneh-tark goes and quarrels with both his wives, and they being mother and daughter, they up and left.'

'Left?' Mrs Paxson said. 'Did they go back to Sitka?'

'No, they went to stay with Kowklux's family, his wife is from the same clan as Tinneh-tark's wives.'

Captain Gordon narrowed his eyes. 'How did Kowklux respond to his nephew's wives showing up?'

'Luckily, he was away visiting one of the other Chilkat chiefs,' Mr

Paxson said. 'So I asked Tinneh-tark to come see me if he would. At first he said no, he was too busy. Then finally, a few days later he comes, his face all blackened like he was ready for war. I sat him down, gave him some grub and told him he deserved great honour for his efforts at peacemaking, and that I wondered if there was anything I could do to help.'

'I'm glad you were able to persuade them to behave, dear,' Mrs Paxson said. She gathered her mouth in a prim line before continuing. 'They need constant reminders of the Lord's view on quarrelling with neighbours.'

'Sometimes words are not enough,' Captain Gordon said. 'Paxson, if you should need our help, you have only to ask. A quick blast across the water from one of my guns and they see reason soon enough.'

Máire's eyes widened at these remarks. Her difficulty in grasping that their culture allowed two wives was quickly replaced by the desire to question the need for such drastic steps to help these people arrive at peace. She glanced over at William to see his reaction and caught his eye. He smiled slightly and raised his brow. His meaning seemed unclear to her. Could she have read an objection there, however silent?

'As it turned out, we didn't need any help,' Mr Paxson said. 'Tinneh-tark spent a few hours ranting and raving about Big Tom, and how he'd been wronged by him until he ran out of steam. I asked him to remember what the minister said about fighting and how it came to no good. He went away quiet and the next day he comes to me and says he's changed his mind and he will accept Big Tom's peace offer, and not only that, he'd make peace with his wives too.' Mr Paxson grinned. 'Boy I can tell you I was relieved. There was Kowklux due back any time and Chief Goutchsha-ee coming in from Sitka to visit with Kowklux, both of them sure to get worked up over Tinneh-tark's quarrel with his wives.'

'The Lord was surely smiling down on us then,' said Mrs Paxson. 'The last thing we need is another war breaking out. It's bad for the mission work and the trading post.'

'Surely things wouldn't have escalated that far,' Máire said.

'Martha, you know nothing,' Mrs Paxson said. 'Things begin and escalate at the slightest provocation. These natives are very touchy about any perceived slight on their honour. You'd best take note. It's all nonsense really, but sometimes you have to be careful to be safe. The sooner we drum these things out of them, the better for everyone.'

'I'm sure Martha will catch on quick enough,' Mr Paxson said. 'And we'll be here to help her.'

'I'm sure she will, too,' William said. 'After all, she's one of us.'

'That's right,' Captain Gordon said. 'And God knows we need as many bodies here as we can get to help tame this wilderness.'

Máire looked around at the gathered group and wondered how much she would become one of them in fact, for at the moment, she resisted William's confident words. When she listened to Mrs Paxson and thought of the many ways in which her companion found her lacking, Máire wondered at her own presumption in coming here. It wasn't the names, the complex relationships or the customs that caused her to pause, but the manner of this group before her. She could not bring herself to think she might eventually feel as they did, though she could not even name what exactly that feeling was they possessed. Perhaps it was that everything was so new and strange to her and its very newness and strangeness made her feel apart from all else here. But did she feel apart from all else? Did she not feel some connection already to her surroundings, a connection that already held her firmly to this land? That she could not deny; she could even take comfort and strength from it. Surely that connection would see her through until she became accustomed to the rest.

CHAPTER TEN

The next morning it was the raven that woke Máire, his deep throaty caw piercing her dreams. She looked out the window, the bright sun lighting up the view, and spied the raven perched on a branch of a nearby tree, the limb swaying softly in the breeze. The sun played off his wing, giving silver-blue hues to the black feathers. He cawed again, his curved beak opening wide. He was large and daunting, feathers ruffling in the breeze, eyeing the world unblinkingly. Then, under some sudden notion, he rose into the sky, great wings pushing downward with swooping grace.

Máire looked beyond the branch to the water, its soft current creating ripples that shone like cut glass. Along the riverbank women pulled in fish lines, their backs and arms bending and stretching in an unspoken rhythm. There was music here too, humming its soft undercurrents. Máire laid her hand on the window ledge and tapped a finger lightly to its beat. The confusion and tension of the day before diminished under such energy and life. She looked to her left. Just up from the bank, beside one of the plank houses some men stood talking, clad in trousers of various coloured cloths and their chests bare of any covering. Some children ran by, laughing and shrieking at whatever game they were playing. Máire could only smile. Some things were not so exotic.

A little while later Máire joined Mr and Mrs Paxson in the little kitchen where the pair had just finished their breakfast. Mr Paxson greeted Máire cordially, his wiry frame hunched over the table while he nursed a steaming cup of coffee. A hunk of bread lay on a platter beside him, a knife propped against it.

'So you're up now,' said Mrs Paxson, seated opposite on a ladder-back chair and dressed in her usual drab brown. She had omitted her bustle, Máire noticed with relief, for she had done the same. 'We have enough to do today. I let you sleep longer than usual, in consideration of your journey. Don't expect to make it a regular habit, though.' She poured a cup of black coffee and pushed it towards Máire. Máire sat down on a stool in between the two of them and stared down at the dark liquid, bracing herself for its bitter taste.

'Oh, I am generally an early riser, Mrs Paxson,' Máire replied as she sipped the coffee gingerly.

'Good,' Mrs Paxson said. 'I don't hold with layabeds.'

Máire declined to comment. It was not a point she felt she needed to press, especially with someone as dogged as Mrs Paxson. She could only hope that time would make her point. Máire switched topics. 'You mentioned there was plenty to do today. Will I be able to look inside the school at all?'

'You'll see the school and the rest of the mission today,' Mrs Paxson said. 'Then we can turn to the subject of getting classes started up again.'

'I look forward to it.'

'Have some bread Máire, Mr Paxson. 'It's mighty fine.'

Máire sliced some bread off the loaf gratefully, as she realized how hungry she was after her meagre repast the night before. She spread the jam across its surface carefully and bit into it, and felt the deep flavours burst in her mouth. 'This is wonderful,' she said, finally. 'What kind of jam is this?'

'It's made from salmonberries, special to Alaska,' Mr Paxson said, his eyes alight.

'Delicious. Mrs Paxson, you are to be complimented.'

Mrs Paxson gave a tight smile. 'I make the jam from a need to be prudent with our food supplies. I also preserve vegetables we grow in the garden. It's one of the many tasks that must be done.'

'I look forward to discovering many more wonders here,' Máire said, determined to be pleasant.

Mrs Paxson gave her a direct look. 'There are plenty of wonders in Alaska. These wonders can swallow you up fine, but if you're not careful they can also spit you out.'

'We don't tolerate waste here,' Mrs Paxson said.

They were in the trading post where Mrs Paxson insisted they begin the tour. She had already showed Máire where each item found its place, from the barrels of dried fish and the sacks of flour to the hardtack and coffee beans used most often by miners on their way to prospecting, or utter foolishness as Mrs Paxson described it. It was as if Máire's work there the day before hadn't occurred. When she showed Máire an item she also explained the exacting method for measuring and weighing each portion, and the notation of the transaction required for the trading post ledger.

Mr Paxson stood propped up against the counter, hands in his pockets while Mrs Paxson held forth about wastage. Mr Paxson casually interjected from time to time. Máire became aware that waste was frowned upon for more than its moral effect since food stores were not only at the mercy of successful tilling, hunting and fishing, but also the vagaries of passing ships. There had been some attempt to establish regular port calls by ship steamers, but more often than not ships were delayed or detoured, or they opted for a more important port. As a simple mission station and trading post, this place did not rate high with most enterprises that conducted business in Alaska.

Just as Mrs Paxson finished her explanation the front door opened, and a young Tlingit man walked in, his shoes scraping the worn wood floor. He nodded over at the group, removing a battered trilby, and pulled at the cuffs of his jacket, a shapeless worsted wool whose edges betrayed tiny frayed threads that dangled along his wool trousers. After greeting Mr Paxson he welcomed Mrs Paxson back from her journey. His English was distinct and polite, betraying only a hint of an accent that denoted its foreign nature. He greeted Máire. 'Good morning, Miss.'

'I'm glad you're back now, Joseph,' Mrs Paxson. 'Was your family in good health?'

'Yes, Mrs Paxson,' he said, his eyes downcast. 'I am sorry I was not here to assist with your arrival yesterday.' He removed his jacket to reveal a linen shirt, slightly yellowed, the paper collar missing from his throat. Carefully he hung his jacket and hat on the hook behind the counter, smoothed his barbered hair back into place, and turned to face them once again.

'Don't worry about that,' Mr Paxson said. 'We managed well enough with the help of our new arrival here.' Mr Paxson introduced Máire to Joseph, his manner friendly and genial, and he gave Joseph Máire's name in return, or rather Martha coupled with her last name. Máire struggled once again over how to reply and whether to correct but as before, the moment was lost in Joseph's reply.

'Pleased to meet you, Miss McNair.' He offered his hand, which Máire took, looking into tentative, but friendly dark eyes. 'We have looked forward to your arrival for some time now,' he added.

'And I've been most anxious to arrive,' Máire told him, and smiled in return. She couldn't help but like Joseph, his shy kindness so endearing at this moment that she felt immediately drawn to him.

'Joseph works here with me,' Mr Paxson said. He patted Joseph on the shoulder. 'He stays in the back, in the kitchen. We've a fold-out cot he uses so he can be close to the store in case there's a need. I rely on him for everything from the accounts to interpreting for the Chilkat who come in and don't speak English. I'd be lost without him, that's for sure.'

'Joseph also helps out in the Sunday school and serves as interpreter for the Reverend Carter when he needs it,' Mrs Paxson said. She regarded Joseph in an approving manner that struck Máire as one that might be used when displaying prize embroidery or perhaps demonstrating a dog taught special tricks.

'You do sound invaluable indeed,' Máire said. She searched for something more to say. 'I only hope I can someday match half your worth.'

Joseph nodded, his face betraying neither pleasure nor disapproval at the comments. Máire suddenly felt her remark to be stupid, not praise at all, but something that sounded far more patronizing than the statements of Mr or Mrs Paxson. She hoped he wouldn't feel them to be so, for she meant the words in their true meaning and not, as they sounded to her, like meagre assurances and praise given to any child. She blushed at her inadequacy.

CHAPTER ELEVEN

Mrs Paxson was called up to the manse to organize the food supplies, so it was several hours before she showed Máire the rest of the mission. After retrieving Máire from the kitchen, Mrs Paxson led her across the field outside the trading post to the other mission buildings at the opposite end of the clearing. At the clearing edge, by several Chilkat homes, stood great carved poles shaped into wings, tails, flailing arms or bulging eyes coloured boldly in blacks, reds and whites to create a terrifying beauty.

Máire asked about the poles, keeping her voice low when she saw a few old men on a bench outside a nearby home. They nodded as she and Mrs Paxson passed by, their arms crossed along the bright calico that covered their chests. A silver bracelet circling a wrist winked in the light.

'They're totem poles,' said Mrs Paxson, her lips pursed in disapproval. 'They indicate the owner's totems, their animal emblems. We encouraged them to leave such things behind when they brought their houses here, but we weren't altogether successful.' Her voice was loud and firm and was easily overheard by any who cared to.

'They brought their houses here?' Máire asked. The houses were striking, but she just couldn't imagine such an effort being made. Mrs Paxson caught Máire's quizzical look and explained the importance they placed on their houses because they denoted affluence and rank.

'When Kowklux decided to come here to the mission from his village, his people took down their houses and reconstructed them on this site,' she added.

Máire looked over at the houses, studied them with fresh interest and marvelled at the care and craft of such actions. They were vertically planked structures with elaborate depictions of leering animals, and other designs she couldn't make out, painted on their sides. Smoke curled lazily up from a centre roof hole of a house they passed, its large expanse heavily adorned with a figure similar to one on the totem pole at its side. Máire recognized the curved beak and piercing eyes of the raven.

'Is that the raven totem?' she asked Mrs Paxson.

Mrs Paxson nodded. 'It's Chief Kowklux's home. But don't pay any mind to that animal nonsense. We don't encourage it at all,' she added.

Máire ignored her disapproval and studied the totem carefully. It towered well above the average person, its dramatic carving reinforcing the power of its height. It struck her as a message of some type, one that more than humans would comprehend.

A woman emerged from Kowklux's house, black hair pulled back in a bun, her hands enveloped in the white apron tied around a startling crimson dress. She smiled at them, showing a small gap in her teeth, then folded her arms across her waist and waited for them to approach.

'Hello, Elizabeth,' Mrs Paxson said. 'I imagine you would like to meet our new teacher, Miss McNair,' she continued, showing a thin smile. She put her hand to Máire's arm. 'This is Kowklux's wife, Elizabeth.'

'Hello, Elizabeth.' Máire stretched out her hand. 'I'm pleased to meet you.'

She took her hand with three fingers and released it quickly, nodding. 'Welcome. We are happy you are here.'

'Thank you. I'm very glad to be here. I look forward to teaching the children and getting to know all of you.' As Máire spoke, other women began to gather behind Elizabeth, their clothes a blending of colours and styles that mixed native and white cultures. It was a startling array, as were the faces that peered at Máire curiously. She tried to smile at all of them one by one. She caught sight of a young woman tucked in behind another, cradling a babe in her arms. She looked so young, almost too young to have a child, and as all manner of reasons for her youthful motherhood came to Máire, she thought of ways she might help her, or women like her. Máire gave her a meaningful smile that she hoped conveyed all her desire to help.

Máire tried to decipher the name of the young woman during the quick recital of names, and she thought Mrs Paxson called her Martha, though the number of names she heard made matching the faces difficult. Martha, the name given her and which was just as ill-matched.

After Máire said a few more friendly words, Mrs Paxson made their excuses, took Máire's arm and guided her past the women over the short distance to the church. It was new, constructed from split logs that contained a set of stairs and double doors. On the far side a bell hung in its wooden tower, a neatly twined rope dangling beside it. Together Mrs Paxson and Máire mounted the stairs and went through the whitewashed wooden door to the room inside. Freshly hewn pine benches scented the air, all of them aligned towards the pulpit up front where light from windows behind it illuminated it in canted shafts. The room was bare of any decoration except for a framed Lord's Prayer hanging in the space between the windows by the pulpit and a few curiously painted pieces of cloth that hung on the wall to the left. Máire moved closer and found that one of them was a crude manger scene, the crooked yellow halo of the baby Jesus edged in mud brown as it mixed with the colours of the manger.

'Our first Sunday school group painted that,' Mrs Paxson said. 'Mrs Carter and I helped them mix the paints and showed them how to use the paintbrush. It is a fine effort, I think.'

'It is indeed,' Máire murmured.

Máire turned from the wall with the manger scene and looked around the room. 'Such a large space.'

'We're proud of our new church,' Mrs Paxson said. 'Before it was built we met in the school. As you'll see, it's old and much too small for a church service.'

'How many attend church now?'

'It varies greatly, depending on the season,' Mrs Paxson answered. 'If the men aren't hunting, or it's not the season for preparing winter stores, we can have close to fifty or sixty, sometimes a hundred at one time. But during their busy season, when the Chilkat are gathering food for winter, the numbers can be sparse. It's that time now.'

'Even with those of Kowklux's people who moved their village down here?'

'They may have moved their village down here, but many still use the summer camps for hunting, fishing and preparing their fish oils and such for winter. But this summer we persuaded some of them to stay at the mission so they could regularly attend church, and school when it starts. They're fishing and hunting from the mission village, but not as actively. We're here to help them out now. Still, we sometimes visit them in their camps, so they're never too long separated from the word of the Lord.'

Máire nodded slowly and thought upon these people whose way of life called them from place to place, their rhythms and homes established by seasons and sea, rather than a tolling bell or a wooden house. How could they line up on hard benches and sit for hours listening to someone preach in a language that was not their own? Many was the time when she sat on hard benches, her own mind in other places while the preacher sermonized in his clipped, careful tones.

'Do you still hold services when the minister isn't present?' Máire finally asked.

Mrs Paxson gave a proud smile. 'Yes. With Joseph's help we instruct them from the Bible, sing hymns and give homilies.'

'You do this yourself?' Máire was surprised that a woman would be allowed to do this. Such an event was out of the imagination of her Belfast church community.

'Needs must, my girl, needs must,' she told Máire. 'The church understands that on the mission, things are not always as they should be. I also lead them in the Lord's prayer in both English and Tlingit.'

'You speak their language?' Máire asked in admiration. She wondered if she would ever be able to learn a language that seemed so complex, its syllables and sounds so breathy.

'I speak some. Mr Paxson speaks it passably, enough to converse a little. It's a tricky language full of ugly heathenish sounds.' She eyed Máire carefully. 'It would be helpful if you could learn basic sentences, for teaching. But if you should find it beyond your capabilities, I'm certain you can get one of the children to translate for you. Joseph will help you for a little while, until you settle on someone, but really his duties are elsewhere.'

'I'll do my best, Mrs Paxson.' Máire felt somewhat bemused, realizing she had never considered the complexity of teaching with an interpreter. A rush of apprehension took hold. Would she be able to ever learn the language? Mrs Paxson was able to learn something of it, though she considered it ugly. The little Máire had overheard seemed far from ugly; rather it sounded full of secret breaths and sounds from another world entirely.

'Well, we had best get on to the school now.' Mrs Paxson headed toward the door. She shut it slowly and carefully behind them. Máire followed her down the few steps and along the grass path to the small building that stood at the verge of tall pine trees. Its weathered vertical planks betrayed a few gaps here and there and the roof had a decided curve to it, the moss clinging to its shingles as it would a tree. Máire loved this little school immediately. It seemed dear and sweet—nothing like the Ladies' Academy with its flower-papered walls and too-fine china, or her own sparsely furnished nursery where, as a child, she sat at a table alone except for the governess, who stood stiffly beside her teaching Máire her sums.

The door squeaked a protest as they opened it, its knob hanging loosely from its perch. Inside, the light poured in from a window on each side. Máire entered deliberately and savoured the feel of the wooden boards worn smooth under her feet. A few rickety benches were lined up against the wall, slates stacked in twos and threes at their ends. A large stool sat at the front of the room, opposite the door, with a small battered stove that provided heat only a few feet away. Overhead, the whitewashed cheesecloth that hung from the ceiling revealed flecks of light where the sun poured in through the holes in the roof shingles. Máire looked around at the floor and benches to see if they showed traces of weather and warping from the vagaries of the roof above.

'Where are the books?' Máire asked, puzzled. Moving towards the front of the room, she could see no storage cupboard, no desk, no chalk board for herself, nor any other sort of equipment she might have expected in a school room.

'Supplies are always short. We must do the best we can. Why, when we first arrived, Mrs Carter, the minister's wife, had no slates at all. She held up pictures from her own books and pointed to them.' Mrs Paxson gestured around her. 'This building was not constructed to be a school. It was a storage shed for the trading post, until it was a church. Then, at Mr Jackson's request, the mission decided to start a school and this was the only space available.' She gave Máire a long, hard measuring stare. 'If you're clever, you'll manage.'

Máire bit her lip, unable to reply. Mrs Paxson moved away from her towards the window on the right. 'Besides,' she said. 'I wonder sometimes if they're ready to tackle such things as reading, writing and arithmetic when they have not mastered the basics rudiments of sewing, baking, and cleaning. Even the adults are as children in such skills and must be taught these things from scratch.'

'You would even have the men and boys learn such things?' Máire's tone was innocent.

'The men and boys, well, of course not. No, they are to be taught through their daughters and wives about such things as proper manners, but they could do with some direct instruction on the ways of basic cleanliness, and perhaps some rudimentary carpentry skills or some such thing.'

Máire declined to bait her further and murmured only some inconsequential words. How much added carpentry skill was needed in the group of men who carved such wondrous large poles? As she mused, her eyes wandered the room and lit upon a framed photograph that hung upon the wall to her left. She rose and walked over to it, intrigued by the four suited young men depicted. Drawing closer she could see that they were not white, but native, their dark tilted eyes staring widely back at her. She examined the photograph carefully and was astonished to find Joseph's face on the far right, wearing a bemused look above a stiffened collar, a tie and the worsted wool jacket sporting the vigour of newness.

'It's Joseph!' Máire said aloud, surprised.

'Yes, that's Joseph there, with the other three who were sent off east, to Philadelphia, to be educated. Their fathers wanted them to become 'Boston Men,' so it was arranged through the Reverend Jackson.'

'Boston Men?' Máire's geography of America was vague, but she knew Boston and Philadelphia were not one and the same.

'They use that term to mean a person civilized and educated in a white man's institution. I believe the name comes from the first group of American men they encountered. They were from Boston.'

'I see.' Máire turned her attention back to the photograph. 'Who were the others that were sent?'

Mrs Paxson moved over to the photograph, and pointed to each in turn as she named them. 'The first on the left is Jackson. Jackson did very well. He went on to marry Bessie, and they are both missionaries in the villages up north. The next is Robert. Robert is a sweet boy and helps his mother a great deal. He lives with her and his younger sister in one of the outlying villages.'

'He isn't married?'

'No, he hasn't found a Christian girl to take as wife yet. But he upholds his principles and leads a good Christian life to serve as an example for his people.'

Máire nodded and wondered what kind of life it must be for Robert, to wait for a girl of sufficient Christian attitude to appear and become his wife. Máire pointed to the next image, noticing something uncommonly familiar about his eyes. 'And who is that?'

'*That* is Daniel.' Mrs Paxson's lips drew into a tight line. 'You remember Daniel. He was there yesterday, when we first came ashore.'

Máire's mouth dropped slightly then began to form words of disbelief as she leaned over to study the photograph closely. Like the other three, Daniel was dressed in a jacket. But the tie and stiff collar that encircled his neck more closely resembled a noose than any kind of mode of dress. Despite the obvious discomfort, Daniel smiled widely, his high boned face bright and shining, a world of hope coming from his eyes. Máire stared long and hard at those eyes, asking of them all the questions that raced through her mind. What gave a boy so much hope and what had happened to it? Had it disappeared or had he grown out of it like the suit, the cut of his hair and the smooth innocence of his face?

'We expected much from Daniel,' Mrs Paxson said. 'His father was a sub chief of some sort. And his mother's people were influential too. Daniel was a bright boy, quick to learn and easy of manner. He seemed the best of those selected for this special opportunity.'

'What happened?' Máire found herself desperate to know, to understand more of this man who seemed so far from a 'Boston Man' than anything she could ever imagine. The man she recalled, the man who carried her with effortless grace to shore, appeared more at home in the sea waves and forest paths than the streets of a bustling city in America.

'He threw it all away, that's what happened,' answered Mrs Paxson, her voice filled with ire. 'Threw it all away and went back to wild heathenish ways, as though he never heard a word of our teachings all these years.' She sniffed and turned from the photograph. 'Still, the other three boys are good boys and we can be thankful for that.'

She walked to the end of the schoolroom, to the door. The tour was finished. 'You can come by later this afternoon and do whatever tidying you see fit. The next few days we'll need to devote to visiting the villages and letting them know the school is reopening. Let's see, today is Tuesday, three days to visit the villages, and that takes us to Friday. We'll say Monday, then. The school will open Monday.' She noticed Máire's look of surprise, for Máire had not expected to begin so soon. 'There is no time to waste. We want to get in as much schooling as possible before the winter weather strikes and the outer villages won't be able to come.'

By the evening, Máire felt the impressions of the day laying heavily on her like the weight of many quilts, so that after the meal she slipped away to the river for some quiet moments by herself to give all of it consideration. When she reached the water's edge she inhaled the scents of the river and dew forming on the grass while the sun's faded light cast weak shadows along the bank. It was only then, in the calm of the lapping water that Máire was able to admit she was overcome by the magnitude of her task. What fool was she to think she could manage this mission work when she had never taught in her life, could speak no word of their language and understood little of their culture? Would they realize that she had come here not for any great noble purpose but only for her own longings? Already these people seemed more than she could understand, their ideas and expectations of her unnamed for the most part. She thought of Cook and all the years of comfort she'd provided for Máire. Was she wrong in her anger? Was she just foolish in her dreams? Her thoughts turned to Daniel and his views on her prospective work as a mission teacher. What would he think of the new mission school, he who'd discontinued his own schooling? What had happened to cause such a change? Máire thought of the image in the photograph, the image that reached out and touched her heart. Was the man so very different from the boy?

A shout caught Máire's attention and she looked up towards the manse to see William hailing Lieutenant Bissell at the edge of the wood. She turned back to face the river, shrinking down along the ground, hoping William wouldn't see her. She had no desire for his company then.

The moment having safely passed, she gazed out upon the river and for an instant there, in the fading light, she could swear she saw seals playing among the rocks, their silky heads catching the remnants of light from the disappearing sun.

CHAPTER TWELVE

It was the third day of their journey around the villages and by this point Máire was on much better terms with the canoe, despite her corset's efforts to hamper that process. Hewn from one long hemlock log, the canoe was long and narrow, its wooden prow an elaborately carved animal. A canoe, she had discovered, is an unstable thing that required a person to sit just so. And only now had she found herself in relative harmony with it, aided by fewer petticoats and looser stays.

'We'll make a sailor of you yet, Miss McNair,' William said.

'Oh really, Lieutenant,' Mrs Paxson said. 'Negotiating a canoe down a river is hardly a grand naval accomplishment.'

'Perhaps not,' he said. 'But it does speak of what can be achieved with determination and practice.' William fixed Mrs Paxson with a benign smile. Mrs Paxson's only reply was to narrow her eyes.

William had joined their party at the last minute as an escort, and also so that he might pursue what he termed 'his naturalist interests.' It was a reason he'd occasionally reinforced with a few halfhearted attempts at naming some plants and wildlife for Máire. She was flattered by his attentions and happy enough to have his company during what was proving to be a journey full of so many extremes of emotion.

Initially she was almost overwhelmed by the lushness of the huge stands of hemlock trees festooned with large vines, moss and mistletoe that lined the path they followed to the river to launch the canoe. On the open water the wind slapped her face with colour as she helped William bail water that sloshed in the canoe from the wake of the paddle.

They arrived at the first village with wet skirts and trousers but Máire hardly noticed, she was so taken by the spectacle in view. Though most of the villagers were away gathering winter food stores in the camps, the remaining elderly group still worked at preparing their own supplies. It was difficult not to gawk at the older tattooed men and women with beringed noses draping fish over drying racks or bending over a few small canoes containing a pungent liquid. Its odour was so strong she had to suppress the urge to retch.

'Why are they heating the liquid in the canoe?' she finally asked Joseph. He somehow seemed the most approachable and knowledgeable of her group. 'Doesn't it endanger the bottom of the canoe?'

'It is not hot enough for it to burn, Miss McNair,' he said. 'They heat the stones on a nearby fire and then drop them into the water.' He shifted uncomfortably. 'A pot is much smaller and would not allow the hooligan to be prepared in such big batches, so it would take longer.'

'Hooligan? Is that what they're making?' Máire asked.

'Yes, it is like lard, I suppose. It is sometimes mixed with berries, especially salmon berries and eaten as a sweet, a delicacy. Or, people also dip slices of fish in it before they eat them.' Seeing Máire's puzzled face he added, 'I know it must seem rather strange to you, but it is the custom.'

It was one of many customs that she called upon Joseph to explain later that evening along with the food she'd eaten. They were seated in a single-roomed house on a platform that wrapped around three sides. The chief, Galge, and the remaining group were gathered there for a meal. Máire found the different food exciting and was eager to try the local method of eating with her fingers.

'It is not so bad, then?' asked Joseph wryly after she tasted the hooligan.

'Different,' she replied, trying not to gag. 'Perhaps it's more of a cultivated taste.'

'I do not have it often,' Joseph said. 'Only if I go to my village. At the store the Paxsons are kind enough to provide me with meals.'

'Have you lived with the Paxsons long?' she asked.

'Since I returned from Philadelphia. They hired me to work in the store about a month later. Mrs Paxson said I could be an example to the others.' His eyes flickered almost imperceptibly. 'I have tried to live up to her expectations.'

'I'm sure you've done that and more,' Máire said. She was silent for a moment, considering his words. She glanced over at Mrs Paxson who was speaking with William. 'What would happen if you marry?' She thought of the little folding bed. A flush crept over Joseph's face. She felt instantly repentant over frankness she would never have dared among her father's friends. 'I'm sorry, I didn't mean to pry, Joseph. You don't have to answer that question.'

'No, do not worry.' He cleared his throat. 'I hope that some day I shall marry and have children and raise them as Christians.'

Máire tried to make up for her impertinence. 'I'm sure there are many Tlingit women who would be eager to marry you, Joseph.' Joseph flushed again, reached across for another handful of berries and only nodded at her remark.

William glanced over at Máire then and offered her some bread, taking her attention. William had only tried the fish oil once, declared it interesting, but apparently not enough to make more than one trip to the bowl. Mrs Paxson reserved the right to decline the delicacy, and though she sampled the berries, she ate her fill of the bread and cheese they'd brought with them in an oilcloth sack.

It was after the meal was over that Máire began to feel discomfort. It began when Mrs Paxson rose and addressed the small group in English while Joseph translated.

'We have great news to bring to you,' Mrs Paxson began. 'News that you will welcome in your hearts. We now have a school teacher at the mission. A teacher who will bring you to the ways of Jesus, the ways of good Christian people.'

She pressed on in her speech, announced the advantages of learning at the school and encouraged the parents to bring their children 'bright and freshly-washed' to the school when it started. They nodded their heads when Joseph finished translating her last words, nods that were neither enthusiastic nor diffident, merely neutral acknowledgment of Mrs Paxson's efforts at presenting her case.

Then the chief, Galge, rose. 'We thank you for your words, Mrs Preacher Lady,' he said through Joseph's translation. 'We will see what we can do. But now we would be glad to sing one of your Jesus songs.' He grinned and waited expectantly.

After a moment she assented and launched into *The Old Rugged Cross*. The group followed her voice, intoning the melody in a rhythm that seemed more like a chant than a rousing hymn. But Máire could only wonder at Mrs Paxson's omission of thanks to their hosts when she began her speech. Mrs Paxson had launched directly into the opening of the school. She seemed so sure of their desire to attend school and learn her way of doing things. Would they want her to teach them to read and write and work sums? They seemed more enthusiastic about hymn-singing than about the thought of schooling for their children. Would an education really help them to make their way in the world? She thought of Joseph and his pride at serving in the trading post for the Paxsons. In some ways perhaps it was a good source of employment, an outlet for his education. Many back in Ireland were never so lucky. It made her uncomfortable, though, to see him uninterested in his own people and to be so determined to do things like white men. But that was what she was here to do. To help the Tlingits adapt to the ways of the whites. And Joseph was a shining example of such efforts.

It was a question that continued to provide an undertone for the next day as they arrived in the second village. Some hours' journey further on, it was bigger than the previous village and contained more substantially built houses, with more elaborately carved totems and painted house fronts. Like in the other village, a few elderly people worked outside the houses preparing a variety of foods, crowding racks with fish, pressing berries between wooden frames, and draping seaweed along rocks. The chief here was Kutchewhe, whose proud bearing filled out the fine needlework cloak that covered his shoulders, and whose manner of address placed him as a more powerful leader than Galge.

'Will we be staying with the chief tonight?' Máire asked after they met him.

'No,' Mr Paxson answered. 'I don't think so. We'll probably stay with Joseph's family. That would be the mannerly thing.'

'This is Joseph's village?' Máire asked.

'I don't suppose you'd have known,' Mr Paxson said. 'Yep, this is his village and his family are all still here.'

'Didn't they want to move down to the mission to be near Joseph?'

'Well, it's not that simple. Their kin, their clan is here. Kowklux's people, they're frog clan and whale clan, among other things. They don't always get on.'

Máire nodded, but she felt the intricacies of the clan relationships would take some time to get used to.

Joseph's family met them just outside their house. Shorter than Máire by half a head, his father stood straight and stiff beside his wife, a round woman with laughing eyes. His father greeted them in careful English, while Joseph stood anxiously beside him, casting him brief glances.

Mrs Paxson answered his greeting and held out her hand. Joseph's father took her hand with his for a moment then let it drop. 'Jimmy and Alice, I'd like you to meet our new teacher, Miss McNair.' Mrs Paxson stepped aside to allow them to see Máire clearly.

Jimmy acknowledged Máire with a nod and a brief smile and Máire murmured her own greeting. Alice, her eyes alight and full of some private humour, looked over at Máire who found herself warming to the older woman immediately. A young girl tugged at Alice's skirts and said something to her. Behind her were an older girl and boy. All three children were dressed in calico shifts, their eyes wide and staring, none of them over the age of eight or nine.

'Hello,' Máire said.

'That's my younger brother and my sisters,' Joseph said.

Máire smiled at them and asked their names. They moved back behind their mother's skirts, too shy to answer.

'That's Tillie,' Mrs Paxson said, indicating the taller and older-looking of the two girls who peered out at Máire. 'This is Annie, and this is Paul,' she added, pointing to the other two in turn.

Máire greeted them. 'My name is Miss Martha McNair.'

'Miss McNair is your new teacher,' Mrs Paxson said. 'She'll be starting the new school for you soon.'

'I hope I shall see you all there.' Máire nodded encouragingly. She looked up at Alice, but her eyes were downcast and Máire couldn't see her response. Joseph's father, Jimmy, gave a quick neutral nod when she looked over at him.

'Our son told us about you,' he said. 'Please enjoy our welcome.'

A little while later Joseph showed them into the house. The home was small on the scale of the chief's house, with a fire pit in the centre and a small sleeping platform. Máire was concerned they would be putting them out of their home and spoke of it to Mrs Paxson, but she assured Máire it was not an issue. The home was a clan home and not a family home in the usual sense, and any refusal of their hospitality would be considered an insult. They would all fit themselves into the house well enough, she explained, while they would provide the group with the best place in the house. These were the rules of hospitality, no different from hers.

The evening proved similar to the one before, only on a larger scale. The people were colourfully dressed in their finest embroidered blankets. The food served was as elaborate as the carved and painted cedarwood boxes they sat on and the screens that surrounded them.

Máire gestured around her. 'How impressive this is,' she said to William.

William smiled slightly and shook his head. 'I must say our host looks rather fearsome.' He cocked his head. 'You don't think he plans to have us for a meal, rather than serve us a meal?'

Máire frowned at him, her pleasure dampened by his remarks.

He hastily apologized. 'I'm sorry, I didn't mean to offend you.'

She accepted his apology, but her disquiet lingered.

'Teacher Lady, do you like our Tlingit food?' asked Kutchewhe in simple English. His dark intelligent eyes cut across the group between them. Máire tried to remain calm under his level gaze and assured him that she found the food delicious. Satisfied, he gave a quick nod and turned his attention back to the group at large. Occasionally he addressed remarks to Joseph in Tlingit. Joseph answered him readily enough and even laughed on one occasion, but underneath the good humour and easy answers Máire could sense some tension.

Eventually, Mrs Paxson called Kutchewhe's attention to the purpose of their visit. Like the previous evening, Joseph stood beside Mrs Paxson to translate as she outlined the plans for the school opening and encouraged all the parents to send their children. At the end of her speech, Kutchewhe promised that all who were able would attend, but that the summer's work was not yet done. When all the tasks for laying down the year's store were complete, he promised there would be more time to send children to the school.

Máire began to wonder if it was such a good idea to start the school so soon. Were the Tlingit really anxious to go to school? Did the parents want their children to learn what she was here to teach them? And what could she teach them with her few supplies, lack of language skills and limited experience?

It was a thought that continued to haunt her on the third day, sitting in the canoe, heading to the final village. During this journey they'd had to cross to the other river, Joseph and William porting the canoe over their heads, stopping to rest occasionally on a fallen log or grass outcropping. William said little conversation during these rests, apparently too tired. Only Mr Paxson offered some conversation. They pressed on and eventually resumed their journey in the canoe once again, paddling upriver until they put into a small bay, below short rapids, where the rush of the water drowned out all speech. The group disembarked, Mr Paxson and Joseph working in familiar accord, pulling up the canoe on the bank with a strength and surety that Máire could only admire.

When the two men had stowed the canoe, the group walked along a trail to the village of Chilkoot. It wasn't much of a distance, and before long Máire spied some Tlingit men coming to meet them, their clothes splashing bright colours against the verdant trees and plants. When they met, the lead man exchanged greetings with Joseph in their language. He was broad-chested and taller than any of the Tlingit men Máire had seen, except Daniel. Under a brightly coloured turban his long, unbarbered hair swung against his shoulders as he gestured back behind him, and for a fraction the light caught the ring through his nose. He turned back round and his glance filtered back beyond Joseph and the Paxsons and to her. His eyes narrowed slightly, intensifying the fierce impression he gave. She lowered her gaze under his close scrutiny.

'You are the teacher lady?' he asked in English.

Startled, Máire raised her eyes to his face and was surprised to see a grin there.

'Chief Kowishte,' Mrs Paxson said. 'We have come with good news that we would like to share with your village. I know we can count on a gracious reception.' She held out her hand.

Kowishte slowly moved his gaze to Mrs Paxson. He ignored her hand. 'You are welcome to our home,' he told her.

'Kowishte heard we were coming and has made time in this extremely busy season to extend his full hospitality,' Joseph explained quietly. 'He offers his home to you for as long as you would care to stay.'

'We accept your hospitality with thanks,' Mrs Paxson said.

Kowishte nodded then turned and, with the other two men at his side, led them to the village. Overwhelmed by the crowds of buildings and totem poles that ranged the bluff above the rapids, Máire couldn't help but be impressed and awed.

The pungent odour of the fish drying on scattered racks filled the air. Men and women worked steadily, a few young children playing at their feet. There seemed more people here than the other villages. When Máire asked Joseph about it, he told her that some of the people had come down from the summer camps for a few days because of their visit. She brightened at those words, thinking that perhaps here there was a real interest in the school.

Still trying to take in all the sights and smells, Máire followed slowly behind as they mounted the high steps to Kowishte's home and entered through the wide-arched doorway that opened onto a small platform above the main floor of the room. Its size was the main feature that first impressed her; it was massive, like a church. Slowly she absorbed the display inside on the wood floor below and the platforms above it. Screens, bowls and boxes smelled strongly of the cedar she had come to appreciate. The display was overwhelming, so striking and grand; it was clearly designed to demonstrate Kowishte's influence and power. Máire stole a glance at him. He stood at a careful distance, erect, feet spread—

the consummate warrior king. Máire paused momentarily at the top of the steps and sensed the display's deliberate nature, a message conveyed with subtle force.

'He seems a chief of great influence. More so than the others,' Máire said to Mr Paxson in a soft tone. He was standing beside her and she hoped only he could hear her words.

'You could say that,' he answered. He glanced over at Máire, his eyes full of humour. 'He's the medicine man, as well as the head man here. That's a powerful combination.'

Hearing Mr Paxson's comments, Mrs Paxson cast a frown in Máire's direction. Máire decided to hold her other questions for another time. She looked at Chief Kowishte and thought she detected a hint of a twinkle in his eyes before they moved to down the steps. He led them to two women who stood at the front of the room, by the platform. The shorter woman moved forward to greet us, her numerous bracelets creating a music that belied her disapproving look. Skin creased in folds around her chin and her mouth.

'This is my wife,' said Kowiste, a note of pride in his voice. The woman cast her mouth into a semblance of a smile, revealing teeth yellowed and decayed with age. But it was her eyes that drew Máire. They were steely and piercing, the sort that could sum you up in an instant, and Máire could only imagine what she thought of her, a pale, thin Irish woman. She was Katchekeeluh, Joseph told her in a whisper, and though she was not Kowishte's only wife, Máire was in no doubt from her bearing that she was his main wife.

The other woman stepped forward after the first introductions and Kowishte presented her as his other wife, whose name she eventually determined was Yedicih. She was young and lovely, her skin smooth, her long hair twined in one long braid down her back. When Máire introduced herself, Yedicih gave a warm, generous smile.

A little while later Máire found herself sharing a curtained area with Mrs Paxson, attempting to make herself more presentable, a difficult task in the cramped space and her distracted state as she mused on Kowishte and his people. They somehow seemed more remote than the other villagers they had visited, though their proximity to the mission station was the same. Perhaps the difference lay in their dress and bearing, more strange and defined than in Joseph's village or Kowklux's; or perhaps it was the strength and power that emanated from their leader, Kowishte. There was a confidence, a certainty she hadn't found present in the other villages. All of these things certainly made them different, but Máire could not escape the feeling that there was something more than these named differences, something that made her hand tremble slightly as she refastened the snood over her hair.

CHAPTER THIRTEEN

They gathered for the evening feast in Kowishte's large hall, he sitting in state on the chest on the high platform at the far end of the room, clothed in blue trousers, a pink calico shirt and, draped around his shoulders, a magnificent fringed blanket woven of goat hair and spruce root, died yellow, black and white. On his head he wore a strange conical grass hat, his long hair curling in loose tangles about his painted face. He looked like some great warrior, a legend from Cook's tales.

The guests were seated in the place of honour, on the platform beside Kowishte—Mr and Mrs Paxson on chairs and William and Máire on feather pallets on either side of the Paxsons. Joseph sat on a rush mat next to Máire, his eyes downcast and his face neutral. Máire had no clear understanding of their placement, but she was under no illusions that it was any less complex than the seating arrangements of any dinner party of her father's social circle.

She gazed around the room. The men and women attending the feast filled the hall with their bright robes. Hats like Kowishte's, only smaller, and others of cedar topped the heads of many men, their faces painted fearsome shades of black, red and white, while the women were clad in calico cloth, revealing bare skin. Everywhere feet, ankles and more were uncovered.

Máire tried to suppress her blushes, to reason silently with herself at such a display of naked skin. She looked around for a more settling view and saw a striking young woman seated to the front side of the platform, close to Kowishte's wives, dressed in a brilliant blue calico skirt and blouse partially covered by a deep red blanket trimmed with pearl beads. Her long black hair hung free and luminous in the firelight, accenting the smooth pale beauty of her face as she sat overlooking the crowd, proud and inexpressive. Next to her, Máire saw with a shock, was Daniel's sister, Rebecca. It was only then she realized that the woman in the brilliant blue was an older copy of Rebecca, and must be Daniel's other sister, Sarah.

She thought to ask Mr Paxson, but decided the distance was too great to pose all of the questions that suddenly arose in her mind. Stealing a glance at Joseph, she saw that he too was gazing at Sarah, but with a look that was filled with a mix of hunger, grief and anger. The moment was so brief that Máire wondered if she had imagined it. And then, after that mild speculation, she realized that not only must this be Daniel's village, but also that he was without question closely related to its powerful chief, Kowishte. Would she see Daniel? Perhaps he was in the hall at this very moment. She scoured the room, her pulse quickening as her eyes reviewed all the faces under the basket hats. It was a fruitless search; that it was nigh on impossible to tell the identity of anyone with certainty given the painted faces, the poor light and the clothing did not reassure Máire.

If he was somewhere in this hall, what would he make of the purpose of their visit? Or the words in which Mrs Paxson couched her invitation? The room suddenly seemed close.

The thought of his possible presence so disturbed Máire's thoughts and body that she found it difficult to concentrate on the huge feast laid out before them. The hall fell silent, distracting Máire from her thoughts as Kowishte rose, commanding attention. He faced the missionary group. 'To the warmest place under my wings I welcome you.' His pronunciation was slow and careful. 'To the warmest place under my feathers I welcome you.'

Kowishte turned to the rest of the gathered group and continued in Tlingit, intoning words that Máire could only imagine were of the sort he said to them in English, with perhaps some further instruction or welcome. She glanced at Joseph again and noted his expression betrayed no hint of dismay or anger that would indicate something out of place, and relaxed a little. The chief's tone seemed pleasant and hearty, and after he sat down, the feasting began.

Platter after platter of food lined the blankets. Máire was nearly paralysed with choice. Rabbit, venison, duck she could recognize and moved to try along with the various berries and squash. There was almost too much food but Mrs Paxson still did not feel inclined to eat more than a few berries, her packet of food still sustaining her. Initially Máire had thought perhaps her views on their washing might be the cause for her refusal of their food, but she could no longer put it down to hygiene. Mrs Paxson watched the food with narrowed eyes, her mouth screwed up as she chewed with deliberate care. This fare was clearly unsuitable, too foreign.

Mr Paxson seemed to enjoy the bounty before him and refilled his own bowl several times. He was given a large carved spoon from which to eat the boiled fish and duck. It acted as a bowl and he used it with practiced ease, the thin broth never spilling from the spoon when he held it to his lips. William concentrated on his food, handling his spoon with some awkwardness as he manoeuvred the food into his mouth. Máire, too curious to eat much, watched her companions and their host in fascination, noting the deft manner with which Kowishte checked each of them with a brief glance and gestures to ensure that all ate heartily, without falling short on his own meal. Occasionally he leaned over to exchange words with Katchekeeluh who watched him intently from her place on the platform.

Some time later, when the feasting drew to an end, or at least came to a convenient halting place, Kowishte held up his hand and the hall fell silent. He rose and declaimed something in Tlingit that inspired nods and affirmative noises from the assembled group. Máire looked over at Joseph quizzically.

'Kowishte would like to acknowledge the honour of your visit by giving you some songs and recitations of his clan history,' Joseph said. His voice was very low, his face and expression tight and withdrawn.

'Oh, lovely,' Máire said, ignoring his demeanour. Joseph's humour had not been restored since she had spotted him regarding Sarah so intently.

In response to her remark Joseph made an attempt at a polite smile. 'I am sure you will find it interesting. But I am afraid you will not understand the full meaning. I will explain it to you later.'

Many of the men rose with encouraging looks and shouts that Máire could only imagine were words of agreement with Kowishte's plans. Kowishte nodded, then held up his hand. The men calmed and eventually regained their seats. Kowishte spoke again, and his words seemed to contain some kind of command and instruction that invoked murmurs and curious glances in the direction of Máire's group. Joseph, his mouth set in a determined line, gave an almost imperceptible nod. Before she could ask him to explain what had happened, the assembled group parted for someone at the back of the room. He had on no adornment or paint and wore canvas trousers and a hide shirt. It was Daniel.

He reached the edge of the platform and stood before Kowishte, his body taut with anger. Kowishte spoke to him in a loud, firm tone. Beside her, Máire heard Joseph's sudden intake of breath. Daniel nodded slightly, looked directly at Kowishte and answered in an equally firm tone. They exchanged more words, still polite but somewhat forced. Kowishte ended the exchange and a long silence followed, Daniel holding his eye for a few moments until, surrounded by a dense and breathless quiet, he eventually shifted his gaze to Kowishte's feet. Kowishte nodded and issued a curt statement in Máire's direction. Joseph rose and looked over at Mrs Paxson.

'The chief would like you to make your announcements before they perform the history for you, Mrs Paxson,' he said. 'He will allow me to translate for you.'

Bewildered, Máire watched as Mrs Paxson rose and moved to the edge of the platform with Joseph in her wake, while Daniel climbed its steps and, without a word or glance to anyone, seated himself on the rush mat that Joseph had just vacated. Numbly, Máire watched Mrs Paxson begin her now familiar speech.

Conscious of Daniel's presence, yet not daring to ask him the meaning of his exchange with Kowishte and its results, Máire endured Mrs Paxson's speech. As she sat there, palms sweaty, she heard Mrs Paxson enunciate the words 'washed and clean' and 'befitting learning of the word of the Lord' and she felt shame. Shame over this speech. Shame at the finely hemmed handkerchiefs she had sewn and the baskets of bounty she had carried. It seemed somehow beside the point. As the full depth of her own culpability in the words now spoken revealed itself, Máire closed her eyes tightly, a meagre denial.

A moment later she opened them and glanced over at Daniel. He looked straight ahead, his face in shadow, unreadable. The firelight caught his hands briefly as they rested on his knees, and Máire could see the fierce markings of his tattoos. She opened her mouth to say something to him, but thought better of it and turned to face Mrs Paxson again.

Eventually, Mrs Paxson finished her speech and awaited Kowishte's response. Kowishte smiled widely, looked her up and down and then replied. Joseph translated for her and Máire caught the neutral words that formed his response. Though they had come in greater numbers to hear the mission group's words, they had made no greater commitment to the school and the mission work than the other villages. Máire wondered if Mrs Paxson's words had affected their reaction.

Mrs Paxson took her seat and Joseph sat down directly behind her on the platform. Máire looked quizzically at Daniel who, after a brief glance at Joseph, regarded her soberly. .

'I am to be your translator for the performance of the clan history,' Daniel said, his voice deliberate and bland. 'I'm to help you understand as much as possible its significance in this world.'

'What about Joseph?' Máire asked him. 'Won't he translate just as well?'

'Joseph will instruct the Paxsons and their companion,' he said, then lifted a brow. 'It seems, Miss McNair, that it is important you understand what transpires as fully as possible in view of your potential position as teacher to the clan's children.'

'Thank you, I appreciate the honour,' she said, slightly flustered by Daniel's quizzical manner and impeccable English. His accent was remarkable only in its being distinctly American. Beyond the flawless execution and demeanour, his command of the language showed such a turn of phrase that Máire could not mistake the irony present. Máire caught William leaning over to look in her direction and she smiled at him reassuringly. He gave her a slight nod. She could feel Daniel's hard glance at the exchange. The silence stretched between them and suddenly became unbearable.

'I don't think Mrs Paxson really intended to express herself in quite those words,' Máire babbled. She wanted to apologize for Mrs Paxson, for their presence, for all of it. She knew they had behaved badly somehow.

Daniel looked over at her, his narrow eyes hinting at the anger his tight mouth conveyed. 'I'm sure Florence Paxson is very conscious of the way she expresses herself,' he said.

'What I mean is, I hope that it was received in the spirit of a wish to help, a wish to teach the children things that will help them in the world,' she said. The explanation sounded feeble even to her ears. She sighed. 'I'm sorry, I don't know what I mean.'

For a moment he said nothing, and then a slight smile crossed his face that briefly lit his eyes. It was during that fleeting moment that Máire glimpsed the young Daniel, the boy in the photograph that hung on the schoolroom wall. The boy that looked full of life and hope.

Two men to the side of the platform began to steadily beat a padded stick on handheld drums. The sound reverberated in Máire's ears and through her body to match her heartbeat. Another man emerged from the back, dressed in a stiff white-fringed cape emblazoned with a large stylised eagle in white, red and black. He raised his arms inside the cape, giving the impression of the eagle in flight and swung his torso from side to side, moving across the floor, while one of the drummers chanted words in a singsong manner.

'This is the time after Raven had brought the light, the light of the sun, the moon and the stars,' Daniel explained in a low voice. 'After he stole them from Nascagiel's cedarwood box and released them into the world. This is the time when The People had to leave their homes and journey far, to a new place.' Daniel's voice, not naturally deep, found a rich and transfixing resonance as he recounted the scene acted and sung before them. Fascinated, Máire watched two men enact the journey, each of them bearing their own highly decorated cape, swaying it back and forth to the rhythm of the drums and the song.

'The People journeyed to the East, the place to begin anew,' Daniel continued. 'After much travelling they came to the edge of the land. Was this the place to stop, wondered The People? Then huge trees surrounding them sang a song. A song of Floating on Water. With great thanks they crafted the trees into seafaring canoes and took to the water. Eventually, they came to a great moving ice mountain, a glacier. They knew the side of this ice mountain was the special place for The People, because it was clear Creator had put the obstacle there so no-one else could enter. But how were they to enter? Then the glacier sang a song to them. It was a song of Going Under. Trusting the song, The People sent three women in a small canoe—all widows. Eventually, the women returned and said there was beauty beyond. Slowly, The People went underneath and eventually came out on the other side.'

Daniel's narrative described the scene before her—the men moving along the water, their capes flowing gracefully as they created a paddling motion with their hands, a fluid action, all of them in accord, then three of them moving away from the canoe and going under the moving white mountain, the glacier of strong angular lines that refracted the sun overhead.

It was then, at this point in the narrative, that Máire's world transformed under the vibration of the drums and the magic of his voice. She became one of the widows, paddling evenly behind the other two, their oars slicing the inky water. Her hands burned with the spray from the sea and her hard grip on the paddle. She struggled to meet the rhythm of the two ahead of her, conscious of their strong strokes, their muscled arms and backs. Above her the white ice walls rose in sheer planes, sounding echoes of their efforts along its sides. The woman ahead, a friend, glanced back at her and mouthed words of encouragement, for she dared not speak aloud, less the mountain become angered. For what seemed like hours they struggled to retrace their journey, until the light ahead grew wider and wider, before opening out into the expanse of blue and The People waiting. The three spoke of the beauty, the purity of what lay beyond. There was no doubt it was where they were meant to go. And the three led them back, each canoe filled with The People, hushed under the tension of going under. They led them to the other side and Máire's muscles screamed with pain, but her heart filled with the pride and awe of what she'd done.

A drum sounded loudly and Daniel stopped his narrative. Máire blinked several times and felt his hand touch her arm briefly. Disoriented she breathed deeply, willing huge gulps of air deep into her lungs. She looked over at the dancers who had paused then reassembled in their pageant to continue the story. Daniel picked up the thread again, telling her of The People's movement north, and their eventual arrival at the great divide, in the land where two rivers flowed. Uncertain about what lay ahead on either course, The People decided to separate into two halves, one group taking the one river and the other half taking the other river, so that if some peril should befall either group, some of their people would survive.

'And so that is how the great Chilkoot People came to be here, the houses that make up the clans of the Kaagwaantaan, the Luknaxadee and the Shangukeidee,' Daniel said. As he said these words the performance came to a close, the drums beating insistently. The people stamped their feet, their praise and approval of the performance clear on their face, and through the sound of the pounding, Daniel's last words echoed in her head and the taste of the sea lingered in her mouth. She blinked again and shifted in her place, covertly stretching her aching arms. Was it the burning pain of the hours spent paddling? Carefully she massaged her arms. She could sense Daniel's eyes on her as she tried to gather herself.

'Chilkoot People,' she said to distract him from his scrutiny. 'I thought you were the Chilkat.'

'We are Chilkoot,' Daniel said. 'The Chilkat are the people who journeyed up the other river.'

'But do you not share the same origins and links?' she asked. 'Surely you speak the same language, Daniel, for Joseph speaks and translates it and he's not from this village, he's from the Chilkat River side.'

'Well, Martha,' he said, laying great emphasis on the use of the name. 'I would say the same of the inhabitants of your islands in Europe. Yet I daresay the Scottish, the Welsh and the Irish who do speak English would not generally count themselves English. But you would say they were one and all British.'

For a moment Máire didn't know what to say, nor how to begin to explain that the Irish did have their own language, a language her mother knew, but of which she herself knew nothing. Only her name.

'My name is not Martha,' she muttered. Her words were a defence of herself that was confused even to her ears. 'My name is Máire.'

'And my name is not Daniel,' he replied firmly.

Máire shifted on her cushion, suddenly appalled at her incredible ignorance. Of course he would not have had the name Daniel at birth; the mission was not there during that time. He would have had a name his own mother gave him, a name that was taken away by the missionaries when they arrived. The name Daniel probably had no more meaning to him than Martha had for her.

'What is your name?' she asked him. Máire suddenly wanted to know what his mother called him. What was the name she called when she bid him goodbye as he went off to join his friends or journey with his father?

'You'll have to find that out elsewhere,' he said. He rose from his position, brushing off his trousers as though it were the question she had just asked.

'But what shall I call you?' Máire asked. She was embarrassed by the tinge of desperation she could hear in her voice.

'Not Daniel,' he replied.

'Fine, Not Daniel it shall be,' she said, suddenly irritated. 'I am Not Martha.'

He paused a moment and a hint of humour crossed his eyes. He bowed slightly.

'I bid you good night, Not Martha,' he said. He left the group and made his way down the steps of the platform to the groups of people who were slowly filing out of the hall. Máire stared after his retreating figure, the tangles of his long hair flashing blue-black as he passed the dying firelight.

CHAPTER FOURTEEN

Máire saw no trace of Daniel the next morning as they prepared to leave the village, though she wandered in the clearing and around the houses. Eventually she moved over to the bluff and took a moment to admire the view of the waterfall where she saw Joseph standing in a sunlit silhouette. He was subdued and spoke only a few words when Máire tried to engage him in conversation. Mrs Paxson came up to them before she could try further, and pressed them to make their farewells to Kowishte.

Once on the river there was little opportunity to speak to anyone, and William and Máire set about bailing again as the occasion demanded, the wind deciding to slap the current with great force against the canoe sides. It left her little time to muse on the previous day with her energy and concentration absorbed by the increasingly demanding task. But the journey was quicker this time, the currents sweeping them downriver towards the mission. They were not on the river more than an hour or so before they drew up alongside the bank to disembark. Before continuing their trek on land, burdened with the canoe and luggage, they decided to stop for a small bite to eat.

The effects of a drink and a bit of bread soon had a cheering effect on all of them. Mr Paxson picked a weed and chewed on it, pointing out birds that sounded calls around them. Mrs Paxson began to recount what she would report to Captain Gordon upon her return. The conversation drifted around Máire as she began to relax in the sun's warmth, lulled by the breeze rippling along the river and among the branches of the trees. She stretched her arms, enjoying the cool air.

'Watch that sun, Martha,' Mrs Paxson said. She fixed Máire with her stern eyes and bid her watch out for the sun, handing Máire the hat she had placed on the grass.

'I'm fine, really Mrs Paxson,' Máire protested. She put the hat in her lap, and raised her face to the sun. Such perversity surprised her, though on consideration she found it a feeble protest against the strong emotions and thoughts Mrs Paxson had evoked in the past weeks in her company. The woman was insufferable in so many ways, yet Máire was in no doubt that she depended on Mrs Paxson's good will for the foreseeable future, at least until she was better acquainted with the mission and her work. Surely then she could find some way of detaching herself, both from her household and her close scrutiny.

'You should heed Mrs Paxson,' William said. 'You wouldn't want your lovely skin to burn and darken, something that happens easily in this sun.'

Máire tried to set aside the stab of annoyance that William would take Mrs Paxson's part. Such a reaction was both petty and unhelpful. Though she knew them both to be right, she found it impossible to set aside her irritation. She turned away from William pointedly to speak with Joseph. 'Do you manage to see your family much?'

'I visit when I can.' Joseph's face tightened. 'But it is busy at the trading post. My family understand my obligations.'

'I'm sure it must be hard for you,' she said. She turned to William, his own hat resting on his knee. 'I would think you can sympathize with him, Lieutenant, separated as you are from your family for months, sometimes longer.'

William's face darkened before he effected a shrug. 'The navy is my family, at the moment. Though perhaps someday that will change.'

'The Lieutenant was raised in such a manner that he understands his duty and obligations,' said Mrs Paxson. 'He knows better than to put his feelings in the way of his service to his country.'

Mr Paxson grunted. 'Still, it's natural enough for anyone to miss their family. Even you miss your family, Florence, though no-one can fault you for your dedication to duty. I bet you miss your family too, Martha.'

Máire considered this briefly before conceding that she did. She found she missed Cook, despite her smouldering anger and hurt, and she missed Polly and Annie. Her father was a more difficult prospect and as such she could only push it to the back of her mind. She hadn't written to him yet and had heard nothing from him since her arrival, and nor did she expect to for some time yet. Not until the people at her Belfast church inquired after her and he would find himself lacking knowledge of her progress. Perhaps she would write to him, just to assure him that her choice was correct, that her purpose still strong and committed. For she realized now, despite all that had passed, she was still resolved in her course. That all these obstacles would be overcome, given time, and she could carve her own place here, a place as strong and clear as the totem poles in the villages.

They moved on a short time later, Mr Paxson and William porting the canoe on the first leg, Mrs Paxson following them, and Joseph and Máire bringing up the rear. A while later Máire felt a sharp pain in her foot and realized a small pebble had worked its way into her shoe. Joseph offered to assist her as she stopped to remove the offending object, supporting herself against a tree. He leaned over to undo the laces of her shoe. His manner, friendly and helpful, gave her courage to pose the question she had harboured since the previous evening.

'Joseph,' she said. 'Could you explain to me something about Tlingit ways?'

'I will try,' he answered without looking up, his tone cautious.

'Last night, when I called Daniel by his name, he told me that wasn't his name. I asked him what to call him, but he wouldn't say. He told me to ask someone else.' Joseph was silent, his expression unreadable from her angle. She ploughed on. 'I realize that he must have had another name, a Tlingit name given to him at birth. Is that what he means?'

'Natsilane is the name Daniel was given when he was young,' Joseph said. He shrugged, removing the shoe from her foot and handing it to her. 'Tlingit names can change as they grow to adults. A change in status or some worthy deed can sometimes also earn them a ceremonial name. Take Kowishte. That is a name of a fearsome leader and now he carries that name to give him prestige and honour.'

'Natsilane,' Máire murmured. She repeated the syllables carefully, wanting to pronounce it correctly. She looked over at Joseph. 'But why wouldn't he tell me his name himself?'

Joseph shrugged again. 'Tlingits do not usually say people's names everywhere and all the time. Names are full of power, full of meaning. When a child is first born, it is weak and the people believe that the spirits in heaven would take the child back, if they knew the child's real name. Later, there are other enemies. You do not always want an enemy to know your power; they might use it against you.'

'What do people call each other if they don't use their given name?'

'We call one another by their relationship to us,' he said. He pursed his mouth. 'Like 'Older Sister' and 'Younger Sister'. Or 'Maternal Uncle' and 'Paternal Uncle'.'

'But why would Daniel, I mean Natsilane, then tell me to ask someone else for his name if he didn't want me to know it, or, as you say, use it and perhaps take his power?'

'I do not know, Miss McNair. Perhaps he wanted to make a point.'

Máire stood thoughtfully a moment, the shoe still in her hand, the pebble forgotten. Eventually, she shook her head, looked down at her shoe, emptied out the pebble and handed the shoe back to Joseph.

'What is your name, Joseph?' she asked him. 'The one given to you at birth.'

Joseph remained silent, quickly lacing up her shoe.

'My name is Joseph now,' he finally answered. 'The other name no longer matters.' He left her then, moving off at a quick pace, attempting to catch up with the others.

CHAPTER FIFTEEN

'Things weren't so quiet here while you were away, Paxson,' Captain Gordon said. 'Not quiet at all. Those Indians don't miss a trick.'

They were seated in the manse parlour: Máire, William, Lieutenant Bisell and, lounging uncomfortably against the wall, Joseph. Mrs Paxson was supervising Betty back in the kitchen.

'Why, what's happened?' asked Mr Paxson.

'It's that Kowklux again.'

'Kowklux? What's he done?'

'A Sitka Indian killed one of Kowklux's relatives and now Kowklux is demanding a certain woman from them as payment for the killing. He'd sent gifts to support the demand, but the Sitka family refused the gifts and said they'd only take a slave as a gift.'

'A slave?' Máire asked. 'Surely there are no slaves here?'

Mr Paxson gave her a grim look. 'Oh, they have slaves right enough. Kowklux don't hold with slaves, though, since he became a Christian.' He returned his gaze to the captain. 'So what happened then?'

'Kowklux said he wouldn't send a slave, and that he still needs payment. The whole thing's a stalemate now.'

'That's no stalemate. Kowklux can still retaliate,' Mr Paxson said. 'Have you talked with Kowklux at all?'

'I had a word with him, told him to behave and forget the whole thing. But he wouldn't listen.'

'These natives take things so seriously,' Lieutenant Bissell said, lounging back in his chair. 'I suppose we should do something.'

'I'm sure a few more sharp words from you will have him thinking,'

William said to Captain Gordon. 'Given time.'

'I'll try and talk to him,' said Mr Paxson. 'Maybe I can convince him to settle for a different kind of payment. Something other than the woman. After all, what's he going to do with her? He can't marry the woman, or keep her as a mistress, he's a Christian.'

'I don't know if more words will help,' Captain Gordon said. 'These Indians don't seem to listen to words. It's force they understand. A gun bigger than their own.'

Máire listened to the exchange, trying to make sense of the events described. Occasionally she glanced at Joseph, wondering what his thoughts were behind his neutral expression. For her own part she found it strange, so alien to think that someone's death could require a payment of another life. Was it written or formally agreed that each life taken required another to replace it? How could such a payment be extracted and what of the life, the person who was required to make the payment? What say had they? What would become of them, especially as in Kowklux's case he could not make her his wife, or his mistress? As she contemplated these implications, she wondered if there were other measures of justice just as strange in this foreign culture.

The group eventually proceeded into dinner. At the door William waylaid her a moment.

'Martha, may I escort you on a short walk this evening before you retire?'

Startled, she could only form an automatic reply. 'Of course, William. I shall look forward to it.' At the moment such a plan seemed unwelcome to her, but perhaps after the dinner, in the close company of the rest of them, she would welcome some moments alone with William.

As before, Betty's service was indifferent, her gait still lumbering, but despite her clumsy handling of crockery and utensils, she managed to give Joseph larger portions.

'How are you, Betty?' Máire asked when she came to her place. Though she found Betty hard to like, she did find her intriguing—one of Mrs Paxson's protégés whose selection to model and perform for the mission seemed at once puzzling as it was also revealing. Máire felt if she could get to know Betty more she might have some better understanding of the extent of Mrs Paxson's influence in the mission and among the Chilkat.

Betty's response was not helpful as she only gave Máire a sour look, her back to Mrs Paxson. 'I am well, thank you.' She pronounced the words carefully and when she'd finished she took her place down at the end of the table near Joseph.

The rest of the dinner was filled with discussion of Kowklux's problem. Though more details came to light, Máire still found the underlying elements confusing. Mr Paxson tried to reassure the group that there was no immediate cause for alarm and she took him at his word, though the faces of Captain Gordon and the other officers remained grim. Mrs Paxson reinforced her husband's comments and insisted on adding her own efforts at talking with Kowklux.

By the end of dinner Máire welcomed the opportunity to enjoy some fresh air before retiring for the night. William led her outside and they made their way down to the bank to stroll along the river, in plain sight of any who cared to watch. For a while they walked in companionable silence.

'How do you feel you're settling in?' William asked her eventually.

Máire paused to consider his question. She didn't feel able to explain fully all that she had thought and concluded over the days, and so decided to demur. 'It's difficult to say at this point. There's been so much to take in, and with our trip to the villages, I feel as though I haven't really had the time to grow used to my new surroundings.'

He accepted her demurral with little comment except a remark on the overwhelming nature of new places. Máire felt he might be trying to reassure her about the events surrounding Kowklux and took some comfort from his concern. She thought again how pleasant it was to have someone attending to her, considering her needs. Máire felt moved to express some positive truth about the mission, to show a response to his concern that she be at ease. 'I am growing accustomed to some things, though. And I must say I am quite fond of Mr Paxson already.'

'Yes. He has an easy, welcoming manner. He is also good with the natives, keeps them calm.' He paused. 'How are you finding the natives? I hope they don't scare you.'

'No. Not at all. I think Joseph has much to recommend him; he is exceedingly kind and patient. On the whole I find both the Chilkat and the Chilkoot remarkable and interesting people. I'm especially drawn to their notion of clan. It's so close-knit, like a family.'

'Chilkoot? Who are the Chilkoot?'

'They're the clans in Kowishte's village. The Tlingit group divided in half and each half travelled up a different river. Kowishte's people paddled up the Chilkoot River.'

William stopped and turned towards her. He frowned. 'How do you know this?'

'Daniel told me,' she said, not giving him his true name for some reason, though she had already begun to think of him in her mind as Natsilane.

'Daniel?' William took her hand between his own, lightly caressing her palm. 'You must have a care when you speak to Indians like Daniel. Their information and understanding are not always reliable. They can be prone to exaggeration and boasting. It's their way.' He drew her hand to his lips. 'You mustn't forget they're not like you. I would hate for you to be led astray by some coarse heathen Indian.'

'I'm sure Daniel knows the name of his own people,' Máire insisted. She felt defensive somehow, as though her own judgment was under attack. 'Why would he lie about that to me?'

William's eyes narrowed, a flicker of anger passing through them. His expression cleared a moment later and he kissed her hand again. 'Come, let's not have cross words. It hardly matters after all what they call themselves.' He drew Máire's hand into the circle of his arm and they continued their walk, but his words remained with her and she found herself pulling away from him slightly. However much she might feel drawn to William at times, she could not like the way in which he mocked the Tlingit people, especially Daniel—Natsilane. Máire repeated the name. His true Tlingit name, for she couldn't help but think of him as anything other than a true Tlingit. A Tlingit who understood the land in which they lived, who moved with the seasons, the thick of the trees, the currents of the sea. These things she could see in him and feel a connection with, a connection that seemed to grow stronger the more she contemplated it.

CHAPTER SIXTEEN

It was Sunday in the mission.

Mrs Paxson arranged flowers on the altar and Máire swept the floors clean of the bits of dust that might have accumulated unseen since Mrs Paxson last attended to it. While Joseph rang the bell in the little wooden tower beside the church, Mr Paxson unpacked the box of hymnals, battle-scarred and torn from years of use.

'They use the hymnals?' Máire asked him. The notion that they might read music as well as the words had not occurred to her until she saw the books.

Mr Paxson chuckled. 'Well, they can't really sing from them. But they want to do it right. And they enjoy holding the book like you're supposed to in church.'

'It's good practice for them,' Mrs Paxson said. 'They get used to how things work in a proper church.'

Máire nodded and returned to her sweeping. It was not long after that people began to come in, responding to the bell. She stood at the door with the Paxsons, greeting each person as they entered. The room filled quickly, people squeezing onto benches or, when the benches were occupied, sitting on the floor. Máire greeted Captain Gordon, William, and Bissell, who entered and arranged themselves along the back of the church by the door. When the church was full and the doors closed, she made her way to one of the chairs beside the pulpit. On the front bench, right under the pulpit, a person she presumed was Kowklux sat next to Elizabeth, his arms crossed along his dark waistcoat and bright yellow calico shirt. He was a stocky man of middle age, his closely cropped hair making his face and body appear rounder than they were in truth. Elizabeth gave Máire a brief smile of recognition before lowering her head.

With Joseph by her side, Mrs Paxson opened the service, beginning with a hymn that everyone present sang with gusto if not in perfect key. Mr Paxson stood up at the pulpit and read haltingly from the Bible, his lips shaping the words, delivering them faithfully into a respectful silence. Máire marvelled at the congregation, a group dressed in variegated clothes and colours, the women's hair neatly pulled back and unadorned. No elaborate hats, frilled dresses and expensive jewellery were displayed here for others to admire or envy. She was suddenly filled with an appreciation for the simple goodness before her.

The service continued, taking a somewhat spontaneous form that Máire had never before experienced, containing hymns that the Chilkat particularly appreciated, alongside various Bible passages. Mrs Paxson requested Máire to read one of the passages, after Joseph's turn, before she began the homily.

Mrs Paxson opened her homily in a familiar vein, discussing the scripture passage Máire had just read on forgiveness. There were no surprises in her words. 'Jesus was a man of *forgiveness*,' she said, placing emphasis on the final word. She outlined the stories of Jesus turning the other cheek, through to the crucifixion. The message was forcefully put, no subtleties or ploys, just a clear and simple statement that could not be mistaken. Máire looked out among the congregation and saw people shifting in their seats, glancing sideways at Kowklux. Kowklux's face was red, his lips pursed in a tight line. Resolutely Mrs Paxson continued, her homily still unfolding as she stared pointedly at Kowklux. A quick glance at Mr Paxson revealed a grim demeanour.

Suddenly Kowklux stood up, and with a flourish, turned and strode out of the church, people scurrying out of his path. His wife followed close behind.

The church fell silent except for the rising pitch of Mrs Paxson's voice. 'Jesus taught us we must treat others as we would be treated,' she shouted, as if to have her message accompany him home.

Quietly, while Mrs Paxson's words still issued loudly, small groups of twos and threes rose and left the church. With only the ship's crew and the manse household remaining, Mrs Paxson soldiered on, finishing her homily and calling for a hymn. The hymn, sung in feeble tones that meandered to its final verse, brought the service to its own end. Joseph threw Máire a rueful look, then moved off to collect the hymnals. She followed him silently, the need for some kind of task suddenly urgent.

Mr Paxson stood and folded his arms. 'Well I reckon Kowklux didn't take too kindly to your message, Florence.'

'He knows he's in the wrong,' Mrs Paxson said. 'It's his guilty conscience that's made him walk out.'

'We should keep an eye on him, though,' Captain Gordon said. 'He might retaliate. Maybe I should send a few of my men to the mission village. Give him a clear message to behave.'

'No, I'll go over later and have a talk with him,' Mr Paxson said. 'It might be with some time to think about it he'll be ready to hear reason.'

'Nevertheless I'll alert the men to be on the lookout for any trouble,' Captain Gordon said. He rose and with a nod left the church. The rest of the men followed close behind, except for William who lingered near Máire.

'Are you alright?' His eyes were filled with concern. 'You mustn't worry. We'll be here to ensure nothing amiss occurs. Put your mind on the schoolwork for tomorrow.'

Máire looked at his compelling eyes, golden as a cat's. How had he come by such a colour, she wondered? She tried to take the calm reassurance they offered, though she could not help but voice her doubts about his assurances. Mrs Paxson's arrogant assumption that her words and approach would soothe these troubled waters surrounding Kowklux and his clan left Máire nearly speechless. She could only hope that Mr Paxson might employ a different and better approach.

'I'm sure it will work out in the end.' William smiled with reassurance. 'I hope your preparations for school won't deprive me of your company at dinner tonight. And perhaps afterwards?'

Máire smiled at him halfheartedly, unable to think so far ahead. Her mind was still full of sympathy for Kowklux. How much more difficult for him when in his culture insults required strong reprisals. But what kind of reprisals would he choose if he didn't listen to Mr Paxson? Suddenly underneath her sympathy a kernal of worry formed.

CHAPTER SEVENTEEN

Máire's nerves were stretched taut as she walked over to the school with her own books and papers in her arms. The air was damp and the dull skies of September promised rain. No raven's call or rainbow colour of wildflowers could distract her as she crossed the small field. The houses were closed; no men milled around chatting, no women tended the nets this morning. All was still. She felt grateful for the escape from any attention. She wanted to focus her thoughts and gather her courage for the hours ahead.

Once inside it only took her a few minutes to organize her things on the little table up front. She laid out the slates on the benches, distributing them two to each one, then decided to collect them all again, thinking perhaps it was better to distribute them when the children were present. The little table suddenly seemed too close to the benches, so she moved it back towards the wall, only to discover that she had too little room for her chair. She returned it to its original position and decided to sit down and review the books one more time. After flipping the pages briefly, she shut the book and put it back with the others. Finally, she decided to wait by the door to greet the students as they came in. Joseph had agreed to ring the church bell to signal school was about to begin before he joined her to translate.

She opened the door to the school and stood for a few moments, undecided if she should meet them outside, by the steps, or just inside the open door where she wouldn't be on view for the whole of the mission. She opted for the latter.

It was fortunate the bell sounded a short while later, for she might have found herself closing the door and barring it, the waiting was so heavy upon her. Forcing a bright smile on her face, Máire looked for the arrival of her first students. It was only a few minutes later that a group of four young children appeared on the doorstep, a man she took to be their father standing a little way off. She greeted the children warmly and told them to take a seat.

The children, three boys and a girl, filed in and made their way into the school. They sat along one of the benches in the front, giggling and stealing glances at Máire. Máire nodded towards them then walked to the front of the room. 'What are your names?' she said, unthinking. Seconds later she wanted to bite her tongue, wondering if it was the right thing to ask. Did these children have Christian names or traditional names? Already she felt out of her depth and wished for Joseph.

As if on cue, Joseph appeared in the doorway and looked around. He frowned.

'Ah, Joseph,' she said. 'Perhaps you could introduce me to our first group of students here.'

He made his way to stand beside Máire at the front and looked down at the small group. He smiled down at them then spoke in Tlingit. The largest boy answered him.

'These four are from Galge's village,' he said. 'Tommy, their uncle, came down to the trading post early this morning and decided to bring the children to see the school.' He indicated the boy who just spoke. 'This is Jack,' Joseph said. The wide, generous smile that answered Máire's greeting reassured her. Next to him his brother wiggled nervously, his eyes peeping from under long lashes. Máire nodded.

'That is Fred,' Joseph said, catching her nod. 'He has six years. Next to him is Mathew, and then Minnie.' Though Mathew was obviously older than Fred, he was shy and looked down at his hands. Minnie, dressed in a red calico underdress and a brown overskirt, her hair in neat braid, put her arm around him. She looked the budding mother already, though she could have been no more than ten.

'I'm pleased to meet all of you,' she said. 'I look forward to getting to know you better and to helping you learn many new things.'

Máire turned to the empty open door. 'Well, I don't see any other students coming yet. I wonder what could be holding them up?' She walked towards the entrance, looking out into the mission. There was still little sign of activity.

'It looks as though Kowklux might be showing his dislike of the service yesterday,' Joseph said. He sighed. 'You may not have any more students today.'

'He would keep the children from school over what Mrs Paxson said?'

'He felt it an insult to his honour, I think, Miss McNair,' Joseph said. He glanced over at the students who were turned around, watching Máire at the entrance. She frowned, then shut the door.

'Very well. We'll begin without them. They'll just have to make it up when they are able to attend.' Máire forced a smile. 'In the meantime, I have my other pupils to think about. The pupils whose family did allow them to come today.' She strode to the front, full of purpose and sat at the table before her four students.

With Joseph's assistance she was able to discover that the children had some English, basic phrases occasionally accompanied by illustrative gestures such as pointing to mouths, eyes or stomach, or walking fingers. They had a somewhat greater understanding of words spoken to them. Armed with this knowledge, Máire began the lesson, printing the letter 'A' carefully on a slate and opening up her book to the place she had marked earlier. It showed a picture of an apple.

'A,' she said, pointing to the letter. She turned to the picture. 'Apple.' She told them to repeat it after her. She began again, stating the letter and then the word 'apple'. They looked at her and repeated the words at Joseph's encouragement. 'Good,' she said, pleased. 'A is the first letter of the alphabet in the English language. Do you understand that?' She turned to Joseph. 'Do they understand what an alphabet is? Do you have a Tlingit alphabet?'

'No, we do not,' Joseph said. 'Our language is not written down, there is no alphabet.'

'Oh,' she said, momentarily at a loss. She frowned. 'Yes, well, let's try something different, shall we?' The children looked at her blankly. Máire took a deep breath. 'We'll stay with words for the moment. Learning English words.'

She looked over at her books, hoping she had enough pictures to show them. She picked up the top book again and leafed through the pages, looking for a suitable picture. It was one of her old school books, one that she had pored over for many an hour with her governess bent over her, watching her progress, a lifetime ago. Máire picked a picture and, studying it, realized it had many things to point to and name, but none of them would hold any meaning for the children. The scene showed a boy spinning a hoop along a road with a policeman standing against a pole and a nanny pushing a pram in the opposite direction. She closed the book with a snap, looked around her briefly, then rose. With a flourish Máire pointed to the chair.

'Chair,' she said. She paused and repeated it, then gestured for them to do the same.

'Chair,' they replied hesitantly.

'Good!' she replied enthusiastically.

She proceeded to name everything in the room, pausing so they could repeat it. After a few rounds of this, she called on them individually to see if they were able to remember the names of the objects. To her delight they missed not one. Eventually she added a few actions, 'sit,' 'stand' and 'walk,' that she combined with personal pronouns. They learned the action 'clap' with such great enthusiasm that she decided to expand the concept and have them clap to a simple children's song. 'Ring a ring o' roses, a pocket full of posies,' she began. They clapped along though Máire wondered if they understood what she was saying. In the end it mattered not for they asked for it again and again.

By the end of the morning, Máire was feeling happy and filled with a sense that perhaps she was not as inept as she first thought. When their uncle appeared at the door, the children rose with eyes sparkling and went to meet him. Máire thanked Tommy for allowing the children to come and told him she hoped he would be able to bring them back soon. He smiled, nodded slightly and spoke something in Tlingit.

'He says that he will try to bring the children the next time he comes to the mission,' Joseph said.

'I hope it won't be too long,' Máire said. 'The children were delightful.'

Tommy nodded to her again, then over to Joseph. 'Goodbye,' he said and guided the children out the door. The children shouted goodbye, a few of them waving tentatively.

Máire bade them farewell in return and followed their progress down the steps and across the grass, her only students disappearing from sight. She breathed a sigh of relief that her first day of teaching had not been a wholehearted disaster, though she couldn't suppress the niggling concern over the lack of students. How long would this situation continue? Would it affect the need for her presence in the mission? The bonds she felt with this place and these people were fragile, but precious nonetheless. She would do her best not to fail.

CHAPTER EIGHTEEN

Máire made her way back to the Paxsons, school books in hand and Joseph at her side. They walked in silence, the heavy grey skies cloaking them with a wet mist that clung to their clothes. Despite the weather, people had emerged from their homes and, though they were somewhat subdued in nature, they were hard at their tasks. Máire saw Elizabeth, Kowklux's wife, and lifted her hand in greeting, but Elizabeth only turned away.

'How long will this go on?' Máire asked Joseph.

He shrugged. 'Until Kowklux's honour is restored.'

'And what will it take to restore his honour?'

'It is difficult to know,' Joseph said. 'A concession, an acknowledgment of his view, or a gift offering, might make peace.'

Máire shook her head. She found it hard to imagine Mrs Paxson doing any of those things. She wondered if the school would founder even before it had a chance to begin. She kicked at the ground, a small gesture of frustration.

Máire arrived at the trading post to find Mr Paxson in the front room attending to a lanky-framed miner. Máire later learned that he, and a few others who had tried their luck with little result in the summer, were camping on the outskirts of the mission, marking time until the next boat home arrived, or the spring permitted them to try their luck once more. The miner, his trousers held up by an odd piece of rope, was bartering anxiously with Mr Paxson. Joseph immediately went over to assist while Máire went through to the kitchen and made some coffee, taking care over the unfamiliar task. Tea was a rare commodity here and she already missed it sorely. It was only a simple thing, tea, but she realized now how much it had permeated her day in the past, its taste, its heat, the quality of its wetness so much more calming than the strong, bitter fare she drank now. Perhaps in time she would grow used to it, like so much else here, but for now it provided no comfort or solace from the strain of recent events. Briefly she raised her hand to her chest where the medallion lay under her blouse.

A few minutes later Máire returned to the front room, three mugs in hand, and gave one each to Joseph and Mr Paxson. The miner had gone.

'Where's Mrs Paxson?' she asked.

'She's over at the manse, talking to Captain Gordon.'

'About the problem with Kowklux?' she asked. 'It seems to have affected the school. No-one from the mission showed up this morning. Just a small group from Kutchewhe's village.'

'Really?' Mr Paxson said. He took a sip from his mug. 'I knew he would take some kind of action. At least now it's done and we know what it is.'

'What do you mean?'

'Well, Kowklux's acted on the insult in a way that won't stir up the other villages,' Mr Paxson said. 'At least I don't think so.' He looked over at Máire. 'But don't you go worrying yourself. The school will be fine. I'll talk to Kowklux, see what I can do. We'll get those children in school.'

Máire nodded, trying to believe what he said. Joseph looked over at them both and shook his head. She took a large drink from her mug, wincing a bit at its taste. Mr Paxson, reading her expression, came over and patted her shoulder.

'It'll be fine, you'll see. In fact I'll go over and speak to him right now.' He made his way toward the door.

'Thank you Mr Paxson, I appreciate your thoughtfulness.'

He ran his hand through his wiry hair, his face red and nodded as he opened the door and left.

'Mr Paxson is a good man,' Joseph said.

The door opened again in a swirl of calico and hide. Natsilane, Rebecca and Sarah stepped through the entry, creating splashes of colour among the dull brown of the sacks, tins and shelves. Both Natsilane and Sarah were silent, their faces expressionless while Rebecca chattered behind them. Their appearance took Máire by surprise since she hadn't expected to see them so soon after the disastrous visit to the village, especially not on the first day of school, after it had finished. Whatever its reason, it suddenly made her nervous.

She smoothed her skirt and attempted some light humour to calm herself. 'Good afternoon, Not Daniel, Rebecca and Sarah.' Rebecca greeted her shyly and stood just inside the door. Sarah nodded slightly, then joined her sister, her posture tall and correct.

Natsilane gave her a wry look. 'Good afternoon, Miss Not Martha.' He turned to Joseph and spoke a brief word in Tlingit. Joseph answered him, his voice subdued. Natsilane moved over to the counter and spoke again in Tlingit, while he pointed to a sack in the corner behind Joseph. Joseph lifted the sack onto the counter, measured out the coffee beans it contained, his fingers carefully smoothing the small brown pellets evenly across the scoop. After he filled the small pouch Natsilane provided, he returned it in silence and noted the transaction in the ledger beside him. Natsilane gave Joseph a nod, handing the pouch to Sarah.

Máire had watched the transaction in silence, wondering what she might say to Natsilane. She felt she had to converse with him if only to exchange pleasantries. For some reason she needed to prove herself to him, but what she had to prove she wasn't sure. That she was not of Mrs Paxson's ilk? That her intentions were good, if sometimes falling short of the mark?

'I'm sorry that Sarah and Rebecca were unable to attend the school this morning,' she finally said. It was not the best remark to make, she realized after it was said, but it couldn't be undone. She clasped her hands firmly in front of her, resisting the temptation to reach for her medallion.

Natsilane moved nearer. 'How *was* your first day of school?'

'A small but enthusiastic group attended,' she told him. 'I'm encouraged and feel sure that it will continue to grow.'

'Kowklux's ire kept away those here in the mission.' It was not a question. It seemed news had travelled quickly.

'I'm sure it will all be resolved shortly. Mr Paxson has gone over this moment to try and get Kowklux to see reason.'

Natsilane gave a grim smile. 'I think it might take a little more than reason to resolve the whole of this.' His expression eased a bit at the alarm plain on her face. 'Though as far as your school is concerned I'm sure all will be well. Mr Paxson understands much about the situation and will more than likely persuade Kowklux to your cause. I was really referring to the root of the problem.'

'You mean the quarrel with the clan in Sitka?' Máire asked.

Natsilane nodded.

'Can't Kowklux find some other kind of reparation? Something more—'

'Civilized? Christian?'

'I was going to say—something more attainable,' Máire replied, flushing. She forced herself to look into his eyes and for a moment saw a flash of regret.

'I'm sorry, I should have let you finish,' he said. He took a deep breath. 'It's a complex affair, but it has to do with Kowklux's honour and his perceived ability to lead his people. He knows he must appear strong—he can't afford to back down.'

Máire nodded slowly, considering his words, until Sarah caught her attention as she moved behind him over to the counter, her long braid swinging slightly with her swift motion. She murmured a few words to Joseph. Natsilane noticed the direction of Máire's glance and turned around to see the pair exchanging words. He spoke firmly in Tlingit and Sarah backed away quickly, resuming her place beside her sister, her head downcast. Joseph moved to clean the shelves behind him.

Natsilane swung around to face Máire, caught her questioning look and sighed. 'That brings me to the issue of your school. Both my sisters have expressed an interest in attending. But there are problems.'

'What problems?' Her mind started racing, trying to fathom his meaning.

'Your lack of understanding of our culture and history is one problem. It may cause some serious mistakes with severe consequences.' He frowned, casting his eyes along her figure. 'I wouldn't want either of my sisters to have the impression that the white women's fashion for squeezing their bodies into unnatural shapes is something to emulate.'

Máire kept her hands forcibly at her side determined to refrain from any contact with her waist where her corset lay beneath her blouse, skirt and petticoats. She was glad now she had omitted her bustle since her arrival. 'I'm not here to teach children about their attire,' she told him, her face aflame.

'I think Florence Paxson would beg to differ,' he said. He lowered his voice. 'Joseph's presence is another problem. Is it permanent?'

'Only until I can find one of the students who would be able to do the translation and any other assistance I might need. Why do you ask?'

'My sister couldn't attend as long as Joseph is there, it's against our ways.'

'Your ways?'

He snorted lightly, his impatience clear. 'Yes, the ways you understand so little.' He glanced over his shoulder at his sisters who lowered their eyes and busied themselves with the folds of their skirts. 'Because my sister has reached maturity, it's taboo for her to interact with men who aren't from an Eagle clan.'

'That's your clan, I take it. Joseph isn't from that clan?'

He paused before he answered her. 'No, Joseph is from a Raven clan and is, in terms you might understand, an eligible bachelor, so my sister shouldn't associate with him. I believe you have a similar custom. You, for example, would not be permitted to keep company with single men without a suitable chaperone.'

'Well, yes, in some situations that's true,' she replied. The conversation nearly overwhelmed her in all its surprises and new concepts she must try to understand and to some degree act upon. She groped for some sort of reasonable answer. 'But then by your own tradition,' she began, 'you should not associate with me, since I'm a single woman and not from an Eagle clan.'

'But you're white. So it matters not that I, or any other Tlingit man, associate with you.'

His remark stung her to silence, her faint short breaths, indicative of her agitation, the only sound that fell between them. The words held far more truth than Máire realized when he first uttered them, understanding after a few moments that in her own world, he, and any other Tlingit man, would be held of little or no account. She flushed hard, glanced up at him and concluded he intended the remark to be understood in both lights. Suddenly she wished him gone, so that she might recover the hopeful outlook Mr Paxson had fostered earlier with his kind words and actions.

'I know you expect little of me, but I'm not here to please you in particular,' she finally said. She moved away from him, towards the wall, where she took interest in a spade that leaned there. Her fingers followed the length of the wooden shaft to rest on the handle. 'As for finding a replacement for Joseph in the school, perhaps Sarah would be the best person to assist me.' She turned to Sarah, her face upturned and eyes alert at the mention of her name.

'Would you be willing to do that, Sarah?' Máire asked, raising her voice. 'I know your English is impeccable and I am certain you would be more than qualified to assist me in any manner necessary.'

Sarah glanced over at her brother. Natsilane shrugged. 'Yes Miss McNair, if you wish, I will assist you,' she said in a calm, precise tone.

'Good, that's settled then.' Máire looked over at Joseph who had remained still and silent by the counter during her exchange with Natsilane. How was it that Natsilane could reprimand him so severely? Why would the necessity to prevent contact between Joseph and Sarah cause such a strong response? But she couldn't let Joseph think she endorsed such harsh treatment. 'I thank you for all your kind help in the school today, Joseph. You were such great support.' Máire said. 'But I'm sure you will be relieved to return to your normal responsibilities now and not be burdened with my needs.' She smiled at him encouragingly while he accepted the thanks. It was difficult to resist the sense that she had bested Natsilane, and she attempted to keep her face and tone neutral as she turned back to him. 'I'm sure Sarah will be an immense help to me.'

'She can come and bring her sister as long as the weather holds. My aunt could accompany them.' There was some humour in his eyes. Was he laughing at her? 'Most of the berries are picked and the fish dried; she can fulfil her other obligations when she returns home in the afternoon.'

Any trace of triumph vanished as Máire realized she hadn't considered that Sarah's age would naturally incur responsibilities to her family and community. She stifled a sigh, recognizing that her use of even the small understanding she had formed of the Tlingit culture had been derailed through her hasty words.

It was only a short while after Natsilane, Sarah and Rebecca left that Mrs Paxson returned from the manse filled with opinions and ideas from her discussion with Captain Gordon about Kowklux's problem. Máire was too absorbed with Natsilane's visit to take in the full meaning of her words. After she appeared to run out of steam, she queried Máire over Mr Paxson's whereabouts and Máire told her about the events at the school and that he'd gone to talk with Kowklux about it. Joseph witnessed the conversation in silence and said nothing when Mrs Paxson expressed her dismay and opined that a few stern words from Captain Gordon wouldn't go amiss. Máire assured her hastily that Mr Paxson was confident about his chances of talking Kowklux around. As if summoned by mention of his name, Mr Paxson entered. He removed his hat and placed it on the counter. All eyes levelled on him.

'Well, George,' Mrs Paxson said. 'I understand you went to speak with Kowklux.'

'That's right,' Mr Paxson said. 'It appears he was ready to let me change his mind about the school.'

Mrs Paxson crossed her arms. 'Oh? And exactly what did you promise in return?'

Mr Paxson calmly assured her there was no cause for concern. 'We talked for a long while. I heard all that Kowklux and the other elders had to say and after a lot of words, we thought of ways to work this all out. Kowklux agreed to have men from both clans say their side of things to me and Captain Gordon. All official, like in a court room.'

'And then what?' Mrs Paxson said, her voice sceptical.

Mr Paxson rubbed his hand across his rumpled waistcoat. 'Why, then we work out a gift exchange both sides can agree to and have a feast.' Mr Paxson grinned, his watery blue eyes filled with humour.

Mrs Paxson sniffed. 'Well, you better go up to the manse and tell Captain Gordon about all this. I don't know what he'll have to say.'

Mr Paxson picked up his hat, a smile still creasing his face and told her he was on his way.

Máire watched him go, marvelling at his skills of persuasion, and that these people were willing to settle their quarrel in such a manner. How strange she found them, but it was a strangeness that was complex. She felt there was something so good about much of their culture. A culture about which she found she was more and more curious. She could never imagine her father agreeing to settle his quarrels with a feast. For him it would be words. Words spoken at length, words written down and signed with some kind of financial part to ensure its worth.

CHAPTER NINETEEN

Betty arrived at the manse dining table, soup tureen in hand, and placed it in front of Mrs Paxson. She peered at Joseph from behind a swatch of hair that hung loose from her bun and, with a tentative smile, she batted her lashes twice before withdrawing to the kitchen. From her seat opposite Máire suppressed a laugh and glanced at Joseph. His gaze averted, he studied his plate intensively, but his rising colour told its own story.

'I must confess I have reservations about this arrangement,' Captain Gordon said after the grace.

'Don't be silly, Captain,' Mrs Paxson said. 'It's the only sensible course of action.'

'Madam, you must remember I'm a representative of the U.S. government and I have a responsibility to ensure the safety of its citizens.'

'Do you think there'll be problems?' Mr Paxson asked.

'There could be.' Captain Gordon frowned. 'The best way to ensure there aren't is for me and the senior officers to moderate this dispute.' He dabbed his chin and looked at Mrs Paxson. 'I don't have much hope for this hearing. These natives really only understand one kind of talk. But since it's set we should make sure we hold it in a neutral location that conveys the authority of the U.S. government. The ship would seem the best place for the event.'

'The ship would be an ideal place,' William said. 'We can enforce our authority easily there, should the need arise.'

'Oh, without a doubt,' Lieutenant Bissell said.

Máire was glad Mrs Paxson had changed her tune and supported her husband. The officers' bellicose attitude dismayed her and made her wonder if just such a location might provide more in the way of provocation than prevention of any trouble.

Mr Paxson licked his spoon clean and sat back in his chair. 'Well now Captain, I don't know about that. You'd probably find it a mite cramped for all the people that'll be at this thing. Maybe we'd be better off having it on the mission grounds. That way there's room for everyone.'

'Yes, I agree with George,' Mrs Paxson said. 'The mission grounds are the most suitable place to hold such an event. Such close proximity to the Lord's house is an appropriate setting to dispense justice, and to remind the Tlingit to be on their best behaviour.'

Betty entered again, this time carrying a large platter filled with duck and potatoes that she placed on the table, grunting under the effort. She wiped her hands along her dress and took a seat. Mrs Paxson picked up the large spoon and began portioning out the servings on the small stack of plates in front of her. She did so with precision, careful to divide the contents evenly among the group, as though they might be fishes and loaves to feed the multitudes.

'We'll have to hold this meeting soon,' Captain Gordon said. 'My men and I will be moving on to Ft. Wrangell before long.'

'I didn't realize you would be leaving us so soon, Captain,' Máire said. She glanced at William and found regret in his expression. Was it for the mission, for her, or that he must once again return to the rigours and isolation of life aboard ship? For herself, she was somewhat surprised to realize she would miss his company. Despite some of his views on the Tlingit, she had really appreciated his assurances as well as the undercurrent of shared experiences, though what experiences she couldn't specifically name.

Captain Gordon spoke of the difficulty in taking leave of people whose company he enjoyed. 'But our duty takes us many places, Miss

McNair, and we must go.'

'Captain Gordon's responsibilities have him all over the Alaska territories and down as far as the California coast,' Mrs Paxson said. 'We were fortunate to have had him and his men here for this length of time.'

'It has been our pleasure,' Captain Gordon said. 'I enjoy our visits here, infrequent though they be.'

There was humour and good will in his voice, and Máire believed it was more than good manners that spoke. If it wasn't for Mr Paxson she might have thought otherwise. Though she had observed he was a man who enjoyed company, she could not imagine that Mrs Paxson's company was such that it would compel someone such as he to extend a stay.

'I must confess I'll miss the great fishing sport,' Lieutenant Bissell said. 'A few of the men and I have caught some fair-sized halibut and only today I hooked one devil of a large salmon.' He turned to William. 'The salmon are everywhere. You must come along some time, Green— you can almost reach down and tickle their bellies.'

'Fishing. Now there is a pastime I've never considered. Though in these waters I might be tempted,' Captain Gordon said. 'Perhaps next visit, if there's time.'

Máire looked down at her plate, covered with stringy duck meat, its sinew and fat clinging desperately to the meagre bone. Perhaps more of them should take up the pastime.

'We'll be sorry to see you all go,' Mr Paxson said. 'I'll talk to Kowklux, Captain. See how soon we can tell the elders of the Kiksaadi clan in Sitka. With luck we might be able to get this hearing arranged for the end of next week.'

'Good,' Captain Gordon said. 'Let me know as soon as you hear, Paxson.'

'I will, don't worry.'

As the conversation moved on to more mundane topics, Máire's attention wandered to the turn of events while she picked at her duck. It seemed a little difficult to imagine that anything serious and life-threatening might come from such a minor dispute, though Natsilane had made it clear that she couldn't use her own understanding when assessing the actions of the Tlingits. Perhaps it was just as well Captain Gordon and his men weren't leaving until after the hearing. She thought again of William. There was without a doubt great value in his protection. And he had shown some real kindnesses. But she couldn't help but feel he didn't seem to appreciate or understand the qualities these people and this land possessed. Qualities she couldn't easily name, but that she felt nonetheless. On consideration she realized that Mr Paxson would possibly understand. And Natsilane might have even been able to explain it to her, though she couldn't, at this stage, imagine herself asking him.

The scrape of chairs signalled the end of the meal. There were no cigars or port here; instead the men enjoyed a discreet cigarette or pipe outside before making off to their respective duties or personal obligations. Máire offered to help clear up, but as usual Mrs Paxson refused. In the absence of the minister's wife, Mrs Carter, Mrs Paxson took oversight of the household in the manse, her personal mission being to educate the natives in the proper wifely skills. Any assistance from Máire was viewed as interference. Máire could only wonder what Betty's opinion on the subject was.

Freed from any duty, Máire made her way to the door to wander back to the trading post. The weather had cleared enough to allow a tentative sun to peek through the cloud-laden sky and tempt her into the evening air. William approached her just as she arrived at the beginning of the path and asked her if she would accompany him on a walk. The evening was so inviting that she accepted his offer with pleasure.

The pair made their way down to the riverbank and then walked alongside it, Máire's hand on William's arm, while the swell of the tidal current lapped gently by their feet. A small breeze blew up and tickled Máire's face, blowing strands of hair in her eyes. She could taste its salt as she gazed out at the water. Over in a cluster of rocks a small pool of water hosted a group of seals. Delighted, Máire pointed it out.

'Aren't they lovely? They look so carefree there. And how they play with each other. Like brothers and sisters.' She laughed. 'Isn't it wonderful?'

William smiled at her. He took the hand that encircled his arm and pulled it into his own hand. Máire turned to face him, filled with the joy of her discovery. William reached up and brushed a wisp of hair from her face, his fingers lingering down her cheek and along to her mouth, where slowly he traced her lips. His face closed in on hers and he placed light teasing kisses on her lips while his hand slipped around to cradle the back of her head. He kissed her harder, deeper, pushing apart her lips, probing with his tongue. Máire stood there, impassive, initially too surprised to resist and then uncertain how to respond. She had never had more than a few chaste kisses from relatives and her father. William's kisses she found disturbing and confusing. Her skin tingled where his lips had been and her mouth softened under his pressure. After a few moments he pulled back a fraction. Máire could feel his breath on her cheek.

'Martha,' he said. He took her hand and brought it slowly to his lips, his eyes still on hers. 'I'm sorry if I surprised you. It was an impulse born of the moment. You looked so happy, so carefree and innocent, I couldn't help myself.' He kissed her hand again, turning the palm to his lips.

'I don't know if this is the time. With our remaining days here filled with events that might sweep us along, I feel I must seize this moment and tell you how much I've grown to care for you,' he went on, biting his lip, 'and how I hope that you might have done so too.'

Máire remained still, waiting for the surprise to pass as well as the annoyance at the use of that horrid name. Should she be surprised, she chided herself? The kiss was surely the biggest confirmation, and some of his solicitude and care in the past weeks had suggested what he only now uttered. But there were other times when she felt some simmering resentment or dislike, though it might be hurriedly covered. Still, the last few moments could leave her in no doubt of his feelings.

Her own feelings were another matter, however. Her life here had only just begun, and though it still appeared uncertain at almost every turn, she still wasn't sure she desired to form any sort of attachment. But what could she now say to William? She wasn't practiced in this situation. She didn't want to earn his scorn, or promise something she was not yet, if ever, able to.

'I don't know what to say,' Máire said finally. 'I must confess you have taken me by surprise.'

William pulled away and turned. 'I'm sorry. Yes, I know it's sudden and I'm not the most practiced of courtiers. I lack the flowery terms and the niceties at times.' He spoke in a low voice. 'But it doesn't mean I lack sincerity.'

'No, no, William. That thought has not passed through my mind at all,' Máire said. 'I too am not used to courting and have no practice in receiving the attentions of a gentleman.'

William faced her once again. 'Have you not?' His face, so handsome now in its earnest appeal moved Máire more deeply than any embroidered words of courtship and romance. She placed her hand lightly against his face.

'No William, I haven't. You must believe my world at home was not filled with suitors and gay parties. I led a very quiet existence and my social acquaintance is not as large as you might think.'

'No,' William said. 'And all the more reason why I feel there are common bonds between us.'

Máire smiled at him. She had not been mistaken. He, too, had felt those bonds. And, given time, she might come to understand their exact nature. 'When will your ship call at the mission again? Soon?'

William's eyes darkened. 'No. And that's part of what prompts my haste with you. It might well be a long time before I see you again. Our visits here are not that frequent since the territory we cover is so large. Sometimes it can be more than a year before we return to Sitka.'

'A year?' It was hard to imagine such a length of time.

'I know. It's much too long.' He took up her hand again, holding it between both of his. 'It's because of this long separation that I ask you to consider this offer now, and hope you won't think it too unseemly.'

'What is it, William?' Máire tried to repress a growing sense of unease.

The words fell awkwardly from his lips, his hesitation and nervous demeanour so much more endearing than a bended knee. 'I realize your father isn't present, and I would wish to proceed correctly, were it possible. But there's no help for it. I-I would ask you to do me the honour of becoming my wife.' There was a careful pause. 'Life for the wife of a naval officer is difficult, but I assure you it wouldn't be for long. For your sake I would resign and obtain a post ashore, somewhere along this coast, or if you like we could live in Ireland. Perhaps I could assist your father, so you needn't be far from him. I would not have you parted from him indefinitely.'

He continued his plea with the greatest sincerity. Máire was grateful for the length of his speech, for it gave her time to collect herself once again. Despite his earlier declaration she had no inkling he would propose so soon. How could she possibly entertain such a notion now, if ever? Marriage had always seemed out of the question and at this point, with her obligations here and her desire to remain unwed, it had been far from her mind.

'William, I'm truly honoured by your proposal,' she told him. 'And I assure you I will give it the deepest consideration, but I can't answer you at once. I have my commitments to the mission. I'm newly arrived and my work has only just begun. I feel it would be irresponsible to abandon it so soon.'

'Yes, yes of course.' A dark flush spread across his face. 'I realize this was sudden, but you understand my position.' He released her hand.

Máire pressed her hand against his arm. 'Don't be offended. There are just so many other considerations at the moment.'

She searched his face in vain for anger or bitterness, but she could detect nothing. He gave her a faint smile. 'I understand. I won't push you for an answer, then. You must give some time to the mission. I could expect no less of one so well bred as you. Shall we leave it for now to think about it until I next come to Sitka?'

Máire felt a surge of relief. In that time the progress of her mission work would be the testimony to any answer she would give. With such evidence and support behind her she would be able to retain his regard and they could continue their connection without rancour. 'Yes, William. I'll do that. But in the meantime we have these remaining days in which to enjoy each other's company.'

Back in her room as she stared out at the sky, still bright in the even northern light, Máire ran her fingers across her mouth, feeling where William's lips and tongue had been. She thought it strange that her initial response to his kiss was so calm. It was only eventually that she'd felt confused. An exciting confusion that now made her slowly run her tongue along her teeth and then suck her finger. What was it that she wanted?

With deliberate care Máire removed her shoes and stockings while she sat on the edge of the bed. She placed her toes on the bare floor and wriggled them, allowing the air to pass between each one. Her fingers found the buttons on her shirtwaist and began to unfasten them, releasing each small pearl disk from its captive hold, the fabric slowly falling away from her neck and the swell of her breasts, where the top of her corset created an unnatural angle. She placed her hands on the corset's rim, recalling Natsilane's words. This corset, donned reluctantly at sixteen, had been part of her daily dress for several years. Despite its discomfort, the corset was now part of her natural modesty along with all her other undergarments, as for any woman of her background.

Sighing, she slipped off her shirtwaist, skirt and petticoats and let them fall to the floor. For a moment she stood unmoving. Slowly, she unfastened the hooks that held the corset tight around her hips, waist and breasts until the flesh was released, free to press gently against the light fabric of her camisole. The corset lay awkwardly in her hands, the rigid bone that pushed and rearranged her body still holding its shape under the soft quilted padding that covered it. She tossed it on the floor, its contrived curves unchanged, the lacings firmly knotted. Máire reached up and untied the little bows that held her camisole closed, and let it join the corset on the floor. Edged with fine Irish lace, the drawers covered the camisole in an airy cloud.

The medallion was the only item that remained on her body and she could feel the metal cold between her breasts as a gentle breeze from her window stirred the air in the room, stiffening her nipples. She reached up and removed the pins from her hair. The braid unravelled and fell about her shoulders and hips, a shawl finer than any silk. Her breath sounded in her ears, shallow and short. With deliberate effort she slowed its rhythm, inhaling slowly and deeply, enjoying the unrestricted movement. Her ribs expanded freely as her lungs drew in air, then pushed it out. Máire cupped her breasts and felt their fullness rising and falling in a rolling rhythm, like waves on a quiet sea.

A gentle humming stirred, a slow slumberous tune that came from within and swayed her body to and fro, rocking it gently with each rise and fall of breath. The rhythm carried her for some time, until the moon shone through the window, and she stood still, allowing its light to wash over her. Somewhere in the distance a bark echoed across the water. Máire smiled.

Later, the seals arrived, the three from the rocks, their velvet eyes wide as they swam closer to her perch on a jagged stone ledge. She reached out her hand, beckoning them closer, the ends of her hair sweeping the water as she leaned towards them. They started to turn away, and she called out, but her voice made no sound. She leaned out more, her breasts brushing her arms while she struggled to signal to the seals. Stretching further, she lost her balance, overturned and was suddenly plunged into the water, deep into the inky black depths, her hair tangling around her, binding her like a fisherman's net and pulling her ever downwards.

CHAPTER TWENTY

Máire awoke in the morning with her hair wrapped around her, and damp sheets entwined among her arms and legs. A cool cloth dipped into the washbowl and wiped along her body left her somewhat restored. She reached to pick up her clothes from the heap she had cast them into the night before and laid them on the bed, smoothing out the wrinkles of her skirt and shirtwaist as much as possible. She donned her camisole and drawers, then, reaching for her corset, she paused. Her hand passed over the corset to the shirtwaist, and slowly she put her arms through its sleeves, fastened the pearl buttons first around her neck, then down over her breasts, noting their swell came softer, fuller and at lower point on the blouse. Máire couldn't deny the comfort as she reached for her petticoats and skirt and slipped them on. With the skirt fastened and smoothed she surveyed her figure. The rise and fall of her chest left no doubt that she no longer wore a corset. And she wasn't under any illusion that Mrs Paxson would fail to notice the omission. Reaching over to the table she took up the medallion from where she'd set it the night before and fastened it around her neck and tucked it inside her camisole. She moved slightly and her toe banged against her trunk, causing a flare of pain up her leg. As she rubbed the toe, she opened the lid of the trunk and saw her garden smock folded neatly underneath her other skirt. Smiling, she lifted the smock out and pulled it on, its generous folds falling well below the waist of her skirt. She fastened the buttons quickly before she could change her mind.

Arriving in the kitchen Máire greeted the Paxsons brightly. Joseph's bed had already vanished as had he, presumably to the front room to open the trading post since, as Mrs Paxson informed her over her eggs and coffee, a small packet steamer was arriving from Sitka early that morning bringing supplies and mail. She told Máire she wasn't needed at the post; the school was her first priority. Mr Paxson cut short Máire's feeble protest and added that she could help sort the post in the afternoon. 'With the miners so eager for news from back home, it won't be long before they're clamouring for their mail,' he said. 'There might even be something from your own kin,' he added.

Máire told him she hadn't had any word since she'd left and would be very glad of news from home. He gave her some kind assurances, for which she was grateful. After gulping the rest of her coffee, Máire excused herself. She was anxious to be away from Mrs Paxson's company and eager to see if there was any improvement in attendance, though she would be content if only the few children from the previous day came since they had been so amenable. She also wanted to have some arrangement in place should Sarah not appear to assist her.

'I'm glad to see you're wearing something practical for your work,' Mrs Paxson said, eyeing Máire's smock as she made for the door. 'Perhaps you have more common sense than I originally credited you with.' She gave a tight smile. 'We'll make a missionary of you yet, Martha.'

Máire walked over to the school, books in hand and her smock billowing gently in the breeze. A hesitant sun peeked out from heavy, watery clouds; mist worried the river's surface. Despite the uncertain weather, men, women and children lined the bank and gazed out at the boat, awaiting the arrival of the steamer. Máire smiled at the thought that she would be on the welcoming side for the people who arrived this time; a tenuous connection to the land and this community, perhaps, but a connection all the same.

Once inside the school, Máire made her preparations with much more ease than the previous day. When the children arrived, she was relieved to see there were a fair number. Rebecca and Sarah appeared too, their hair neatly braided and tied with thongs. Kowishte's younger wife, Yedicih, escorted them. After a brief nod in Máire's direction, Yedicih quietly slipped into a bench at the back.

Máire's hopes for a good day were realized. Sarah proved an able translator and assistant, as did Rebecca who immediately became indispensable, quietly coaching the very young while Sarah and Máire took on the older students. In all there were twelve students, most of them under ten years of age, for the older children in the mission were still helping their families with winter preparations.

When the lesson had concluded, Máire watched in satisfaction as they filed out, leaving only Sarah, Rebecca and Yedicih remaining. 'Thank you, Sarah, you've been most helpful this morning,' she told her.

'You're most welcome,' Sarah said in a careful tone. All morning Máire had been struck by the formality present in both Sarah and Rebecca, though in the younger sister Máire felt this could be traced to a natural shyness common within her age group.

Máire began to gather up the books the students had left. Yedicih rose quietly from the bench at the back and made her way to the door with no sense of haste or impatience. She waited at the door quietly. Máire debated whether she should invite her to join them at the front, but after a moment Máire decided to let her be. She turned instead to Rebecca.

'I don't know how I would have managed without your work with the young ones. You were very good with them.'

Rebecca smiled tentatively from her pile of books at the table then murmured some thanks. Sarah moved beside her and picked up one of the books on the desk, thumbed through it until, conscious of Máire's scrutiny, she handed it to Máire.

'Would you like to borrow that book, Sarah?' It was a book of Irish fairy stories. 'You may take it with you and bring it back each morning should we need it for class.'

'Thank you.' Sarah calmly took the offered book. She looked at the cover, tracing a finger over the embossed fairy image. 'It looks interesting. Is it the clan tales of your own place?'

Máire's first reaction was to laugh, but then realized Sarah's question held some truth. 'I think you might describe them as such.' She looked at Rebecca. 'Perhaps you could read them to your sister. I'm sure she would enjoy them.'

'Can you dance them, Miss McNair? Like our own clan tales?' Rebecca asked.

Máire paused and smiled. 'Why, I don't know. I suppose I could try. It's possible that some people do, but not in the manner that you dance your clan tales.' Máire thought of the tinkers and their wild steps that felt the music and wondered if she knew rather less about it than she realized. 'Perhaps some time we could make up our own dance to one of these tales.'

'Could we?' Rebecca said. Sarah rested her hand on Rebecca's shoulder, but remained silent. Sarah's face betrayed neither approval or disapproval and Máire found her whole countenance difficult to read. Glancing over at Yedicih revealed little. Máire decided she would have to keep trying despite this lack of encouragement which might be due to a cultural issue she had no grasp of at present. Perhaps Joseph would enlighten her. Or Mr Paxson. She realized yet again it would all take time. Time for her to learn more fully their ways and traditions so she could perhaps be effective in improving her relations with them.

They left the school soon after and Máire walked with Yedicih and the girls as far as the trading post, where they parted to make their way back to their village along the winding path through the woods and fields. A canoe journey took only just over an hour, but since there was no spare canoe, it was a good two hours by foot. Despite their assurances that the journey was not overly difficult, Máire couldn't help but be impressed by their dedication.

By the time Máire arrived at the trading post the packet steamer had unloaded its goods and passengers and was already heading back downriver. A few miners and Tlingits carried boxes inside, while others milled around the front steps. Máire noticed one lone Tlingit man making his way to the steps, battered shoes slung around his neck. He was tall though somewhat stooped, and his lank hair hung past the frayed collar of his soiled, ragged jacket. Máire watched as he sat down and took the shoes from his neck and slid his grimy feet inside them. One of the soles was secured with a bit of string. Slowly, his large fingers working clumsily, he untied the knot that fastened the string and reworked it, creating a tighter fit. He muttered something, then pulled himself up, groaning slightly with the effort. He noticed Máire's stare as he glanced around, and fixed his watery eyes on her, the rims yellowed and dull with years of hard living. Máire nodded self-consciously in his direction and made her way up the steps past him.

He followed her inside and shuffled over to the counter while she went through to the kitchen to set down her books. Mrs Paxson was there filling the sugar and coffee canisters. After a brief exchange, Máire returned to the front room where Joseph was taking inventory and Mr Paxson was finishing with one of the miners. She saw the stack of mail over on a barrel and went over to pick it up, seeing a letter from her father on the top. The Tlingit man stood just inside the door, unmoving.

'Benny,' Mr Paxson said when he noticed the Tlingit man. 'We haven't seen you for a good while. What brings you back home?'

Benny nodded to him. 'Mr Paxson.' Beads of sweat gathered at his forehead. He ran his tongue over his lips. 'Need any jobs doin'?'

Mr Paxson frowned, peering closely at him. 'Well, let's see, Benny. You know I don't hold with drinking hoochinoo, or any liquor for that matter. You dry?'

'I know, Mr Paxson. Sure, Mr Paxson. Sure, I'm dry.' Benny looked down at his feet, his hands trembled slightly. 'I got nowhere else to go, Mr Paxson,' he said, his voice barely above a whisper.

'Hmmm. I guess we could use some help here right now,' Mr Paxson said. 'Joseph is run off his feet here, what with more miners just come in, and the Chilkat starting up the trading for the winter stores.' He looked Benny up and down. 'Think you could sweep up the store, keep the shelves stocked and tidy?'

Benny nodded slowly.

'We can't pay you much though, Benny. You know how things are here. But we can give you food.'

'Okay, fine, Mr Paxson. Thanks.'

They shook hands on it. 'Why don't you go back in the kitchen and Mrs Paxson will fix you something to eat first. Then when you're finished you can come and sweep up around here.' He gestured towards the corner. 'Broom's over there.'

'Thanks, Mr Paxson.' Benny nodded towards him and made his way through the room to the kitchen, shuffling a little, the string on his shoe hampering his walk. Máire heard Mrs Paxson greet him. She glanced at Mr Paxson who stared at the kitchen door, a frown on his face.

'Will he be alright?' Máire asked. She kept her voice low, refraining from the question that really was in her mind. Joseph looked up from his work, waiting for Mr Paxson's answer.

Mr Paxson sighed. 'I don't rightly know. I hope so. If past experience is anything to go by, though, it doesn't look good.' He tugged lightly at his beard. 'But I can't but feel sorry for the poor man. Things never seemed to go right for him after his wife and two of his young 'uns died in a fever back along.'

'How tragic,' Máire said. 'To lose all your family at one time.' She thought of her own loss and her heart reached out to Benny.

'He still had Daniel and the two girls left, though. That's the thing. He just lost himself in the bottle instead.'

A small gasp escaped Máire. 'You mean he's their father?' She found it difficult to believe that the decaying old man she had just seen was father to someone who appeared to be in such command of his surroundings as Natsilane.

'He's their father right enough, though you wouldn't know it now. When he turned to drink after his wife and other two children died, Daniel came back home and took the girls to live with their uncle, Kowishte.' Mr Paxson shook his head. 'Shame though, they were all getting on so well in the mission. The girls and the mother were learning quick enough, and the boys, especially Daniel, were real promising. Daniel was going to be a college boy.'

'That's why Natsilane gave up his schooling? Because his mother died and his father took up drinking?' She felt she'd finally found some clues as to Natsilane's behaviour, a reason to make sense of the choices he had made.

'Natsilane?' Mr Paxson knit his brow. 'Oh, you mean Daniel.' He frowned a little. 'Someone tell you his old name? Not him, I'll bet, though I'm not sure he likes being called Daniel anymore.' He rubbed his chest lightly. 'I can't say that those reasons are exactly why Daniel gave up his schooling back east, but it was after that he started taking up his native ways again, living the old tradition. Though he don't really mix with the others of his clan. Can't seem to settle with them, nor they with him. Except his uncle. His uncle wants him to be a medicine man, like him.'

Benny entered at that moment, halting any further questions. As much as Máire might try otherwise, she could not help but stare at him, her eyes following him across the room as he headed toward the broom. 'Hello,' she said. 'I understand you're Benny. I'm Miss McNair.'

He looked over at her and nodded slightly, then reached for the broom, wrapping his fingers slowly around its handle to grip it hard in his large hands. He went off with it, moving with deliberate action while Máire forced herself finally to look away, trying to not to stare, to compare his stooped and broken body with that of his son's.

CHAPTER TWENTY-ONE

Later that afternoon, Máire stole a few moments to read her letter on a dry spot, eventually settling on a flat rock free of moss, away from the mission. She unfolded the pages, her hands trembling with anticipation and some anxiety about what her father might have to say. His familiar spiky handwriting sprawled over the pages she smoothed across her lap. She held her breath while her eyes scanned the letter, searching for important words and meanings. Her breath gradually released, a grim smile forming on her mouth. Beyond the greeting, 'My dear daughter,' her father could have been writing to any one of his acquaintances. The weather was somewhat cool for the time of year, the business was doing well (another strike had been averted), the Comptons were in good health (Mr Compton sending his regards) and he trusted Máire was well. She picked up the next page and found that it was covered with carefully rounded handwriting. Cook's name was written at the bottom.

Dear Miss Máire,

Your father let me send you a letter (Eddie is riting for me). We are all well. Annie had a bad foot. She is better now. Polly took over her chores and is glad to be back in the kichen now. Me and Eddie went to the musik hall and hurd a singer. Lovely she was. Hope you are well and you are eating good and keeping warm. I am nitting you a scarf.

PEG (Cook)

Tears formed and spilled over. She brushed them away quickly but as soon as she managed rid herself of them a new batch coursed down her cheeks. She could hardly tell herself what exactly prompted this display. Did she really miss Cook, or Polly and Annie? Did Cook's actions really matter now?

'Letter from home?' William squatted down beside Máire to offer a handkerchief. 'I'm sorry to intrude on your privacy, but I saw you sitting under the tree and I thought to ask you for a walk. It was only when I came closer that I realized you might want to be alone. But then I thought perhaps you would prefer a handkerchief?' He smiled tentatively.

Máire took the handkerchief, dabbed her eyes and attempted to suppress her irritation at his interruption. 'Yes, William, of course, I'm grateful to you.' He was being very kind and thoughtful, and she felt niggardly in her lack of appreciation. She attempted a smile, folded her letter and put it in her smock pocket. 'Perhaps a walk would be just the thing to bring me out of my gloom.' William offered her his hand and she allowed him to help her rise.

They began an amble along the bank, heading back towards the mission buildings, her hand resting on the inside of his arm. Máire could see Mrs Paxson working in the little garden plot beside the trading post. 'I trust your Indian school went well today?' he asked.

'It did. I had a nice group of children. Sarah was there, with her sister Rebecca. Both of them were a big help.'

'Sarah?'

'Yes, you know Natsilane's sister. We saw her at Kowishte's village.'

'Natsilane—pardon me, but I'm confused with these names. Who is Natsilane?'

'I'm sorry, I mean Daniel. Sarah and Rebecca are Daniel's sisters.'

'Oh I see.' He paused a few moments. 'They were helpful at your school today?'

'Very helpful. I'm fortunate to have them. And they travel such a distance every day. I admire such dedication, especially in the face of all the misfortune in their lives.'

'What misfortune is that?' William asked, his tone polite.

Máire recounted the sad events, feeling their sorrow anew. 'It explains much about Natsilane and his actions. It must have been dreadful to have been so far away when his mother and brothers died, then to come back to find his father could no longer care for his family. So much loss.'

'I'm sure it was difficult for them,' William said. He gave her a neutral smile.

'But now Benny, his father, is back,' she persisted, despite his lack of interest. She wanted to make him understand the tragic events that influenced this family. 'He came in on the steam boat from Sitka. He looked ill and ragged. It was such a shame.' Máire pulled lightly at his sleeve. 'But Mr Paxson gave Benny a job after he gave Mr Paxson his word that he no longer drank, so perhaps he will turn himself around.'

'You mustn't trouble yourself about these Indians too much,' William said. 'You're doing enough, teaching them. These people have their own ways, and though I hate to say it, sometimes you can't change them.'

Máire withdrew her hand from his arm and frowned at him. 'It's not a question of troubling myself, William. It's a question of helping someone to regain his or her wellbeing. To assist him back into the world. A world where people can help him become what he was meant to be.'

William's puzzled look halted the words that poured from her. She realized she had not been speaking of Benny at all, but of Natsilane. Máire flushed.

'I'm sure it will be fine,' William said. The puzzled look remained as they resumed their walk. They arrived at the trading post some moments later and greeted Mrs Paxson and Betty as they came around from the garden. Mrs Paxson looked up from the basket she had slung over her right arm and gave them both a frown. She had yet to say anything direct to Máire about William keeping company with her, though she made her feelings quite clear in other ways. Máire thought Mrs Paxson liked William well enough, but she felt Mrs Paxson would be glad when he was gone and would no longer present a distraction to her and the work she was sent to do.

'These lettuce are not what they should be,' Mrs Paxson said, fingering a feeble green specimen. 'And the carrots are rotting again this year. Betty agrees with me. I shall have to get Joseph to dig up the whole lot of them.' She held up a small orb, the odour of its decaying flesh strong. Betty wrinkled her nose.

'I'm sorry to hear your garden has not been a success, Mrs Paxson,' William said. 'Perhaps if you tried some other vegetables? I think cabbage would do well here. Or potatoes.'

'Nonsense,' Mrs Paxson said. 'You sound like George. It just takes perseverance and determination. And I can assure you, Lieutenant, I have plenty of that.'

Máire suppressed a smile while William hastened to smooth things over. 'Of course, Mrs Paxson. I'm certain you will have success.' Máire looked at the vegetables and wondered how, unlike William, they dared to disagree with her.

CHAPTER TWENTY-TWO

Máire watched the children file out of the room and smiled in satisfaction. She could add another successful school day to her growing count. Beside her, Sarah and Rebecca began to collect the slates and books the children had left on the benches. Struck by a notion, she placed a hand on Sarah's arm.

'Why don't you take the lead in the next session?' It seemed a wonderful idea. Sarah's help was especially invaluable to Máire. She was quick to suggest new methods to teach the children, to select words that were a part of the world they understood, or overcome a troublesome sum by counting objects rather than repeating them by rote. That the children had responded so well to the idea had prompted Máire to make the offer to her now.

'Oh, no, Miss McNair, I wouldn't do that.'

'But of course you must. You're so good with the children. I'm sure they'd enjoy it very much.'

Sarah smiled politely and shook her head. 'I thank you for the praise, Miss McNair, but I'm here only to assist you in the translation.'

From the back, Yedicih spoke to Sarah in Tlingit. Yedicih had accompanied Sarah and Rebecca each day and sat silently in the back for the duration of class. She had smiled and nodded to Máire at the beginning and end of each class, but nothing more.

Sarah replied to Yedicih with a few brief words. Yedicih nodded.

Máire could only guess that the exchange concerned Máire's offer, and assumed that Yedicih approved Sarah's answer. She sighed. 'I think you'd be an admirable teacher, but I won't press you further. If you should change your mind, you only have to say.'

Máire couldn't understand why Sarah refused to lead the class. She couldn't detect any shyness or anxiety when Sarah translated during class, only calm assurance. The woman was a puzzle, but Máire still found that she wanted her as a friend. She'd never really had a friend before, but it appeared Sarah didn't feel the same towards her. The fleeting connection over the fairy tale book had ended with its return, and Máire could extract no comment from her over the contents. Rebecca had provided all the questions and insights that, though humorous, did little to alleviate the disappointment Máire felt over Sarah's silence.

Máire looked over at Rebecca fondly. She had a natural talent for working with the younger children, especially the shy little Mathew and young Minnie. Now Rebecca sat unusually silent on the front bench, waiting for her sister. She'd been subdued during all the lessons.

'Come, Rebecca, why don't you, Sarah and your aunt walk me back to the trading post?' Máire took her hand. 'Perhaps I can persuade Mr Paxson to find a barley sugar to give you.' Rebecca looked up at her and brightened a little.

'Oh yes, Miss McNair.'

With Rebecca and Sarah beside her and Yedicih following behind, Máire walked back to the trading post, halting occasionally for greetings from some of the women and children in the mission. As they neared the trading post, she could see Benny shuffling up the steps to the door. Since Mr Paxson had hired him he had come to the trading post every afternoon to sweep and tidy the shelves. The tins were dusted and restacked carefully, and the bare floors were spotless. Máire was glad to see that Benny had managed to remove some of the grime from his face and hands, and had found a clean, less ragged shirt to wear under his jacket. He looked so much better. She wondered if Mr Paxson's own wardrobe had provided the shirt. Or perhaps it was one of the miners from the small camp where Benny was staying that had sprouted just outside the mission.

'There's your father, just entering the trading post,' Máire said, gesturing towards it. She gave Sarah a look full of warmth and compassion. 'He returned a few days ago and Mr Paxson has given him a job. He seems to be doing quite well. Perhaps you would like to speak with him while I get Rebecca her barley sugar?'

Sarah eyes darkened and she shrugged off Máire's hand. 'I'm sorry Miss McNair, but I have only just remembered that we promised to return as soon as possible. Perhaps another time.'

Before Máire could say another word Sarah took up Rebecca's hand and, with Yedicih close at her side, walked briskly away from Máire, her back firm and straight, Rebecca struggling to keep up. Máire realized her mistake and her heart sank.

She walked into the trading post still numb from Sarah's hasty retreat. Joseph was behind the counter eyeing Benny with a slight frown. He looked over at Máire and attempted a smile.

'Good afternoon, Miss.'

'Good afternoon, Joseph. Hello, Benny. How are you settling in?' she said brightly.

Startled, Benny shuffled his feet at his place by the corner, his eyes on the floor. 'Okay.'

'Good. I'm so glad.' Máire searched for encouraging words to say. She felt a strong desire to compensate for his daughter's avoidance. 'I'm sure the Paxsons are glad of your help. I can see the difference already.' Benny mumbled a reply and fell silent. The silence stretched as Máire tried to search for something more to say.

'How did the school go today?' Joseph asked finally.

'Very well, thank you, Joseph. The children are making a little progress I think. Sarah has been so helpful. And Rebecca.' Máire frowned. 'In fact

I hoped to persuade Mr Paxson to reward Rebecca's help with a small treat just now.'

'They are coming here?' Joseph's face brightened. A loud bang halted Máire's reply. She turned to see Benny lift up a small barrel his broom had knocked over. He glanced in their direction and muttered an apology before righting the barrel and resuming his sweeping.

'No, Sarah couldn't spare the time. She had to return to help her aunt.' Máire glanced over at Benny.

'I see,' Joseph gave a grim look over Máire's shoulder. 'Maybe another time.'

'I hope so, Joseph. I hope so.' She wanted the breach with Benny's family to be healed and would do all that she could to help bring about a reconciliation, but she realized she must go slowly and carefully. There could be more harm done than she knew if she proceeded with haste, especially since there was so much she didn't yet understand. Wouldn't they rather have their father back, after all? Especially with their mother dead so many years.

Mr Paxson returned a short while later with the plans for the hearing. Kowklux and the Kiksadi clan agreed to hold it the next Tuesday. If the weather was fine it would be outside, otherwise they would have to use the church because of the large numbers expected to attend.

'Mr Paxson looked over at Joseph. 'You won't mind translating, will you, Joseph? It's not your clan, so they won't think you'll take sides.'

'I will do my best, Mr Paxson,' Joseph replied.

'Good, that's settled then.' He rubbed his forehead. 'Anyone know where my wife is?'

'She is at the manse, sir, giving Betty instructions about curtains, I believe,' Joseph said.

Mr Paxson grinned and shook his head. 'I'll just go up and give Mrs Paxson the news.' He stopped at the door. 'You and Joseph can keep an eye on things here. The miners coming down from the pass seem to be growing in numbers. They're welcome to come in here, but we don't want any trouble.'

'I'm sure it will be fine, Mr Paxson,' Máire told him as he turned to leave. She could hear Benny's broom swishing vigorously along the bare boards. He seemed to have improved in his short time with them. She suddenly felt more hopeful about persuading Sarah and her sister to see him. She could not bear to think of them separated from their father who seemed such a broken person.

CHAPTER TWENTY-THREE

Captain Gordon cleared his throat and put his hand on the wooden pulpit. 'Jesus went to the well,' he began. He tugged at his collar and fiddled with one of the brass buttons as he looked out over the assembled congregation. 'Yes. He went to the well and there the women were assembled ready to draw the water for the day.'

As the homily continued, Máire drifted away from the sea of words, pushing her mind outwards like an eddy from a boat. The ease she felt was in part due to the continued omission of her corset, a fact hidden by the voluminous smock she tucked in generous folds about her as she sat ensconced between William and Mrs Paxson. Mrs Paxson had given her a strange look when she appeared in the smock that morning, but Máire had told her that her good dress needed mending and her shirtwaists were all stained. Máire tried not to take pleasure in her unplanned slight against Betty, but there was truth to the statement. Now Máire wondered how she could get material for another smock so that she might wash this one without returning to wearing her corset.

Mrs Paxson shifted in her seat and Máire could feel Mrs Paxson's firmly upholstered figure rub her own. She shifted slightly away, towards William. He turned and smiled at her and in panic she smiled back. William had taken her down to see the seals again yesterday. She'd laughed and watched them splash and play in the rock pools, and she told William she felt them to be her friends. She knew it to be true because they came to her at night in her dreams. Dreams as vivid and real as anything in her life had been. Dreams in which she swam naked with them, her hair unbound, just like before, the water flowing over her skin, smooth and silken. They knew her.

But William could only laugh and give her a light kiss on the cheek when she mentioned it.

The homily ended and Mrs Paxson signalled the final hymn. 'All rise.'

The singing began, an enthusiastic if off-key rendition of 'Jesus Gentle Saviour' filling the room. Kowklux sang with gusto, a sure sign that he approved of the homily and the hymn. With the hymn concluded, Kowklux made the first move and made his way over to Captain Gordon.

'Your talk I liked,' Kowklux told him, and shook his hand hard. He nodded to Mrs Paxson and moved down towards Mr Paxson and shook his hand as well before making his way out the door.

The genial atmosphere continued as the rest of the group filed out. Máire bade William a brief farewell and remained behind to help the Paxsons and Joseph to tidy up the church. Mrs Paxson briskly piled hymnals and straightened benches.

'I think we might need to use some of the benches from the school for the hearing, George,' she said. She turned to Máire. 'So there will be no school that day, Martha. And we should probably cancel school the day before, as well. That will leave time to move the benches into place.' Máire nodded. She realized any argument was useless under the force of Mrs Paxson's organizational energy.

As Máire and the Paxsons made their way out of the door, Mr Paxson told them that Captain Gordon had agreed to have his men help shift the benches. Mrs Paxson grunted an approval before taking herself and Joseph off to the manse to compile a list of all the supplies.

'Wouldn't Kowklux provide the food?' Máire asked Mr Paxson. 'It's his dispute.'

'It's because it's his dispute that he wouldn't feed everyone. It's got to be someone who ain't partial to either side.' He grinned at her. 'That way there's no danger of poisoning.'

Máire smiled in the hope he was only teasing, though she wasn't certain that the Chilkat would deem poisoning to be such an outrageous action. 'Wouldn't one of the other clans play host to this hearing?'

'Well, maybe, backalong, if they had these kind of things, but they asked us to judge it, not another clan. So it's our job to feed them.'

Máire's questions were cut short by the sight of Natsilane waiting patiently by the trading post steps. He was leaning against the wall, his arms and legs crossed casually. The sight of him took Máire by surprise, giving her no time to hide the flash of pleasure she felt.

Mr Paxson raised his hand and called a greeting. 'Well now, Daniel, I wouldn't've expected to see your face here on a Sunday,' he said when they came alongside of the steps. Natsilane rose slowly, his legs unfolding with fluid grace. Mr Paxson laughed and patted him on the shoulder. 'You're welcome, anyhow.'

'It must be a special day if I can surprise you, George.' Natsilane flashed a grin, an action that lit his face. It was a startling sight, his usually hardened, angular, steely eyes now softened with humour. The result was a handsomeness that was undeniably magnetic.

He turned to Máire. 'Good day to you, Miss Not Martha.' His face was still alight and his voice was pleasant. Suddenly tongue-tied, Máire could only nod.

'I'm guessing this isn't a social call, Daniel, but that you're wanting something from the store?' asked Mr Paxson.

'As much as I hate to admit it, I haven't come for Sunday afternoon tea with you. I've come for some more coffee beans.'

'Coffee beans? You're not a coffee drinker, Daniel. I don't think I ever saw you drink coffee.'

'I know. You're right. They're not for me.' His tone was almost shy. He glanced at Máire. 'They're for my uncle. As payment. It seems he actually likes coffee.'

'What're you paying your uncle for? You been up to no good?' Mr Paxson's mouth twitched. Clearly, he found the line of questioning enjoyable.

For a moment Natsilane looked embarrassed. 'It's for Sarah and Rebecca,' he said, his expression carefully contained. 'They asked me if they could come to the school. It was the only way my uncle would give permission.'

Máire was stunned as she realized that the whole ploy to get Sarah and Rebecca to the school had been a farce. He had known all along they were coming when Máire requested Sarah's help. He had just been toying with her.

Mr Paxson threw back his head and laughed. 'Well that's a new one on me. There I was thinking you had taken up one of the evil vices of us white folk.' He shook his head. 'Though I'm amazed Kowishte has a taste for it.' He turned to the steps motioning for Máire to precede him. 'Come along in then, and I'll fix you up with your beans.'

They made their way inside, Natsilane bringing up the rear. After taking Natsilane's proffered sack, Mr Paxson went over behind the counter and hefted it onto the wood surface with a resounding thud. Máire stood just inside the door, subdued and confused by the mixture of humiliation and frustration that Natsilane had aroused, yet unable to excuse herself and go to her room.

While Mr Paxson measured out the coffee, Natsilane turned to face Máire. He ran his eyes over her figure and raised his brows. 'Your dress is very interesting.'

Máire folded her arms around her waist, pulling in the smock, only to drop them a moment later, feeling certain that he knew her secret. She stiffened, determined to bluff it out. 'I thought it might meet with your approval, since you spoke of your concerns over your sisters being unduly influenced by unsuitable attire.' Máire paused and raised her chin a fraction. 'I was certain they were serious concerns, so I took them to heart.'

Natsilane nodded, a gesture almost imperceptible, if not for the glint that flickered in his eye. 'I approve,' he said in a low voice.

Máire looked down at her hands, embarrassment replacing any need to retaliate for his trickery. 'I'm glad your sisters are able to come. They're both very helpful.' Máire had a sudden thought and put on her best smile. 'Sarah has a real talent for teaching. I'd like to learn the Tlingit language and I thought perhaps Sarah might help me. Do you think she'd agree?'

He shrugged, his face expressionless. 'You'll have to ask her.'

'Here you are then.' Mr Paxson held out the pouch. 'That should do you for a while.' He paused. 'You know about the hearing?' Natsilane shook his head and said he'd not been to his uncle's village for several days. Mr Paxson filled him in. 'It might be a good idea if you and a few others from your clan came,' he added. 'Some of you've got relations in Sitka, don't you?'

Natsilane smiled. 'We all have relations in Sitka.' He took the pouch from Mr Paxson. 'Perhaps you're right, it might help guarantee a peaceful outcome if some of our clan were there. They know my uncle won't permit anything untoward. I'll speak to him about it.'

Mr Paxson nodded, marking the transaction into the ledger. As Natsilane turned to leave, Mr Paxson looked up and frowned slightly. 'Oh, by the way, Daniel,' he said in a low voice. 'Benny's back. He's sober, so I gave him a job here. Sweeping. He's staying with the miners.'

'Yes. I know.' He nodded to Mr Paxson, his demeanour stiff, his jaw hard once again. 'Thanks for the beans. I'll be off now.' He glanced at Máire as he made for the door, a dark brooding look that froze the farewell she was about to utter in her throat. She couldn't mistake its warning, though she was not entirely clear the nature of it. Did he know about her attempts with Sarah and Rebecca? She was certain that any further attempts she might make to help matters must be carefully handled.

CHAPTER TWENTY-FOUR

The day of the hearing emerged wet and soggy, the clouds smearing the sky grey. Máire shivered as she dressed. The first signs of winter had finally arrived. Looking down at her obviously soiled smock, she sighed and reached for her corset. Betty had, with her usual sunny disposition, grudgingly agreed to wash and iron Máire's shirtwaists the previous day. Máire promised herself she would launder the smock at the earliest opportunity. She pulled a shawl around her against the chill.

When Máire arrived in the kitchen, she saw Mrs Paxson had donned her good jacket and skirt for the occasion, but a buttoned waistcoat and a battered jacket seemed Mr Paxson's only concession. Joseph's worn suit was freshly brushed and his hair was plastered to his head. After a quick breakfast, they made their way to the riverbank to await the arrival of the Sitka clan. They had camped downstream the night before, etiquette apparently dictating the formal greeting be conducted the day of the hearing.

Máire, Joseph and the Paxsons reached the riverbank to find Kowklux's men lining the water's edge, their faces painted black, and hair caught up in bright cloths. There were no women present. A few men had heavily embroidered blankets draped over their shoulders, while others wore stiffened leather vests.

'Have they painted their faces for a reason?' Máire asked Joseph in a low voice as they neared the group.

'It is to show that they are ready to fight, if things do not go well.' Joseph's mouth formed a tight line across his face.

Máire surveyed the group closely. It was subdued, low murmurs from a few of them the only sounds as they shifted under the wet sky. Kowklux stood in front, his chest bare despite the rain, his painted face fearsome. Captain Gordon, the ship's officers, and about six of his men stood in full uniform a few feet apart. Máire picked out William among them. As she watched, the rain began to penetrate her hair, giving her a sudden chill. Máire pulled the shawl over her head, despite Mrs Paxson's frown at such a common gesture.

An equally sombre and colourfully clad group arrived from Sitka amid tension no less evident for the insistent spatter of rain across the wooden paddles they lifted out of the water in preparation to come alongside of the bank. Mr Paxson stepped forward to greet them, Captain Gordon close behind.

'Chief Goutchsha-ee,' said Mr Paxson. He held up a hand to a broad-muscled man in a carved cone hat and blackened face. 'You're welcome to our home.' He turned to indicate Captain Gordon. 'This here is Captain Gordon, from the American warship, *U.S.S. Jamestown*. He's going to help out at the hearing today.'

The chief nodded solemnly and disembarked with the others at a spot just ahead of Kowklux's men. Slowly, Goutchsha-ee's group proceeded towards the church, following Mr Paxson, Captain Gordon and his crew. Kowklux's group brought up the rear. All of them were silent and grim amid the heavy rain. Máire followed Mrs Paxson up to the church behind the last of Kowklux's men, noting her determination to ensure no stragglers might create some 'accident' with Goutchsha-ee's canoes.

Inside the church, Goutchsha-ee's men, about thirty in all, lined one side of the room. Kowklux and his men faced them, all fierce glares and frowns. At a table between the two groups sat Captain Gordon, Mr Paxson with Joseph at his side, and William, taking out his pen to record the testimony. Máire took a seat beside Mrs Paxson, at the back of the room by the door. Just as everyone seemed settled, the door opened again and in walked Kowishte, Natsilane and a few other Chilkoot men. All eyes turned to these newcomers while Kowishte calmly took one of the two remaining seats by the door. Natsilane, after a brief nod in her direction, sat in the other seat, which was next to Máire's. A moment later he crossed his leg over his knee, a simple, natural gesture but one that brought his thigh in closer proximity to Máire. Máire folded her hands in her lap and forced herself to concentrate on the proceedings up front and ignore the corset biting hard at her waist.

The room fell silent once again as everyone settled onto their benches, their expectant eyes directed at Mr Paxson. Carefully, with Joseph translating, he explained the process for the day. One by one, each person on the prepared list was to give their testimony about the events, as he understood it to be true. When Mr Paxson had concluded, Captain Gordon rose and cautioned them about telling the truth and to refrain from misbehaving.

The first person to rise and speak was Tinneh-tark, Kowklux's nephew. With a fiercely painted face, he came to the table confidently and spoke forcefully, while Joseph translated for the benefit of the whites present. He explained that last spring, Goutchsha-ee's cousin had killed his own cousin in a fight. Tinneh-tark had witnessed the fight, and it was clear to him Goutchsha-ee's cousin must give reparation. As Tinneh-tark described the events of the fight, Goutchsha-ee's men began to hiss and mutter. Some of Kowklux's men shifted in their seats, while others grunted, their faces increasingly stormy.

Tinneh-tark stood beside the table, his legs splayed wide and his arms crossed. 'My cousin was a valued member of the clan, so Kowklux, our strong and fierce leader, could only settle for an equally valued member of Goutchsha-ee's clan.' He paused, looking over at Goutchsha-ee. 'Seeing Goutchsha-ee's position, though, he decided to select a woman for his brother to marry.'

The hisses increased, one of Goutchsha-ee's men shouted words at Tinneh-tark, eliciting a noisy response from Kowklux's side. Many rose in their seats, a blade flashed amid angry shouts and stomping feet. More knives appeared, and everyone was on their feet, shouts and gestures issuing from a raging sea of angry, painted faces.

Mrs Paxson rose. 'Silence!' she shouted as she tried to make her way to the front.

Mr Paxson pounded the table and Captain Gordon issued angry commands to his men to establish order. In response William and Lieutenant Bissell brandished their pistols, but no-one took notice.

Máire looked at Natsilane who seemed to view the chaos in front of him with steady calm. Then after a signal from his uncle they both stood. Kowishte made his way to the table, his gait dignified and solemn, his nose ring glittering in the light. Natsilane followed behind. When Kowishte reached the table he looked around room, his eyes seeming to touch on every person standing. Gradually the shouting and pounding died down, and one by one the men resumed their seats.

The room silent, Captain Gordon spoke. 'How dare any of you bring weapons into this place of God, to an event sanctioned by the U.S. government. I will remind all of you that these are official proceedings. If there are any more loud outbursts—' he motioned to Lieutenant Bissell. 'This officer, Lieutenant Bissell, will go among you and collect all weapons. You can retrieve them later. I'm empowering Lieutenant Bissell to shoot anyone who dares so much as rise from his seat.'

'Now, Captain,' Mr Paxson said. 'I'm sure all that ain't necessary. These folk have calmed a bit, and things will go fine now.'

'No, Mr Paxson, I won't have this kind of behaviour.'

'Captain, I'm telling you, it'll be fine.' Mr Paxson's voice had a sharp edge to it. 'Chief Kowishte will vouch for them and so will I. And Florence.' He looked over at his wife and then to Kowishte who gave a dark look and nodded.

'Yes, everyone will be calm,' Kowishte said.

Captain Gordon pursed his mouth and shook his head. 'Alright Paxson. I don't like it though. And I'll hold you responsible if anything goes wrong.' He sat down and motioned to William to resume his record-keeping. 'We'll continue now.'

Mr Paxson nodded toward Tinneh-tark who had remained standing beside the table throughout the upheaval. 'Go on,' he said.

Tinneh-tark resumed his testimony, his words more measured in tone and his stance less arrogant and sure. Kowishte stood beside him, his arms crossed and his gaze fixed on Tinneh-tark's face. Natsilane moved off to the side, but remained standing.

Tinneh-tark continued his version of the events, emphasizing points here and there, but largely giving a less inflammatory account. Kowklux's men greeted Tinneh-tark's conclusion with approving noises. Captain Gordon and Mr Paxson conferred briefly, then called a man from Goutchsha-ee's group, Gac, to give his account of the events. Gac had apparently witnessed the fight that had resulted in death of Tinneh-tark's cousin. He spoke at length about the fight, stressing how much Tinneh-tark's cousin had provoked it, heaping insults on the Sitka man. Gac sketched over the events following the fight. His account was second-hand and seemed to shed no further light upon it, but he was permitted his say.

And so it continued for the next few hours, witness after witness rising to testify, with only an occasional outburst or argument interrupting the proceedings. William recorded each word and Mr Paxson listened carefully while Captain Gordon fidgeted often, his eyes continuously scanning the group with suspicion. Through it all, Kowishte stood impassively overseeing the event, his looming presence acting as a silent warning to them all.

At one point Máire found her eyes on Natsilane, studying him thoroughly as if by such close examination she might understand him more. She tried to imagine him as a child, teasing his friends, affectionate with his mother. What had his mother been like? She must have looked something like him, her hair dark and long, black eyes and a generous mouth set in a face with high cheekbones. Such a loss for him. She thought of her own privileged childhood, the perfectly sewn clothes of fine fabrics and trims, the expensive furniture, the elaborate meals. Such advantages, yet without the benefit of any motherly attention. There was more of a sense of her mother's presence here than at any other place, except perhaps at the house by the sea. It was an idea that some of the native people might understand. She regarded Natsilane again. As if sensing her thoughts Natsilane looked over at her briefly, gave a faint smile, then calmly shifted his gaze to Mr Paxson.

Finally, many hours later, the last person finished speaking. Mr Paxson rose.

'I'd like to thank everyone for their cooperation today. Everyone had their say, I think, and there's lots to think over. We'll all have something to eat and drink and that'll give Captain Gordon and me time to sift through all that we heard and come up with a solution.'

Everyone rose amid murmurs and filed out of the church. Once outside Máire followed Mrs Paxson to the manse to help bring out the food. The rain had stopped, and there was enough of a watery sun present for everyone to feel that the best place for the food was on tables outside. With the help of Betty and some of the other women, Máire carried heavily laden plates and bowls to the tables. There was chicken and bread and Betty's squash soup thickened with flour and lard. Some of the Tlingits picked at the food uncertainly, but many were hungry and ate heartily.

Máire made her way around the various groups, ladling soup into their large, carved wooden spoons that acted as bowls. She noticed Natsilane standing on his own outside these groups, surveying the people, his face impassive. She thought nothing more of it until, backing out of one of the groups, she turned and found herself face-to-face with him.

'Would you like some soup?' she asked, making an effort at calm.

He looked down at the cook pot Máire held and wrinkled his nose. 'I don't think so, do you?'

Máire looked at the soup, a thick skin of congealed lard and flour floating on its surface, not a piece of squash in sight. Máire grimaced. 'It isn't very appealing,' she said.

'No. Have you tasted it?'

'Well, no. I've had little time to eat anything. I've been busy assisting Mrs Paxson.' Máire looked up at him and laughed. She felt like some orphanage matron handing out tasteless gruel. She shared the thought with Natsilane and he laughed too. Startled by such an open reaction, she choked and began to cough.

'Here, let me take that,' Natsilane said. He reached for her pot and set it on the ground. Before she knew what he was about, he clapped her on the back vigorously. Her surprise at his touch, and the restraint of her corset, only caused her to cough harder. He led her to a small rock away from the crowded tables and busy feet.

'Wait here a moment, I'll get you something to drink,' he said eventually after her coughing had subsided. He returned seconds later with a tin cup filled with water. Máire sipped carefully, finding the liquid refreshing and cool on her stressed throat.

'Thank you.' She looked down into the cup. 'You're very kind. I do feel silly after such a performance.'

'Oh, I think there were one or two performances inside the church today that were far sillier than yours.'

Máire looked up into his face and smiled at his small joke. There was no trace of mockery in his eyes, just a glimmer of humour that was so surprising in his normally solemn face. She felt gratified that he felt he could share this humour with her. In fact, she wondered that he had spoken to her at any length at all, despite her earlier observation about his solitude. Before it hadn't struck her as anything other than his choice, but she now wondered if that was truly the case. Mr Paxson had described his people's inability to 'settle' with him. She couldn't recall any of the other Tlingit present greeting him or talking with him, yet she observed that his uncle seemed to effortlessly engage in conversation with any one of the Tlingit. She looked at him with a fresh eye.

'I'm not certain if you're referring to any particular person,' she told him. 'I can only say I'm glad that there were some who managed to keep a cool head.'

'It might have become extremely unpleasant, resulting in a scene that would have doubtless shocked you.'

'Thank you for your concern, but my life hasn't been entirely sheltered. I know it got quite dangerous there at one point and if not for you and your uncle it might have been very ugly,' Máire said. She touched his hand lightly. 'I am not the only one who should be grateful for your cool head.'

He allowed her the touch, appraising it, his face placid. She tried to catch his eye. 'I do not mistake the person before me, Natsilane. No matter how much you may pretend otherwise I know you are a compassionate man.'

He looked up at Máire then, his eyes unreadable. 'I think you do mistake it, Miss McNair.' He gave her a wry smile and turned and walked away.

Máire frowned. What could he mean? Tears stung her eyes, but she chose to ignore them. Well, Natsilane was not everyone here. There were others now who counted on her good opinion, who were happy to converse with her. Despite these assurances she couldn't set aside the feeling that there was more to Natsilane's reaction than rejection of her remarks.

CHAPTER TWENTY-FIVE

'A Deer Ceremony. That sounds so interesting,' Máire said. 'Do they exchange deer, to signify peace?'

'It is a Deer Ceremony because deer are peaceful,' Joseph said. 'After each side has agreed to the gifts to be given, they will have men pretend to be deer, to show peaceful behaviour.'

'Later, the deer dance, sing songs, and then there is a feast,' Benny added in a soft voice.

'I see,' Máire said. It seemed such a unique manner in which to settle differences. She was surprised and gratified by Benny's contribution to the conversation. And he'd been so helpful just now as they unearthed the remains of the garden and packed the tins and small sacks of flour and other grains into the burlap bags. She was looking forward to witnessing everything Joseph and Benny described. But there was much to do in the way of trying to organize food for all these people for the next few days, and to supplement Kowklux's food supplies for the feast. He had fewer food stores for winter since Mrs Paxson had persuaded him to spend more time at the mission instead of fishing in the summer camps, away from her daily watchful guidance. Máire gathered up the sack Benny had packed and told him she had laid out some food for him in the kitchen.

'Why don't you join us in the feasting for the next few days, Benny?'

'No thanks, Miss. I'm fine,' he mumbled. 'I'll just take a little bread with me, if that's okay.'

Máire assured him it was and he shuffled off to the kitchen while she and Joseph picked up the sacks of food. As they made their way across the clearing, Máire saw Mr Paxson, Kowishte and Natsilane watching

189

two groups of men being ushered in opposite directions. Tinneh-tark was among the group going off with Goutchsha-ee's men. Máire told Joseph she'd join him later at the manse, set down her sack, and joined the three men.

'Is something amiss with the peace settlement?' she asked.

The three of them turned to her, Kowishte eyes narrowing slightly. Natsilane ignored her. Mr Paxson grinned.

'Don't worry Martha, this is all part of this here Deer Ceremony.' He pointed to the men. 'Each side has given the other a group of hostages. They're the 'deer,' see, and they'll spend the next few days with the other side. Seems they'll be treated with great honour, while they do dances and songs. Then it's time for the feast.'

'Have the negotiations been successfully completed?'

'Not yet. We'll do the real nitty-gritty stuff tomorrow,' said Mr Paxson. He gestured to his companions. 'We've Daniel and Chief Kowishte here to thank for it going so well. The ceremony was all their idea.'

'The ceremony is how it should be,' Kowishte said.

Mr Paxson nodded. 'Well, I suppose there's enough to do now over at the trading post. Goutchsha-ee's folk are bound to keep us busy over there. Not to mention the miners.'

Máire told him of Mrs Paxson's plans to supplement Kowklux and the Kiksadi clan's food supplies from the trading post and the fishing efforts of Captain Gordon's men. When she inquired about Natsilane and Kowishte's arrangements, Mr Paxson told her as *nakani*, a sort of barrister, they would be honoured guests of the clans.

'Before you go to Kowklux's place, Kowishte, can I get you some coffee by way of showing my appreciation?' Mr Paxson asked.

Kowishte gave him a puzzled look, and after a glance at Natsilane, gave a nod. The two of them moved towards the store, leaving Natsilane standing beside her. Mr Paxson looked over his shoulder at Natsilane.

'Daniel, you still aiming to catch some fish for us for this feast?'

'If I can manage it tomorrow, before the final negotiations start,' Natsilane said as he made a move in the opposite direction. Máire put her hand on his arm to restrain him.

'Please, let me apologize for my words yesterday. I overstepped myself and I'm sorry.'

He glanced down at her, then her hand, his face studied indifference. 'Don't trouble yourself. It's of no consequence.'

'It's of consequence to me,' Máire told him. She removed her hand. 'Can you at least be gracious enough to accept my apology? After all, I was only expressing admiration, I was hardly biting your head off.'

He avoided her eyes. 'As I said, it's of no consequence.' He turned and walked away. Máire stared after him feeling she had made no headway. It would have been better if she had not said anything at all to him. She could not fathom why he was being so difficult.

Though Máire was not overly busy the next day, there seemed little spare time for William, who sought her out. She had stopped in the kitchen briefly to check with Betty the amount of sugar needed from the store when he appeared behind her and greeted her.

'Oh William, you startled me,' she said as she caught up a wisp of hair and placed it behind her ear. She felt bedraggled and could hardly suppress her annoyance at his appearance. 'I'm all in a rush, now. Was there something you wanted?'

He held up a feeble little fish and smiled. 'I've brought my contribution to the feast.'

She glanced at his meagre offering and sighed. 'That's good of you. If you could just pass it over to Betty there, she can deal with it.'

'I was hoping you might be able to express your gratitude on a short walk.'

'Thank you, but I'll have to refuse, there's just too much to do,' Máire said.

William nodded. 'I see,' he said in an even tone, but a flicker of anger crossed his eyes. 'Maybe another time.'

'Yes, of course,' Máire said.

He pressed his hand on her arm. 'Don't let the cause of these ignorant savages wear you out.' He cast a glance over her clothes and hair.

Máire looked at Betty before returning her glance to William. 'I have to go now.' She turned and left. It was becoming clear why she wished to avoid William's company. If only she could stop wishing for Natsilane's. She hoped she would see him when he handed over his contribution to the cook pot. But she was not to be so lucky, for he made his delivery into Betty's hands when she was absent.

The ceremony began in the early evening, a weak wet sun still in the sky despite the autumn month. Everyone gathered in Kowklux's house, he being the host of the event. Some of Kowishte's village appeared, including Sarah and Rebecca. Máire raised her hand to greet them from where she sat. She was squeezed in the back, seated between William and Captain Gordon, the only other whites besides the Paxsons, allocated precious space within the house.

Settled in with as much comfort as she could manage given the situation, William leaned over towards her. 'I hope we may manage some time together soon. I depart the day after tomorrow,' he said in a low voice.

'I'm sure there will be some time,' Máire said. Suddenly she found his close proximity suffocating. She shifted slightly, easing her weight away from him.

'This seems like a circus show, don't you think?' remarked Captain Gordon as she stirred next to him. She followed his gaze around the room, taking in the riot of colour and design. Tlingits covered in blankets, capes, carved and woven hats, trimmed headbands and flashing jewellery filled every possible space. Clan crests were painted on faces, and tracked across tunics in pale ochres, blues, blacks and reds.

Captain Gordon leaned forward slightly. 'Look at those fellas upfront.'

The two chiefs, Kowklux and Goutchsha-ee, were both garbed in blankets banded and buttoned in a whirl of dancing colours, their heads each framed in fur-trimmed headbands. Nothing could dispute their rank and status.

In front of the chiefs, Natsilane and Kowishte formally directed people to their seats. Máire stared intently at Natsilane. His hair was still a tangle, but his face was painted boldly in black and red, and he wore a hide tunic dyed a dark blue, an intricately beaded figure of a wolf's head leaping from its front. He was almost unrecognisable, so strange-looking in this ceremonial dress it made her uncomfortable. Máire looked over to his uncle, equally elaborate in his own dress, and felt her discomfort ease, for Kowishte seemed noble, a regal warrior king, inspiring obedience. Máire kept her eyes on Kowishte, admiring his erect bold posture as he indicated to each person the correct place to sit, keeping Kowklux's people on one side with the women against the wall, and Goutchsha-ee's people on the other side, seated in the same manner.

Some people shifted in front of her and she could finally see the 'deer', seated with their backs to her on richly dyed and worked blankets, dressed from head to toe in the most finely wrought clothes. They wore feathers in the form of a 'V' held against their foreheads by a band, and fluffy down was sprinkled across their heads. Since the day before, servants had attended the 'deer,' seeing to all their needs.

The ceremony began when all were seated appropriately. Natsilane and Kowishte made some short speeches in Tlingit, Natsilane's solemn delivery in contrast to his uncle's more animated approach. Máire had little idea what was said. Joseph had been seated too far forward to translate and Sarah and Rebecca were over by the wall. Máire resolved again to ask Sarah to teach her the language.

The speeches ended. One of the 'deer,' a man from Gouchsha-ee's clan, rose with his back to the group and began a kind of singing chant, raising his feet in rhythm. It was mesmerizing, its thrumming rhythm vibrating across the room and through her chest. The unfamiliar sensation was uncanny, close only to what she had experienced in Kowishte's ceremony. When the man finally finished he circled in a clockwise direction, turned to face the group, then paused a moment before beginning a dance.

Accompanied by a hand drum, the 'deer hostage' swayed his elaborate cape, beating the air like the wings of a bird, feet stepping high as if ready to land. Máire sat motionless, her breath catching in her throat at such a show of an animal's grace, an appreciation captured in a dance that mirrored the world around him, telling its own story. Then it was if she and the man became the bird as it lifted off the ground and soared up over the trees, looking down upon the brightly coloured crowd. The wind caught her feathers; she lifted her wings to catch its force, then glided gently round in ever tighter circles, drifting closer and closer to the ground again, pulled by the insistent beat of the drum.

The drum sounded a great flourish. Máire blinked her eyes and the hostage dancer stood before her, his cape still and silent over his shoulders. Máire watched him walk solemnly to his blanket and take his seat while she fought a racing heart and rapid breath. Carefully she glanced around trying to connect to what she saw now in the room. Had anyone noticed anything?

She glanced at William and he frowned at her. 'This is all too much,' he said. 'Barbaric. Too much for your sensibilities, Martha. Shall I escort you away?'

Máire bristled. The name, the assumption, were all too much. 'No, I'm fine William. I prefer to remain. But you go if you must.'

William's frown deepened. 'Yes, well, if you insist.' He rose and with some hasty excuses to Captain Gordon, climbed across limbs and feet to the entrance. Máire could only stare after William in wonder. Captain Gordon gave her a little shrug and returned his attention to the front.

Tinnheh-tark was the next person to perform. He stood with heavy dignity, head high, back facing the group, and began his own chant-like song. The song's cadence was somewhat different to his predecessor's, though the gestures were not unlike his and the plaintive sound was the same. Máire eventually relaxed under his sounds and found herself swaying slightly as the soothing rhythm filled her body and connected to the beat of her heart. Tinneh-tark finished eventually, the accompanying drum sounding loudly, recalling Máire to her surroundings. She watched half-conscious as Tinneh-tark completed the circling motion like the man before, then entered a dance.

The evening progressed, each 'deer' rising and performing his own song-chant and dance. All of them performed their piece with careful dignity, enacting his role to the best of his ability. Máire hardly dared move, cautiously attentive. She wasn't certain she wished to repeat her early experience.

Beside her, Captain Gordon dozed, his slight snore hardly discernible. Despite her earlier resolve she lost herself in the magic of the dances and songs which took on lives of their own. The dancers and singers became the animals, the mountains, the trees and the sea around them. As the flames flickered across their faces it seemed all the spirits of the land answered the performers' calls and filled their bodies to become one with them.

CHAPTER TWENTY-SIX

'Is William going to join us?' Máire asked.

'Not until later, after the ceremony. He's in charge of the watch on the ship,' Captain Gordon said.

'Oh.' Máire reflected on the truth of this news as she tucked her smock carefully around her. Captain Gordon sat beside her, she in the same place as the previous day, but Lieutenant Bissell in what had been William's seat. It was obvious William was avoiding the ceremony. Was she the cause of William's increasing dislike of all things Tlingit?

'Captain, do you know what the Coptic religion is?'

'Isn't that a Hottentot thing?'

'North African, sir,' Lieutenant Bissell said. 'Hottentots are South African.'

'Ah, yes,' Captain Gordon said. 'I knew it was some kind of nigger religion. Why do you ask?'

'Oh, no reason,' Máire said. 'I heard someone mention it and wondered what it was. I thought a man of your experience might know.'

Captain Gordon gave her an absentminded nod and turned to the front where the ceremony resumed. Máire puzzled over the captain's information. How was it William's mother had practiced an African religion in Baltimore? Once again she realized there was much about William she didn't know.

The drumming struck up with a thunderous beat. The ceremony continued in much the same manner as the night before. Each 'captive deer' rose and gave a brief song followed by a dance. The songs were shorter this time and seemed a little happier than the deers' previous efforts, but no less exotic or stirring for Máire. She was sorry when it ended and they announced it was time for the feast. Some of the women and girls of Kowklux's clan rose proudly and took various bowls of food to distribute among everyone. Natsilane and Kowishte, seated on either side of the chiefs, were served with the chiefs. Máire could see by the formality of the offerings to Goutchsha-ee's group there was much etiquette involved as each of the recipients of the food acknowledged their servings with great solemnity. She did her best to behave with as much seriousness as she accepted her own fare from a young girl that she recognized from the school.

Later, after much food had passed through everyone's hands, people began to rise and move outside to talk and exchange banter with the other groups. Máire took advantage of the general movement and decided to stretch her legs and perhaps seek out Sarah.

Máire moved off to the edge of the clearing and took in the elaborate costuming and the exotic sounds of the breathy language that surrounded her. Then she glimpsed the face and flash of braid she was certain belonged to Sarah, and she set off to waylay her. Sarah vanished from her sight for a few moments, but Máire saw her again near a wooded outcrop by the river's edge just before she disappeared behind a tree trunk. Curious, Máire followed her path, slowing down as she neared the trees and voices reached her ears. Someone was talking to Sarah, a male, and as Máire strained to hear the words she realized with a slight shock it was Joseph.

Máire halted in her tracks and drew a deep breath, not certain how to behave. She could not make out his words as he was speaking in Tlingit, so she couldn't assess the intent of their meeting. She did know that it was against Tlingit custom for them to be alone and Natsilane would certainly not approve of it. Was it her place to interfere, though? Máire sighed and stepped forward with as much noise as possible as she made to clear her throat.

Joseph's voice ceased and after a pause he stepped out from behind the tree and greeted Máire.

'Hello, Miss McNair.' He ran his hand through his hair distractedly. 'Are you enjoying the feast?'

'Oh yes, Joseph, very much. But my legs were somewhat cramped so I thought to take a walk and give them a stretch.' Máire smoothed her skirt. 'I was looking for Sarah and happened to see her head in this direction. I wanted to put a request to her.' Máire looked pointedly at the tree trunk. 'Perhaps she would hear my request now?'

Slowly, with a quiet dignity, Sarah emerged from behind the tree. Joseph glanced over at me, a sheepish look on his face. 'I am sorry, Miss McNair, I did not mean to deceive you,' he said. 'You will not say anything to anyone, will you? There was no harm in it, I promise you.'

Máire looked from Sarah to Joseph, trying to read their faces. Sarah greeted her scrutiny with a certain amount of calm, though something lurked at the back of her eyes.

'Please, Miss McNair,' she said quietly.

Wordlessly Máire nodded, then turned to Joseph. 'Perhaps you should be getting back to the festivities. There might be some need of your translating skills.'

Relief crossed Joseph's face before he expressed some quick thanks, and with a glance at Sarah, he left.

'Thank you for your kindness,' Sarah said. She smiled a little. 'You had a request for me?'

'Yes, I was wondering if you might be able to help me—' Sarah's faced paled as she looked past Máire. Máire turned around and saw a grim-faced Natsilane approach, Rebecca trailing worriedly behind him.

Máire greeted them both. 'I've enjoyed the ceremony,' she said. She wanted to direct the conversation on an even keel and hoped he was not still annoyed with her. 'But it has gone on for quite a while so I decided to come here to ease my legs and put a request to Sarah. I was just asking her, when you arrived, if she would be kind enough to teach me Tlingit.' Máire looked directly at Sarah. Sarah's eyes were downcast, her toe digging the earth.

'Of course, Miss McNair,' she said. 'I would be happy to help.'

'Good, I look forward to it. Perhaps we can arrange to have the lessons following classes each day.' Máire turned to face Natsilane and saw to her relief that his expression had eased considerably and displayed something close to amusement.

'Are you enjoying the festivities, Rebecca?' Máire asked after a few moments.

'Oh yes, Miss McNair.' She beamed a smile at me. 'The jokes are very funny.'

'Jokes?' Máire asked.

'Oh yes, they were telling some very funny jokes.' She frowned slightly. 'Of course you would not have understood.' Rebecca smiled again. 'But now there will be more be dancing and singing. You'll enjoy that.'

Máire looked down at Rebecca, pleased that she had considered her lack of language skill. 'I'm sure I shall enjoy it. I love dancing.'

'Do you dance, Miss McNair?' she asked.

Máire laughed. 'I do dance, but not the kind of dances you're used to.'

'What kind of dances do you perform?'

'They're partner dances, between a man and a woman. They don't tell a story, not really, they're just for enjoyment.'

'A man and a woman?' Rebecca sounded disbelieving.

Máire nodded. She looked over at Natsilane, uncertain if she should continue. Rebecca followed her gaze. She moved over and tugged his arm.

'Older Brother, did you dance when you were among the Boston people? Can you show me? Please, please?' Rebecca added some more pleading words in Tlingit. Natsilane looked down at her with a crooked smile and removed her hand from his arm. He spoke a few words in Tlingit then turned to Máire.

'Now Younger Sister, you will note there is a certain amount of ceremony required in this foreign dancing, too.' He bowed low in front of Máire, his hand making a grand sweep in front of him. 'May I have the pleasure of this dance, Miss McNair?'

Joining in the spirit of this comic display Máire waved an imaginary fan and curtsied deeply. 'Oh sir, my dance card is full, but I will free this one for you, since you insist.' She batted her eyelashes with exaggerated slowness. She could hear Rebecca giggle.

'I am deeply flattered, Miss McNair.' Natsilane held out his hand for hers and Máire placed it firmly inside his palm then leaned over to lift her skirt. His other hand slid around her waist, fitting firmly at the small of her back, pulling in her smock. Máire looked up at him and he raised his brows, his eyes flashing humour. A smile curled slowly across his mouth. Máire's mouth dropped slightly, the dismay at his discovery of her missing corset no doubt written clearly across her face.

'A waltz, I think?' Natsilane said, clearly enjoying her discomfort.

Máire nodded, too flustered to speak, and felt him move her off into the dance's familiar rhythms. Natsilane guided her with expert ease, twirling and swaying to an imaginary band while she tried to forget the warmth of his hand at her waist, its heat penetrating the layers of cloth to her skin. The hand that held hers was dry and warm against her own clammy fingers, and she wished for the protective cover of evening gloves.

Rebecca clapped, crowing with delight while Sarah relaxed enough to give a genuine smile. Máire felt her own discomfort ease and she was soon losing herself in the sheer enjoyment of the dance. As much as she loved dancing, she had had only infrequent opportunities to enjoy it back home since her father was not entirely in favour of the pastime, deeming it frivolous. It was only when someone socially prominent hosted the occasion that her father would relent and allow her to dance. Máire smiled up at Natsilane, grateful that he provided this opportunity, albeit in slightly unorthodox circumstances, and for a brief moment the humour she saw gave way to a look of deep longing.

'What kinds of festivities are going on here?' William's voice cut into the revelry.

'William. Hello.' Máire broke away from Natsilane. 'We were just giving a demonstration of a dance for Rebecca and Sarah.' Máire smoothed her dress and reached up to tuck a stray hair into place, conscious of her flushed face and rapid breathing.

'Could you spare a moment for a word?' His jaw tightened perceptibly. 'That is if you're finished with your demonstration.'

'Yes, of course.' Máire turned to Natsilane. 'I'm sorry. Would you excuse me please?' Natsilane nodded imperceptibly, his face closed, the humour vanished. Máire looked at Sarah and then Rebecca. 'Thank you, I enjoyed showing you the dance. Perhaps you can show me one of your own sometime.'

'You were both very good, Miss McNair. Wasn't she good, Sarah?' Rebecca said with a mischievous smile. Sarah tilted her head slightly and nodded. 'Yes. You dance very well with my brother, Miss McNair.'

Feeling flustered and suddenly guilty, Máire walked away meekly at William's side and didn't resist when he drew her hand through his arm. With the hand safely settled William seemed to relax a bit.

'I was looking for you. You had me worried.' He stopped and turned to Máire, taking both her hands between his. 'You must take care with whom you associate. You must realize you have a position to maintain.' He leaned down and kissed her hands. I say this only because I care very much for you and how you are perceived. I would not want others to think ill of you.'

She suppressed the irritation his remarks aroused. There was nothing untoward in what she had been doing. Rebecca and Sarah had been present and it was hardly a private room in which they had danced. But she must not raise his ire. He was leaving soon and she had no idea when she would see him again, a thought that saddened her for she had grown used to his company and his assurances. 'I'm sorry,' Máire heard herself say. He looked at her, his eyes searching her face. Máire realized that for all he might be above her in height, Natsilane was taller.

'I have to take my leave of you now. We're going back to the ship and we depart first thing tomorrow.'

'Really? That early?' She hadn't expected him to return to the ship until tomorrow, after he had made his farewells.

'I know. It's much too soon for my liking. And it leaves me little time to put into words what I would wish to say to you.' He brushed a hand along her cheek. He leaned down and kissed her, his mouth insistent. His lips pressed firmly, resolutely and his hands began to wander along her back. Máire pulled away, suddenly remembering her missing corset.

'What is it? Is something wrong?' He closed his hands around her arms.

'No, no. It's nothing, William. It's all the excitement of the past few days.'

His eyes narrowed and darkened and his fingers gripped her a little tighter. 'Of course, you've been doing quite a bit for this hearing, helping Mrs Paxson. And just now, showing that group of Indians a proper dance. But as I said before, have a care. It doesn't pay to get too familiar with the natives. They can misunderstand it.' He looked down at Máire, a hint of pleading in his voice. 'Can I have your promise on that before I go, so I can rest easy while I'm away?'

Máire opened her mouth to protest and he stopped it with another kiss. Máire sighed and met it with resignation rather than any commitment to his request for a promise. She smiled at him weakly, deciding to refrain from any further words and followed him slowly back to the feast while the heat from Natsilane's hand lingered across her back.

Part III

CHAPTER TWENTY-SEVEN

Alaska, Autumn/Winter 1890

With William's departure it was as though Belfast became a place of things that used to be, a place only to lodge memories. Máire's thoughts were firmly directed on Alaska, the people, the places all becoming increasingly familiar to her. She could feel her mother's approval in all she touched. Her laughter echoed in the trees. Her sweet fragrance lingered in the salt breeze that came off the water when the wind was in a certain direction. Alaska was part of Máire, or so it seemed.

She wondered how the Tlingit measured her progress. Her only option to gauge her success was to fumble along with awkward methods and take pride in her growing understanding of the language and the manner in which the children responded to her. It was only later that she understood it was easy to seize even little triumphs and call it progress.

A few weeks after the deer ceremony school resumed. On the day, Sarah arrived with Rebecca and her aunt in tow and presented Máire with a cloth-wrapped bundle, a trace of a smile on her face.

'My brother said I should give this to you.' She placed the bundle on the table.

Embarrassed, Máire looked down at the plain dark cloth, tied with a strip of bold red and blue calico. She could not imagine what kind of gift Natsilane would send her, or that he would even think to give her one.

Máire's heart started pounding as she gingerly worked at the knot, conscious of Sarah's scrutiny. 'Oh, it's something for the school I imagine.'

When she'd unwrapped it fully she set out its contents. Lying before her were two smocks, reworked from the gathered yoke dresses the Tlingits wore with their skirts, and finely sewn. Both smocks had newly fashioned pockets at the hips and were shaped in the general style of hers. The dark blue one had served as the wrapping and was a fair match to Máire's own smock. Its companion, however, was of such a brilliant red shade of calico Máire could only blush at the sight of it.

'They're wonderful. So finely sewn. But who made them?'

'I did. With my aunt's help. But it was my brother's idea.'

'Thank you so much. It was kind of you. And kind of your brother to think of my needs.'

'My brother thought you would find them useful,' Sarah said. 'Shall I mention that you like them?'

'Yes, please tell him that I do, very much.'

Sarah nodded and for a moment her eyes twinkled. Perhaps there was some hope of a friendship with Sarah.

Máire covered the smocks with her shawl as the children began to file in. She wouldn't risk any distractions for herself or the questions the children might ask. Despite her resolve she couldn't help but think about the smocks at various times while she taught.

When the class was finished, and all the children were filing out, Máire approached Sarah.

'Would you consider teaching me the Tlingit language on afternoons when you're available? We could do it after class.' She wanted to start as soon as possible. 'I realize you have many obligations, Sarah, but perhaps lessons two or three times a week, for an hour or two, would not take up too much of your time.' She gave a sheepish smile. 'I do know one or two phrases already.'

'I think that could be arranged. I could work with you perhaps an hour or so today, if you wish.' Sarah turned to her aunt and spoke with her in

Tlingit. 'Yes, I could do that, my aunt will permit it.'

'I would be grateful.' Máire smiled. 'Before we start, would you like to come over to the trading post for a bit of food? It's only Joseph and Mr Paxson attending the store today, and I'm sure they won't mind our company for a short while.'

Sarah's face brightened. 'Yes, we would be glad to accept your hospitality,' she answered without thought. She spoke briefly to her aunt, a barely detectable tone of pleading present. Yedicih sighed a little and then nodded.

It was then, as they walked back to the trading post, that Máire saw the seals. They were playing in the river by the bank, rising up along the current, sleek bodies scything the water. She was elated to see them, but when she pointed them out to the others, the seals were gone.

'They must have come up from the inlet,' Sarah said, pensively. 'You like seals?'

'Yes, I find there's something about them that draws me. Perhaps it's their eyes, they're —I don't know—mournful. Don't you find them so? They seem to understand so much and are filled with such compassion, yet they can also be so playful and lively.' Máire gestured futilely to the empty space, the still, silent river the only thing in view.

'You have some connection to them,' Sarah said. 'It may be that your ancestors were Seal People. Our own people were descended from Brown Bear. He taught the People much about themselves.'

'Oh yes, he was good,' Rebecca chimed in. She came up along side of them in a skip, taking up Máire's hand. 'Brown Bear helped a poor man whose family and friends had all died. It's a wonderful story.'

Could she actually be one of the Seal People? Was she mad to even consider such a thing? Máire looked at Rebecca and tried to recall her words. 'Are there any Seal People in your clan?' Máire finally asked her.

Rebecca frowned. 'I don't think so, but maybe. You must ask my brother. He could tell you.' Sarah made some low doubtful noises, but Rebecca just shrugged.

Máire laughed a little uncertainly and caught Yedicih's glance as she briefly raised her brows and smiled, a fleeting but friendly gesture Máire appreciated.

Each morning from that point on, Máire went to the riverbank and stared at the inlet, the mist clinging to her lashes and hair, hoping to catch glimpses of the seals as they looped the rocky outcrop. Occasionally one of the Chilkat men would see her watching them and nodded or smiled at her vigil.

Máire bit her lip when she caught sight of herself in the mirror before making her way downstairs. The smock was so very red. She grabbed up her jacket and made her way downstairs, harbouring the brief hope that Mrs Paxson might already be at the manse. Slowly descending the stairs she jammed her arms through the sleeves of her jacket and had it almost buttoned by the time she reached the bottom step. Some things she wouldn't leave to chance.

Once inside the schoolroom she refrained from picking at the buttons and fiddling with the collar when the children filed in. Sarah entered with Rebecca and her aunt. Sarah smiled when she caught sight of her and gave her a quick nod. Rebecca wasn't so subtle.

'You look very pretty, Miss McNair.' Rebecca turned to Sarah. 'I knew that colour would brighten her face. Did I not say as much to our brother?'

Máire was certain her face matched the smock, but she knew that Rebecca meant it kindly. 'Thank you. I'm glad you like it.' She hoped that would be an end to it. It was enough that it had taken her over three weeks to work up the courage to wear the red calico. Once she faced down the attention this morning it would hopefully attract no further notice.

As the lessons progressed, and no other remarks came from anyone else, Máire relaxed and almost forgot she was wearing such a strong colour. It took her by surprise then when the children filed out at the end and Henry's sister stopped in front of her and fingered the red cloth. 'Miss Teacher looks very pretty today.'

'W-why thank you.' The blood rushed to her face to match the smock yet again.

Sarah moved to her side and put a hand on her arm. 'She is right. The colour becomes you.'

Máire managed another 'thank you' and busied herself gathering her books and materials together to cover her embarrassment. With some relief she reached for the relative safety of her jacket and donned it quickly. 'Why don't you come up to the post today for our picnic?' she asked. 'This time I'll provide the food.'

'Oh, speeleeendid,' Rebecca said. 'Splendid' was Rebecca's latest word. She'd admired its mixture of sound when Máire had used it the week before.

Sarah murmured her delight at the opportunity to eat up at the trading post. Yedicih frowned but nodded her assent. It had become their habit to picnic in the classroom before the Tlingit lesson and treating Máire to Tlingit dishes Yedicih and Sarah brought with them. Today, though, she knew Benny was elsewhere and Mrs Paxson was either up at the manse hounding Betty or working among Kowklux's people.

Pleased, Máire walked with the three of them and planned the little feast she would spread for the group. She knew Mr Paxson wouldn't mind even if he was there. As it happened it was only Joseph tending the store and she made a careful note of the light in his eyes when Sarah followed her through the door.

'Joseph, you don't mind if we have our little meal here with you, do you? We'll make it an easy picnic.'

'A picnic?' Joseph turned from Sarah and looked at Máire quizzically. He took in her smock that her open jacket revealed, smiled slowly and nodded. 'Very nice,' he said.

Máire resisted the urge to clutch her jacket around her and headed towards the kitchen. 'Rebecca, if you'll give me hand we'll only be a moment. Sarah, you and your aunt could clear a space on the counter and Joseph can set a bench beside it.' Máire smiled to herself, certain that if Joseph was worth his salt as a suitor he would find at least ten different ways to talk to Sarah or at least brush her arm.

In the kitchen she cut slices of bread that she passed to Rebecca to butter. After watching Rebecca, with grim concentration, maul several slices, she stopped. 'This isn't what you normally eat of course.'

Rebecca looked up from her work. 'No.'

Máire bit her lip. 'Well there's some venison in the larder, I think. I could cut that up. Maybe we should put some of your own dishes with this as well.'

'Yes, I think that is a speeeleeeeendid idea.'

Máire smiled and went in search of the venison.

Later, while she watched Sarah's coy little smiles to Joseph as she played with the venison, Máire tried to assure herself that it was a good idea eating at the trading post for a change. Sarah certainly was enjoying it. And Rebecca. She looked over at Yedicih and her doubts returned. Though she displayed polite attention, her posture was stiff and she ate little. Would she tell Natsilane? Even if she was inclined to tell him, Natsilane didn't visit his uncle's village that frequently. Sarah had mentioned that it had been a few weeks since she'd seen her brother. It would be fine. No harm could come from this little meal.

Her concerns flew out of her mind after she returned to the classroom to start her Tlingit lesson. She loved the language, the breathy sounds that came deep within the chest, but it was difficult. Sarah was patient but Máire felt her progress was slow, no matter how hard she worked. This day she seemed worse than ever.

'Repeat after me.' Sarah pointed to her smock and grinned. 'I am wearing a red smock,' she said in Tlingit.

Máire looked down at her smock and all the words she heard flew out of her head. 'Can you say that again?' She was determined to ignore the little teasing. Sarah said it again and she made an effort to copy it.

Rebecca roared with laughter. Máire could see even Yedicih tried to cover a smile with her hand. Yedicih repeated the words.

'Try to make a sound like this,' she said, and shaped her mouth slowly to form the words. Her own English had improved from her time in Máire's classes.

Máire tried again. Sarah shook her head.

'Try another phrase. We'll leave the smock out of it today.'

Sarah tilted her head. 'Perhaps that is best. Maybe you're not ready for that phrase yet.'

'Joseph, I want you to accompany Betty to see her aunt. Take a sack of flour with you. Betty says she's running low.'

Máire winced when she heard those words as she paused outside the trading post door. There was no need to see Joseph's face to know how he would feel about those instructions. Betty was difficult to avoid these days since Mrs Paxson had shut up the manse and put Betty's dubious housekeeping talents to work at the trading post. The door opened in front of her and Betty stepped through the threshold swathed in a dark shawl, a pleased smile on her face.

'Betty, please tell your aunt I say hello,' Máire said in stumbling Tlingit. Betty frowned at her. 'What?'

Máire sighed. 'Give your aunt my regards.'

Betty's frown turned to a smirk. She nodded briefly. Behind her Joseph appeared a resigned look on his face.

'Miss McNair, hello.'

'Hello.' She eyed the sack over his shoulder. 'You're very good to take the time accompany Betty like that.'

He shrugged and followed Betty silently down the steps and along the path.

Máire turned and made her way through the door. Mrs Paxson stood behind the counter, her arms crossed.

'What was that you were attempting to say to Betty just now?'

'Oh, just a bit of Tlingit I was trying out. I thought if I spoke it as often as possible I could learn it more quickly.'

'It's all very well to be learning it. It's a necessary tool for teaching the Lord's word and anything else they might need. But never forget, it's a tool, nothing more. To pretend anything else is foolish and can only harm our cause here.'

'I'm sure I appreciate that, Mrs Paxson. But you must agree that to know the language is halfway towards understanding the people, and that can only increase our ability to help them.'

Mr Paxson appeared from the kitchen. 'It'll be real useful to her to learn the language.'

'I'm not saying it wouldn't. I just mean she should have a care when and how she uses the language. You don't want them to get the wrong idea.' Mrs Paxson sniffed. 'You must be careful the way you phrase your ideas when you write your mission reports, Martha.' She eyed Máire carefully. 'Have you written any of your first quarter report? It will be due at the end of this month. Along with the letter to your sponsoring church.'

Máire bit her lip. She had completely forgotten this task and now it loomed large. What on earth would she say to them? They would want to hear about the souls she'd saved, the children she'd rescued from the dangerous grasp of primitive customs and brought to Jesus' loving embrace. Would they appreciate the beauty and richness that surrounded her here? The fifteen glaciers she could see from the garden, the interesting children in her little school, or the exotic and moving celebrations that figured so prominently among these hospitable people? She knew they wouldn't. Perhaps she could write about Benny. Mrs Paxson had recently managed to persuade Benny to attend church on Sundays. Would he count as a saved soul?

'I haven't written the report or the church letter yet, but I have thought of things to write,' Máire said. 'I plan to set aside some time to do it soon.'

'Perhaps you would like me to read them over before you send them,' Mrs Paxson said. 'It would be a good idea, since you have little experience in writing them. I assisted the Carters a few times when they were too busy to complete their reports in full.'

'I appreciate the offer Mrs Paxson, but I'm certain I will find the time and be able to manage on my own.'

'Well, you should be able to. You've fewer responsibilities than the Carters had. I just thought to offer my experience, but if you're determined to write them by yourself, I won't interfere.'

'She'll be fine, Florence,' Mr Paxson said. 'She's caught on real quick here.'

Máire smiled at Mr Paxson, grateful for his defence, and pleased in his estimation of her adjustment to life here. Máire felt that, coming from a man like Mr Paxson, such praise held some weight, but she couldn't help but wonder what Natsilane would think—would he feel she'd made progress?

CHAPTER TWENTY-EIGHT

The smell of the sour wool, stale tobacco and liquor fumes threatened Máire's stomach. She licked her lips and swallowed, looking around from her place at the counter to distract herself. If only the minor repair on the manse window could have waited for another day she wouldn't have had to face these two in front of her. Was it the smell that really upset her? Or was it Carl's crushed nose and surly manner that made her uneasy as he stood beside his gnarled old companion, Pete? The miners were no different in cleanliness to many she'd encountered here. And they were a common enough sight of late with the onset of winter calling a halt to their work up north. So many of them just seemed so unsavoury, hanging around gambling and drinking, waiting for the steamer to Sitka. She looked at Benny over in the corner, sorting nails. Did he know these men? She eyed Mr Paxson next to her. He didn't seem affected by the two men at the counter. He handed Carl a pouch of tobacco.

'Hey George, you play cards, dontcha?' Pete asked.

'Course he don't Pete, he's got religion. Them kind don't play cards,' Carl said. 'Ain't I right George?'

'Well boys, now that ain't entirely true. Some of us have been known to play a hand or two. I'm just not that lucky, so I stay away from all that.'

Máire heard the door open and looked for some relief. Natsilane entered. She smiled at him a little nervously and watched as he walked towards her, his face pleasant, a smile on his lips.

'*Ma sá iyati?*' Máire asked proudly, sounding each syllable carefully.

Natsilane hesitated only a moment, a flash of surprise crossing his face. 'I'm fine, thank you,' he responded calmly. '*Wa.e de?*'

He said the words quickly, much quicker than Sarah or Yedicih ever spoke them to her, their own enunciation careful and clear so she would understand. Máire paused a minute, reviewing her response in her mind. '*Xhat yak'e*,' she said finally, for she was fine. She glowed under Natsilane's approving nod.

'I've been hoping to have a word with you,' Máire told him. 'I wanted to thank you for the smocks. I appreciate them very much. I just hadn't the time to do my own and Sarah is such a fine needlewoman.'

'My sisters mentioned that you were pleased with them. Both smocks,' he grinned.

Máire laughed. 'Yes, they're both lovely. The children have especially liked the red smock.'

Carl's grating voice broke into their conversation. 'Looky here, Pete. We got us Benny, over in the corner there, as quiet as a mouse. You think Benny plays cards? Whaddaya say Benny, you play cards?'

Benny sprung from his squat over the neatly arranged packets and knocked over the small barrel that held the others, the nails raining noisily across the wooden floor. Frozen, his eyes darted around the room until they rested on Natsilane's back. Natsilane remained facing Máire, his fingers fiddling with the empty leather pouch he had placed on the counter, staring at the shelves. Anger, hurt and pain played across his face for a moment, until he visibly schooled the emotions to indifference.

'I would like some of the coffee beans again, please,' Natsilane said, his voice low and careful.

Máire glanced behind him again and watched Benny hastily gather the spilled nails back into the barrel, while the two miners stood over him, quizzing him intently. Natsilane repeated his request.

'Yes, of course, I'm sorry.' Máire took up the pouch to fill his order, still stunned over his reaction.

'How are you, Daniel?' said Mr Paxson.

'Fine, thank you, George.'

'I guess you'll be off hunting soon?'

'I've done some already,' Natsilane said. 'But I'm hoping to go again in a few days.'

'You had much luck? Any extra you might want to trade? We could sure do with some more meat here, especially after that feast.'

'The hunting hasn't been too bad, so far. If I have anything to spare I'll keep you in mind.' Natsilane picked up the full pouch Máire placed on the table, nodded to them both, turned, walked past his father and out of the door without a further word.

'How can he do that?' Máire whispered.

'How can he do what?' Mr Paxson said.

Máire looked over at Benny on his hands and knees, still struggling to gather the nails back into the barrel while Carl and Pete chatted over him.

'Ignore his father as though he doesn't exist.'

Mr Paxson frowned. 'He doesn't exist,' he said in a low voice. 'At least as far as Daniel and the clan are concerned.'

'But why? I don't understand.'

'Benny's been exiled. That means, according to the clan, he's dead.'

'For what reason? How could they possibly do something so cruel?'

Mr Paxson gave her a hard look. 'I know it don't seem charitable, but they see Benny as someone who forgot his obligations to his clan and family. That's a mighty powerful thing to wrong.'

'But his own son? Surely he would have sympathy for his father. After all, he finds it difficult to live among his own clan.'

'Though Daniel might have problems settling and getting some of them to accept him, that don't mean he isn't traditional is his way of thinking.' He put his hand on Máire's shoulder. 'Sure, he could have been the next chief, if things hadn't gone so wrong. But he understands that the traditions are there for a reason. Don't forget that.'

Máire glanced at Benny again, hunched over his packets, his grimy fingers resuming their slow progress through the cache of nails as he painfully counted each one into the packet. How could she understand such an action that cut a person off from his home and family, leaving him with no connections, no-one to understand the pain he must be feeling? Was she wrong to condemn such judgements out of hand, when she had witnessed enough exclusion in her own country, for want of the proper faith, for want of a good family name, of for want of a husband? She could only remember her own sense of exclusion and feel that somehow it could never be justified.

Máire smoothed her hair, pulled stray wisps back into the snood that held the braid coiled at the back of her head, and gathered up her Bible from the table in her room. Downstairs, Mrs Paxson waited for Betty to finish tidying away the noon meal before the three of them set off to Kowklux's house for the Bible lesson. When Máire joined them Betty was removing her apron, her chin jutting the air and her eyes a glittering black. They headed off, Betty trudging alongside Mrs Paxson, while Máire walked slightly behind them, running various Tlingit phrases through her head. She pulled her shawl closer around her, glad for the thick jacket she wore underneath. The weather had become decidedly colder, the wind carrying a sharp bite. How did they appear to the Chilkat as they approached their homes, three women clad in shawls each with such different gaits, such different expressions—determination, anticipation, and reluctance—and such different intentions?

Regardless of how peculiar they might have seemed, Elizabeth welcomed them with formal but sincere hospitality, and ushered them into the house to a section in one corner, where about fifteen women sat on blankets. Máire followed Mrs Paxson and Betty to the blanket provided for them and took a seat. She sat like the Tlingit women around her, her legs crossed under her skirts. Elizabeth sat next to Mrs Paxson, folding her hands quietly in her lap.

'It is nice to see the teacher lady,' Elizabeth said.

'Yes, Miss McNair decided to come with us today,' Mrs Paxson said. 'She wanted to tell you how important Jesus is to her as a teacher.' She continued speaking, sprinkling Tlingit words throughout, Betty attempting a little translation, though her English was little better than Máire's Tlingit. Mrs Paxson pressed her index finger into the cover of her Bible. 'Jesus, as we know, was a teacher. He taught his disciples, the twelve apostles. He taught the high priests, those men who thought they had all the answers. He taught the sick, the lame, the old and the poor. Jesus was everyone's teacher. Miss McNair will tell you more.'

Máire suppressed a small gasp. Mrs Paxson had not mentioned that she would require her to speak to the women, let alone on the aforementioned topic. Máire had been thinking only in terms of asking about their families, their children and to perhaps share something of her own home with them. She had no idea what Mrs Paxson would have her say to them on the subject of Jesus.

'Mrs Paxson, you've explained it so well, I feel I hardly need say more,' Máire said, floundering for words. Near her, a child wailed in a mother's arms, squirming to be free from her grasp. It was the young woman called Martha, the Chilkat Martha, the girl with a child that Máire met on her first day in the mission village and took for an unwed mother. It was a mistake, the first of many she'd made in the short time she'd been here. When Máire had asked Mrs Paxson about her she had promptly informed Máire she was the wife of one of the elders and had given birth to his first son. The native women had a knack of looking like children, when in fact they were not, she'd added.

Martha's child was about a year old, anxious to explore the world, while she herself tried unsuccessfully to enclose the child in a firm embrace in her lap. Máire turned to the distraction and greeted them.

'What a bonny babbie,' Máire said, Cook's own expression coming to mind. She reached out for a little fist that grabbed the air. The child smiled at her, its dark eyes alight with interest. Martha offered the child to Máire and she leaned over and lifted him to her arms. Máire could see now that it was indeed a boy, his short little shift hiked up with her effort, leaving him bare below the waist. She closed her arms around him while he hugged her neck. She inhaled his warm milky scent. He gurgled sweetly in her ear, patting her face, pulling her ears. Máire laughed and spoke little baby words to him, crooning the sounds that came to her from the far reaches of her memory.

Máire hugged the moment to herself, closing her eyes, while the child responded to her voice, putting his hands on her mouth and nose and then along her hair. With a gentle tug he loosed her snood, its unfamiliar shape and size attracting his curious little fingers, then pulled it from her head, along with all the pins. The braid tumbled down her back. He crowed with delight at his successful conquest and, unable to resist, Máire planted a kiss on his cheek. Martha reached for him, clearly embarrassed at his assault on the teacher, but he waved his trophy towards her, babbling his victory. She took him from Máire then, and tried to pry the snood from his captive fingers, but he protested.

'Let him have it,' Máire assured her. 'I don't need it.' She swept up the few hairpins from her lap and tucked them in her smock pocket. She would not bother with trying to reassemble her hair. It was too tiring and required concentration.

'Don't be ridiculous,' Mrs Paxson said. 'You shouldn't have let the child be so free with you. They must learn to behave, even at that early age. Martha, take it from the child.' She held out her hand for the snood.

Which Martha, thought Máire for a moment. 'No, really Mrs Paxson, it's fine. I take responsibility for it.' Máire turned to Martha. 'He may have it for now. I'll collect it from him when we leave. I'm sure his fascination will have waned by then.'

Mrs Paxson sniffed, but let the matter go. After a dark glance in Máire's direction she opened her Bible to read and explain scripture passages that showed Jesus as a teacher to the children and abandoned all pretext of including Máire. Máire watched the little boy continue to explore her snood until Mrs Paxson's mournful off-key alto voice began a Bible song. The women clearly enjoyed it and sang with her, sounding word approximations with Mrs Paxson's clear enunciations.

The meeting ended on that note. Mrs Paxson tucked her Bible in her arm and rose. The rest of them joined her, milling their way to the door, Betty beside Mrs Paxson while Máire lagged behind with the other Chilkat women. She made her way over to Martha and her son. When he saw Máire, he chortled and reached out his hand. She couldn't help but smile at such a greeting and she leaned over to give him a little kiss on his cheek, her braid sweeping out in his direction. He latched onto the braid, entangling his strong little fist in it and tugging her towards him. Máire stifled a brief cry of pain and, with his mother's help, worked to pry his fingers from her hair.

'I am sorry,' his mother said, her round face embarrassed again.

Máire placed her hand on her arm. 'Don't apologize. He's only a child. A lovely, curious child.' She smoothed down his hair and kept her own out of the reach of his hand.

'You are very kind,' Martha said. She reached out for Máire's braid and touched it gently. 'You have pretty hair. It is like my sister's.' She smiled, then added something else in Tlingit Máire couldn't quite translate. Máire thanked her and bid her goodbye.

She joined Mrs Paxson and Betty outside and they turned to make their way back to the trading post, Mrs Paxson leading the way. Máire came up beside Betty.

'Did you hear what Martha said to me in Tlingit as we left?' she asked in a low voice. Betty turned to her and cocked her head.

'Yes.'

'What was it? In English, I mean.'

Betty muttered her explanation then moved on quickly to Mrs Paxson with a question. Máire barely caught the words but heard enough of it to piece together the meaning. Was it true? Had Martha really said she could almost be taken for a Tlingit woman? What was almost as startling as the statement was how pleased she felt about it.

Three girls with joined hands circled wildly in the clearing and chanted loudly. The words of *Ring a Ring O' Roses* brought a smile to Máire's face but she could see Mrs Paxson's back stiffening; they neared the clearing. Máire scanned the girls and recognized them from her class. She marvelled at their joy in the game and watched as they all screamed and tumbled down at the same time.

'Whatever are those girls shouting about?' Mrs Paxson said.

'It's a game,' Máire told her. 'You remember, *Ring a Ring O' Roses*? I taught it to the smaller children. I thought it would be helpful to use rhymes to teach them English.'

'You're responsible for teaching them that unseemly gibberish?' The last word was all but spat out. Her bosom heaved against her jacket in a threatening manner. Betty looked at them both with interest.

'I don't see how it could be unseemly,' Máire said. She was confused. Though it might have at one time described a horrible death, it was now harmless children's play. 'It's a game. They don't know its meaning from long ago.'

'If this is your attitude, I see we must have a long discussion,' Mrs Paxson said. She threw Máire a dark look. 'I can only imagine the other things you've been teaching the children. Since you don't seem to understand what's appropriate for our mission school I see I shall have to go over your lessons myself. We'll do it this evening.'

'Really, Mrs Paxson, that won't be necessary...' But Mrs Paxson had walked off. The subject was closed.

Máire sighed. How would she ever explain her work with the children to a person who could only think in terms of saving their souls, when at times Máire felt it was they who were saving hers?

CHAPTER TWENTY-NINE

The words unsaid and words to be said hung in the air as they suffered Betty's clumsy meal around the cramped kitchen table. Máire poked strategically at her bits of venison, excising the burnt sections with the tines of her fork and trying to plan her response to Mrs Paxson.

'A bit less water in the gravy, next time, Betty,' Mrs Paxson said. 'But this is a great improvement. Don't you think so, Joseph?'

Máire looked up at her. She wouldn't raise a brow, no she wouldn't.

Joseph made no response.

'We should really do a supplies inventory, Joseph,' said Mr Paxson. 'We'll try and tackle that tomorrow. With winter closing in we need to get a good sense of what we'll be needing. Since the miners have come we're going through things a lot quicker than normal.'

'I have been keeping a kind of record already. It is in the back of the ledger on a loose sheet of paper. I meant to tell you. It is enough to give you an idea of what is left.'

'Great. You're one step ahead of me. In fact, I don't know what I'd do without you, Joseph.'

Mrs Paxson reached out and patted Joseph's hand. 'You've become an indispensable part of the trading post, not to mention the mission.' She cleared her throat. 'But we can't have you dedicating every part of your life to the trading post and the mission. It's about time you thought of yourself a bit. Of your future.'

'I assure you Mrs Paxson, I am very happy here in your service.' Joseph shifted a little uncomfortably under her intense scrutiny. 'I would not change things.'

'Nonsense. I'm sure there are times you have thought about adding things to your life. Like a wife and family.' Joseph reddened perceptibly, while Mrs Paxson charged on. 'Don't you think it is about time you took a wife? There are a few suitable women who would make you a good partner.' She looked over at Betty who was spooning a helping of venison into her mouth, and smiled archly.

Máire was horrified. Could Mrs Paxson actually consider Betty a 'suitable' wife for Joseph? Though she knew Mrs Paxson wanted Joseph to marry a Christian, was she blind to Betty's slovenly attitude, her general lack of effort and interest in anything that might be construed as work? Máire looked at Joseph, alarm slowly replacing shock on his face.

'I can see you find the notion surprising,' she continued. 'It's only natural that you wouldn't have considered it seriously since your quarters here at present aren't suitable for a married couple. But we could change that. We could convert one of the other little storage sheds into a room for you both, couldn't we George?'

George reluctantly looked up from his plate and glanced at Joseph. 'I think you need to give the boy a chance to breathe, Florence. Seems like he has to get used to the idea first, before you go and make all the arrangements.'

Mrs Paxson eyed Joseph and pressed her lips together firmly. 'Well, perhaps it is a lot to take in.' She looked over at Betty again. 'But you have no need to look far for a good Christian woman, and we would support you fully in this decision.'

'I appreciate your concern,' Joseph mumbled. He fell into a deep silence.

More words loomed in the air now, heavy and oppressive with their dark promise and sucking hope away from the future. Máire brooded, sipping the coffee that ended the meal and barely noticing it scalding the back of her mouth.

Mrs Paxson cleared her throat and looked at Máire. 'Well, now, perhaps you would be good enough to show me your school lessons and we can decide a plan of action.'

'Really, Mrs Paxson. There's no need. I assure you that there's nothing else in the lessons that might cause you upset.'

'No, I insist, if only so that I can write my own letters to the board with a clean conscience.'

Máire rose slowly and retrieved the material. Mr Paxson, Joseph and Betty left, escaping to other tasks elsewhere. Máire presented Mrs Paxson with a general outline of the methods and content of her lessons. Mrs Paxson sniffed and clucked her way through Máire's explanations, reserving her comments until Máire had completed her overview.

'That's everything?' she asked. Máire nodded.

'This won't do, Martha. This won't do at all.' She drew herself up, her shoulders expanding as she folded her hands in front of her. 'Do you understand why this will not do? After watching my own approach among these people, can you not fathom why your lessons are lacking?'

Máire hesitated. She had some inkling, but she refused to give in. 'No, Mrs Paxson, I don't see why my lessons are lacking.'

'My dear girl, that is all the more reason why you need guidance.' She pointed to Máire's material. 'Among all those fine ideas, is there any sign of our Lord and his importance in the world? How can you teach them English and not teach them about our Lord? This is a mission, Martha, a mission whose central purpose is to bring them into communion with Jesus. To do that we must teach them English and basic Christian ideas of cleanliness, maintaining a good household and other such things that enable them to live in a Godly manner.' Her voice had reached a level that covered twice the distance it needed, as if to pierce Máire's dull brain with each rising note.

Máire was angry. Mrs Paxson was not an official missionary, yet she constantly tried to direct the mission work. She didn't mind most times, but she cared about the teaching and she enjoyed it. Despite that she knew Mrs Paxson had influence with the Mission Board and she had to respect that. Calm was required. She retrieved the patience cultivated at her father's knee and at Mrs Engelton's side. 'I understand, Mrs Paxson. I imagine you have suggestions about suitable material to add?'

'In a word, scripture. You must teach them Bible verses, not some rude rhyme. And they should sing nothing but hymns, or Bible songs such as the one we sang today. Surely you know those songs? Didn't they teach them back in your country?'

'Of course, Mrs Paxson. Yes, I am wholly familiar with those songs.'

Mrs Paxson snorted. 'Then I'm more surprised that you haven't taught them. Perhaps you need assistance.'

Máire froze in horror. Would Mrs Paxson take it upon herself to 'assist' her lessons and sap all the joy she experienced in those few hours every morning? 'I assure you, Mrs Paxson, I don't need assistance. I thank you for the thought, though.'

'No, I think it would be helpful to you, at least for a while. And it would set my mind at rest.' She smiled. 'I'll ask Betty to attend you there. She's been invaluable at my Bible meetings. She can help you select verses and teach the songs to the children. Betty has a wonderful voice and now knows many Bible songs.'

Máire stared at Mrs Paxson in disbelief. She couldn't imagine Betty assisting in any other way than to occupy a part of a bench. And yet, it was possible that this solution Mrs Paxson insisted upon was less offensive than it initially seemed. 'As much as I'm sure you think Betty's help would be invaluable, I wouldn't keep her away from her duties very long. A few weeks should be enough.'

Mrs Paxson gave Máire a quizzical look. 'Yes, that might be all that's needed.'

The next day, wrapped warmly against a damp wind, Máire made her way to the school. Betty followed close behind, porting Mrs Paxson's Bible, carefully marked at appropriate verses. Máire had spent the rest of the evening before revising sections of her lessons so they would pass Mrs Paxson's scrutiny while she secretly hoped Betty's drifting attention would enable her to modify or omit the most heavy-handed sections.

The two of them pulled up by the steps when Máire heard someone call her name. She turned to see Rebecca coming up to the school, followed by Sarah and Natsilane. She tried to cover her surprise and initial delight with a cheerful wave that turned to a muffled groan when she remembered. Betty. How would she manage to teach these ridiculous lessons under Natsilane's scrutiny? He was sure to mock the Bible verses and their pointed references to Christian cleanliness, work ethic and rules for living.

'How is it you're playing chaperone today?' Máire asked him when they had all exchanged greetings. 'Your aunt isn't ill, is she?'

'Yes, she's ill, and my young sister here pleaded for my company today.'

'Oh, dear. I hope it's not serious?'

'No, it's not. In fact you might say that it is a happy illness. She's going to have a baby.'

'Oh, but that is marvellous news. She must be very glad.'

Rebecca laughed. 'She doesn't seem so happy at the moment.'

Máire smiled. 'Oh, give her my best wishes.' Behind her Betty shuffled. Máire turned and indicated Betty. 'Oh, you must know Betty. Mrs Paxson has asked Betty to join us for a while.'

Sarah and Rebecca greeted Betty. Natsilane raised his brow then nodded to Betty. Máire kept her face bland; she wouldn't bite the bait. Would he decline to join them? Betty was, after all, a Tlingit single woman. But no, Natsilane followed them up the steps and through the door so Máire could only guess her clan was acceptable. Or that her

Christian faith negated the custom in Natsilane's eyes.

With a large amount of resignation Máire watched the children file in the room. Natsilane's presence caused great curiosity as he took a seat at the back of the room and folded his arms across his chest. Betty arranged herself on the front bench, narrowing her eyes in studied concentration. Máire took a deep breath.

'Today I thought we'd begin with something a little different. Something Mrs Paxson thought you would find helpful.' The children looked at her expectantly. She glanced nervously at Natsilane. He raised his eyes heavenward. She cleared her throat. 'It's just a little Bible verse, from Isaiah. *Behold, God is my salvation; I will trust and not be afraid, for Jehovah is my strength and my song; he is also become my salvation.*'

Natsilane coughed quietly in the back.

'Now children, just repeat after me.' Her voice cracked slightly. 'The first sentence, *Behold, God is my salvation.*' Her voice was firmer.

The children chanted after her, mimicking her cadence. What am I doing, she thought? What do these words really mean? What do they mean to these children? Will they ever hold any kind of meaning for them? She looked down at their trusting faces then over at Natsilane again. Arms still folded and ankles crossed, he eyed her carefully. Was she more a hypocrite for teaching them something that she wasn't certain she believed herself? A glance in Betty's direction showed her closed eyes and a nodding head.

'That will do, children. We'll move on to our numbers now.' She kept her voice low and even.

And so her strange lesson progressed, Bible songs or verses inserted when she thought Betty might be attending, then reverting to her usual content when Máire knew her to be asleep. It made for a trying few hours. She was glad when the lesson came to an end and she was able to dismiss the children. Máire sent Betty on her way at the same time.

While Sarah and Rebecca collected the slates, Natsilane wandered up to Máire.

'I must say I never experienced a lesson quite like that before.'

Máire fiddled with the books on her table. 'Well, it wasn't my usual lesson, I assure you.'

'I thought as much, since my aunt indicated you have a real gift for teaching and her judgement isn't usually lacking.'

'Was it that bad?'

'Not bad so much as contradictory in approach, perhaps.' He gave a half-smile. 'Though it seems you had extenuating circumstances in your new student.'

Máire laughed weakly. 'Betty was not my idea, I assure you. Mrs Paxson has it in her head that I need some guidance for my lessons and she chose Betty to provide it.'

'And do you—need guidance?' He smiled fully now.

'Of course I don't. It's Mrs Paxson's view, not mine. I tried to put her off, but she wouldn't have it.'

'She can be difficult to put off anything she has a mind to, I know.' His smile became kinder and Máire relaxed a little. 'But I've noticed a few occasions when some tactics have proved successful against her.'

Such tactics were not hers to know just yet. Natsilane called to Sarah. 'You've brought the lunch?'

'No, it was my turn,' Máire said. 'I've a basket up at the trading post. I'll go and fetch it.'

'Stay here,' Sarah said. 'We will get it.' She looked at Natsilane and he nodded. Without further words she grabbed up Rebecca's hand and set off.

'I'm sorry, I, ah, forgot the basket this morning.' In truth she'd left it behind so that Betty wouldn't eat with them. 'But will you all be staying the whole afternoon, with Yedicih absent?'

'Yes, carry on as you would normally. Lunch, the lesson—I'm prepared to remain for the duration and escort the girls back to the village. That is if it's agreeable to you.'

Máire wasn't certain how she felt. A bit of panic, apprehension over how he'd judge her progress at Tlingit, could all explain her sudden sweating palms and racing heart. 'Of course you're more than welcome to remain,' she said. 'I would hate to miss out on the Tlingit. Will your aunt be able to come tomorrow, or do we have the pleasure of your company for a time?'

'I don't really know. She does wish to come. She's told me how much she enjoys the lessons.'

'Tell her thank you, I appreciate her praise.' Máire felt on safe ground, now. 'I could not teach half so well without your sisters' help. Sarah has a real gift with children.' She looked at him tentatively, struck by a thought. 'I suppose the time is approaching when she will be thinking about beginning her own family.'

Natsilane made some noises that committed to nothing. Máire took a deep breath and tried again. 'Is she spoken for? That is to say, is there someone…' Máire searched for the proper words from his culture.

Natsilane laughed. 'I'm sorry. You're irresistibly amusing when you try to phrase your words in a manner you think appropriate to Tlingit custom. And the answer is that my sister's marriage requires much careful planning. It is not so simple as choosing a man who will provide for her. She is high-ranking and it's important for my uncle to select her husband carefully so that it reflects his standing and forms an important alliance. Such an alliance can ensure peace, as well as enhance the clan's prestige.'

'I see some things are no different here.'

Natsilane snorted. 'Aren't you just the typical white woman that indulges in fancy romantic notions.' He drawled the words with deliberate care, his tone mocking. 'There are many reasons for our traditions and they're based on a deep understanding of the clan's best interest.' His eyes darkened and a short bitter laugh escaped. 'No matter how I or my sister might feel about it as individuals, we must accept that.'

His words hung in the air, heavy with meaning. Máire looked down, stunned at the naked pain she saw in his face, and studied his hands that toyed with slates on her table. The wolf eyes of his tattoo seemed to reprimand her. She'd never considered what Natsilane must endure.

The two of them continued to stand there silently, each burdened in their own way by Natsilane's words.

CHAPTER THIRTY

Her hair hung down around her, heavy like a curtain, cloaking her nakedness as she perched on the rock's edge. A fiddle tune played around her like a breeze, lifting her hair. She hummed and it grew louder, filled her head, spread down to her toes, a strong pulsing movement. She rose to the challenge, arms lifting as she twirled. She spun round while feeling the music in her, around her, and she spun again and again, catching the swirling vortex of the song. Her foot missed a beat and she was flying through the air, her hair fanning out behind until she hit the water and the frantic rhythm transformed to a slow and sensuous waltz.

It was the fiddle tune that Máire searched for the next day as she prepared for the lesson, the dream still fresh in her mind. She found she hoped Natsilane would be present again. Once Sarah and Rebecca had returned with the basket and lightened the mood she'd enjoyed herself immensely. She'd even relaxed enough to tease him when she saw him pull out a tobacco pouch and start to roll a cigarette.

'I didn't think you would indulge in such a non-traditional pastime.'

He patted the tobacco carefully into the paper with one finger. 'Tobacco is traditional enough,' he said. He rolled the paper back and forth between his two fingers to pack the tobacco more as he shaped it into a cylinder. 'It was here long before any white man arrived.'

'But we don't use tobacco like that,' Rebecca said. She studied the bit of jam on her bread then took a bite.

Natsilane gave her a sidelong glance, shrugged, pulled out a box of matches and lit the cigarette. 'It's still part of the tradition.'

'Coffee is not traditional, though,' Rebecca said. There was a hint of defiance in her tone.

'Coffee?' Máire said. Natsilane glared at Rebecca.

Sarah gave Máire a wicked grin. 'Our brother has a great weakness for coffee.'

Máire looked at Natsilane who inhaled his cigarette slowly and fixed her with a nonchalant look. She burst out laughing. Sarah joined her, then Rebecca and, finally, Natsilane.

It was the laughter and the easy Tlingit lesson that followed that made her hope that Natsilane would be at the lesson the next day. But Yedicih was there. Máire had no idea when she might see him again to recapture the easy camaraderie or perhaps even to broach the subject of Sarah's marriage again.

However a few days later, before she had another chance to speak to Natsilane on the subject of Sarah's marriage, Máire found an opening to pursue it indirectly with Joseph. She was keeping him company at the trading post when it occurred to her to ask him about Betty's parents.

'Her mother is dead. She was a L'uknaxadee clan. Her father…' Joseph shrugged.

'Her mother was a servant in Kowklux's house. She died of fever, about the same time as Daniel's mother and brothers. So Betty was taken in by her aunt. Another servant.'

'I'm sure it must have been hard for her,' Máire said. 'How was it Mrs Paxson came…'—she searched for the right words—'…to rely on her so much?'

A smile played at Joseph's mouth for a moment before he answered Máire. 'I think Mrs Paxson found Betty a very willing pupil. Mrs Paxson explained to her that if she became a Christian her life would change.'

Máire refrained from commenting on Mrs Paxson's influence or Betty's enthusiasm for Christianity. 'I imagine if Betty is such a committed Christian than it would be important for her to marry a Christian.'

'Yes, I think so.'

'As it would be important for you.'

'Yes, I would like to marry a Christian.' He gave Máire a questioning look. 'Would it not be important for you, when you marry?'

'Of course, though I doubt that I shall marry.' She gave a guilty laugh. She'd suddenly realized weeks had passed and she had not thought once of William. She made a mental note to write him that evening, but then relaxed when she remembered there had been no boat to take the letter. Perhaps William had been so busy with his duties he wouldn't have found the time to write himself. It was a feeble thought, she knew, but she really couldn't work up an interest in writing him at this point, though she knew she must and would.

She pushed these thoughts aside for Joseph's problem. How much did he care for Sarah, a woman who might not even be a Christian? Máire knew that Natsilane had renounced his faith and, like his uncle, held to traditional ways, but she wasn't absolutely certain that Sarah and Rebecca were no longer Christian. They kept their Christian names and sang the Bible songs along with the children in class, yet she had never seen them at any of the church services.

'How was it that Natsilane and his family came to be Christians?' It seemed strange in a clan so firmly traditional as Kowishte's.

Joseph looked up from the ledger he was marking. 'It is a long tale.'

'Can you give me some idea of it?'

He sighed, shut the ledger, and put down his pencil carefully. 'Benny was a *hitsaati*, headman of his house. It was a strong house, but not as strong and powerful as Kowishte's. Benny envied Kowishte, and though he married Kowishte's sister, he could not put aside his bad feelings. He tried to challenge Kowishte's honour, but lost his own in the end, and they told him he was no longer fit to be *hitsaati*. So he brought his family here to the mission, and the Carters and Paxsons took them in.'

'Oh, I see. Thank you for explaining.' As Joseph said, it was a long tale, and not because she could see there was much he'd left out, but because of its vast reach into the past and future of the community.

Any thought she might have had that Mrs Paxson wouldn't question Betty about the school lesson was quickly dispelled at dinner that evening. Crowded around the small table, the four of them pushed the food around their plates, all except for Mrs Paxson. She scooped each mouthful from the plate with a miner's determination while Betty stood near her, ready to dole out a second helping.

Mrs Paxson waved Betty back to her seat. 'Betty gave me a full report on the school lessons. It seems they still have frivolous elements to them.'

Máire glanced over at Betty who studied her plate.

'Really, Mrs Paxson, I've included Bible verses as you instructed. In fact I begin each day with one.'

'It's the balance that must be right. And from what I understand you still haven't achieved it. I think if I review your plans for each lesson you'll understand what that perfect balance is.' She pursed her lips. 'Betty can let me know how successful you are at implementing the balance.'

'That's really not necessary. I assure you I'll implement your suggestions. There's no need for Betty to attend.'

Mrs Paxson narrowed her eyes. 'But there is a need.'

A soft snort from Mr Paxson and a shift in posture from Joseph were the only comments offered in Máire's defence.

The weather soon seized control from even Mrs Paxson's grip on events. Snow ripped across the land, blowing blizzards and drifts that layered quickly across the mission grounds. The unusual November weather brought no praise from the mission inhabitants for the purity of the heavy white blanket of snow that burdened the roofs, grass and tree tops with its weight. Uneasy mutterings and whispered accusations circulated, prompted by the certainty that only violations of taboo could have caused weather this severe. Mrs Paxson worked hard to stop these rumours that, like any fire, having been quenched one area would ignite in another.

Her efforts were inhibited by the weather itself. Any travel required snowshoes, a case of strapping on implements shaped like tennis rackets to the feet and walking splay-footed in a loping motion. The action produced little grace and added considerable time. Without them there was no hope of going more than one step or two before sinking hip-deep in the snow. Máire, awaiting her own pair of snowshoes, sat cooped up in her bedroom for three days, and from her window watched Mrs Paxson lope awkwardly to the cluster of Chilkat houses and then back home, like some crippled bear in a hopping game.

The sun emerged finally and the snow shone like brilliants sparkling on the rooftops and along the banks. Such light made for optimism, and with her new snowshoes in her possession Máire hoped she might resume the lessons, even though she didn't expect Sarah and Rebecca to attend. However, only a few children managed to attend the few days following the lesson. Concerned, she finally broached the subject with Mrs Paxson after consulting with Joseph.

'Joseph seems to feel that many of the children are at home because it's winter time, the time for sitting around the fire and telling stories and clan history.' Máire frowned, uncertain if she should add the other reason, then decided she should. 'He also says they feel that one reason it's snowed so much is because the children attend the school.'

Mrs Paxson pulled a grim smile. 'Oh, for heaven's sake. The weather is not directed against the Tlingit personally.'

'I know, of course. I was thinking that if we could get the children back to school in some sort of regular routine, that might help stop these runaway thoughts.'

Mrs Paxson considered Máire. The tension eased from her mouth. 'You might be right. We'll go there now and talk to Kowklux. See if we can get these silly notions out of their heads once and for all.'

A short while later Máire was wondering what she'd started as she trudged behind Mrs Paxson, her snowshoes strapped to her boots, her skirts held high. Her own efforts with the snowshoes soon took all her focus, moving not so much like a loping bear but a crippled one-legged bird.

Kowklux, seated on his cedarwood box, greeted them with reserve but honoured all the rituals of hospitality she'd come to expect in his house, making them comfortable and offering food.

Mrs Paxson came right to the point. 'I understand that some of your people feel that the school might be the cause of the weather. I'm sure you know that's utter nonsense. The school is important for these children. It is the best way for them to do well and to learn of all of God's blessings.'

'I'm sure you understand and support the help I'm trying to give the children,' Máire added. 'It's not a bad thing, at all. It's for the children's good.'

Kowklux's face remained passive as he listened with equanimity to each of the women. 'You must see the blanket my wife is making, Miss Teacher,' he said when they finished. He motioned to Elizabeth.

For a moment Máire wondered if he'd understood her and she looked across at Mrs Paxson who frowned briefly before turning to view the blanket. She had to admit it was beautifully wrought, woven with strips of cedar and goat hair.

'Very fine quality, Elizabeth,' Mrs Paxson said. 'You show great skill, my dear.' She turned back to Kowklux. 'Can we count on your help to encourage the children to attend the school, Chief Kowklux?' Máire noted the deliberate inclusion of his title.

'I think we will wait. It will be best to wait.'

'Wait? Wait for what, may I ask?' Mrs Paxson said.

'We will wait to see what the winter brings, Mrs Preacher Woman. No more school, thank you.' He folded his arms across his chest and looked at her darkly. Máire could see it was no use pressing the issue further and Mrs Paxson seemed to conclude the same. She sighed.

'All right, Kowklux. We'll suspend the school for now, because of the weather. But we will still have Sunday services. God does not hear such feeble excuses.'

A little sniff escaped her as she rose and gathered up her snowshoes and coat. Máire followed suit, her heart sinking a little. She found it difficult to understand how he could link the school with the heavy snows. Was it that he feared the snow would be too difficult for the children to walk through? Yet they still managed to get around in the mission. And there was enough fuel to feed the stove and keep them warm there, despite the drafts. The belief, whatever it was, ran deeper than the new Christian faith he practiced. A belief that even Mrs Paxson, at least for the moment, couldn't shake.

CHAPTER THIRTY-ONE

From the snow-covered riverbank Máire contemplated the yawning stretch of ice transformed to milk white from its crystal clarity of the week before. So opaque was it now she could not imagine any life beneath it, no sluggish fish clinging to the bottom, no crawling crabs or even lichen hanging at its edge. Certainly no seals or any creatures that might require air to breathe. There was only the solid surface, rock hard as the mountain behind her.

She glanced down at the skates strapped to her feet and then looked over at Joseph who was skimming the ice with his skates in slow loops that grew larger with each circle. He cocked his head in silent concentration for a single sound that might betray the ice's strength. A few moments passed and he smiled and nodded to her.

'Yes. It is very firm. And should be all the way to the village.'

Máire steeled herself and took her first tentative steps on the ice. This was not a new experience, but many years had passed since she'd spent one late afternoon with Annie on a small pond in the park, her ill-fitting skates borrowed from Annie's younger brother.

Her ankles wobbled as she tried to gain her balance, but then, after a few more wobbles and small steps she lengthened her stride and managed a graceful glide. She laughed, wobbled again, and then regained her balance. She moved out onto the ice and lengthened her stride, feeling the wind rush against her cheeks and play in her hair. She twirled a little, gained confidence and twirled again; her arms out wide, she savoured the rush of cold. Sheer joy and the tinker's tune, strong inside her again, whirled her round and round until, dizzy, she collapsed on the ice.

It was laughter that helped her rise again before Joseph arrived, that and the tune still buzzing in her feet that made her forget about any future bruises. With a prim little smile and a few sober glides on the ice she proved her readiness for the journey north. Joseph arranged the bundles of food, snowshoes and blankets on his back and they set off. She'd no idea how long it would take to get to Kowishte's village, but it couldn't be slower than walking and it might even be as fast as a canoe. She matched her strides against Joseph's long ones, eager to get to their destination and have a chance to talk again with Sarah and Rebecca. She was glad that the more turbulent waters of the river to Joseph's village prevented it from freezing so Mrs Paxson had had no choice but to abandon her notion of visiting Joseph's village in favour of a visit to Kowishte's. Máire felt no qualms about agreeing to try and garner more interest in the school and teach a Bible lesson if it allowed her to see Sarah and Rebecca. It seemed that in the last few days the only people that she'd seen, besides the Paxsons and Joseph, were the miners.

'Have you always had so many miners gathered here in the winter?' she said, panting a little. Trying to talk and keep up with Joseph's sweeping strides proved more difficult than she thought.

'No. Each year is different. Some years there are more than others. But this year the snow made it impossible for the boat to come and take them to Sitka. They may be here now until spring.'

'Spring? Oh, dear.' She thought of all the miners who straggled in regularly, their hands clutched under their folded arms and trouser legs soaked up to their knees from the trek to the trading post. They brought little custom, just gathered around the wood stove and basted themselves as long as they dared. It wasn't that she minded so much. It was the likes of Carl or Pete who pestered Benny with stories about their imaginary gold and badgered him to come and play cards. Benny didn't usually respond, just kept his head down and tended to his task. What worried

Máire more was that the way they talked to Benny made it clear he'd played with them on occasion. The grey tone of his skin and the return of the yellow cast to his eyes didn't bode well either.

'Is there any way Benny could go and stay with people in your village? I'm worried about him.'

Joseph looked over her and frowned. 'No.'

Further discussion was out of the question. Máire sighed and turned her mind to other possible solutions, but soon the trembling ache in her legs took her mind to the journey and a determination that she wouldn't collapse before the end.

An hour after they had set out, the clearing near the village came into view. With great relief Máire reached the bank's edge, sat down and removed her skates. Her calves burned and she hoped they wouldn't make it impossible for her to make the short journey to the village loping like a one-legged bird in the snowshoes.

When they came through to the clearing, Máire saw Rebecca standing outside Kowishte's house arranging a pair of snowshoes alongside other pairs of various sizes. Bundled up against the cold snow in a large shawl, to Máire Rebecca looked like a large raven looming by the door until, hearing their tread, she turned to view Joseph and Máire's approach.

'Hello, hello!' she called, waving wildly. 'Welcome.'

They returned her wave and made their way to the steps. While Joseph and Máire removed their snowshoes, Rebecca sat on the top step and chattered with great animation.

Máire laughed at her energy. 'It's so wonderful to see you, Rebecca. I've missed you.'

After his initial courteous greeting Joseph had fallen silent, his body tense as he unstrapped his snowshoes with studied care. She longed to put a reassuring hand on his arm, but knew that he wouldn't appreciate it. It was sweet that he might feel nervous around Sarah's family, like any suitor.

With the snowshoes and ice skates safely stowed, the three entered the house. Máire blinked against the dim light after the brilliance outside. From the central roof hole a shaft of light poured down as a veil of smoke created by the fire beneath filtered up through it.

Over in one area clusters of women were busily weaving baskets of all sizes and shapes out of softened spruce roots, their fingers working nimbly while they chatted to each other. Máire recognized Yedicih among them. She looked up at their entrance and smiled. Her face glowed with life. After a few words to her companions she rose smoothly and made her way over towards Máire and Joseph, her figure carrying more fullness than when Máire had seen it last.

Máire greeted her with her hesitant Tlingit and she returned the greeting with a new graceful dignity that Máire could only admire.

After they exchanged pleasantries she led Máire over to another part of the house, near the fire where Kowishte's older wife, Katchkeelah, supervised Sarah at the loom. Sarah worked diligently, her head bent over her fingers, weaving the strands of wound goat hair and cedar strip while Katchkeelah sat at her side. A moment later the older woman reached over with her gnarled fingers and straightened a thread. She focused on her task, calmly describing her action in Tlingit before she looked up at Yedicih and Máire. Sarah cast a glance beyond Máire, spied Joseph, then lowered her head.

'I very sorry to interrupt, Older Sister, but we have some visitors,' Yedicih said in Tlingit. She smiled tentatively. 'It is Miss McNair and the Tlingit man from the trading post.' She'd said a clan name that Máire didn't recognize, and Máire glanced over at Joseph. He looked down at his feet, his face growing redder. A flutter of anxiety arose in her stomach.

Katchekeeluh nodded towards Máire and Máire repeated the greeting she'd given to Yedicih, stumbling a little over the words in her sudden nervousness. Katchekeeluh returned the greeting and rapidly added something Máire didn't understand, so she had to turn to Joseph for a translation.

'She says you are welcome in this house and invites you to sit by the fire and take some food. You must excuse her, an old woman, from attending you personally. Her sister and niece whose limbs are not heavy with experience will wait upon you.'

'Her sister? Does she mean Yedicih?'

Joseph nodded, slipping an anxious glance at Katchekeeluh, and Máire cursed herself for stating Yedicih's name in front of them all. 'Are they really sisters?' Máire could not think the two of them could be from the same family, let alone be sisters.

'No,' he answered quickly. 'Not in the manner you understand.'

Katchekeeluh cleared her throat, recalling Máire's manners.

'Thank you,' Máire said hastily in Tlingit. 'I am honoured by your hospitality.'

Sarah rose. 'Aunt, I thank you for your time. I will waste it no more and join my friend over by the fire.'

Katchekeeluh took Sarah's place at the loom and with Yedicih leading, they made their way over to some empty pallets close to the platform. Máire took a seat in between Sarah and Yedicih, grateful to be removed from Katchekeeluh's scrutiny. Joseph found a tactful spot behind Yedicih. A few moments later Rebecca joined them with some hot drinks and a plate of dried fish.

Máire scanned the groups engaged in various tasks around the room as she nibbled her fish. 'Is your uncle here?' She struggled to keep her tone nonchalant. It wasn't their uncle she was really asking about.

'The men are out hunting, but they should be back some time today if they are successful. My brother is with them,' Sarah said in English with a slight smile. 'So. We're very glad to see you, but what brings you here in such weather?'

Máire laughed a little nervously and searched for words that didn't make her out to be as foolish as she felt. 'I know it may seem a little reckless to undertake such a journey in this weather, but I've missed you both. And the school has been suspended for a time, because of the weather. The weather is making the people at the mission uneasy.' She turned to Joseph. 'But the journey wasn't so bad—in fact it was enjoyable. Wouldn't you say so, Joseph?'

Joseph gave a slight smile and nodded.

'It is true the bad weather is not a good sign,' Yedicih said in English. She had followed the conversation with determined concentration and sensing that, Máire had spoken slowly.

Máire looked over in delight at her response. 'Your English is so good, now.'

'I have been practicing with my nieces,' she said, a note of pride in her voice.

'Joseph has been helping me with my Tlingit, in Sarah's absence,' Máire said. 'I didn't want to lose the words I had.'

'I can see you have improved,' Sarah said. She glanced over at Joseph. 'Your new teacher is good.'

'But now you can practice with us,' Rebecca said. 'We can all help you. You must come again.'

Máire gave a wry grin. 'I would love to and, well, Mrs Paxson thought I might manage a bit of teaching while I was here and maybe a Bible lesson of sorts. So if I did that I'm sure my visits wouldn't be a problem.'

'That would be wonderful,' Sarah said. She looked at Yedicih who murmured something.

Máire watched the exchange and looked over at Katchekeeluh. 'That is if your aunt wouldn't mind. And your uncle.'

'I don't think they will, no. Especially if you begin with stories. But I will ask my uncle.' Máire caught Yedicih's brief look of doubt.

'Yes, ask your uncle.' She rubbed the slight mound at her belly. Her face cleared.

The door opened and a gust of wind swept in. A moment later Kowishte stepped through the entrance, followed closely by Natsilane and two other men Máire didn't know. The group made their way to the fire amid some general greetings, while children clutched at their arms and pulled at the sacks of game. Three women rose from a far corner and hurried over to shoo them away then relieved Kowishte and the two men of their sacks. Natsilane offered one of the sacks for the women to take. The three women exchanged glances, and then looked over at Kowishte who narrowed his eyes. The youngest and slimmest of the women moved forward with reluctance and took the sack from Natsilane whose posture had gone rigid and tense.

Sarah and Rebecca jumped up from beside Máire and rushed to relieve the woman of Natsilane's sack while Yedicih, moving slower, went to her husband's side. With the women tending to the sacks, Kowishte and Natsilane made their way to a pallet close to Máire's. She started to rise, uncertain if she should move to a less intrusive place in the room.

Kowishte caught sight of Máire and motioned her to remain where she was. Máire thanked him in Tlingit.

'Your Tlingit is good.' He was clearly surprised. He studied Máire's face.

'Thank you,' Máire told him, speaking the Tlingit carefully. 'Your niece and wife have been helpful in my efforts to learn the language.'

His eyes held hers for a moment. He chuckled. 'Very good. We'll see how you progress.' He motioned to Natsilane to sit beside him. Natsilane took the seat indicated, the tension in his body eased.

Máire watched him fold his legs on the pallet, wishing there were something she could say or do that would alleviate the pain of the scene she'd just witnessed. Was this all the result of his father's actions? She looked down at his moccasins, the beads sewn in a finely wrought design of a grey wolf. It matched the design on his hands, though now with the tendons, warm from the fire's heat, those wolves seemed almost alive.

Natsilane cut in on her thoughts. 'I'm surprised to see you here.'

She raised her eyes with guilty speed and blushed. She looked over at Joseph who was talking with Kowishte quietly. 'We, ah, thought to come because the frozen river made it easy to skate here. It was a pleasant journey.'

'Skating, eh. I thought I noticed skates by the door when we came in.' He smiled a little and for a brief second it reached his eyes. 'I can just imagine you flying along the ice like some large raven.'

She laughed a little uncertainly. 'Well maybe not quite a flying raven. More like a hobbling crow.'

He joined her in laughter and she felt his tension ease further just as Sarah rejoined them and sat beside Máire.

'Miss McNair would like to share some of her stories with us, Uncle,' she said to Kowishte in careful Tlingit. 'In her land it's the custom for women to tell the stories to the children. If you permit, I'll help her translate.'

Kowishte turned to Máire. 'You have tales of your land? We have many tales too and we never tire of hearing them. They're filled with courage and honour,' Kowishte said. 'It will be interesting for the children to hear the tales of a clan from a land so far away. To learn what courage and honour they might have.'

'I would enjoy hearing your clan tales, too,' Natsilane said, his brow raised. 'I hope you won't mind if I sit in on this little storytelling?' His last remark was in English.

Máire repressed a grimace. 'Of course you're welcome to join us, but

I'm afraid I must leave it for another time. We should go back now, before it grows dark.' Máire and Joseph rose. Sarah and Natsilane joined them. With a smile and a possible wink Sarah bade her farewell and Natsilane, with a mocking grin, took her hand and shook it. With her hand still warm from the shake, she waded through the rest of the formal leave-takings, practicing her Tlingit each time she could. Eventually she and Joseph left the house after promising to return in a few days, if possible. It was a promise she hoped she could keep, for more reasons than she would willingly acknowledge.

CHAPTER THIRTY-TWO

Máire regarded her audience and tried to suppress the deep anxiety that seized her suddenly. Beyond the small group of children with eager, upturned faces that clustered around her in the corner of the far platform, a group of women wove baskets, the reeds spilling in all directions, and nearer the fire a group of men talked in quiet lazy tones. Near the centre of the room Katchekeeluh sat at her loom, back straight and fingers working the strands of wool.

In another corner Natsilane wielded a knife on a piece of wood, fashioning a large-eyed bird with a curved beak from a section of cedar. Occasionally he stroked the wood, as if to feel the placement of his blade, to sense the wood's intent. Absorbed in his work, he appeared not to show interest in the story she was about to tell.

With Sarah positioned near her to translate and Joseph behind her, Máire closed her eyes to recall the images Cook's stories always painted. She reached up and touched the medallion under her clothes. Still there, resting at her breasts, it calmed her. She began her tale.

'This is the tale of my people, the Milesians, a people who, like the Tlingit, travelled across the open sea to arrive at their destined home, a lush and emerald-coloured land. The inhabitants, the Tuatha De Danaan, met them at the shoreline and told the Milesians they would not share the land of their ancestors with newcomers. But Amairgen, the all-powerful Milesian bard who could command the seas, the winds and the other earth elements met with the three goddesses of the Danaan and promised to name the land after each one of them. With the power of Amairgen behind them the Milesians demanded the Danaan either submit, give battle or accept judgement. The Danaan insisted that Amairgen judge the terms. He told the Milesians to depart the shores, go beyond the ninth wave, the point of exile, then return to take the land by force.

The Danaans called up furious winds that buffeted the Milesians when they reached the ninth wave. Amairgen rose and sang to the winds:

> *I invoke the land of Ireland.*

On he continued, invoking all the bounty of Ireland, the waterfalls, the wells, the lakes and rivers, the woods and hills and the tribes until, ending it, he sang,

> *Let the lofty bark be Ireland,*
> *Lofty Ireland, darkly sung,*
> *I invoke the land of Ireland.*

The winds dropped, the seas calmed, and the Milesians sailed onward and landed on the shores. As they landed Amairgen proclaimed himself and sang rhapsodically:

> *I am the wind upon the sea,*
> *I am a wave upon the ocean,*
> *I am the roar of the sea*

Amairgen went on, proclaiming himself as a stag, a bull, a hawk, a teardrop of the sun, the fairest of blossoms, and on he continued, showing his power, his all-encompassing presence. On he proclaimed:

> *Who but the poet, the singer of praises,*
> *Who but I divides the Ogham letters,*
> *Separates combatants, approaches the Faery mound?*
> *I, who am the wind upon the sea.*

Máire ended her tale. There were tears in her eyes, for her words had conjured not only the power of a moving tale, but she felt truly for the first time the greatness of the Irish people, despite her father's claim to a homeland and heart in the glory of Britain and the empire.

A little girl tugged her skirt. 'Very good, very good!' she said. Around her other children nodded and added their own enthusiastic words.

'Amairgen is a great hero,' Sarah said. 'You must be proud to have him as your ancestor.'

She smiled, delighted and glanced over at Natsilane. He caught her glance and bowed slightly, an acknowledgment that sounded louder in her heart than any of the shouted praise.

Though there were requests for another tale, Máire was forced to decline, not only from her understanding of Tlingit etiquette, but also because she knew she was unable to   sustain another tale with as much passion. Rebecca decided to attempt one of the tales herself, retrieved from her memory of Máire's book Sarah had read to her. Gratefully, Máire relinquished her seat to Rebecca and moved to the back of the group.

'This is not a tale from Miss McNair's clan,' she began. 'I think it's another clan, a clan short in stature.' She spoke in Tlingit, almost winking with the joke. She continued on recounting her own version of a leprechaun playing a trick on a lazy good-for-nothing man.

Engrossed in trying to make out the Tlingit words of her tale, Máire didn't notice Natsilane at her side until he spoke in a low voice. 'I stand corrected.'

Máire looked at him in surprise. 'I don't understand.'

'I had long held that your people had little to commend them in the way of courage, power and daring, and I can see I was wrong.'

Máire could only mutter a barely distinguishable 'Oh', momentarily at a loss over the exact meaning of his statement. 'My people? My people, the people of Ireland?'

He looked away a moment. 'I'm sorry. I take your point. You are an able storyteller, you have been taught well. Was it your mother who taught you? Is that your custom in Ireland?'

Máire gave a low choked laugh. 'No, my mother didn't teach me it was someone else, a servant.' She looked at him, holding his eyes, the rhythm of her tale still singing within her. 'I lost my mother when I was young. To the sea.'

She looked away, over to Rebecca who chattered away with her own tale.

'The servant told me my mother was a selkie, one of the seal folk.' She spoke the words in a low voice almost before she knew they were on her lips.

'She couldn't help it, you see.' She slipped into Cook's phrases. 'She had no choice, so. The seal folk live ashore for a brief spell, following human ways, until the pull of the sea comes over them, strong and forceful like. It's their true folk, the selkies, calling them.' Máire's voice trailed off, barely audible.

'I've heard of the seal folk,' Natsilane said.

She looked up at him. His eyes darkened and filled with sympathy. 'I'm sorry.'

Máire's chest tightened and she turned away, confused and regretful about her disclosure. She tried to brush away her fear and forced a small laugh, attempting to make light of the words that hung heavily about her.

'Really, I'm sorry,' Natsilane said again. He laid a hand on her arm, his fingers warm through the cloth of the smock and blouse, comforting. A large gesture. Máire fought back the tears that clouded the view of her skirt and shoes and closed her throat to speech. The silence stretched between them, reshaping and finding a form that became comfortable, so that eventually, she was able to raise her head and offer him a weak smile of thanks. They continued to stand together, side by side, enclosed in the air of words and quiet thoughts that somehow linked them, the essence of it balm to her mind and heart, and she remained still in the hopes she might prolong its ease.

Over on the pallet Rebecca continued her story. Sarah sat on the floor opposite Joseph, her eyes on him rather than Rebecca, expressing all her emotion for one brief moment before she lowered them to her lap. Máire could not doubt her feelings any longer.

Natsilane, his attention fixed on Rebecca, gave a soft laugh. Máire took heart in that sound. 'I have discovered Mrs Paxson has a penchant for matchmaking,' she said in a low voice. 'But I don't think the recipient of her attention would consider it favourably.'

'Florence Paxson has a penchant for dabbling in many things that are not necessarily in the best interest of the recipient.'

'In this case she has it in her mind to form a connection between Betty and Joseph.'

'A connection?' He snorted. 'A very delicate term for such an unlikely match.'

Máire pulled a slight face at his teasing. 'Yes, I thought it a very unlikely match, and I'm certain that Joseph agrees.'

'I would imagine so. He is from an entirely different rank than Betty.'

'A different rank?'

'Joseph's family is high-ranking among his clan.' He paused. 'Betty's is not.'

'I think Joseph may reject Betty on other grounds as well,' she said and nodded towards Sarah. 'His affections are engaged entirely in another direction. And they seem to be returned in equal measure.'

Natsilane stared ahead, his eyes fixed upon his sister. 'No,' he said finally. 'That's not possible.'

'Could it truly not be possible?' Máire pleaded. 'When it is both their wish?'

He turned his head slowly and gave Máire a hard look. 'Do not meddle in affairs you don't fully understand. Or you put yourself in the same category as Florence Paxson.' He fell silent, his face and thoughts closed to any further discussion.

During the journey back to the trading post Natsilane's rebuke lingered in her mind, dispelling any desire for the lighthearted antics she'd engaged in before. Joseph sensed her change of mood and remained silent for the most part. He uttered only a few words of praise for her storytelling and her success at awaking the children's curiosity in some English words. 'Interesting word, 'leprechaun',' he said.

The following day Mr Paxson inquired about the visit when they were alone in the trading post, and unlike the vague report she'd given Mrs Paxson Máire confessed to him the nature of the tales Rebecca and she had told.

He gave a roar of laughter. 'I'll bet they enjoyed them. Those kinds of yarns are right up their road. Still, you got them interested and that's a start, Martha girl. That's a start. But I wouldn't be letting on to Florence just how you've got their interest.'

'Thank you for your kind words, Mr Paxson. And, no, I hadn't planned on giving Mrs Paxson specific details.'

Máire looked around the counters and floors, noticing for the first time they weren't in their usual immaculate order. 'I hope my journeys with Joseph haven't been depriving you of necessary assistance here?'

'Nothing doing. Don't worry about us. We're fine.' He sighed. 'It's Benny. He hasn't showed up for a few days, now. It ain't that I mind about the shelves and things, it's that it's a bad sign.'

'You mean you think he's drinking again?'

'That and maybe worse. Those miners, now they're just too tempting for him, I think, what with their cards and liquor.'

'Benny plays cards for money?'

'You could say that, and more. Benny was a real gambling man. He had some run of luck in the past, but that was long ago, before the liquor started affecting him so bad he couldn't remember the cards.'

'I had no idea it was that serious. Is there anything we can do?' Máire suddenly felt guilty she hadn't spoken to him much, hadn't shown him that someone cared what happened to him and believed he could reform.

'I asked the miners that were here this morning if they'd seen him, but they said no,' said Mr Paxson. 'I'll go down to the camp first thing tomorrow though and see what I can find out there.'

True to his word, Mr Paxson visited the miner's camp the next day while Joseph and Máire minded the trading post. In between serving the few customers, Máire reviewed her book of tales to select another story to present to the children on her next visit. She thought she might involve Joseph somehow in the telling. Anything that might show him in a positive light. She was hopeful that, given time, Natsilane might come to accept the notion of a marriage between Joseph and Sarah. But for now, she would keep any further comments to herself, and hope that Mrs Paxson would move slowly with her own plans.

She considered the various stories listed in the contents, then leafed through some of the pages.

'Perhaps I should bring the book along and show them the engravings while I tell the tale. They might enjoy that.' She pushed the book towards Joseph with its pages open on an image of a boy leaning over a riverbank, talking to a fish. 'What do you think?'

He glanced down at the page. 'I think it would be much more entertaining if you were to act this out.' He raised his head, looked over at her and gave a little smirk.

She narrowed her eyes. 'Joseph, you are not suggesting I become the fish?'

'In Tlingit tales we act all the parts,' he said with deadpan seriousness.

'But how on earth would you act like a fish?'

He raised his hands to his shoulders, flapped them and made guppy motions with his mouth. 'I would think these actions would convey it well.' He lowered his hands. 'Will you try?'

She stared at him a moment then laughed. 'I will view that as a jest, and nothing else.' She made a brief guppy motion with her lips. 'No, you see, it's impossible. I'll just have to do it in the manner of my own people.'

Joseph smiled and shook his head just as the door opened and Mr Paxson entered.

He removed his hat and ran his hand through his hair. 'Well, no news,' he said. 'I talked to a lot of the miners and the only thing I could find out is that two days ago some of them saw Benny with Pete and Carl heading for Pete's tent.'

'Were you able to talk with either Pete or Carl?' Máire asked.

'I couldn't find Carl, and Pete was passed out in his tent. I'll try again tomorrow. But I told the others to let me know if they see him. And there was a free meal in it for them if they did.'

Máire nodded. She knew that the free meal would be sure to tempt them to tell them Benny's whereabouts, now that most of them were virtually penniless and unable to buy or barter much food. She hoped something would come of it, though, and they would locate Benny.

Máire sat on the pallet once again, poised to tell another story. This time she wouldn't just be reciting as she'd done with Amairgen's tale. Nor would she show the book with the engraved images that hid her face and cued her next lines as she did earlier this day. She gathered her thoughts in earnest, reaching deep inside for the passion and courage to tell this tale. Above her the rain pelted the roof in heavy sheets, its sound setting the drama for her telling. The sound explained the reason that she sat here this evening unable to return with Joseph to the village until it was safe to do so. The men were out hunting again so there was plenty of space.

It was Rebecca that had persuaded her tell another tale. 'Winter is the time for tale-telling, Miss McNair. Joseph can tell us a tale from his clan and then you can tell us one more.'

'Why don't you tell a clan tale?' Máire asked Rebecca.

'No, I only know the general tales and not that well. Joseph, he's supposed to be good. He trained with his uncle before he went to that school.'

Máire was surprised, for she hadn't really considered Joseph's life before he came to the trading post. She looked at him, suddenly seeing him in a new light. She'd come to see his humour, his quick mind, but now there was more to consider. So many qualities that seemed to sit uneasily upon the character she'd originally perceived. Now that perception had shifted, as though she had been viewing Joseph through refracted glass, a view full of sharp angles and distortions.

'I look forward to hearing Joseph's tale, then. I'm sure he'll be good.'

Joseph rose slowly, looking around at the group as if to gauge their temper. He stood a few moments, tall and dignified, his arms at ease by his side, then began his tale, his eyes lighting and arms rising and falling with the action as he told a tale that belonged to all the clans, the story of Raven and the flood. Sarah sat beside Máire, softly translating the words so that Máire could share in the tale with the rest of the group. But Joseph's tale came more surely through his hands, arms and the rest of the body as he described the rising waters, the people's fear and their attempts to go to higher ground. His voice rose and fell as the waters came and finally left, leaving the animals on land, the sea creatures in the water.

The audience showed as much appreciation for Joseph as they did for Máire. Though Máire was certain it was a familiar tale for them, having caught sight of the occasional nod or words being mouthed along with him, she could see the delivery was a power in itself that prompted their warm praise.

And now it was her turn. She glanced over at Sarah and then to Joseph. Their tale must not end as this tale. She took a deep breath.

'Long, long ago, a woman gave birth to a child, a girl, and it was said that she would become the fairest woman in all the land. And with such beauty came danger. She would cause the destruction of her country. They called her Deirdre. The king, hearing of her promised beauty, decided he would marry her and safeguard her from her terrible fate. And a beauty she became, with her fine fair hair that tumbled down her back and her eyes so full and long-lashed. But she didn't want to marry the king, so old and bent that he was. Why would she so? No. she pined for Naoise, a young man so handsome with his hair the colour of a raven's wing and skin as white as snow. Oh yes, he was worthy of any woman's love, so why not hers? Ah but no, he couldn't look at her, could he? She was betrothed to the king. Could a man of honour do ought but turn away from such a path that meant betraying his own king? La no. Oh, no. Please the gods no.

'But sure what chance had he, for her beauty it was such that it poured over him, poured in him, filled him up like. What could he do? She couldn't hold back her love no more than she could hold back the sea. So off they went the two of them, escaping in the night to a foreign land, for they couldn't remain in their own. Ah no, no indeed. And in this foreign land of Alba, that be Scotland, they settled.

'After many years this same king sent a message that he promised to forgive them if they would only return. Naoise was happy to hear this, for he missed his friends and the land of his birth. 'Oh stay, oh stay, *mo chroí*,' said she. 'I do not trust the king.' But he would not listen. No, he would not. With fear in her heart Deirdre prepared for them to go.

'Oh dearie dear, but he was wrong. So very wrong. As soon as he landed, one of the king's men met him and, drawing his sword, killed him dead. Deirdre, wild with grief, was taken to the king to be married against her will. Such treachery, such evil could not go unpunished. Not in this world. Naoise's friends and family rose up and fought against the king. And Deirdre, what of she? Ah now, such pain and grief you hope to never know or bear, and no more could she, for when bound in hands and feet and sent in a chariot to one of the king's men, she cast herself upon the rocks to die. Buried she was, beside her love. And out of those graves arose two trees, that bent and grew until entwined they be.'

Tears filled her eyes. The tale was always so sad, so very sad with every telling, but still it captured her, the love and grief, and the fateful doom. What was that fate that held Deirdre's story? She looked around her. Sarah had tears in her eyes. Of course she would understand such a story.

'Well I don't think that hero was very wise or able,' Rebecca said. 'Could he not have fought that fellow off and killed him and then fought the king?'

Máire smiled at her. 'Ah, then it would be a different tale altogether,' she said with Cook's intonation.

Around her the children murmured, doubt on their faces.

'But a clan tale is there to inspire and teach us,' Rebecca said.

'Oh, I think there is much to be learned from this tale,' Sarah said. She looked at Máire sadly.

The next day dawned clear and bright, and somewhat warmer than it had been for several weeks. Joseph and Máire departed with reluctance, but promised to return in a short while, if possible.

CHAPTER THIRTY-THREE

Máire entered the trading post with Joseph following close behind. A miner with a tattered shirt and faded twill trousers stood at the counter and waved his hands as he talked. 'I saw him, I'm tellin' you. He was up yonder walkin' along that path over there. You know, the one to the woods.'

Mr Paxson nodded. 'Now you're sure about this, Len? You're not just making this up?'

'Sure as I'm standing here. Now what about that supper you promised?'

'You can show me where you saw him go first. There's plenty of time for your supper later,' said Mr Paxson. 'Besides, my wife ain't here at the moment. She's up at the manse.'

'Shall I go up and let her know?' Máire asked. She thought it might be an opportunity to broach her own request.

'If you like, Martha. Though you don't have to go tramping in all that wet snow if you don't want to.'

'It's not so bad in the path areas. The snow is packed down, making it quite tolerable.' Máire strapped her snowshoes on to her boots again and made her way out of the door, careful to hold her skirts well away from the water-laden snow that squelched up through the mesh. Máire realized she had made an unrealistic assessment of the path's condition. The effort to walk in the snowshoes was tiring, the wetness making the snow slippery and difficult to grip in places. She paused halfway to take a short rest, taking in the view beyond her feet for the first time. Over to the side, in the woods that lay on the mission's outskirts, she caught sight of a flash of red hanging from a low tree limb. It was some kind of cloth, fluttering gently in the wind.

With renewed energy, Máire changed her direction and headed towards the red cloth. She made her strides as long and as quick as she dared. As she drew closer, the red became more vibrant and eventually she could see it was a thick, wool muffler, one she recognized. Máire moved closer, her breath coming in great gasps, beads of sweat gathering across her brow. Through squinted eyes she made out a dark shape, a few paces along from the muffler.

A sob tore through her, warring with her laboured breathing as she stumbled towards the heap. Her feet tripped on her skirts and she fell to her knees. With determination she steeled herself and rose, pushing onward, finally reaching the bundle of clothes piled across the path. Her vision cleared enough and beyond the clothes to the feet, the hands and finally the face, white and bloated in death. She reeled, suddenly nauseous at the sight of a dead body. She forced herself to breathe slowly. This body was a person, this body was Benny.

Máire knelt beside Benny and carefully removed the empty liquor bottle held tight in his fingers. 'May you find some peace, Benny,' she said. Tears streamed down her face and she attempted to brush them away. She could only feel sorrow for such an end to a very troubled life. How awful that Benny should die cold and alone, without any kind words. She tried not to think about all the things she might have done to prevent this end while, with as much care as she could manage, she arranged his limbs neatly, to give some ease for him in death that she wasn't able to provide him before.

The tears continued and Máire fought to contain them. There was still much to do. She rose, briefly brushed her skirts and retraced her steps to the trading post, only looking back once at the outline of Benny's body. The wet snow hampered her progress, and she wailed in frustration at her slow pace. Finally, she arrived and clambered up the steps, not bothering to remove her snowshoes. She went through the door with such a noise she had no trouble attracting Joseph's attention from his ledger.

'I've found him, Joseph. I've found him. It's so terrible.'

'Who have you found? What is terrible?'

'It's Benny. Over in the woods. I noticed his muffler hanging from a tree, and when I went over to investigate, I found him. He's dead, Joseph. He's dead.'

'Dead? How?'

'I think it was drink. I don't know.' Máire struggled to make sense. 'We must let Mr Paxson know. He's out there looking for him now. In the other direction.'

'Yes. You are right.' He started to walk to the door. 'I will go. You stay here while I fetch him,' he said, reaching for his coat.

'Alright. But shouldn't I go tell Mrs Paxson?'

'Just stay here. I will be as quick as I can. Do not worry.' He shut the door behind him and Máire watched him through the window as he strapped on his snowshoes and took off in a strong purposeful gait. A moment later she grabbed her skates and plunged out of the door.

Minutes later Máire had strapped on the skates, slung the snowshoes across her back and glided off on the ice. She knew the way and there were several more hours of light left. She could foresee no problems. The ice was slicker than before, occasionally causing her skate to slip once or twice, but she made good time gliding up the river with the steady sloping strides she'd cultivated over the previous trips. Benny's poor sad face warred with her efforts to form convincing arguments as her legs worked hard to complete the journey.

Máire arrived at the path entrance somewhat out of breath and overheated from all her efforts, but her desire to make amends for Benny and bring him some kind of peace helped her cope with the increasingly treacherous path that led to Kowishte's village. Her breath came in heavy pants and her legs stumbled occasionally. She could see a sheen beginning to form on the snow's surface under the effects of the approaching dusk's falling temperatures.

'What are you doing here?' Máire turned and saw Natsilane come up behind her. 'Where's Joseph?'

'He's back at the mission. I had to come, I had to tell you, I felt you must know, it was only right. He needs peace, it should all be mended now, in death, to give him peace.' The words poured from her in a confused jumble, but she could not help herself. All the emotion and strain from the past few hours seized her and she started to tremble. Natsilane held her by her arms and stared into her face, his own knotted with concern.

'Who needs peace? Is someone dead? What is it?'

Máire took a deep breath and fought the rising tide of grief inside her. 'Your father. It's your father. I found him dead, in the woods. You must come. You must. Can't you see it's all finished now? You can at least bury your father, and bury the past, but with a care to him.' Máire started to tremble. A dry sob escaped her.

He paled, his face stricken. 'No.' The word came out as a wail. He turned from her, put his hands to his face. 'No, no, no! It can't be done.' He turned back to her. 'Don't you see that?' He put his hands on her shoulders and gave her a shake. 'Will you ever learn not to meddle in things you don't understand? My father has been dead to us for a long time. He was an exile. A person that didn't exist for us. That is our custom, a custom you may not understand, but it is not for you to question it or try and change it. Is that clear?'

His words rang in her head and his eyes held Máire for a moment, until he threw his hands from her, the disgust and anger written across his face. He turned away and, deaf to her racking sobs, strode off towards the village.

She stood there, her chest heaving, tears drenching her face, and railed at his words and harsh judgement. Could she be so very wrong? Was her understanding so misguided? She had no idea. Perhaps it was all foolish nonsense, born of her silly ideas.

Slowly she turned around and retraced her steps back to the river while inside her despair and self-rage rose. At the river's edge she removed her snowshoes and fumbled on her skates, her eyes still blinded by tears. The wind picked at the loose strands of hair that hung along her cheeks and chin, flinging them up in her nose and eyes. She brushed the strands aside with her gloved hand.

On the ice her legs worked slowly as she skated along, their muscles protesting from the day's exertion. She tried to steady her pace, but her mind kept recalling Natsilane's words, his face dark and looming with anger. Perhaps she was wrong to come to Alaska. Wrong to think she might find a home here. There were so few times when she felt she might belong somewhere. How was she to find such a place when her own understanding proved so faulty?

The blades under her feet slipped against the ice, her long strides arrested mid-stroke. Long grey streaks crossed beneath her, fissures ruptured in myriad directions that groaned plaintiff tunes for those already dead. The tunes rose up, their high-pitched notes sounding harsh, strident. They swallowed her feet and then, still not sated, swallowed the rest of her body. Burdened with her petticoats, smock, skirt and coat, she sank further and further into the inky black water. Her hair unfurled, then twined round her, lacing in the heavy clothes, trying to capture her extended arms that reached upwards for help.

She rose up slowly from the water, reborn and new from the deep journey to the river's bottom. Her hands were grasped and she was pulled into this new world, a world in which she could wear her new selkie skin. Her flesh cold and wet, her lips tasting of blood and salt, she was carried from the water to a darkened cave, a womb of walls painted with brown and red figures of a tale of others' passing. Here she would awaken and greet those who'd waited for her for so long.

One by one, her heavy clothes were carefully removed; each layer unwound like the threads of a moth's cocoon, with a tenderness that spoke of ritual. With only a fur beneath her, she lay naked except for the medallion tucked between her breasts. A new skin was pulled over her and heated her blood as a deep, dreamless sleep overtook her.

She awoke. Behind her a small, smoky fire had little effect on the inky darkness. She turned her head toward the fire. Black velvet eyes and smooth sleek skin glistened in the light—she touched the figure beside her, her fingers tracing each contour with longing, smooth and selkie-like, until her hands encircled the head and pulled it down to hers.

'Natsilane, Natsilane,' she whispered hoarsely. She gasped his name over and over as her lips traced arcs across his brow, down his cheek, to rest hungrily on his mouth. She pulled him closer, wanting his skin to become hers, to match their selkie forms against one another. An initiation. Greedily she sucked and licked his lips, her hands continually seeking all the crevices of his skin now grown hot and slippery under her touch, the moans of their courting sounds echoing along the cave.

She pulled at his hide trousers, as he pushed her tunic skin high under her arms. He entered her, a rhythmic joining of pain and pleasure that seared through her. She folded her legs around his body, rocked them into the rhythm of the sea, rocking until the wave rose and spent itself inside her and left her gasping for breath. Then, warmed in a cocoon of circling arms and legs, darkness took over. She was transformed.

She awoke still entwined in his body, the lingering taste and scent of their binding stirring her from her sleep. She opened her eyes slowly, like someone drugged. The fire, now almost embers, cast their shadows in sharp relief against the cave wall. The shadows rose and fell with the fire's movement, as though caught up still in the sensuous motion of their bodies. She raised her head slightly from Natsilane's chest and studied him, drinking in the beauty of his smooth, tight skin, the dark fringe of his lashes against his cheeks, and the curve of his full lips. She kissed his mouth, running her tongue along its soft fullness, then insistently inside. Beneath her he woke, his lashes brushing her face. His skin, covered with salt from their lovemaking, became alive and slick under her wandering tongue and stroking fingers, denying the soft protests he issued through his mouth. He murmured her name over and over while she caressed him with her hands, mouth and tumbled hair, moaning softly, until she could only cover his body with her own, press him inside her to rediscover the blissful rhythm.

Afterwards she stroked his face, crooning and planting soft kisses on his naked ear. He ran his hand along the length of her hair and sighed. 'Oh, I'm so sorry. So sorry. This is a grievous thing that's happened and it's my fault.'

She lifted her head, sought his eyes for comfort and found only pain. 'How can you say that? How can you even think it might be anything other than perfect? It was meant to be.'

He groaned and cursed himself. 'Ah, no, Máire, no.' His eyes darkened, the pupils shrinking to nothing. 'It could only be a mistake.'

'A mistake? How can that be? I can't accept that.' She tried to control the tremble in her voice.

He set his lips firmly and looked away. 'We're different, you and I. Your people and my people have nothing in common. We have different customs, beliefs, language and almost entirely opposing views of the world. We could never escape that, no matter what lies between us as individuals.'

She sat up now and seized upon the knowledge that overrode all he had just stated. 'But you came for me, you returned, like the selkie's promise, and brought me here so we could become our true selves.'

Natsilane pulled her into an embrace. 'Oh Máire. I came after you. After we spoke, I let my anger get the better of me for a while, until I realized you had not come to the house. I rushed after you, annoyed with myself that I was so careless over your wellbeing.' His voice darkened and he stroked her head. 'I caught up with you just as you plunged into the water.'

He fell into a brooding silence. She said nothing for a few moments, trying to find some way to convince him of the truth. But he spoke before she could, his words barely above a whisper. 'There were no selkies. If anything would have come for you in the depths of the water it would have been the *Kooshdaakaa*.'

'The *Kooshdaakaa*?'

He frowned. 'They're the Land Otter People, dark underwater creatures who take the souls of the drowned. They assume the shape of the dead and prey on the living, enticing them into the woods or down into the deep reaches of the water to their caves. They're much feared.'

Máire shivered. How different they seemed from the selkie folk, so dark and evil. The selkie folk would not take one that was not of their kind. 'But I'm here now, with you. Not with the Land Otter People. You're my people now.'

He didn't answer her, but she could feel his body tense slightly and a distance, not of any physical size, formed between them. She looked around the cave for some clue, something to inspire her to bring him back and caught sight of the faint figure painted on the walls. 'What are those figures?'

'It's the tale of my people, our beginnings here in this land. This cave is special, sacred to us for the truth it contains. I stay here now, the times when I need that truth.'

She leaned closer to the walls and he put more sticks on the fire so that she might view it better. Slowly she began to make out shapes, light and dark, that danced across the cave walls. Natsilane wrapped his arms around her, and with a fur hide draped across their shoulders, he recounted the tale the pictures told, the tale he'd spoken when she first visited his village those few months ago. He spoke the words softly in her ears, weaving a magic of worlds that took form on the wall in front of her. She sighed at its perfect creation.

His words ceased, as she knew they must, deep in her heart. The tale had ended, and with it their time together. She could not move him otherwise, no matter what words she used to change his mind. He only shushed her with a gentle finger to her lips and shook his head. Then, tenderly, he wiped her down, using a cloth damp from the snow outside the cave, and clothed her in the fur tunic and trousers that topped his own clothes against the weather. He spoke no words, his motions speaking all to her, as she silently pleaded her case with her eyes and heart. Smothered in the deep fur, she watched Natsilane bundle her wet clothes, dowse the fire, and scatter the embers along the cave floor with his feet. He led her out of the cave's mouth, back to his village, while the dawn broke slowly over them.

At the village she walked behind him to Kowishte's house, still following a wordless waking dream, until the cries and concern of Yedicih and Sarah pulled her into the life they spoke. Natsilane gave them a brief account of her mishap and fortunate escape while they drew her to the fire and plied her with hot drink and food. Máire tried to sip the drink and answer their questions, but she found her voice had left her, all power to express her thoughts smothered by grief when they had left the cave.

She allowed them to change her into Sarah's clothes, to comb and braid her hair in two, tying off the ends to hang down her back, like their own hair, yet not quite. Carefully they bundled her, speechless and swollen with grief, into a sledge, tucking furs around her sides and head. Sarah and Rebecca attended her on either side, walking carefully by the sledge while Natsilane pushed silently behind, the three of them comprising her escort back to the mission.

They delivered her to the Paxsons, unharmed in all manners physically. She stood silently in the kitchen while Mr Paxson attempted to calm Mrs Paxson who railed at her for undertaking such a foolish journey. Nothing mattered at that moment, only Natsilane's voice as he cut short the diatribe and told them Máire must be put to bed at once. He instructed Sarah to help her and she moved quickly to Máire's side, her arm encircling Máire as she escorted her up the stairs. With each step Máire strained to hear the fading sounds of Natsilane's voice, reluctant to release her last connection to him.

Once inside the room, Sarah silently removed her clothes and slipped on her nightdress, while Máire's thoughts drifted back to the cave where she had been undressed not long before. A sob wrenched her throat. The noise of the grief brought Sarah's eyes to Máire's. She smiled and stroked Máire's face briefly, then took her hand and folded Máire gently into the bed.

'Do not despair,' she whispered to Máire. 'All will be well.'

Máire looked into her eyes, warm and tender with compassion, and attempted to smile. Sarah pressed Máire's hand then rose, leaving her to fall into a deep, fathomless sleep. A sleep as deep as the deepest sea, her body sinking heavily into its lowest depths, where the shadows hung inky black to hide any *Kooshdaakaa* that might be lurking.

CHAPTER THIRTY-FOUR

The leaden sky, heavy with unshed rain, cloaked the group circling the grave, clung to lashes, dampened shawls and rimmed noses. Heads bent in respect and bared to the air showed hair slick and wet.

'May the Lord rest his troubled soul,' Mr Paxson said.

'Have mercy on this sinful man. Amen,' Mrs Paxson said. Around her echoes of 'amen' rippled through the group.

Mrs Paxson stood erect beside her husband, meticulous in her black, her Bible completing her outfit as a perfect match. Behind her Betty shifted in her place and the large shawl that wrapped her slipped back from her head to reveal a bored expression.

But Máire didn't care. She could find no anger inside her to rage at Mrs Paxson's self-righteous words, or Betty's indifference. Her own sorrow lay too heavy upon her, as heavy as the sky, so heavy, so very heavy. She looked down at Benny's coffin, hastily built to lower into this makeshift shallow grave, the best they could manage in the cold weather. The others moved away slowly, and only Joseph lingered beside her, waiting for her to move. Movement seemed impossible. Contemplating Benny's grave seemed only barely possible.

Finally, she picked up a handful of snow and threw it on the coffin. 'Ashes to ashes,' she said, voicing the words that reflected her own condition more than Benny's future state.

The snow began again, heavy and insistent; it cloaked the landscape in a blinding whiteness that immobilized the mission. The snow no sooner ended than it began again, thick heavy flakes piling new layers on the mounds that crept past the windows. Mr Paxson and Joseph pushed and shovelled the thick layers of snow, creating great battlements to provide passage to the sheds for wood and the depleted stores. The meagre fare they ate each day reflected the perilous state of their food levels. They had little idea when the weather would permit any hunting or fishing.

The women passed some of the time getting ready for Christmas, stitching odd bits for the children and fashioning some decorations for the church. It was less than a week away and Mrs Paxson feared the weather would compel her to postpone the service, a situation she was not prepared to accept easily. Finally, the snow stopped and Mr Paxson and Joseph worked hard to clear a passage to the church. When they finished that task they worked on the path to the village houses. Mrs Paxson was delighted. She announced she would visit Kowklux and that Joseph and Máire would go with her. Máire made no objection. She had no care for what she did.

Mrs Paxson entered Kowklux's house with an officiousness slightly diminished by the clatter of her snowshoes against the wall. The room fell silent. Máire's eyes struggled to become accustomed to the dim light after the brightness of the outdoors, but after a while she could make out the grim looks and averted faces. Elizabeth greeted them with a wordless nod and led them solemnly to the front of the room. Kowklux sat on the small platform, a frown creating a deep furrow across his face.

'Mrs Preacher Woman,' he said when they were seated. There was no preamble, no offer of food or drink. Máire shifted uneasily. Joseph translated the conversation. It was too important to leave to the chance of poor interpretation. 'You have asked us to live in the ways of Jesus of the book. We have done so. We have moved our families, given up our ancient ways, because your Jesus said we must.'

'You have been good and faithful followers of the Lord,' said Mrs

Paxson, her voice strong and clear.

'Yet your Jesus does not seem pleased with us. No, Mrs Preacher Woman, he seems anything but pleased.'

'What on earth do you mean?'

'Your Jesus has covered us with big snows, sent the game from our doors and shut the fish underneath thick ice. Our stores are all but gone. What have we done, Mrs Preacher Woman?'

Mrs Paxson pressed her lips together. 'Our Lord has not visited snow upon this mission to punish you. Our Lord does not work in such a manner, I assure you. Have we not had the same snow upon the trading post and the church? You must not assign the whims of the weather to the Lord's work.'

'Your Jesus has no say over this terrible weather?'

'I assure you he does not.'

Kowklux shook his head. 'Then it must be as my nephew said. We are being punished. Punished for following these ways of Jesus. For burying our people in holes instead of burning them to ashes, ensuring their passage to the otherworld and their next life.'

'Don't be ridiculous,' Mrs Paxson burst out. She took a breath. 'What I mean to say is that there is no connection between the heavy snow and the Christian burials. One does not cause the other. It has just been an unusually bad winter thus far. Surely you've had bad winters before?'

'We have had bad winters and with these bad winters there have been causes. And each time we have learned that cause and made it right. This time it seems the only way to make it right is to remove the bodies from the holes and burn them in the way of our people.'

'What? That would be impossible, Kowklux. It would be sacrilege. The only way you could possibly make it right in this case is to wait until the weather clears and go hunting. Mr Paxson and Joseph will accompany you and bring their rifles.'

'You do not understand, Mrs Preacher Woman. The game will not be as plentiful. There is little for them to eat that is not covered in deep snow.'

'Well, we'll help you fish, then.' She gave a short impatient sniff. 'We'll go up to Kowishte or Galge or even Kutchewhe's village and see if they can spare some food until a ship comes. We won't let you starve, Kowklux.'

'We will see, Mrs Preacher Woman.'

Mrs Paxson shifted in her seat. 'I'm sure you'll realize there is no truth in Tinneh-Tark's words. In the meantime you can come and share food with us at Christmas. The celebration of the birth of our Lord is in a few days. We'll have the service at the church and then a feast afterwards for you and your people. There will be presents for the children. They'll enjoy that.' She looked around the room at the solemn faces then turned back to Kowklux and smiled. 'I will count on you to be there.'d

Mrs Paxson was refused comment. Máire could feel no pleasure or concern at Mrs Paxson's discomfiture. She could feel nothing. The conversation had rolled over her and barely registered. What was there to do anyway? And how could it matter whether they took action or not? It certainly mattered not at all to her.

Mrs Paxson rose and shook Kowklux's hand to leave. Joseph nodded and he and Máire followed Mrs Paxson silently out of the door.

Christmas dawned dull and grey, but clear enough for Mrs Paxson and the rest of them to don their Sunday clothes and make their way carefully to the church for the service. Betty and Máire had used the time in the days before to help Mrs Paxson meet her promise; they cooked and prepared as much food as they dared for a feast. The simple homely presents were wrapped in brown paper and tied with twine.

Betty joined them on their tramp to the church, a plain large blanket clutched around her. She lumbered on, breathing great clouds of air in front of her as she greeted the group, giving particular attention to Joseph. Joseph was clearly uncomfortable at such notice, an observation that reminded Máire she wasn't the only one who might need comfort.

Inside the church, Joseph lit the stove. He stoked it high against the room's cold and desolate appearance which the weeks of disuse had created. Mrs Paxson placed the sack of presents at the front, beside the pulpit. The rest of them set out hymnals and laid some festive greens upon the pulpit and window-ledges. When all the preparations were completed, Mr Paxson rang the bell and then joined them while they awaited everyone's arrival. The room grew warmer, the comfort of its heat lulling Máire into a contented state that lasted for a while, until Betty's foot knocked against her leg. The church was still empty, the door shut firmly against the cold. Mrs Paxson drew her lips together into one thin angry line.

'Right,' she said after a moment. 'We'll conduct our service now.'

She hummed a few notes to find her pitch and began a joyous hymn. After a few lines the others joined in, their voices making a feeble choir in the large room. With steely determination she continued the service, Mr Paxson and Joseph taking turns to read the scriptures while Betty and Máire formed the rest of the congregation. Máire barely attended to the Bible readings and homily and made only feeble attempts to sing. A queer silent group they were as they filed down the church steps onto the path, to be greeted by a group of Chilkats gathered in the small cemetery staring down at two large gaping holes. Tinneh-tark and another man crouched over shovels, digging furiously.

'What on earth is going on?' said Mrs Paxson.

'I don't know. I'll find out.' Mr Paxson walked over to the group, Joseph following close behind. Mrs Paxson paused and went after them; only Betty remained beside Máire.

'Do you know what they're doing, Betty?'

She gave Máire an appraising look. 'They are digging up the bodies.'

'But why? What good will that do?'

'To burn them. It is the Tlingit way. To send them on to the otherworld.'

Máire registered mild surprise. 'Surely it's too late for that?'

Betty shrugged, leaving Máire to guess what they might achieve by it. She felt a mild discomfort, a sense that it somehow disturbed Benny, interfered with his dignity. She had no notion how she might stop them, and could find no real energy for it.

Mrs Paxson obviously felt no such helplessness. 'This must cease at once. You have no right to conduct this wanton sacrilege.' Her voice rang out with conviction. She moved to take the shovels from the diggers, grasping hold of the handles. 'Stop them, George. Stop them.'

'Now let's be reasonable here,' Mr Paxson said. 'Why don't we go somewhere and talk about this? Come up to the church and have something to eat first. It'll be easier to think, then. Betty and Martha will bring over the food we prepared.'

After much murmuring and consultation Kowklux relented. The diggers ceased their work, Tinneh-tark looking sulky and resentful. With a nod from Mrs Paxson, Máire turned and motioned for Betty to follow her to the trading post, while the group slowly and reluctantly made its way over to the church.

In the kitchen the aroma of smoked fish and simmering stew greeted Máire. She lifted the pot lid and looked inside at the thin layer of fat that swirled on its surface. Her stomach surged and bile rose to her throat. She turned away, grabbed a bowl and retched into it. Betty eyed her closely before turning to lift the large basket of bread lying on the table. Máire flushed under her scrutiny. This was the fourth day in a row her stomach had turned at the sight of food. Máire pressed on with her task, refusing to give voice to the thought that crept up in her mind. There was no time to dwell on anything but the meal at hand. With quick efficiency she rinsed the bowl, then found a cloth and lifted the pot of stew off the stove onto the table.

Joseph came through the door at that moment and took the handle from Máire's grasp.

'Let me help you,' he said.

She smiled at him gratefully as she tried to quell the turmoil in her stomach.

The villagers consumed the meal in uneasy silence. Mrs Paxson dispatched her own food with great efficiency while Máire could only manage to eat a few bites. She blamed the tension and anxiety that surrounded her for her lack of appetite. Kowklux ate slowly, considering each mouthful before swallowing, his eyes focused on the floor in front of him.

When the meal had finished Máire assisted Betty in clearing up. She welcomed the activity amid the growing tension in the room. Mrs Paxson cleared her throat and looked pointedly at her husband.

'Mrs Paxson says your food stocks are low, Kowklux,' Mr Paxson said. Joseph translated his words.

Kowklux nodded slowly. 'The winter has been hard so far. We have not been able to hunt or fish as we need. Because we did as your Jesus asked, staying here instead of moving to our summer camps to stock winter stores, our food is scarce. Because we have not followed our ways, we are being punished. To make amends we must now take the bodies and send them to the afterlife in the ways of the People.'

'But we'll help you the best we can,' Mr Paxson said. 'Joseph and I will hunt, we'll find game. We'll help you cut holes in the ice for winter fishing. I'll go to Kowishte and Galge and get their help. We'll find a way, Kowklux, don't worry about that.'

Kowklux studied Mr Paxson for a moment, his eyes dark and piercing. 'No, we have gone too far from our ways for your Jesus. In this matter I am firm. We must burn the bodies.'

Mr Paxson shook his head sadly. 'I'm sorry you have to do that, Kowklux.'

Mrs Paxson grew red, her chest swelling under the force of her anger. 'This cannot be allowed. It is against all Christian dignity.' Mr Paxson laid a hand on her arm.

'My wife naturally feels obliged to remind you that it ain't the most Christian thing to do.' Mr Paxson gave her a meaningful look. 'But I know it's a hard choice for you and you got to do what you think is best.' Mrs Paxson remained silent, her face and hands a maelstrom of emotion and activity.

Kowklux rose, and the other villages took their cue and made ready to leave. Slowly they filed out of the church, their dark, solemn faces showing no joy or celebration of a Christmas day. The sack of presents lay undisturbed on the floor beside the pulpit.

It was such a peculiar Christmas to experience so far away from home, where year after year, Máire had attended a large church filled with people dressed in elaborate clothing and singing rousing hymns. Returning home, she and her father would exchange functional presents before sitting down with aged aunts to a food-laden table. It was later, down in the kitchen with Cook, Annie and Polly that her Christmas became festive. She giggled and joked over remaining food, danced a quick jig with Annie, and sang the wren hunting songs with Cook. Here, a feeble tentative service, a hurried feast and then exhumation of two bodies made up a day that held them all prisoners with qualms and anxieties. It was a Christmas like no other she had ever spent, and wouldn't likely ever spend again.

Máire remained for some time, standing between Joseph and Mr Paxson, while Tinneh-tark and his companion struggled to remove the layers of snow and dirt. Mrs Paxson had declined to watch the exhumation, declaring she would not be party to such sacrilege on any day, let alone the day of the Lord's birth. The large group from the mission village looked on, only occasional murmurs and words of guidance breaking their grim silence. It was a difficult job; the cold had frozen the ground nearly solid.

After a while, the cold chased Máire in, and it was not until she saw sparks shooting up hours later in the darkening sky that she realized they had finally uncovered the two bodies and were burning them according to their custom. She could smell the stench of the fire through the glass pane of her window, while the dark grey clouds of smoke billowed in the wind. She thought of Benny and his poor, wretched body and grieving mind, and hoped that he, like his bones now licked clean of the weak and ruined flesh by the flames, would be at peace.

Máire sat in the silent schoolroom and toyed with the slate on the table before her. It wasn't the first time she'd sat here, staring at nothing. Not at all. Several times since New Year she'd come here, and several times to the manse, and the church, to any place where she could sit in silence, away from probing eyes, to think, and lately, to pray. Pray to what she asked herself. Her mam? The God she never knew?

She placed her hand on her belly and looked down at her fingers, lying straight across its flat surface. Her belly seemed so innocent, so unchanged, giving no hint of the turmoil inside. Perhaps this turn of events would change Natsilane's mind. She smiled tentatively, letting the thought take hold. A small kernel of hope.

'May I come in, Miss McNair?'

Máire looked up with a start and saw Joseph at the door, a large bucket in his hand.

'Yes, please do,' she said, collecting herself.

'I came to see how well the roof is holding up. Mr Paxson mentioned you said it seemed fine, but I thought there might be a lot of snow piled in the gutters and water in the buckets and they would need to be emptied.'

'Oh. Yes.' Máire looked over at the buckets placed under the few small gaps in the roof that dripped through the sheets. The buckets were nearly full. 'I suppose it does need some attention. Thank you, Joseph.'

Joseph looked at her and nodded slightly. 'I am glad to help.'

He picked up two buckets and went to the door and emptied them outside. He repeated the action around the rest of the room, until all the buckets were empty. Máire watched him in silence, finding a soothing comfort in his calm, considered motions.

She waited until he was finished with his task to speak. 'Joseph, do you think we could go up to Kowishte's village again soon?'

He paused, studying the bucket's handle, then raised his eyes to hers. 'Are you feeling up to the journey, Miss McNair?'

'Call me Máire, Joseph. Please, you must call me Máire. Yes, I feel up to it.' She tried to smile. Her fingers twined nervously around one another. 'I am somewhat restless, Joseph. I feel the need to pick up some of the threads of my purpose here. I thought perhaps at Kowishte's village I could tell some stories, teach a little English. It's difficult to say when the school here will resume.' She looked down at her hands, away from his gaze.

'Of course I will accompany you. If the Paxsons will permit it.'

'Thank you, Joseph,' Máire said, her eyes still fixed on her hands. She was afraid to look at him. She was fearful he would see everything in her eyes. He would know what had happened, how she had changed and that she now had a new life growing inside her.

CHAPTER THIRTY-FIVE

There was no-one to greet them at the door, and when they entered, after a tentative knock, the dark room seemed to engulf Máire, as if she were swallowed whole like Jonah in the whale's belly. The fire flickered in the room's centre but she could feel no warmth from it as she stood next to Joseph waiting for her eyes to adjust. Murmured conversation and low muttering reached her ears and for a moment she wondered if perhaps she'd come to the wrong house.

Sarah appeared at her side. 'Ah, Miss McNair, this is a surprise. Come in.' She glanced over at Joseph and gave a shy smile and nodded. She drew her over to where Rebecca and Yedicih sat, on a pallet near the fire. Máire could see Yedicih's belly swelling generously under her skirt. Joseph made his own way over to Kowishte and settled into a discussion with him.

After Máire had exchanged greetings with the three, Yedicih rose to fetch some refreshments. Sarah took Máire's hand and looked into her eyes. 'How are you feeling, now?'

Máire pulled her eyes away from Sarah's. She was unused to such direct looks from any Tlingit woman, especially someone as perceptive as Sarah.

'I'm quite well now, Sarah, thank you very much.' She scanned the room carefully. 'Is your brother here?'

'My brother? No, he hasn't been here for weeks. He left to go hunting shortly after we took you back to the mission.' She gave Máire a reassuring pat. 'He doesn't usually spend that much time here. Not everyone finds his company welcome.' She cast her eyes around the room, stopping at

Katchekeelah then turning back to Máire and smiling. 'It was only lately, since you arrived that he had been visiting more often.' She studied Máire again. 'Why do you ask?'

Máire looked down at Sarah's hands grasping hers. 'I need to speak with him. There is something I must tell him, directly, face to face.' Her voice cracked slightly. 'Will you tell him this, when he returns?'

'Of course, Miss McNair. I'll be sure to tell him.'

'Please, don't call me Miss McNair. I am Máire.'

'Not Martha?' She smiled at Máire gently.

'Not Martha.' Máire returned her smile, grateful of Sarah's attempt to lighten her spirit.

Yedicih joined them then, a drink and small bowl of food in her hands. Máire looked at the food, a mixture of dried berry cake and salmon eggs, and quietly placed it by her side, praying her stomach would not make any protests.

She turned to Yedicih. 'How are you keeping? You look very well. Is everything going well with the baby?'

Yedicih smiled and rubbed her belly lightly. 'Yes, we are both doing well.' She reached over and took Máire's hand and pressed it against her belly. 'There. Can you feel the baby move?'

Máire felt the small quick pressure against her hand and for a brief moment felt the marvel at such a thing. Tears gathered in her eyes and it was all she could do hold them back.

A figure loomed large over her and Yedicih. She looked up to see Katchekeelah, her face thunderous, speaking rapid Tlingit to Yedicih in an angry tone. Yedicih gave her own quick retort but then removed Máire's hand carefully. Katchekeeluh turned to Máire and with narrowed eyes she muttered some words, turned and moved away.

Sarah broke the silence. 'You must not mind her. She is old and follows many of the traditional ways.'

'Oh, I see,' Máire said. 'You would not normally touch a pregnant woman's stomach?'

Sarah exchanged a glance with Yedicih. 'Something like that.'

'You would hardly do it where I come from either,' Máire said with a nervous laugh. 'In fact it wouldn't be mentioned in public, nor would you really appear in public if you were that far advanced.' She knew she was babbling, but there was something more going on. The undercurrent of tension in the room and between the two women was strong, but she was not in the best frame of mind to make sense of it. She'd achieved what she needed to here. Perhaps it would be best to take her leave. She caught Joseph's eye and could see he was finished as well. She only hoped that his errand produced better feelings than hers had.

It was later, on the journey home, that Joseph confirmed his success. 'He heard our needs and will give us some of the food from their village. It will be sent down to the mission as soon as he can arrange it.'

Máire squeezed his hand. 'Kowishte is a good man.'

Kowishte proved true to his word. A few days later he sent some men loaded down with dried fish, game and potatoes. The Paxsons offered some things from the trading post like pots, utensils and cloth, in return for the supplies, so great was their gratitude and relief at the sight of such welcome gifts. Mr Paxson added a generous helping of coffee beans, with the claim that Kowishte's own store must have long disappeared since it had been a while since Daniel had purchased any for him.

Máire looked for Natsilane among the men, an anxious few moments of scanning the approaching group, only to be disappointed. He was not there, and from as much as she could tell, he had not yet visited the village.

It was weeks later that he came, suddenly opening the door of the school, startling her out of deep thought in her seat by the window, a blanket wrapped around her.

He shut the door and leaned against its frame. 'My sister mentioned you wanted to see me.'

The moment she'd long awaited was here, and after all this time, all her preparations, all thought fled from her mind at the sight of him standing there, face carefully neutral. She cast her eyes down to her shoes stained grey from the countless exposures to the snow. She drew her breath. 'Yes. I had to see you. I'm sorry. I needed to talk with you.'

'Is there something amiss? My sister mentioned it seemed urgent.' His voice was so remote, his words so crafted. She wanted to go to him, feel his arms around her, hear his voice murmur soothing words and know that it would be fine. That the life growing inside of her was something born of two folk now become one.

She willed her thoughts to him and swallowed hard. 'Well, possibly.' She tried to raise her eyes again to look at him, but she couldn't manage it, the fear of what she might find there was too great. 'There's something I must tell you. I-I think I might... that is to say...' She swallowed again. 'My courses have not come. Not since... not since I saw you last.'

Silence greeted her words. A silence that lasted for long moments that fixed her eyes to her shoes and the floor around it. Eventually, she raised her head a fraction and her eyes moved slowly over to him. He was sitting on a bench, his head in his hands. She shrank a little into herself.

After what seemed an age, he raised his head and looked directly at her, his eyes dark and full of pain. 'Are you certain? Could it perhaps be something else? The shock of your accident?'

'No. I don't think so.' She bit her lip. 'You see, there have been other signs. Unmistakable signs.' Her eyes dropped to the floor again. 'I'm sorry,' she said in a small voice.

A stricken look filled his face. 'No,' he said, his voice softer. 'It's not you who should be sorry. No. It's my fault. I must take responsibility for this.'

She felt heartened a little by his words and gentle tone. 'We can find a way to make this work, to be together, can we not? Surely we could be married, find somewhere to live. You could find work. It will be fine, won't it?'

His face hardened and he laughed, a long bitter sound, full of the weight of unhappy years. 'I could not live in your world. Not as your husband, someone of your standing. We would never be accepted. Believe me Máire, I know this from experience. Do you think I learned nothing back east? Do you think I was welcomed in every house as a man, a man with a proud heritage, equal to their own? I assure you I learned that I am well suited as a curiosity to people of good or indifferent society. Interesting to invite to all manner of functions, to engage in conversation. But I am not to go near any marriageable daughters. They may observe me from afar, as they would any animal in a zoo, and perhaps, on occasion, under suitable chaperonage, hear what I might say about the strange animals of my homeland.'

She realized suddenly the bitter pain of his years away from home. 'That was in Philadelphia. If we went somewhere far away, remote, say in the wilds of America, surely it would be different?'

'Máire, this is the wilds of America. And you know as well as I, it would not work.'

Tears started to well in her eyes. 'It might work, maybe in Ireland,' she said softly, but she knew she was wrong. In such a place where Catholics and Protestants could not readily mix without criticism, how would they accept the two of them? 'Could we not live among your people? Would we not be accepted among your family and clan?'

He looked at Máire directly, his eyes hardening slightly. 'Even if they favoured it strongly, it would not work. They barely accept me now, if at all. And you don't understand what you are asking of yourself. It may seem quaint and interesting to you as an outsider, but it is a hard life at times, and in years to come it will get no easier.'

He didn't understand. He had it all wrong. She didn't desire this because it was quaint or interesting. She wanted to be with the people she cared for and whom she thought cared for her. Her folk. 'I would learn all I needed to know. I promise you. I would do it.' She took his hand. 'Please, please let me try.' Tears spilled down her cheeks unchecked.

He looked away from her. 'No, I'm sorry. I know you would wish to, but it wouldn't be enough. I couldn't let you do this, and regret it later as the toil and strange customs become a burden to you. You were not bred for such a life.'

He took a deep breath, then turned to look at her, his jaw tight. 'I won't desert you, though, you mustn't worry.' He paused again, and it gave her a brief moment of hope. 'Perhaps my family is the answer. They could ask you to come to the summer camps. When you are nearer to your time you could stay there, until you have the baby. We'll tell the Paxsons you're to teach the children. My aunt will look after the baby. She'll have had her own by then and would be able to nurse it. I'm sure she would.'

Tears continued to flood her face, spilling onto the blanket, creating small damp patches in its folds. 'You could return to the mission then, your reputation and position still intact. No-one here need know.' His voice softened. 'It's the only way, Máire, the only way I can protect you.'

She nodded then and sank to into the chair, the burden of his words and the months before her suddenly too much to bear. 'Go. Just go,' she told him. Her tears ceased and she turned to stare once more out of the window. She knew her only choice was to accept his plan, the arrangement of her life for the coming months, the years to come. What alternative had she? She couldn't return home, for she would surely be ruined. If she remained in the mission without Natsilane she would be disgraced, unable to continue her work for the mission and they would send her home where an even bigger disgrace would await her. She could not escape this turn in her life, to find a remote place, to find folk of her own. She had done that already and now it seemed they didn't want her. Behind her, the door opened and closed softly.

Part IV

CHAPTER THIRTY-SIX

Alaska, Spring/Summer 1891

After Natsilane closed the door, Máire's world sank into darkness, mirrored by the thick dreary fog that cloaked the mission and obscured the river. She found no comfort in her dreams, no comfort anywhere, only a blank and yawning emptiness that filled her nights as well as her days. There was only the lingering echo of Natsilane's words, as heavy and oppressive as the fog outside her window.

In the ensuing weeks Máire's sickness lessened somewhat, but she was still not tempted by food, a habit the Paxsons found cause to remark upon and which caused Joseph to send her probing glances. Betty smirked and muttered when Máire was within her hearing, but she said nothing. Mr Paxson assigned Máire's disinterest in food to the dark, dreary weather and the close quarters to which it confined them, a situation compounded by the decided gloomy undercurrents that still prevailed among Kowklux's people, despite the distribution of the food Kowishte had provided.

Máire trudged behind Betty, Joseph and Mrs Paxson towards Kowklux's house for another attempt to bring Kowklux's clan to heel under the guise of a Bible lesson. She felt the pinch of her skirt around her waist though she'd left the top hook undone. She fiddled under her coat to unfasten the next hook. Though there was little enough to show for her pregnancy with her generally slight frame and poor appetite, she was glad for her smock to conceal the loose hooks. The smock hid a multitude of sins, she thought with wry humour.

Once inside Kowklux's house and ushered with the rest of them to be seated on the side platform, she was careful to arrange her skirts and smock with diplomatic care in consideration of any untoward glances from Betty. Around her she was surprised to see that besides Kowklux, Tinneh-tark and some of the other men were present. Only a few like Betty and others of the lower ranks had attended church lately, so she'd assumed Kowklux and the other high-ranking men would have absented themselves.

'I thank you, Chief Kowklux, Tinneh-tark and everyone for attending this Bible meeting,' Mrs Paxson said.

The men gazed sombrely at Mrs Paxson, standing at the back, their legs planted wide. Kowklux looked drawn and tired, his posture weighted by the presence of the men around him, especially his nephew Tinneh-tark. The severe expression on Tinneh-tark's face carried such a chilling intensity that when his eyes found Máire's she averted her gaze. Even Betty shifted her bulk uneasily.

Mrs Paxson did not seem deterred and, despite the lack of any offer of hospitality, immediately launched upon a piece of scripture, illuminating its finer points and meaning for the group, while Joseph translated in a neutral voice. The women's eyes remained fixed on their laps, their bright scarves the only view of their heads. Eventually, Mrs Paxson's words petered out and she fell silent. She looked at Kowklux expectantly.

He heaved a sigh. 'You have said some good words, Mrs Preacher Woman. Good words that came from Jesus, who has wisdom. I can like your Jesus, but I am not so sure your Jesus can like our people.'

'My nephew says he is a spirit for the white man, and we should have nothing to do with a white man's spirit. We have our own spirits, spirits that are here, that know us, and we know them. We would not be facing food shortages and would not be dependent upon your people if we had not deserted *haa kee haa yegi*, our spirit above all spirits.'

'Jesus loves all men.' Mrs Paxson pointed to the text in her hand. 'He tells us here in the Bible. There is no mistake. He calls all men to be Christians, not just white men.'

'Does it say in there he calls Tlingit to become Christians? For Chilkat to become Christians? For L'uknaxadee? For me, the Hit Saati of the Gagun Hit, L'uknaxadee of the Chikatkwaan?'

'Well no, of course not. It mentions no-one specifically, nor does it call any one particular group to be Christians. Not in the sense you mean.' Mrs Paxson folded her lips together. 'He calls all of us in the world, in a general way.'

Kowklux shook his head. 'That is like smoke. Not clear. How is it this Jesus thinks we Tlingit can have a spirit who is not familiar with our ways, like our own spirits with whom we have lived for many ages?'

The pitch of her voice rose a notch. 'Jesus can see all people in all places, not just white people.'

'I do not think that can be possible.' Kowklux sighed. 'My nephew thinks we should give up these Christian ways, and there are many here who support him. He says while the white men seem here to stay, we do not need to take their Christian ways. We must take from them what can help us, not what hurts us. That is our way. The Tlingit way. What do you think, Mrs Preacher Woman?'

'Yes, we should find ways to live together, white man and Tlingit. But we, the white men, can also help you, as good Christians.' Mrs Paxson spoke firmly, her words clipped. 'We bring so much good to you, if you could only see.' Her words seemed mild enough, but her tone implied that his failure to see was entirely a fault of his own.

Kowklux folded his arms. 'I know you think this, it is your way. But we have our ways, and at this time, they are ways we must follow.' He glanced at Tinneh-tark, then stared hard at Mrs Paxson. 'For now, we want you to stay here. To run the trading post and the school. They are useful to us. But I can say no more about your Jesus.'

'But Kowklux, you are baptized in the faith! You cannot discard it like some unwanted cloak.' Mrs Paxson rose, her face flushed, her lip thrust forward. 'I insist that you reconsider. I will bring my Bible again and we can go through the scriptures until you're satisfied.'

'I have made the decision and spoken of it here. It is done, it is final. You are welcome to stay and talk with the women. They will provide you with some food, such as it is.' Kowklux began moving away.

Mrs Paxson lifted her chin even higher. 'No, I think the only alternative we have at this juncture is to leave, Kowklux.' She gathered up her things from the platform and motioned Máire and the others to follow her. Máire drew her coat and Joseph and Betty followed suit.

Máire thought about his reasoning as they made their way back to the trading post through the muck and mire. It was startling, and at first laughable, that they would think the Bible would name them specifically. And that his limited world view would give him the idea that Jesus should know him. But Kowklux had spoken of the spirits that inhabited the place in which they lived, spirits that they understood and that understood them. She wished then that they could be her spirits and that they could help her.

Perhaps, in response to Kowklux's own invocation, the spirits took hold and the weather turned mild. Once a lifeless frozen slab, the river slowly came alive, great fissures forming from its centre, spreading outward to its edges until, too fractured to support itself, sections broke away and slipped into the inky depths. The remaining sheets of ice that clung tenaciously to the banks eventually fell apart under the effects of the endlessly licking current, and were carried along the river, becoming increasingly transparent, until finally they dissolved.

Máire watched the impact of the milder temperatures on the river with some fascination. The warmer weather also melted snow as well as ice, leaving the mission a mire of mud and puddles. Visits to the school, church and manse became a tiring struggle to negotiate boggy paths that sucked at her feet with every attempted step and caked her skirt hems and boots. Mr Paxson eventually laid some planks that made progress easier for a time until the mud swallowed them, the weight of the many journeys they had borne driving them under.

Sitting on her bed Máire stared at the two letters in her hand, one containing her father's familiar script. With deliberate care she broke the seal and removed the contents from the envelope. It was two pages, well-spaced, a careful distillation of news that seemed to have no place in her life at this moment. It was between those spaces that she felt the most pain. Spaces so wide she could almost fall into them.

She sighed and began to read its contents. There was no mention of Cook, Polly or Annie. There was a reference to Mr Compton who had asked after her health, an inquiry, her father pointedly reminded her, that had occurred after many months of placation and assurances on his part.

Máire worried her lip as she read the remarks concerning Mr Compton and fought the urge to laugh. If Mr Compton knew about her present condition it would certainly extinguish any interest in her and cancel all need of placation.

She read on and in his final paragraph she read news that caused her some mild surprise.

After many years of silence my own sister, Eunice, has written me to say she is recently widowed and to ask if she and her young child could come to live with me. Naturally I felt it my duty to offer her our home.

She wasn't certain what surprised her more: that an aunt she'd never met would want to live with her father; that she had a cousin, a girl with whom she might have shared some friendship; or that her father had said '*our* home'. But what hope had home for her now? She bit her lip, stared down at her lap and saw the other letter, addressed in a bold script. William.

She picked it up and traced her name across the paper. Yet another lifetime to put aside. She steeled herself and opened the letter. As she read the contents her mouth formed the words and she tried to take them in. She knew she no longer had rightful claim upon his affections, and that he never really had any claim upon hers. In the end the words made no sense to her and she folded the letter away, attempting to fold away the guilt with it.

She had neglected to remove her own letter to William from the bundle of letters and her heavily scrutinized mission report that now made its way on board the steam packet to find William at some point on his tour of duty. It was a letter full of vague good wishes, written so very long ago. Máire hadn't been able to face writing a new letter. No thoughts had shaped themselves, no letters formed words.

She rose from the bed and went downstairs to help unpack the stores, leaving her letters scattered across her bed.

Mrs Paxson stood in the front room reading out one of her letters.

'This is excellent news,' she said. She handed the letter to her husband. 'The Reverend Carter and his family plan to return to the mission at the end of the summer.'

Betty hung in the background, leaning heavily against the kitchen door. With the uncertainties and tensions at her village that cast her own Christian leanings in a dubious light, she'd spent more time here with the Paxsons.

'Finally, we'll be able to run a proper mission again,' Mrs Paxson said.

'I think we've done pretty well here, Florence,' Mr Paxson said. 'All things considered.'

'Yes, we have. And we will no doubt get Kowklux back on track soon enough.' She waved her hand towards the letter. 'And with the minister returning to the mission he'll able to fulfil functions that you and I cannot.' She looked over towards Joseph. 'Such as officiating at wedding ceremonies.'

Joseph reddened visibly under her gaze.

'Perhaps we could do something about that suit of yours, Joseph. I think it might be time to measure you up for a new one. We could send off to Sitka for it. I'm sure it would be here by the end of summer.' She turned to Betty. 'I think you could use a new dress too, Betty dear. A proper dress.'

Betty looked down at her skirt and tunic, fingering the faded yellow calico that seemed to emphasize her thick, muddy features. 'Yes, thank you, Mrs Paxson.' She stole a glance at Joseph, her eyes calculating.

Joseph turned his back on the group, picked up some food tins and stacked them purposefully on the shelves. There could be no doubt about Mrs Paxson's plans. Máire was horrified. Resentment and compassion stirred inside her, a small wellspring of emotion.

'Mrs Paxson seems to have thought much about your future.' Here, in the trading post with just the two of them, she decided she would broach the subject. She watched Joseph's face carefully as he bent over the ledger, writing meticulous entries.

'She has.' He continued his work.

She decided to probe further. 'Do you support the direction of her thoughts? I had thought perhaps you had inclinations in a different direction.'

He looked up, put his pencil down and sighed. 'No, I am afraid I do not wish for the same thing Mrs Paxson does. Though she seems determined.'

'Have you given any thought to what you might do? I don't wish to pry, it is only that, as you say, she does seem determined, and ideas are taking a definite shape in her mind. They may take such shape that events will overtake you and there will be no outlet.'

Joseph's eyes darkened. 'You know the way things are. There is not much chance that my wishes will come to pass. Daniel does not consider me a good match for Sarah, so I am sure his uncle and the rest of the clan agree. I am a Christian, I have friends among the whites, so I have no standing, no rank in his eyes. My family, my clan mean nothing against that.'

'Is there no other way? Is there anything I can do to help?'

He looked at Máire and his eyes softened. A sad ghost of a smile crossed his face. 'You have many burdens yourself. Do not concern yourself with mine. You have been a good friend, Máire. I thank you for that.' He paused, looking down at the ledger. A moment later he straightened, his jaw tightening. 'I have not given up all together. I will try and see Sarah. Ask her to come away with me.'

Máire ignored his reference to her burdens, reluctant to contemplate what he might suspect. 'Where will you go? What will you do?'

'We could go to Sitka. I might be able to get work there, as a clerk or even in the cannery.' His voice was firm. 'I will find something.'

Máire nodded encouragement, though his plan seemed more desperate than practical. She could only imagine what life they might find, for she doubted if such a strong mission town as Sitka would welcome anyone who had seriously disrupted one of Mrs Paxson's plans. Though it was possible she was wrong.

CHAPTER THIRTY-SEVEN

Perhaps it's true the spirits look after the innocents. It was a thought that struck Máire when she next saw Joseph after he opened the door to the schoolroom where she sat reading her Shelley. He'd travelled to Kowishte's village and had visited her at the school after he returned. His whole face was alight with a joy she'd never seen in him.

'It will all be arranged,' he said as soon as he was in the door.

'You mean you and Sarah are going to elope?'

For a moment his face showed confusion, it cleared and he laughed. 'No, no. Not that at all. We are going to be married. Kowishte has approved it. It is only a matter of the formal negotiations between the two families.'

'Kowishte approved? How?'

He gave her an odd look. 'Daniel pleaded our case in such a manner that his uncle decided it would be a wise choice. He told him I was part of the future of the Tlingit, because I understand both worlds. I did not know Daniel thought such things. Or his uncle.'

Máire was so stunned she could hardly take in the full implication of the words. What could this change of heart mean for Natsilane? Had he realized Joseph might consider running away with Sarah? Or had he really thought about their situation?

'I also have a message for you from Sarah and her aunt,' Joseph said. 'They want you to come teach the children at the village and then at the summer camps when they go there.' His face gave nothing away and his tone was neutral. 'They also want you to see the new baby. It has only just arrived.'

'She had the baby? Oh, how wonderful.' She continued to enthuse over Yedicih's news while her mind considered Joseph's other words. Natsilane had arranged things as he promised. She felt some relief, but couldn't help feeling a twinge of disappointment that his arrangements hadn't taken a different turn.

'I leave tomorrow to visit my family,' Joseph continued. 'I want to tell them how things stand between Sarah and me as soon as possible so we can begin formal offers. I know it must be done by the old ways. Sarah's uncle made that very clear. But I must ask you not to mention anything to the Paxsons. I will tell them in good time. When the formal steps have begun.'

Máire pressed his hand. 'Don't worry, Joseph. I give you my word on it.' She resisted the urge to hug him, knowing he would not have felt at ease with such a gesture. 'I am so pleased for you. You have my best wishes. Both of you.'

'Thank you. Your help in the past few months has meant much to me.'

It was news of another kind that wound its way across the water and along upriver from Sitka in a little fishing boat, landing on the shore only to spread among those who milled along the shores and then through the village up to the trading post to be delivered to the Paxsons' ears.

'Mickey O'Shea, we haven't seen you in a good while,' Mr Paxson said. 'What brings you here?' Máire glanced over at the kitchen door and saw Mrs Paxson's pursed lips and narrowed eyes.

Behind Mickey, groups of miners and Chilkat men jostled for space and talked loudly, each trying to compete for attention. Mickey raised his hand and they fell silent.

He turned to Mr Paxson, ran his hand through his coarse fair hair and winked a large blue eye. 'Now Georgie, haven't you been missing my fair face, so?' He smiled. 'But I'm here now, like. And such news I've got.

News yer granny could only imagine.'

'What news?' Mrs Paxson asked in her most severe voice.

'The Northwest Trading Company are looking to build themselves a place just along from here.' He indicated vaguely with his thumb. 'It'll be grand, so it will, with a whale fishery, oil works and trading post.'

'Impossible.' Her tone alone would surely make it so.

'Ah now, not so impossible. They're going to start building the wharf come spring.' Mickey looked around the room. 'That's what I heard in Sitka. From a company man. And he wants men. Labourers who can handle a hammer, to help build the wharf.' Mickey straightened and cleared his throat. 'He's after making me a foreman, so I come here. To recruit as many as I can, like. Any takers?'

'What'll it pay?' asked one miner in the group.

'More than yeh'll ever make at yer played-out little water hole up north,' Mickey said with an easy laugh. 'Come on men, there's free meals, living quarters and a decent wage into the bargain.'

'Mr O'Shea, unless you have specific business to transact with us directly, kindly take your wheeling and dealing elsewhere.' Mrs Paxson, all rage and heaving bosom, stepped into the room to bring the full weight of her presence to bear upon Mickey O'Shea.

Mickey raised his hands and backed slowly to the door. 'Now, now, Mrs Paxson. I can understand ye'd be upset like, but I'm only after telling yeh what's already done. They're coming for sure.'

'No matter what's done, Mr O'Shea, I still have say over who is to come on my own premises.'

'Alright, alright, I'm going.' He opened the door. 'Any of yeh interested in working with me, just come along here and I'll sign yeh up.' The large group, pushing to get inside the trading post only moments before, began to push their way out again, shouting questions and names at Mickey O'Shea.

Máire shifted under the weight of the deafening silence that greeted the group's departure. Such news, and brought by one of her own countrymen. How strange it was to hear the familiar accent, the cadences and tones she associated with Cook, Annie and Polly. As much as she might enjoy the speech cadences it couldn't hide the significance of the words. A commercial trading company so close to the mission would no doubt have some impact on their lives. She just didn't know exactly how.

Máire put down the skirt she was trying to alter and rested her hand on her rounded belly and felt it quiver. Her breath caught in her throat, startled at such a queer feeling as a slow tentative bud of joy blossomed and spread to her heart. Their child. Was this how Mam had felt when Máire moved inside her womb? Suddenly, she wanted the child more than anything in her life.

But she would have to broach the visit to Kowishte's village soon. She couldn't hide her widening girth much longer. With a last wry glance at the unaltered clothes that lay in a discarded heap, she rose and made her way downstairs.

The Paxsons were sitting in the kitchen drinking coffee in silence, their faces grim. There was no doubt Mickey's news still weighed heavy on them.

'Would you like me to look after the store for a few minutes?' Máire asked.

'No, don't bother, Martha. Nobody's coming for a while,' Mr Paxson said. Her voice was bitter. 'They're all down at the mining camp waiting to sign up with that O'Shea man.'

'Ah.' She tried to keep her voice neutral.

Mrs Paxson frowned at her. 'Did you want something?'

'Yes, if you have a minute.' She steeled herself against the daunting look, took a chair and declined the offer of a drink. 'During Joseph's visit to Kowishte's village they put a request to him.' She gave Mrs Paxson a direct look and tried to remain calm. 'It seems they found the few lessons I taught very interesting and helpful. They would like more.'

Mrs Paxson gave a grim smile. 'So you've finally done something right.'

Máire clamped her teeth a moment, determined to ignore the jibe. 'Yes, well. Since the school here is temporarily suspended they would like me to come and stay there. Under such an arrangement I would be able to give longer lessons, and devote more attention to their preparation.' She paused and glanced at both of them, wondering if she should add more.

Mrs Paxson's gaze sharpened. 'Why has Kowishte shown so much interest now? He's always made it clear he has little time for the Lord's word.'

'Let's have a little faith in the girl, Florence,' Mr Paxson said. 'She's done well here and we should be thanking her. After all, he's interested enough to ask Martha to come and visit. The least we can do is oblige him in this.'

'I think it would be good for the mission if I go,' Máire said carefully. 'At the moment it would seem I could be of more use in Kowishte's village than here. And Kowklux and his people might look to Kowishte's request as an example to follow.' She forced a smile.

The front door opened, slamming against the wall with a bang. Mr Paxson rose and started through to the front room only to return. 'It's just Betty.'

A few moments later Betty stood at the kitchen door and sniffed. 'Good afternoon, Ma'am.' She reached up and wiped her hand across her nose. Máire resisted the urge to hand her a handkerchief from her pocket. 'I got somethin' to tell you,' she said.

'What is it, Betty?' Mrs Paxson said politely.

'That man who come. Many go with him now.'

'What man? You mean Mr O'Shea?'

Betty nodded.

Mrs Paxson snorted. 'I suppose most of the miners would go with him. The winter was hard and most of them must be desperate. I'm sure the money and room and board seems more attractive than wasting any more time on foolish dreams of striking gold.'

'Not just camp men. Chilkat go too.'

'Our Chilkat? From the mission? Impossible.' Mrs Paxson's voice had become so shrill Máire winced. Betty shrank back to the doorframe.

Mr Paxson put a hand on his wife's arm. 'Now, Florence. Let's hear what Betty has to say. It might be a few of the young ones. Course they'd want to go. You know them Chilkat. They like to see what's going on, see if they can get any trade from it.'

Mrs Paxson turned her gaze slowly to her husband. Her eyes softened a little, a smile formed on her lips. 'Yes. You're right. It's probably a few of those young men, filled with foolish curiosity. Still, we should talk with them, make them see sense. It's not a wise course for them to go off and spend time around such dubious company. I'm sure Kowklux will agree.' She rose from her seat. 'I'll talk to him now. Before it's too late. Come, Betty.'

Máire sat and watched them go, puzzling briefly over this piece of news Betty had troubled to pass on to them. Then she turned her thoughts to her own impending journey. She hadn't settled when she would go to Kowishte's village because of Betty's interruption, but she decided now that it was best not to delay. She would ask Joseph to make the journey with her soon. He was visiting his own village now, but she'd ask him when he returned.

'In spite of the fact that most of the men are going, Kowklux said he couldn't forbid it,' said Mrs Paxson that evening at dinner. There were tears in her eyes. 'Would not, is more the case.' She stabbed the fat-encrusted potato on her plate. 'Betty, you have sliced these potatoes too thick again.' She picked up her knife and sawed at the offending piece.

'That Mr O'Shea has no business coming here, preying upon the Chilkat like that. No business at all. And his language was deplorable. He knows full well we carry the authority of the mission with regard to the Chilkat. And the government, for that matter.'

'Well as much as that might be true, we still don't have the right to make him leave, Florence. He knows that. It was no use telling him. Besides, as much as I hate to admit it, that letter of his says he's got authority too.'

Mrs Paxson sniffed. 'It wouldn't surprise me if that were a fake. You can hardly trust an Irishman, George.' She looked at Máire. 'I'm sure he's tricked someone along the line. Once he has them working on this wharf, he'll probably take all the money for their wages and run off somewhere.'

Máire felt her face redden, any sympathy she might have felt now vanished. The woman's rudeness knew no bounds. But it would do Máire's cause no good to say anything about it now. She took a deep breath, instead and decided to change the subject.

'Perhaps it would be best if I begin my lessons at Kowishte's village soon. I could try to enlist Kowishte's help to persuade Kowklux to recall the men. Kowishte seems to have some influence over him. At the very least my presence there as mission teacher would give Kowklux some pause.'

Mrs Paxson looked at her husband in what seemed a moment of indecision. 'Yes,' she said, her voice somewhat subdued. 'Maybe you're right. Maybe that will help.'

'I'll make preparations then. When Joseph returns he can accompany me.' Máire returned to her meal, hiding a small smile of triumph. Though her girth had thickened she felt lighter now and still nurtured the small hope deep inside her but which she dared not voice.

CHAPTER THIRTY-EIGHT

From the window at the trading post Máire could see Mrs Paxson by the riverbank, shoulders slumped, staring at the fishing boat as it slipped its moorings and pulled away from the shoreline. On its decks miners and Chilkat stood making farewells to the others who remained on the bank. Mrs Paxson's efforts to halt or mitigate the numbers of men enlisting to work for the North West Trading Company had produced no results. Kowklux had refused to see her when she visited and she could convince no-one else of the company's danger. The battle was lost.

Mrs Paxson turned from the boat and walked back up to the trading post, her face grim. Though Máire couldn't see the harm in the men working for the company, she could nearly feel sorry for Mrs Paxson now. Such an awful lot of effort she'd put into her work and with little to show. But surely it would be better for the men to be working than hanging around here getting into trouble with drink and gambling.

Máire caught sight of Joseph in the distance. He'd missed much in the few days he'd been away to his home village. She hoped everything had gone well, but could only imagine what kind of impact his news would have on Mrs Paxson.

By the time Joseph reached the trading post Mrs Paxson had arrived and divested herself of her coat and boots, and was filling the room with complaints. Joseph didn't seem to notice her grim countenance, nor the tense air that hung around her. He greeted everyone and set down his small bundle after he had eased off his mud-caked boots.

Mr Paxson nodded. 'Joseph,' he said in a tired voice.

Máire tried to ease the tension. 'It's good to have you back, Joseph. I hope your journey went well and your family are in good health?'

'Yes, thank you.' He smiled at her, his face light and full of energy. There was no need to say anything more. 'I would like to speak with you Mr Paxson, Mrs Paxson.' He missed Máire's warning look.

'There has been a serious turn of events since you left,' Mrs Paxson said.

'I have news too,' Joseph said, pressing on. 'Happy news. And I would like to share it with you both.'

'Yes, I'm sure,' Mrs Paxson said, brushing aside his words. 'The events here were most severe in nature, and were not in the least joyous. And they will affect all of us.'

'I'm sorry to hear it,' Joseph said. She had his attention now.

Mrs Paxson told her version of the events of the past days, railing against the trading company and O'Shea, her face tight with fury. Behind her, Mr Paxson looked drawn and tired.

She ended her account. 'Joseph, we have much work to do,' she said. 'The company can't build nearby, bringing men with low morals to entice the Tlingit into dangerous habits. We must still work to persuade the Tlingit to stay here at the mission. In the meantime I will write to Mr Jackson and the Mission Board. They will be able to put a stop to the trading company's ill-considered plan to build.' She turned to Máire. 'Martha, you must of course write too, they would expect a letter from you.'

'Certainly I'll write them, if you wish.' She'd no objection to writing, but she was sceptical of its benefit.

Mrs Paxson's face cleared, the tight lines of anger around her mouth eased. She turned her attention to Joseph. 'Now, what was it you had to tell us?' Her voice was pleasant, the hard edges only barely detectable.

Máire shifted uncomfortably. There was a long pause while Joseph ran his hand through his hair and patted down the sides.

Mr Paxson broke the silence. 'Why don't we all go in the kitchen a moment? I'm sure we could all do with a sit down while Joseph tells us his news.'

They made their way into the kitchen. Betty looked up from her place by the stove where she stirred a pot and smiled. Or pretended to. Máire suspected she'd not been far from the kitchen door before they entered. At Mrs Paxson's request Betty reached for the coffee pot and slowly filled their cups. Mr Paxson picked his up and sighed deeply.

Joseph ignored Betty and cleared his throat. 'I was grateful for the opportunity to visit my family. This past winter has brought hard times for everyone and I was glad to see they have managed well enough.'

The Paxsons nodded and Máire smiled. His village still kept much of their traditional ways, though some of them were Christian. They seemed to have worked out a manner in which to live with both.

'While I was with my family I also talked to them about my wishes for the future. About marriage.'

Mrs Paxson smiled at him, patting his hand. 'That's good, Joseph. It shows respect for your parents and elders, an important commandment in the Bible. Are they agreeable?'

'Yes, I am happy to say that they are agreeable to my wishes. And my aunt is happy to act on my behalf.'

'Good,' Mrs Paxson said. 'Once the formalities are concluded we can look to renovating that shed. The weather's getting warmer so we should be able to finish it in good time for the wedding. Don't you think so, George? If it's in September, after the Carters arrive, we'll have all summer to get things ready. But I'll have to look into getting some material for curtains, and maybe even a tablecloth. It would be nice to have some refined touches to start off married life.'

Máire looked nervously at Joseph.

'And then there's the wedding outfit.' Mrs Paxson eyed Betty. 'We must not waste any time getting started on that.'

'I think Sarah's family will make those arrangements.'

'What's Sarah got to do with it?'

Joseph's face remained neutral. 'It will be her wedding outfit.'

'Don't be ridiculous...' Mrs Paxson stared at him. 'What do you mean?' Her voice was steely.

'My aunt has agreed to approach Sarah's aunt on my behalf to arrange our marriage.'

A spoon clattered to the floor. Betty bent over in clumsy haste to retrieve it.

'Why would you do that? You cannot think to marry her. She doesn't live a proper Christian life and her family don't support our work here. It's impossible, Joseph. You cannot waste your life in such way.' Mrs Paxson sat stiff and erect in her chair, her eyes fixed on Joseph.

'It would not be a waste,' Joseph said calmly. 'I care deeply for Sarah, and she does for me. We want to be wed. As Christians. Sarah has agreed to come and live here with me. She accepts that my life is here, in the mission and she wants to share it with me.'

'Her uncle will never agree,' Mrs Paxson said flatly. 'No, I'm sorry Joseph, but it will not happen, though you might wish it.' She smiled tightly and extended her hand once again to his arm. 'You must not grieve over much. We'll see you wed. To a proper Christian. I'm sure you must know we put as much store by Betty as we do you. I don't think she would be adverse to an attachment with you.'

Betty turned around and smiled at them uncertainly. Máire could almost feel pity for her.

'No, Mrs Paxson. I am sorry, but you do not understand. Sarah's uncle has already agreed. At Daniel's recommendation. He only awaits my aunt's visit as a formality, he insists we follow traditional ways in that.'

'No.' Mrs Paxson closed her fingers around Joseph's arm. 'I can't believe that. Joseph, you're making a mistake. You must listen to me.' His neutral, calm expression seemed to drive her on. 'This is not the wisest course for you. We have only your best interests at heart, and you must heed me when I say that you can't marry Sarah.'

'Florence.' Mr Paxson finally spoke, but his voice was edged with fatigue. 'Give the boy a chance. He is a good boy and has done us real proud up to now. There's no reason he won't continue to.'

Mrs Paxson turned to her husband. 'But everything we planned for, everything we decided for him, he's undoing all of it.'

'It can't be that bad, Mrs Paxson.' Máire said. 'Sarah is a good woman. I know she will make Joseph a good wife.'

Mrs Paxson turned to Máire, all rage and indignation. 'You. What do you know about it? If not for you, Sarah would never have come here, enticing Joseph, turning his head from his duty. We have you to thank for all this.'

'No, Mrs Paxson,' Joseph said. 'I have known Sarah since she was a young girl. You know that to be true. She is Daniel's sister, do not forget. And one time Daniel and I were as brothers.'

Máire gave Joseph a grateful look and thought to add some more words, though she didn't know if they would hinder his cause more. 'Sarah is a good teacher. Perhaps she could be an assistant in the mission, become part of the work here. That can't be a bad thing, Mrs Paxson. Especially in Mr Jackson's eyes. Didn't you say to me once that Mr Jackson admires a mission with enterprise?'

Mrs Paxson looked at Máire with cold eyes and frowned.

Joseph placed the bundle in the canoe with care. He turned to Mr Paxson and took the small sack of books from him.,placing it beside the clothes bundle. Máire watched each action from her place in the prow of the canoe, each shift in movement and weight manifesting in the varying flutters in her stomach. She wasn't certain if the tears in her eyes were from the thought that she wouldn't see Mr Paxson for some time, or if it was her nerves, taut over what lay ahead for her.

Mrs Paxson stood behind Mr Paxson in sullen silence. Her only words to Máire all morning had been, 'Try not to make a hash of things'. She'd hardly said a word since Joseph had announced his news and had made no comment when Betty failed to appear the last few days.

Joseph climbed into the canoe and, with Mr Paxson's help, pushed off from the bank. Máire faced upriver, towards her destination, while behind her Joseph paddled the water with swift, sure strokes. Despite his vigorous efforts, progress was slow against the strong spring currents. Such currents didn't make for a smooth journey, as the canoe lifted slightly with each paddle stroke. Máire reached for each gunwale to steady herself, the fine balance achieved in other journeys vanished under her new shape and weight.

There were no gentle rhythms to comfort her or soothe her fears. This was a determined journey amid uncertain currents. Her hopes and fears lay bare in this canoe. Could she weather these threats? Would she tip over and sink like some random stone? She rested her hand on her stomach. There was a possibility she could die. Giving birth in the wild without any doctors or midwives. She reached up to the medallion that lay, as always, between her breasts. Ah Mam, she thought. Watch over me.

Eventually, they arrived at the mooring area for Kowishte's village. Joseph helped Máire ashore, and with great effort, pulled the heavy wooden canoe up on the bank. She bent down to help him, but he motioned her away, his eyes drifting down to her belly. She reddened at his glance, and stepped away to allow him to finish the job on his own. After he had seen the canoe safely overturned upon the bank, he sat on its underside to catch his breath.

Máire fingered the bundle in her hand, careful to keep her glance averted from Joseph's. In a few minutes, he stood and reached for the rest of her belongings. She stepped over to him and moved to take the sack of books she would use for her teaching, as well as her volume of Shelley.

Joseph reached down and put his hand over the sack. 'I will take those. You must have a care. You should not be lifting heavy items now.'

Máire dropped her hand from the book sack hastily. 'I'm fine Joseph, really.'

'Yes, but you must take care.'

'Thank you for your concern.'

She began to walk on towards the village. 'Will you stay long at the village? You must have some things to discuss now that your marriage is settled. And I'm sure Sarah would wish you to.'

'I still have my duty to the Paxsons. I will have to return there in a few days.'

'Oh.'

Máire suddenly didn't want him to leave her. Part of her felt he was her last link to the life she knew, a life that was relatively safe, and though she knew her condition made her absence necessary, she found it difficult to let that link go. And she liked Joseph very much. He might know why she was coming here, but she had no fear he would disclose it to anyone. She just didn't want him to think any less of her.

'Joseph, don't you miss your family? You so seldom see them. Wouldn't you rather live with them? It might be easier for you and Sarah.'

'Yes, I miss my family. But I chose to live in the mission and they understand that. It may seem that my own life there is not much, but the life for my children will be better. They will learn English early, go to school, maybe even college. They will be able to do much more than I. That I can do this with Sarah as my wife, I think I have you to thank. I am certain it was because of you that Daniel changed his mind.'

Máire said nothing, just wondered at his words. Though she could not imagine that she had any influence over Natsilane, it was nice of Joseph to credit her for some part of his happiness. Here was a good friend. And he was to marry another such friend of hers. She fervently hoped that his plans would come to something.

When they arrived at Kowishte's house her nervousness suddenly returned in full force. Sarah was the first person to greet her, moving to the door as soon as she saw Máire and Joseph at the entrance. Máire leaned forward to clasp her hand, her heart beating wildly, her eyes scanning the room. 'He is not here,' Sarah whispered in her ear.

She forced herself to smile and look directly at Sarah. 'I am so glad that it worked out well for you and Joseph.'

Sarah nodded and squeezed Máire's hand, her eyes moving behind her to Joseph. 'We have you to thank for that, I think.'

'I'm happy that something positive has come from these past months.' The words slipped softly from Máire's mouth before she could recall them.

Sarah looked at her in concern and put her arm through hers. 'Many good things have come from these past months,' she said softly. 'And much of it to do with you. You must have patience; some more good things will come. In the meantime let me take you to one of the blessings that recently arrived. Yedicih is anxious to show you.'

She pulled Máire forward into the house, while Joseph went off to deposit her things and pay his respects to Kowishte. They found Yedicih in a quiet corner of the house, sitting beside a large woven basket. It was the baby's cradle. Máire knelt down carefully beside it and looked inside. The baby, round-cheeked and black-haired, lay asleep in a pile of furs and blankets. As if sensing her presence he opened his dark eyes and his tiny mouth gurgled.

'Oh look, he's smiling.' Máire leaned back on her feet and rested her arm across her own girth unconsciously.

'He sees another mother,' Yedicih said quietly in English, her hand reaching out to the arm on Máire's stomach. 'You are well?'

Máire hastily pulled her arm away from her stomach, breaking the contact. 'Yes, yes I am well.' Though Máire realized Yedicih knew, it was difficult to openly acknowledge her pregnancy. She didn't know if she was ready to do so now.

'Do not worry, we are here to help you. You are as my niece now, and I must look after your welfare, and the baby's.' She smiled. 'You are carrying a Tlingit, of the Chilkootkwaan.'

'And you are as a sister, now,' Sarah said.

Máire nodded, her eyes lowered, still unable to look at either of them.

'We will give you time to recover from your journey,' Yedicih said. 'To have a drink and some food to eat. Then we can examine you and make certain all goes well with the baby.'

Máire glanced over at the small child curled up in the small basket and felt a wave of longing come over her. She raised her head and looked across at Yedicih. Their glances—one compassion-filled, the other pleading—held until caught by some movement. Máire saw Katchekeeluh come into view, her face glowering darkly.

Words rattled overhead, Katchekeeluh's menacing and low, Yedicih's response calm and just as firm. The exchange continued until Katchekeeluh gestured to Máire with a flourish then turned and left.

CHAPTER THIRTY-NINE

'What does a bride in your country wear when they marry?' Sarah asked.

Máire considered for a moment in her place beside Sarah on the pallet in the corner of the room. She felt best here, more removed from prying eyes and unwanted attention. Now, in her third day here, she still wished she could become invisible.

'Well, usually we would wear a long white dress, a veil and carry a bouquet of flowers.'

'A white dress? Why?'

'The white symbolizes the bride's purity.' Máire blushed. This was something she could no longer claim.

'Purity?'

How would she put this? She looked over at Yedicih who was nursing the baby so openly in front of everyone. Really, she supposed there was no need to be delicate with Sarah.

'I mean that the woman hasn't had any intimate relations with a man.'

Sarah gave her puzzled look for a moment and then laughed. 'Oh, I see.'

Máire looked up behind her where Katchekeeluh now stood. She muttered a few words, waved her hand at Máire and left just as suddenly as she'd appeared.

'Is something wrong? Am I behaving incorrectly?' Máire searched her mind for any possible misconduct. She'd tried so hard these past few days to behave as any Tlingit woman. Sarah and Yedicih had answered all her questions about a Tlingit woman's obligations and tasks, and though they wouldn't let her help them much with food preparation and she was unable to do any of the crafts, she thought she'd avoided any kind of cultural trespass. She could tell that the women were still suspicious of her presence. They avoided her most times, though she wondered if this was due to Katchekeeluh.

'You are not to worry about my sister,' Yedicih said. She patted Máire's arm. 'It is hard for her to shed very old traditions.'

Reassured for the moment, Máire watched the baby's hand curl at Yedicih's breast. Sarah had told her his name was Brown Owl. 'It's a shortened form of his birth name, given to him so the spirits will not hear his real name and call him back.' At the moment Brown Owl's strong suckling dispelled any notion he might leave this earth and return to the spirit world.

Máire felt a strange tugging at her own breasts as they strained at the already over-tight camisole and blouse under her smock. She pulled at her clothes. Yedicih caught her action.

'When this little one is finished I think I will fetch the birth woman. It is time to see how things are with your baby.' Yedicih said, her voice gentle.

Máire's hands stilled. Despite the gentle tone Máire was filled with anxiety. She'd no idea what to expect. She'd never been fully examined. Even doctors at home had done nothing more than look at her throat or feel her pulse on the rare occasions she'd been ill. 'Please, could it just be you? And Sarah if you need her? Please.'

She looked at Máire closely. 'If you wish it, for now. But she must look at you eventually. I know little compared to her.'

Yedicih rose, laid the baby in his woven cradle and gestured for Máire to follow her. She headed to the blanketed off corner next to Brown Owl's basket. Behind the blanket was the pallet where she slept and Kowishte too, most times. Now that Yedicih was nursing, he spent the bulk of his nights with Katchekeeluh where he could sleep undisturbed. Máire stood beside the pallet, unsure of what Yedicih wanted her to do. Yedicih said nothing in the end, just undressed her with a tenderness that brought tears to her eyes, removing first her smock and badly fastened skirt and then her blouse, petticoats, camisole and drawers, and finally her boots and stockings, until Máire stood naked before her, belly swollen and breasts enlarged, the medallion resting on top of them. Máire placed her hands over her waist in a feeble attempt to cover her girth.

Gently Yedicih moved her hands and began to feel Máire's belly, pushing gently against it, her face filled with concentration. She pulled Máire down to the pallet and continued her examination along to the entrance of Máire's womb, asking Máire questions about the pregnancy. Anxious over her serious face and the slow nods she gave in response to Máire's answers, Máire began to worry about the baby. 'Is everything alright? Is there something wrong with the baby?'

She smiled at Máire. 'It is fine. You have a slight frame, but the baby is small, so all should be well. I think you should see the birthing woman, though.'

Máire nodded, too relieved to do anything more than agree. The examination had not been so unpleasant, just the anxiety that accompanied each pressing and probing motion.

'Come, let us get you dressed now,' Yedicih said. She picked up the under garments and fingered them carefully. 'It might be better if you left off these clothes for now. They are tight for you to wear and I can see they're uncomfortable. It's not good to constrict the baby in such a manner.' She laughed a little. 'Or you.'

So they omitted Máire's undergarments, and her blouse too, and at Yedicih's insistence Máire donned one of her skirts. Though its easy fullness made it more comfortable than her own tight woollen one, its waist came under Máire's breasts and pushed the full gathers of the skirt out over her belly to form a bulky curve along her smock. Máire looked down at her new attire and grimaced. 'I look nothing like a lady now,' she said in English. 'Mrs Paxson would have a fit. And my father.' Máire bit her lip at that statement. Her father would have more than a fit. If he could see her now, he would disown her without a blink of his eye.

'You look lovely.' Yedicih smoothed a wisp of hair from Máire's face and tucked it up in her snood. 'You are blooming with health. Your own health and that of the baby. It suits you.'

Máire took her hand and squeezed it and tried to push aside any distressing thoughts. 'You're very good to me, I can't thank you enough.'

'What else would I do for my niece?' She pulled Máire's hand through her arm. 'Come, shall we see what my son is up to?'

She parted the blankets and they went through to the little cradle. Máire could hear the coos and gurgles that comprised Brown Owl's mysterious language. She put her hand to rest on her own curving belly, now large with its extra bulk of the skirt's gathers and tucks, and felt a surge of contentment and joy.

'Oh little one, you just don't like to sleep much, do you?' Yeidicih laughed and picked him up, enfolding him in her arms and nuzzling his face. 'Are you afraid you will miss some event?'

Máire watched her coo and smile at her small son, her own hand still resting against the curve shaped by her own little one. 'May I hold him?' Máire asked. She suddenly wanted to know what it was to have a baby in her arms, to feel its head nesting against her elbow.

'Of course.' Yedicih placed him in Máire's arms, tucking in folds of the blanket around his little face. Máire handled him carefully, trying to support his head and all the delicate parts that made up his small body. 'You are so beautiful, little one,' Máire said in English.

'Just like his mother.'

Máire looked up to see Natsilane standing beside her, his face dark and unreadable. Her breath caught in her throat. He'd finally appeared. Unconsciously she squeezed the baby tight to her side, fearing she would drop him in her sudden nervousness. Brown Owl screwed up his tiny face and began to howl in protest. Yedicih took him from Máire quickly, then turned to greet Natsilane.

'Welcome back, Nephew. It is good to see you, though it is not above time.' She looked pointedly at Máire.

'I had much to attend to, Aunt. But I can see you and your son have only grown healthier in my absence.'

Máire stood silently by Yedicih's side, not knowing what to say, but unable to take her eyes from his face, or suppress her longing. She craved for his touch, his voice and all the sense of him that had pressed in on her these past months and nearly smothered her with its fierceness. Unconsciously Máire's hand slipped to rest on her stomach. He glanced over her then, taking in her posture, her clothes. His eyes flickered.

'You will be glad to know that Máire is in good health,' Yedicih said.

Natsilane turned his attention back to Yedicih and forced a smile. 'Good. I have made the arrangements for the summer. We'll go to the upper camp on the lake. We'll leave at Kiyanee.'

'When is that?' Máire asked in a small voice.

'At the Moon of the Land Flowers. A week's time.' He said it in English, her ignorance underlined.

'Is that not a little soon?' Yedicih asked. 'Won't you go with us for the hooligan run?'

Natsilane glanced over at Máire's stomach. 'No, we'll head to our own camp. With any luck, there might be a small run there.'

Máire swallowed hard, the longing suddenly transformed into a smouldering anger she found comforting.

Though Natsilane remained in the village over the next few days he did his best to avoid Máire, a difficult task given the close quarters. He slept in Kowishte's house, in a corner as far away as possible from Máire's sleeping area next to Sarah and Rebecca. During the day he found tasks outside, or in another house to keep him occupied. Máire watched his behaviour and her anger grew. Was she to be the only one held at fault for her appearance?

With this thought in mind she approached Yedicih.

'May I borrow one of your underdresses to wear with this skirt?' she asked. 'The skirt is so comfortable and I think the underdress would be too. The smock provides some comfort but it is a bit loose under here.' She gestured towards her breasts.

Yedicih looked up from the basket she was weaving and eyed Máire carefully. 'Please, sit down,' she said in English.

She remained while Máire eased herself down. Behind Yedicih, Brown Owl gurgled a greeting. He no longer spent his time in the basket, staring up at the dark timbers of the roof, but was now strapped into a wooden cradleboard decorated with fine little shells. The cradleboard was propped against the wall, which allowed him a view of all the room's activity and, Yedicih explained, kept him from wriggling or rolling into danger, especially when they travelled up to the summer camp and conducted work there.

She smiled at Máire when they had settled, her hands still working the spruce roots with deft movements. 'I am glad you are finding the skirt comfortable. It is not always easy to achieve comfort when you are pregnant, especially near the end,' she said in Tlingit. 'I think you would benefit from wearing the underdress, it would help you keep warm in the first few weeks at the summer camp and, as you say, it would also give your breasts more support than wearing just your own overtunic. But you may find it bulky to wear under your smock.'

Máire lifted her chin a fraction. 'I would wear it without my smock.'

'Oh.'

'I don't see that it would be a problem. They will all know about my condition soon, why not now?'

'I think what my nephew would have them know is something else.'

'But I don't understand.'

'Normally we would never reject a child or a child's mother. A child has his identity, his clan, through the mother. They would remain part of her clan. But this is different. My nephew seeks to protect you, to look after your interests. You must realize that. Your own people think differently.' She reached over and touched Máire's arm. 'You must not worry. I will look after your little one as my own, but I will tell everyone it is a child of a cousin who has died. My husband has agreed to that. When this is all over you will be able to return to your people with an eased heart.'

The words hit Máire like a slap. She knew that Natsilane had said he would arrange it in this manner, but she'd still harboured the hope he would change his mind. Sarah, Rebecca and Yedicih's warm welcome since her arrival had fed that hope.

'What of the birthing woman you mentioned? She will know. And your nieces. Don't they know already?' Máire reached desperately for some little flaw in Natsilane's plan.

'Yes, the birthing woman will know, but she will say nothing. Birthing women know many secrets that they are bound not to tell. My nieces will say nothing. They care for you.'

Tears filled Máire's eyes and spilled over her cheeks. Yedicih put aside her basket and took her hands. 'You must not be upset. Everything will be fine.'

'How can that be?' Máire said in a broken whisper. 'I'll lose all. The baby, your nephew.' She spoke the last words so softly she hardly heard them herself.

Yedicih squeezed her hands. 'These things take time. You must have patience. My nephew shows concern for you. You can see that.'

She left Máire with those cryptic remarks to go and fetch the underdress. Máire remained seated and played idly with Brown Owl, speaking little baby words and dangling a little cloth ball in front of him while she mulled over Yedicih's words. She was so engrossed in her thoughts she didn't notice Katchekeeluh's approach until she was upon Máire, staring hard, her mouth working, muttering unintelligibly.

'Is there something wrong, Sister?' Máire used 'sister', uncertain how else she should address her.

She ignored Máire's query, bent over Brown Owl and scooped him up in her arms. 'We know when there are *Kooshdaakaa* in our midst. Stay away, Land Otter Woman,' she said darkly. She marched off with Brown Owl in her arms.

Máire stared after her, holding the little toy, too stunned to move from her place on the floor. Yedicih returned a few moments later and found Máire still holding the toy.

'What is wrong? Where is my son?'

'She took him,' Máire said in English. 'She called me a Land Otter Woman and then picked him up and took him. As though I was a poison, something that would harm him.' She looked up at Yedicih. 'I would never, never harm him. You know that, don't you?'

Yedicih knelt down beside her. 'Yes, of course. You must not mind her. She is only a little apprehensive of you since your accident in the river. It is nothing.'

She looked over at Katchekeeluh's figure huddled over the cradleboard, across the room. Yedicih drew her brow together. 'I thought that after my nephew had spoken to her, she had given it up, forgotten it.' She sighed and rose. 'I will go speak to her now. Tell her that she is mistaken.'

Máire nodded and wordlessly watched her leave, then looked down at the underdress that now rested across her lap. She drew no comfort from Yedicih's words. Katchekeelah had reminded Máire that she was an outsider here, that they were not her kin. But she was no *Kooshdaakaa*.

Rebecca found Máire in the same spot a while later, fingering the cloth ball.

She tugged at Máire's sleeve. 'Come Miss McNair, share some more stories with us. Some tales about those funny creatures, the leprechauns. Or the ones about faeries.'

'I don't think so,' Máire replied. 'It will disturb the others.' In truth, she wanted to do nothing that would call attention to herself.

'Please, Miss McNair. The other children would enjoy it, I know they would.'

A few minutes later Máire found herself seated on a side platform, near the storage area with six or seven young children clustered in front of her. Sarah had joined them, taking a seat beside Rebecca, a smile on her face. Máire had decided on the tale only moments before, when she'd eased herself down onto the pallet and felt the baby kick. With her hands folded carefully in front of her, she began.

'This is a tale of my people,' Máire paused to find her rhythm, the swoosh swoosh of the sea. 'It's a tale of the selkie folk, the seal people who shed their skins and take human form.' She spoke in English, the words rolling off her tongue, while Sarah quietly translated. Her voice was low, almost a whisper.

'It happens on a moonlit night, it does so, at the time when night equals day. A time of magic, a time of possibilities. Midsummer, we call it in my homeland. The special people, the seal people gather there in the northern corners, along our rocky shores. Ah, and what draws them there? Is it the rockpools so deep and clear and teeming with life? Or the spumey spray that tickles your nose and clings to your hair like polished pearls?

'Not one of those things is it, wondrous though they are. No, it's the music so it is, the music of the sea and the music of the land come together, inviting the seal people to one fine dance, one fine night.

'And one fine dance, one fine midsummer night, a man spied upon them from his hiding place behind a large rock. Among them he saw a woman, the fairest of the fair. Her hair, of deepest black, shone silver in the moonlit night. He'd watched her remove her skin, her silken seal covering that came away with one fluid motion to reveal herself in all her beauty, oh lah, oh lah.'

'Down along the shore came she, dancing and twirling, the music singing through her, soaring out to her legs, her arms and down her hair, wild and free. The others danced behind her so, but the man minded them not at all. And who could blame him with such a wonder to behold? No, who could blame him at all. And who could blame him so, when he crept out from his rock there and snatched the fair maid's sealskin?'

'With the sealskin tucked deep inside his coat he approached her. 'Ye must come with me now, so,' he told her. 'Ye are the fairest of the fair and I love you so.'

'But why would I come with ye,' said she, 'when all the music of the world this night calls me?'

'Ye will come with me fair seal maid,' said he. 'Your sealskin is mine, so you have no choice.'

'Oh lary me,' said she, 'oh lary me.'

'But follow along did she, for she had no choice, you see. He had her skin, her precious skin and without it she could not return to the sea.'

'They were married so and long years did she stay with him, lonely and pining for her kin. And then, just before the seventh year, this selkie woman, so sad and pale, gave birth to a child. Oh lah, such a wonder, such a dream, this little child so small and dear. She sang her song to the child, so mournful and true, the song of the selkies, the *coi ran oi ran oi roing*, that called them in.'

'And then, one night, while the child lay sleeping, all milk-cheeked in the cot, she found her sealskin, deep within her husband's chest. In her hands the sealskin came alive, as the sea and music rose in her, with its *coi ran oi ran oi ro* cry.'

'She kissed her babbie goodbye, promised some day to return, then ran down to the sea and plunged deep into the water.'

Máire closed the tale with her eyes fixed on her stomach. A sigh closed over the group and she looked up. Rebecca looked beyond Máire's shoulder.

'Was that not a wonderful tale, Brother?' she said in English.

Máire turned quickly and saw Natsilane move from the edge of the platform.

'A very moving tale, Sister,' he answered, his face unreadable.

He gave Máire an odd look, then asked Rebecca a question about Brown Owl's cradleboard. While Rebecca answered Natsilane the other children crowded around Máire and asked her about the story. Eventually, Máire slipped away, but Rebecca and Natsilane had disappeared.

She went outside, in the hope she might see the pair, but there was no sign of either of them, or anyone else that she knew who wasn't too busy at some task. She stared into the trees, recalling the tale she'd told, the selkie story that was as much her mam's story as it was a tale to be told around the fire. Rebecca, Sara and Yedicih seemed to understand its meaning for her. She thought of what Katchekeelah had called her, Land Otter Woman. Natsilane had mentioned them to her before, the *Kooshdaakaa*, the underwater beings that took the souls of the drowned. Why Katchekeelah thought Máire was such a creature she could only imagine. She shivered. She could only hope that in time she would prove it not so.

CHAPTER FORTY

Máire could barely hear Natsilane's even paddle strokes as they sliced through the water, pulling the canoe further upriver towards their destination. Up front, at the prow, Sarah paddled too, providing additional speed and support to Natsilane's efforts. Máire admired Sarah's strength and skill: that she could dip and lift the paddle, pushing the water, for such a sustained time period. The years of experience it suggested were almost daunting.

The group continued in silence, the two paddlers caught up in their rhythmic task, Rebecca dozing behind Máire, while Máire studied the towering trees that lined the river, lost in thought. Though she was glad to be away from Katchekeeluh's dark looks and constant mutterings, she was nervous about this next stage of her life. At the upper summer camp where they were headed, it would only be the four of them. There would be no escaping Natsilane's withdrawal. And despite the fact Yedicih and Sarah had explained that she would journey with them to help Sarah plan her Christian wedding and instruct her in her upcoming duties in the mission, she knew that she would feel obligated to help them as much as possible with the fishing and drying. It was more than obligation that she felt, though. She wanted to help; she wanted to learn how to be useful. But Natsilane would surely see how useless she was.

Eventually the canoe left the river for a lake where the current lessened but proved no less choppy as they ploughed their way across the surface to the far shore. The shore drew close and Máire could see a clearing with a rough shelter of woven branches and wooden poles. Near the door drying racks stood vacant and waiting while further down the shore she could see a large pit. This was to be their camp. Her heart sank.

'Such hard work, Brother,' Sarah said when they pulled alongside. She grinned. 'You spoil us with this much comfort. Our uncle would say you are becoming soft in your old age.'

Natsilane stepped out into the water, his bare feet hardly making a splash. He held the canoe steady while Sarah and then Rebecca followed without hesitation, neither of them wearing shoes or stockings to protect from the wet.

Natsilane turned and scooped Máire up in his arms, clasping her firmly to his chest. She leaned against him, looking over his shoulder, trying to make herself as small as she could in her impossible bulk. She inhaled his scent, making the most of this brief moment of closeness. Now he felt more distant than the last time she had been like this in his arms, when they first met. The silence hung between them as he swung her across the canoe's edge. Her foot caught the rim, nearly tipping it on its side.

Rebecca's laughter rang out. 'Careful, everything we have for the summer is in the canoe,' she said.

Natsilane set Máire on the shore and returned to the canoe to draw it up on the small clearing. She watched as he carefully unloaded the packs and bundles and placed them on the ground for Sarah and Rebecca to carry to the shelter. She reached down for a bundle, but he stopped her, placing a hand on her wrist.

'No. Go rest over there.' He indicated a rock at the edge of the clearing. His eyes were averted but his meaning was clear.

Fighting tears, she did as she was told and took a seat on the rock and watched the others unpack. Sarah and Rebecca arranged the fur skins under the shelter for the four of them to sleep on, then created a small hearth area and started a fire. Natsilane meanwhile stowed the basic food stores of dried fish and smoked meats safe from any curious bear and unpacked the fishing gear.

Máire watched them with a growing sense of helplessness. Except for the nights when she'd sleep in the shelter, was she to sit here for the duration of their stay?

Rebecca came over to her, grinned and grabbed her hand. 'Come, I'll show you my favourite place where we pick strawberries. We must be careful though, the bears love to go there, too.'

Máire allowed Rebecca to take her with her, past the little shelter and along the path to the woods beyond it. She appreciated Rebecca's thoughtfulness. Her misery must have been clear for all to see. She must make more of an effort.

'Hold the net like this,' Sarah said.

The three of them were knee-deep in water, their skirts hitched up in their waistbands away from the water below, their feet bare. On their heads they each wore brightly coloured scarves to keep their hair from blowing in the wind.

Máire grasped the dip net firmly, Sarah's hands over hers while she guided the motion of the net into the water. She released her hands and took up the basket Rebecca handed her.

'Now bring it up quickly and hold it for a few minutes while the water drains.'

Máire did as she was told, delighted with the results. She laughed as the water poured away and some of the fish jumped out of the net. There were so many around her that she knew the next time she'd get just as much. After the net had drained sufficiently she swung it towards Sarah who stood ready with the basket.

'You've got it now,' Rebecca said. 'That's a good haul.'

Sarah retreated to the shore where the pit lay ready to receive the catch. Máire dipped her net in and pulled it up laden again with more fish and poured it into Rebecca's basket. Rebecca retreated to shore as Sarah returned with her empty basket. They continued using this system for a good while.

During a pause Máire asked Rebecca the question that had pressed her for some time. 'This is such work for you two. Do you do this every year?'

'Usually we are here with Uncle and the servants do much of the work. But this year my brother feels an obligation to Uncle and will add this catch to their own at the other camp.'

There was no need to state the reason for the obligation, Máire knew. For the first time she realized the amount of hardship Sarah and Rebecca as well as Natsilane were enduring for her sake.

As the net work progressed Máire found she could just about manage it, especially with her bulk, but she was determined to be useful. She was glad she'd insisted on learning the nets now, even over the objections Natsilane had given on one of the few times he'd spoken directly to her. She looked further down the shore where Natsilane worked tirelessly on his own, away from her, clad only in shortened canvas trousers, grease-stained and salt-stiffened from years of use. Even from her vantage point she could see the corded muscles working in his arms as he gathered in the seine net filled with hooligan.

Though the four of them slept together on the furs in the shelter at night, Natsilane was careful to keep his distance. She tried to accept his actions and ignore the tightness in her chest, lightened only marginally by Rebecca and Sarah's warm companionship.

Hours later, her muscles screaming, she raised herself up and put her hand to her back to give it a rub. She heaved a sigh and wiped her brow. On the shore Sarah helped Natsilane empty his latest catch into the pit. He looked up and caught her eye. She tried for a smile. He dropped the net, said a few words to Sarah and strode out to her.

'You've done enough now,' he said when he reached her side. He took the net from her hands and led her back to the shore to the rock at the camp's edge.

She nodded, too tired to protest and took her seat. He leaned over her and for a few brief seconds massaged her back. His hands were gentle and probing and the relief they produced was deep. She didn't dare move or look up at him, afraid of disturbing the welcome touch. A touch that brought not only relief, but also a connection she couldn't deny.

His fingers were gone almost before they arrived, though his touch lingered. 'Thank you,' she said. She stole a glance up at him and saw the concern that remained for only a moment replaced by something more neutral.

'Stay there for now,' he said. 'We can manage fine.'

Before she could reply he turned and left to resume his tasks. She rested there and tried to ease her back and arms, but there was no ease for her soul.

Just as quickly as it began, the hooligan run was over and they were left with a pit full of food, preservative and lubricant. Before any further preparation could be done they had to wait for the fish to ferment for nine days, a process that sent odours throughout the camp that grew stronger every day.

While they waited they turned their attention to other tasks. They prepared nets, fashioned salmon weirs and created fishing lines, and Natsilane hunted the ducks, geese and other small game that now started to reveal itself in the late spring weather. Sarah and Rebecca showed Máire how each task was done. They helped her twist and weave the spruce roots to mend the nets, fasten the hooks on the lines and explained how to block the little inlet to create the weir.

It was when they were constructing the weir that Máire first saw the seals, their barks echoing along the inlet. Oh Mam, she thought. The seals are here. She reached up for the medallion that lay beneath her tunic dress in its place of safety and watched them leap and play in the water, slicing the current, whiskers twitching and mouths wide. Rebecca and Sarah paused in their labours and joined her vigil. Who could resist such joy? Who indeed. Máire smiled.

The days passed and Máire helped with more of the tasks as her skills progressed. Sarah showed her how to gut fish and indicated the unused parts to return to the water as thanks for its bounty. Máire also cut up fish for the cooking pot, gathered wood for the fire and cleaned their bowls and the pot after their meals. With Rebecca she helped pick some of the greens, like wild celery, that grew close to the camp, their young shoots just beginning to show themselves in the warmer weather.

It was just after she'd put some wild celery in a pot of water one morning, sitting by the hearth fire, that Sarah pulled down the rabbit hanging from the rack and placed it in Máire's lap. Máire looked up and saw Sarah grin.

'Something a little more difficult to try.'

Máire fiddled with the rabbit, uncertain where to begin. She supposed Sarah meant for her to skin it. But though Cook had done it more times than she could count she had to confess she never really took notice of Cook's method.

Sarah sat down beside her. 'Here, I'll get you started.'

With a deft stroke she cut into the fur and began the process, explaining each step. After a moment or two she handed it over to Máire. She tried her best, but she found she took more flesh than skin away with the knife. When she was finished Sarah calmly took the rabbit from her and with a few sure strokes improved Máire's poor efforts as best she could.

'I'm hopeless at this I'm afraid,' Máire said. She pulled the shawl she wore up higher around her neck to cut the breeze blowing there. She had it crossed along her chest and tied at the back so it freed her arms, like the workwomen at home in Ireland. 'I fear I'll never be very good at this.' She still spoke in a mixture of Tlingit and English, though her grasp of their language was growing by leaps and bounds.

'Have patience. You will find your way soon enough. Skinning takes practice, that's all. And you are quite deft at keeping the fire at an even burn now.'

Máire picked at her bare toe, then tucked it up under her skirts as she watched Sarah work with speed and skill to finish the task. She tried to take comfort in Sarah's words.

She straightened up, wiped the sweat that poured down the side of her face with the back of her hand and inhaled the summer smells of fresh cedar and dried grass that assailed her. With her heightened senses she found such odours restored her and eased the discomfort of her ever-swelling breasts and belly. She felt a kick and jumped a little, surprised. Such events seemed to occur more when she rested than when she worked, as if the baby knew all there was to do.

'What is it?' Rebecca asked. She continued at her work at the next tree, carefully removing the cedar bark for later use in the weaving. Beneath her lay a respectable bundle cut previously.

'It's nothing. The baby kicked.' She wiped her brow again and pulled her scarf further down to better absorb the sweat. 'It's so very hot.'

Rebecca looked over at her. 'It's the pregnancy. It makes you feel the heat.' She grinned suddenly, walked over and grabbed her hand. 'Come with me.'

Before she could say anything Rebecca led her through the trees to a secluded spot by the water. With a few deft movements Rebecca pulled off her tunic and splashed her way into the small pool.

'Come on,' she shouted.

She laughed then turned and dived under the water. Though Máire looked longingly at the water, after all these weeks at the camp she was still stunned by Rebecca's absolute lack of modesty. But who was she to worry about modesty, for she stood clad in nothing more than a shift, in an advanced state of pregnancy. What would Rebecca think of her body? She'd hardly allowed herself a close examination and was always quick about her ablutions, lifting her tunic for a brief daily wash.

She removed her clothes with great hesitation and eased her way into the water. Looking down at the taut skin along her engorged breasts she noticed the ruddy brown area that circled her reddened nipples. She traced the faint pattern of fragile blue veins along the pale skin and rested her finger on the medallion. The baby kicked again as if to remind her of its strength.

The water flowed over her, feeling cool and silky against her skin as she turned her face up towards the warmth of the sun. She loosed her hair, removed the snood and pulled out the pins so that she could give it a much-needed washing. Rebecca swam over to her and, with some leaves she found and crushed, she helped her with the task. Máire submerged her body fully to rinse her hair and watched it stream out in front, floating like flotsam on the water's surface. A lullaby drifted through her mind and she began to hum along as she turned over and pushed her way through the water, her body no longer cumbersome, but buoyant and graceful in the water. She sang more and broke her head through the water, certain she would catch sight of the seals; they would recognize her call. But there was no sight of them.

The cold eventually compelled her to give up and join Rebecca on the shore. She climbed out of the water, sat on the grass, and set about untangling her hair. Rebecca took a seat beside Máire, her own hair a wet streak down her back. 'Don't bother with your hair now. Let me comb it for you when we get back. Will you allow me?'

Máire looked at her, surprised at the request. It seemed like such a sisterly action and she was flattered and heartened by such a wish. 'I would love to have you comb my hair. Thank you for asking.'

Rebecca smiled at her, a great show of teeth and bright eyes. Her gaze then flickered down to Máire's bare, stretched belly. 'Does it hurt?' she asked.

Máire felt her face redden, her arms automatically going down around it. 'No,' she said quietly. 'It doesn't hurt. Not yet.'

She asked Máire no further questions, simply shooting another bright smile in Máire's direction and catching up her tunic over her head, anxious to be off to fetch the comb. Máire hastily pulled on her underdress and snatched up her skirt and scarf and followed her.

Back at the camp Rebecca sat Máire down in front of the shelter and, with comb in hand, she began to separate sections of Máire's hair, working the tangles with slow careful precision. Her touch was gentle. She pressed lightly against Máire's head with her fingers as she trailed down slowly through Máire's thick hair. It was a restful experience, something she had not encountered as a child, when severe brushings by her nurse were seen as chores rather than pleasures. It was only under Annie's care that she discovered its soothing quality. In Rebecca's hands the experience was so calming, Máire closed her eyes and drifted off into a half-sleep.

'Look Brother, her hair is nearly as long as our sister's, and just as thick.'

Máire's eyes flew open. She couldn't see him and she dare not turn around but she could feel his presence, weighing her down, igniting her emotions. A wave of desire washed over her. She licked her lips, and then bit them in shame at feeling such things with a child in her belly. Natsilane moved away, his footfall sure and deliberate.

Rebecca tapped her shoulder. 'My sister is considered to have very fine hair, you know. That counts for much among us.'

Máire muttered her thanks to Rebecca and tried to draw her bare legs slowly up under her tunic.

'You must keep still. I don't want to hurt you.' Rebecca pulled the comb through the right side of Máire's head down through to the end at her waist, then placed the comb down beside her. In the cool breeze and warm sun Máire's hair was nearly dry. 'Will you let me braid it and pin it up for you?'

'Of course. Let me get my hair things.' Máire reached over to look among her hastily grabbed bundle for the pins and snood, but couldn't see them. Had they been in her hand when Rebecca helped her clean her hair? She couldn't remember.

'Never mind,' Rebecca said.

She took Máire's hair and began to braid it, deftly dividing the hair and twisting the strands among themselves. When she had finished Máire had two braids tied neatly at the ends with thin strips of rawhide.

'There,' she said. 'It suits you. You look just like a proper Tlingit woman, now.' Máire could only nod, suddenly feeling much less than any kind of Tlingit, proper or otherwise.

The seals appeared again at the inlet, attracted by the fish that gathered in the weir. Máire was glad they'd returned and went to feed them to lure them from the weir. They came to her, their barks begging for the fish she dangled from her hand. And so it became a regular event, a ritual of her own making that grew each day. She talked, then sang and then patted their heads. She gave them each a secret name. They kissed her hand and then eventually her cheek when she gave them their fish. A kiss hello. A kiss goodbye.

Natsilane caught her at it once, but only shook his head and walked away. She was certain she saw a shadow of a smile.

In the days that followed Máire found a small pile of fish by her basket, ready for the seals.

Rebecca twisted the last bit of hide on the end of Máire's freshly braided hair. Máire looked up and spotted figures coming toward them. They emerged from the woodland some yards from the campsite.

'Hello!' Máire cried.

She raised her hand to greet Yedicih then eased herself up from her seat. She fought the lumbering gait of her eighth month and made her way towards the figures, but the sandy soil made it impossible. Rebecca raced ahead of Máire to join Yedicih and an older woman wearing a bright-coloured scarf. Lines carved the woman's face like weathered wood, but her eyes were kind for all that. She eyed Máire closely as she approached.

Yedicih smiled and embraced Máire when she reached her. Brown Owl peeked sleepily over her shoulder from the blanket that tied him to her.

'Welcome, Aunts,' Rebecca said. 'You're over at the summer camp now?'

'Yes,' Yedicih said. 'We arrived a few days ago.'

After a few moments' fuss over the baby, Yedicih introduced the woman beside her. 'This is our birthing woman. I've asked her to come and examine you, since the time is nearly here for you to deliver the child.'

'Where is your camp?' Máire asked as they walked on towards the shelter, her steps feeling heavier, the weight and size of her belly almost too much to carry. She tried not to think about the birth.

'It's not far, an hour's walk from here,' Yedicih said. 'So we have some time for a good visit before we have to return.'

When Máire reached the camp, Yedicih led her inside the little shelter and helped Máire remove her skirt, leaving her underdress to cover her, while the birthing woman looked on. Rebecca remained outside with Sarah and Brown Owl and watched Natsilane make his way back to the camp. Máire hoped the exam would be over before he arrived.

Under the birthing woman's eagle eye, Yedicih lifted the underdress high up by Máire's arms to allow her access. Grim-faced, Máire endured the probing and pushing, both standing and seated on the blankets, holding Yedicih's hand for comfort. The birthing woman grunted and muttered while her large worn hands worked expertly along Máire's body.

Finally, she looked up and asked Máire questions about the baby, her bodily functions and her dreams.

'Dreams?' Máire was puzzled, thinking perhaps she had translated incorrectly. She nodded. Máire stared at her then shook her head. 'Nothing.' Her dreams were nothing she would have her know.

She shrugged and left Yedicih and Máire together while she accepted Sarah's hospitality outside. Máire could hear Natsilane talking to them and teasing Brown Owl.

'She is pleased,' Yedicih said. 'You are in good health and so is the baby.'

'You could tell that from her mumblings?' Máire asked, her voice a little tart. She pulled down her underdress and reached for her skirt.

Yedicih touched her shoulder lightly. 'Don't worry. My nephew will come for me and the birthing woman when it's time. We're only a short distance away.'

It was a halfhearted thanks that came out of Máire's mouth. She tried to appreciate all of Yedicih's kindness, but she could not help the sense of grief that suddenly swelled in her like a great tide. This would all end when the baby arrived. She would have to leave here, leave Sarah, Rebecca and Natsilane to go back to the mission to a life she knew she could no longer endure. Natsilane and her child would be near her, to watch and perhaps to speak to, but never to touch. Never to hold it as her own child in her arms, to kiss its face as a mother would. Or to kiss Natsilane as a lover would. Máire would still see them, but it would not be the same.

She looked down at her chapped, reddened hands with their broken nails, and took some pride in what she had managed to do in the few months since she'd arrived. But it was not enough. Soon everything would change. And she could not bear it.

Yedicih took up Máire's hand, led her outside and away from her thoughts. They talked for a short while until Yedicih rose to depart.

'We must go if we are to get back to our camp before dark. My husband will worry.' She turned to Máire and glanced at Natsilane who stood on the other side by Sarah.

'One thing I should mention, though it is probably nothing. Just before we left the village, Betty accompanied Joseph when he came to speak with my husband. She spoke at some length with my sister. But I am glad to say that my sister has ceased to make those foolish accusations about you.'

While Yedicih discussed Katchekeeluh's comments about Máire with Natsilane, Máire sat in silence, mulling over her news. Her heart started beating rapidly, the earlier despair replaced with a sharp sense of panic. She'd become so consumed with her life here she had forgotten to send word to the Paxsons that she was spending the summer at the camps. Máire could only hope that someone had seen fit to explain to Betty a credible reason for her early departure.

CHAPTER FORTY-ONE

She stood under the trees just away from the shoreline, out of site of the camp, and watched him cast the net across the water. The motion was fluid, full of such practiced grace, and for a moment the net hung there, suspended in the sharp breeze that blew from the west, until it fell feather-light to sink gently into the water. He stood there, patient as any eagle, and waited before gathering it up, hand over hand, filled to the brim.

She watched him when she could, greedy for all the moments she could find. He was always working like a demon, pushing his body to its limits, while the food stores piled to impressive heights. They all worked hard, she had enough calluses to prove it, but none worked harder than he.

She turned from her vigil and picked up her basket of berries, her usual excuse for her spying trips. She picked her way through the trees, taking care not to step on anything that might cut her bare feet. They were hardened to most things, but now and then a sharp stone could still bring a wince of pain.

Reaching the camp she handed her basket to Sarah and sat beside her with a groan. The baby had dropped now, which made sitting much less comfortable, even in the sandy soil. Sarah gave her a sympathetic smile and began to remove the berries from the basket and place them in the drying tray next to the others.

'Why don't you sing one of your Irish songs?' she said. 'One of those your cook would sing.'

Máire searched her mind for a tune. 'The Spanish Lady' came to mind. She looked down at her bare feet. Maybe that was what inspired the notion. She heard the first note in her head and began.

As I was walking through Dublin City
About the hour of twelve at night
It was there I saw a pretty fair female
Washing her feet by candlelight.

She continued the song, getting the rhythm and enjoying the lilt. Sarah clapped and Rebecca came over and joined in as Máire told of the lady who tempted a man as she washed her feet over the 'ambry coals.' They all laughed at the words and she blushed at their probing questions as they insisted she explain the idea of 'a lady of ill repute.'

'Was not one of Jesus' women such a type?' Sarah asked. 'Why would Christians find such women offensive?'

Máire struggled to explain. How had she become entangled in a religious discussion? 'Yes, but you see, Jesus forgave her despite her actions.'

After a few more comments they let the topic go and pressed her instead for another song. She searched her memory and came up with a song that had no harm in it as far as she could detect. Máire was just midway through it when a loud voice interrupted her singing.

'I would expect nothing more than to find you singing like some hoyden,' Mrs Paxson said.

Máire looked up from her task and rose awkwardly, self-consciously tucking a small strand of hair under her scarf. 'Mrs Paxson,' she murmured. A puzzled and weary looking Mr Paxson stood behind her.

'So, it's true. Betty wasn't mistaken,' Mrs Paxson said.

Her voice was hard as steel as she surveyed Máire, taking in her belly, now pushed out far beyond the folds of her skirt. Máire's hand went there now, as if to protect the child within from what she knew was to come.

'Look at you, dressed as a heathen. Acting the whore that you are.'

'I am not a whore,' Máire said loudly.

Máire's words only seemed to incense her. Her face, mottled with anger, flushed deeper with each sentence.

'You are most certainly a whore. A wanton manipulative whore. At first I couldn't believe it when Betty told me what you had done. I didn't think that anyone would bring such shame upon the mission and its work, bring shame upon the Presbyterian Church. Even you. But I was mistaken. You, who we took in and made a part of the mission, a part of God's work. And how do you thank us? You betray us.'

'I did not betray anyone,' Máire told her, her anger flaring. 'It was not planned, I did not do it to shame anyone.'

She clenched her hands at her sides to stop them from shaking. Her legs were suddenly drenched and she shifted them closer together. She would not be cowed.

She looked over at Mr Paxson but he just shook his head, his eyes dark and sad. Though she knew she shouldn't have expected his support, it still hurt to see his disappointment. Máire wanted him to understand, to see that she had not failed him, that she was not what he thought she was. As if sensing her struggle, Sarah moved to stand beside her. Rebecca had vanished, slipping away at Mrs Paxson's first words.

'Máire is a good person,' Sarah said. 'She is my friend and the friend of many of us here. She will remain so.'

'I did not ask your opinion, Missy.' Mrs Paxson momentarily transferred her hard stare to Sarah.

'I have nothing to thank you for either. If not for your friend's interference Joseph would have married Betty, a woman much more suited to the work ahead of him. As it is now, I fear the Mission Board will not advance him as quickly.'

'Joseph is happy.' Máire's voice found strength after Sarah's defence. 'He will be a good husband to Sarah, and she a good wife to him. That's what matters.'

'And you, what do you propose to do with yourself, now that you are ruined? Don't think the Mission Board will have you, or your bastard. You'll have no home back with us.'

'It is none of your affair.' Máire flung the words at her. 'You have had little care for me from the start, so I would not have expected anything from you or your mission. A mission that will fail if you do not put a leash on your pride.'

'Oh, it is indeed my affair, young lady. I will write to the Mission Board the instant I return and inform them of the state of things. They shall know in Sitka soon enough, and no decent person there or anywhere in Alaska will look upon you, except perhaps a poor miner, desperate for some warmth at night.'

'She has no need to look for a home, Madam,' Natsilane's voice boomed from behind Máire.

She turned around to find him striding towards them, Rebecca not far behind. He came up to Máire's side and put his arm around her shoulders. Máire tried to hide her surprise as he pulled her close to him.

'Máire will stay with us, with my clan. She is my wife, and it is my child she carries.' Natsilane looked directly at Mrs Paxson, his gaze unwavering. Máire remained still beside him, too stunned to move.

'You are married? When? How?' Mrs Paxson narrowed her eyes, her voice steely and controlled once more. 'Forgive me if I find it difficult to believe, but there has been no opportunity for you to be wed. The minister has not set foot outside Sitka since Martha arrived.'

'We are married under Tlingit law. A law that has weight and meaning among my people. And since it is among my people that we live, that is the law that will serve us. We do not need your Christian babblings to make it a true marriage.'

So stunned was she by his words that Máire could only stand beside him blankly, and wait to be told that it was all a joke, that his words were just for show.

'It is true,' Sarah said. 'They are married. As married as any couple I know.'

Mrs Paxson looked from Natsilane to Sarah and then finally to Máire. 'Well, it seems you have found your bed and now you must lie in it. But as far as the mission is concerned, you are finished. I will send Joseph with your things and a resignation letter I expect you to sign.'

Without waiting for Máire's reply she turned and retreated down the path, Mr Paxson following behind, limping slightly. Máire wanted to go after him, to at least thank him for all that he'd done for her, but she had no energy to move. The strain had been too much. Máire sagged against Natsilane.

'Are you alright?' Natsilane asked, his voice filled with concern.

Máire allowed herself a moment to feel his arms around her and savour the soft words directed towards her.

'I'll be fine in a minute.' Máire put her hand to her stomach, feeling a dull ache at its base. 'I just need to catch my breath.'

'Here, come sit down.' Natsilane drew Máire to the small rock and eased her on to it. She felt a twinge and grimaced. 'You must not let her words upset you, Máire. They mean nothing.'

'Nothing?'

Though Máire put on a brave face, she was starting to shake, as she began to truly understand her situation. 'She'll eventually get to my father, I have no doubts on that score, and he will never accept me back.' Her mind spun. What would she do? Where would she go? Máire had to think.

'There is no need to worry about what she will do. You will stay with us, as I told her, as part of the clan.'

'But you told her that we were married.' Máire looked behind him at Sarah. 'Sarah even supported your statement. You both lied to her.'

'We will make it truth.' He leaned down and brushed the hair back from Máire's face. 'That is if you wish to make it the truth.'

Máire stared up into his eyes, seeing her own face mirrored there. The words she had so long hoped for had been spoken. Could he mean it? Máire swallowed hard.

'What about your doubts? What about our differences?'

Tears spilled down her cheeks and she gulped for air. A sudden pain seized her and she gasped, doubling over with its sharpness. The baby was coming.

Their son was born as the sun was setting, there on the shore facing the lake, upon blankets woven with the finest quality goat hair. Sarah rubbed him in seal oil and rolled him in soft dry moss and pieces of old blanket before she presented him to Máire who pulled him against her naked, sweat-soaked body, all pain forgotten in the joy of holding him.

She looked over at Natsilane. 'Our son,' she said, and smiled. Nothing could shake her mood.

'Our son, Wife,' he said, and he leaned over and kissed Máire on the forehead.

She felt the baby stir beside her, small gurglings that pierced her light sleep. With a sleepy yawn she sat up, the fur coverings slipping from her bare shoulders, and pulled the baby to her lap. The baby rooted around at her chest until he found her nipple. Goal achieved, he suckled greedily. She sighed and looked down at his dark hair and eyes in contentment. Her little selkie boy.

'Hungry again?' Natsilane asked. He pulled back the fur skin and sat up beside her and watched with shy interest.

'Yedicih says it won't happen so often in the night after a month or so.'

'A month?' He gave a wry grin.

She laughed softly. Though it was only the three of them in the shelter, she was conscious that Sarah and Rebecca were sleeping nearby, in their own newly constructed shelter. She also acknowledged that she selfishly wanted to keep these moments just between herself and Natsilane.

Natsilane rubbed her back. Since the baby's birth this supportive gesture had become a nightly routine and it thrilled her. She'd been a little self-conscious at first under his watchful gaze, but now she loved it so that every night she almost felt disappointed when the baby finished and she had to place him all sleepy-eyed back into his nest of furs.

'Have you given any thought to a name for the baby?' she asked.

'Have you?'

'It's for you to choose, Husband.' She said the word tentatively, but she meant it. 'It's the custom after all.'

He brushed a strand of hair from her face. 'We'll make our own custom now.'

'I would like you to choose.'

She smiled and looked down at the baby. He was dozing now, finished with his meal. She covered her breast and was about to lay the baby down when Natsilane put a hand on her bare shoulder.

'May I?'

She placed the baby in his arms, taking care of its head. Natsilane held him gingerly. He looked over at her and encircled her with his free arm. She remained there until tiredness overcame her and her head started to bob. Natsilane eased her down into the furs and then, after placing the baby between them, he lay down beside them.

She reached carefully through the branches for the large salmon berries that hung ripe and lush at the back of the bush, taking care not to jolt her son who was strapped to her chest with a blanket. He stirred in his sleep, snuggling down deeper against her. She found that, strapped in this manner in the heat of late summer, he dozed contentedly against her while she moved along the shrubs, picking berries, cutting spruce roots to weave for baskets, or carrying out any other task that took her away from their camp. Lately, though, she found he was getting heavy. His weeks of his greedy nursing had put weight on him.

She turned at the sound of someone or something approaching. 'La, la, la,' she sang, in case it was a bear. In truth she'd not seen one yet, but that didn't mean there wouldn't be a first time. She breathed a sigh of relief as Yedicih came into view.

'Niece, you're looking well.'

Máire found she still blushed with pleasure at the name 'niece'. 'I feel well, thank you.' She looked down at her arms, browned thoroughly from the sun. No more ladylike paleness.

'Sarah told me that you were here, so I left my son in her care and came to find you.'

'I'm delighted you've come.'

Yedicih moved beside her and peeked over her shoulder to view the baby. 'If it's possible, I think he's grown in these last few days since I saw him.'

The baby stirred against her at the sound of Yedicih's voice, a movement that caused a slight ache. She laughed. 'He certainly feels as if he's grown.'

'Here, let me take him while we walk back to the camp.' She reached over and helped Máire unstrap the baby, and took him into her arms. Máire picked up the basket of berries and followed Yedicih, chatting and exchanging news.

It was a little while later, after the two were settled by the hearth fire along with Sarah and Rebecca and the two babies on the blanket beside them, that Yedicih shared her real news.

'We have heard that Mr Paxson is very ill and has taken to his bed.'

'Oh, no,' Máire said. 'That's awful. I hope it's not serious.' She could only imagine what Mrs Paxson would make of such a turn of events. However much she might appear self-sufficient, Máire knew she relied on her husband for much.

'I understand that it is. But we must hope for his recovery.'

'What a shame, he's such a nice man.'

'Will that affect my sister's wedding?' Rebecca asked. She glanced at Sarah who frowned.

'I don't know,' Yedicih said. She lay a comforting hand on Sarah's. 'There are still many weeks until that time. Your holy man and his wife have returned, so that won't be a problem.

'And there's other news too. The trading company have gone ahead with their plans and have hired many Chilkat to build a wharf. Mrs Paxson is very angry about it and is asking the holy man to help her stop it.'

'But what can he do?' Sarah asked.

Yedicih shrugged. 'I don't know.'

Máire saw Natsilane emerge from the woods, his arms filled with a bulky item wrapped in a skin and tied with spruce root cord. When he arrived at the camp he greeted everyone and lay the mysterious package down in front of her.

She gave him a quizzical glance. 'What's this?' she asked.

'It's for you,' he said, his voice shy. 'Well, for you and our son.' Carefully she removed the cord and unwrapped the skin to reveal a finely wrought cradleboard. The leather straps were carefully worked, decorated with small shells, and the board itself was painted and carved with a distinct image of a wolf.

'It's beautiful,' Máire said. She looked up at him and took his hand.

For the moment she could say no more.

'Your son has a fine cradleboard, Nephew, but he has no name,' Yedicih said, her voice firm.

Natsilane laughed and smiled, then crouched down beside Máire, his eyes twinkling. 'Well, by rights it should be 'One Who is Always Hungry', or 'Big Fat Cheeks'.' He laid a hand on her shoulder. 'But since he has my wife's eyes, maybe we should call him 'Little Seal'.' He said the words in English, to mark in his own way, in deference to the custom.

Rebecca clapped her hands. 'Yes, yes,' she said. She reached over and tugged her brother's arm. 'And now you two must have a marriage feast. It is only right.'

Natsilane gave Yedicih an uneasy glance. She smiled at him. 'Of course you must. I can see no reason why you can't have a small feast right here.' She gestured around her. 'There is enough food to give many feasts.'

'A marriage feast? Here?' Máire asked. Though Natsilane had said they would be married under Tlingit law, she assumed that it would really not be possible, given Katchekeeluh's influence and Natsilane's own dubious position. That he called her 'Wife' was enough.

'Yes. A small feast. I will come with Brown Owl. I will bring Kowishte too. He will want to be present at his nephew's feast.' She said the words with conviction and Máire could only hope it was true.

CHAPTER FORTY-TWO

Yedicih removed the silver bangles from her arm and slid them over Máire's wrist and the silver rings that now adorned her fingers. Beside her Sarah threaded silver rings through her newly pierced ears and Rebecca brushed her hair that hung loose down to her waist. The medallion rested against the bright-coloured calico tunic, a perfect match for the other jewellery that adorned her.

'Aunt, do you have a nose ring?' Sarah asked.

'A nose ring?' She fought a wave of panic.

Yedicih shook her head solemnly. 'No, I didn't bring one.'

Sarah laughed. 'What a shame,' she said.

Máire studied her face and gave a weak laugh. It was a jest, after all.

Her hair finished, Yedicih crowned her head with a wide beaded headband trimmed with ermine, and Rebecca draped a heavy blanket woven in hues of pale yellow, black and blue on her shoulders, its edge covered in fur. It was very fine, the design so elaborate she could not make out its emblem.

'This is lovely. It's too good for me, surely.'

'It is mine,' Yedicih said. 'It is not too fine for you. For are you not my niece?'

Máire looked across at Yedicih's beautiful face with its high cheekbones and dark, slanting eyes. 'I am honoured that I shall be your kin. I couldn't wish for more.'

'Ah, but you shall have more.' Yedicih smiled and reached inside the sack beside her. She pulled out a pair of moccasins, made of the softest, whitest doeskin and elegantly beaded with tiny shells.

'My nephew asked me to give these to you. To wear at the feast.'

Máire took them from her, too moved to speak, and placed them carefully on her feet. 'They're perfect. This is all perfect.'

And perfect it was. When she was dressed, Sarah and Yedicih led her to sit at Natsilane's side at the place of honour, in front of the small group headed by Kowishte. She was gratified to see a few other Chilkoot had chosen to come as well, one of them holding a drum.

After she was settled, Kowishte rose and spoke words of welcome. She reached under Natsilane's own blanket for a reassuring hand. Natsilane seemed unperturbed by the ceremony. He sat calmly beside her, cloaked in his own blanket, his arms lined with bangles, his fingers and ears full of rings. She was grateful for his attention to all the details and appreciated the honour it indicated.

It was the last detail, though, that caused her to stare for a moment. Like his uncle, Natsilane had chosen to wear a ring on his nose. He glanced at her sideways and for a brief moment he winked.

Máire couldn't help but smile in return and settled into her seat to enjoy the ceremony. Feasting was the central tenet of the ceremony; a meal shared between a couple and witnessed by their relations sealed the link and made them husband and wife. Máire ate little, each bite she brought to her lips accompanied by the sonorous tinkle of her bracelets. She tried to keep her eyes downcast, like any proper bride, but couldn't help but steal periodic glances at Natsilane. He remained calm, chatting with his uncle and the other guests present.

When a baby's wail broke the chatter she couldn't help but look up, wondering if it was her own. Yedicih had placed him in the care of one of the servants who nursed a baby of her own so that Máire might be free throughout the feast and the night to follow. It was the longest time she'd been away from her son and she missed him terribly, despite the joyous occasion.

The feasting ended eventually and they all left for their beds, Natsilane and Máire retiring to a private shelter. There she carefully removed her finery and lay with him on their bed of blankets and furs, a wife in truth.

The occasional bite in the air and the faint smell of decaying leaves and plants signalled autumn's approach and with it the need pack up the camp and return to their winter homes. It also heralded the imminent approach of Sarah's wedding. Joseph had sent reassuring messages to confirm that all would go ahead as planned. To Máire, in some ways, leaving the camp also meant the real start of her new life; she would go with Natsilane to live in his cabin, a short distance from Kowishte's village.

It was a journey made with joy, Sarah anxious to tackle the final preparations for the ceremony and greet the guests that would soon be arriving from far-flung villages, ready to honour a niece of Kowishte's high status. Máire's own happiness she owed to the others in the canoe and the dramatic turn of events since last she'd journeyed on the river.

When she arrived at the cabin, Little Seal in the cradleboard on her back, she hesitated at the doorway, suddenly uncertain. Natsilane came up behind her, laden with provisions.

'You'll have to take off the cradleboard if you want me to carry you across.'

She turned her head to look at him and laughed. 'Not at all. I was just surveying your little castle.' She looked back and peered inside. 'Well, not quite a castle.'

'I can make some improvements if you like. I hope to make some furniture. A table and whatnot.' His voice held a hint of anxiety.

'No, it's fine,' she said.

She made her way in and swung the cradleboard from her back and set it against the wall. The baby was still asleep. That was something, then. She looked around her. It was bare of furnishings except for a small bunk filled with furs on the side and a stove for heat and cooking in the corner. She raised a brow. She'd not expected this much, in truth. She remembered the coffee beans. Exactly how traditional was her husband?

'You might start a fire in the stove, while I bring up the rest of our things.' He indicated the store of sticks by the stove. She took a deep breath and nodded. This was it. She would begin with laying the fire.

Some time later, Máire heard someone enter the cabin. She looked up from the pot she stirred and saw that it was Yedicih.

'Aunt, you are well?'

'I am well, Niece. And you?'

Máire nodded. They'd fallen into a mixture of Tlingit and English that suited them both. 'Would you share in this soup I've made? It's ready now and Natsilane won't be back for some time.' She reached for a two large ladle spoons that lay in the basket beside the pot.

'Yes, thank you.' Yedicih made her way over to the bunk and sat down. Máire handed her a ladle filled with soup.

When they were both settled and had taken sips, Máire asked after Sarah and Rebecca.

'They are both well. Sarah is busy hosting all the guests that have arrived. So many gifts they've brought. She'll need a whole room just for them.'

Máire smiled at the thought of Mrs Paxson allowing the extra room. 'Have you any news from the mission? Did Mr Paxson recover?'

'Joseph tells us that he is still ill, but there is hope he will recover.' She frowned. 'But there is other news, that's not so good. The chief's nephew is dead.'

'Kowklux's nephew? How?'

'It happened when he was working on the wharf for the trading company. A tree fell on him and killed him instantly.'

'Oh, no. How awful. Kowklux must be very upset.'

'He is. They say he has demanded reparation from the trading company. Many, many blankets, canoes and silver. The company have refused to pay it.'

'That sounds serious. What will happen? What will the Chilkat do?'

Yedicih shook her head her face grim. 'They will not take it lightly.'

Máire bit her lip, wondering how the trading company would handle any response the Chilkat might make.

Sarah's wedding day finally arrived. Máire rose early and donned her skirt and tunic top and braided her hair as she always did now. She looked at the medallion that lay in the little basket beside the bed and decided to leave it there with the other silver pieces. Better to keep her dress as simple as possible in front of Katchekeeluh.

In his basket Little Seal fretted softly, picking up her tension as she made him ready, strapped him into his cradleboard and hefted him on her back. She glanced over at Natsilane, just stirring under the skins that protected him from the chill autumn morning. She'd let the fire die, reasoning to herself that they would be away for a day and night. Was that the right decision? She still had so much to learn.

Natsilane's eyes fluttered open. 'Are you off, then?'

She nodded and bent down to kiss him shyly on the head, the full weight of Little Seal pressing on her back. He seemed to get heavier each day. Soon he would be crawling and getting into everything. She glanced briefly around the cabin and noted the many hazards. The cradleboard took on a whole new meaning for her.

With a brief clasp of Natsilane's hand she left the cabin and made her way through the underbrush to the village outskirts, then along the path that led to Kowishte's house. The boards shone bright with the freshly renewed Kaagwantaan wolf crest. She entered the house tentatively, glancing around for any sign of Katchekeeluh. There were a few men donning capes and hats and women making adjustments on their own finery, but no sign of Katchekeeluh.

Quickly she made her way over to Sarah's side of the platform and the voices that came from behind the blanket. She pulled it aside and saw a small group of women, Yedicih included, clustered around Sarah, combing her hair and adorning her arms, fingers and ears with silver bangles, rings and hoops. Katchekeeluh stood behind them all and watched. When she caught sight of Máire she gave a pointed frown, muttered something under her breath and strode past her, back out into the large room.

Yedicih nudged Sarah who turned around and smiled at Máire. 'Welcome, Sister,' she said and stretched out her hand. 'I'm so happy you've come.' She handed Máire a small silver ring. 'You can help me with this.'

'What is it?'

Sarah's smile became mischievous. 'It's a nose ring.'

Máire stared down at the object in the palm of her hand. How on earth was she to put it on Sarah's nose?

Sarah's laughter rang out. 'No need to look so worried. I was only teasing you.' She removed the silver ring from Máire's open palm and with some dexterity and fixed it onto her nose. Máire stared at the result, struck not only by its impact, but that she should find it somehow regal.

While the other two women murmured their own approval Máire backed away and surveyed the whole result. The embroidered and beaded hide tunic fell in soft folds around her lithe figure. Her dark hair draped her shoulders and hung down her back.

Yedicih squeezed Máire's hand. 'Doesn't she look beautiful?'

'Very beautiful. Like a queen.'

Yedicih touched her shoulder. 'I have something for you.' She reached over beside Sarah's sleeping pallet and unfurled a red blanket edged with a single line of pearl buttons. She handed it to Máire. 'Put it on. It's for today.'

Sarah, Yedicih and the other two women helped Máire drape it around her shoulders, arranging the folds so that it covered her completely. 'There,' Sarah said. 'You look fit to attend any wedding.'

Máire was speechless at such kindness. With the blanket she would more likely blend in with the others. The last thing she wanted to do was call attention to herself at the mission.

Katchekeeluh came then, imposing in her heavy blanket and tall headdress, and told them it was time to leave. Máire followed behind the group as they filed out through the crowd of onlookers to the waiting canoe. Kowishte was there, with Natsilane and other relatives. They settled Sarah in the middle of the large carved canoe, the silver jewelry glistening in the bright sun. Kowishte climbed in, near the prow by the front paddler, and Katchekeeluh and Yedicih sat behind him. Rebecca took a place behind Sarah, at the back, where a young Chilkoot man lifted a paddle out of the canoe, ready to push off.

Máire watched the canoe leave. Sarah looked so happy now, but was that enough to endure Mrs Paxson's company down at the mission? Or was she just manifesting her own dislike of Mrs Paxson through these misgivings and the knowledge that she'd miss Sarah? She hoped Sarah would keep her promise and visit often.

Finally, when all the canoes had been launched, Natsilane and Máire prepared to climb into their own. They both thought it wise to arrive separate from the rest of the wedding party in the hope they could slip quietly into the church unnoticed among the crowd of onlookers.

Natsilane settled Máire in the canoe, her cape tucked securely around her, then handed her the cradleboard containing Little Seal.

They made their way down the river, the current carrying them with a fair speed. Máire watched the other canoes moving along ahead, their carved prows slicing the water with force. It was an impressive sight, and she felt a surge of pride to be a part of it. She looked back at Natsilane, twisting carefully against the balance of the canoe and gave him a wide smile.

He grinned at her. 'Wife, you must turn around and behave like the dignified matron you are.'

She laughed and resumed her position and looked down at Little Seal, drowsy with the rolling motion of the canoe. She let her hand drop into the water and watched it rush over her fingers, noticing the play of fractured light on the spray. Diamonds, she thought. These were the jewels she would treasure now. Moments of quiet beauty. She continued her reverie, studying the water and the life that teemed beneath while the canoe made its way rapidly downriver until, lulled by its rhythm, she dozed off.

It seemed only a brief moment later, but it must have been much longer when Natsilane called her name and pointed ahead. She turned and saw the approaching mission buildings and nearby, in the middle of the deep river, a large ship.

She strained to make out its identity through the mass of canoes that were pulling alongside of the riverbank. Its shape was familiar, but she waited until the canoe drew close enough to make out the letters before she allowed herself to acknowledge what she knew in her heart. *U.S.S. Jamestown.* She bit her lip, but reasoned that she had nothing to fear from that ship, or its crew. Her circumstances had changed. She had started a new life, and they were all in the past. Nothing could alter that.

Beyond the ship Máire could see other canoes, large ones filled with Tlingit men, black paint smeared across their faces. They brandished spears, long knives and a few rifles. Shouts rang out from the ship and as Máire and Natsilane pulled closer, she could see the men scurrying across the decks. A porthole opened and a black gun muzzle appeared, pointed out at the water. In horror Máire watched a man give orders to set fire to its fuse. It was William, his face contorted in anger. The canon's boom roared across the river, echoing against the snow-capped mountains above them.

It all took place in a matter of seconds. The canon ball thrust deep into the river while its wake surged along Máire and Natsilane's canoe and overturned it. They plunged into the water and the prow slammed into Natsilane's head, knocking him unconscious. Wave after wave of water poured over them, swallowed them whole.

'Little Seal!' Máire shouted, thrashing the water, desperate to see through the churning sea.

Natsilane's leg glanced off her thigh; she reached for it, and for a moment clutched the fringe of his hide trousers in her fingers, but then it was gone. She paddled furiously towards him. Her mouth opened to give voice to his name, but water poured in and swallowed any sound. For a moment she drifted downward, all breath gone. In that breathless moment she caught a glimpse of her son above her, securely bound in his beautifully wrought cradleboard, his long lashes closed against his perfect round cheeks, his mouth still. She reached up and pulled the cradleboard to her, while around her bubbles floated, growing larger and larger, until she could see they were grey and sleek with eyes of velvet brown. Softly the song rose up and, like a lullaby, it soothed her, surrounded her and pulled her down. And then she knew. Like her mam, she was selkie too.

THE CHOSEN MAN

J.G. HARLOND

KNOX ROBINSON
PUBLISHING
LONDON • New York

CHAPTER ONE

Cornwall, England, early March 1635

Using her clever knife and humming the necessary chant, the woman scored a circle into the turf beneath the ancient cross. The beginning at the end at the beginning. Into the circle she placed an acorn for him and marked a tree growing from its shell. Beside the tree she placed the flowers for her, blue periwinkle, an early primrose then a twig of wine red hawthorn buds for the future. Gradually, she began the sequence:

Blow the wind blow, rain the rain down ...

She had timed it exactly, the first drops of spring rain pattered on the weathered stone of the Celtic cross.

Blow the wind blow and rain the rain down,
Bring us a summer to grow more than grain.
Growing and growing, circle give life...

Aggie hummed meaning into the words, the shape, the petals and buds then scraped soft green turf back over them. The rain would do the rest.

For a moment she rested on her haunches and looked about her. Had she been seen? She put her knife in its special pocket and struggled to her feet. A storm was brewing up over the sea to the south, the wind in her face.

"Well, how can that be?" she asked the small dog waiting at her side. "How can she come from all the way over there?"

Aggie now peered through the blustering rain at the line where the old river met the sea. "That's not right," she said. "Not from foreign lands."

The Vatican, Italy, early March 1635

"Another particularly tenuous idea from Spain. Grasping at straws this time."

"Stems."

"What?"

"You mean grasping at stems."

"Is that supposed to be amusing?"

"Well the whole thing is ridiculous."

"Perhaps, but it could do significant damage," replied the younger man, who had been made a cardinal at twenty-three. He sat down behind his desk and picked up the Spanish envoy's gift to examine its jewels.

The Pope's other, less effective nephew watched his cousin raise an exquisite crucifix to the light; silver on mahogany, emeralds and purple-blue lapis lazuli from the New World: a gift from Spain – or a reminder of their territory.

"A set back in finances won't damage established Dutch tradesmen very much. I certainly can't see it having any significant effect on their war with Spain," he said.

"It will if they're using this new banking system. If the hard-working middle-classes, artisans and the like are selling tulip flowers at high prices then putting their profit in banks, and the Dutch government is using that money to finance resistance to Spain – when the market suddenly collapses there'll be a run on those banks. And if the money isn't there ... Can't you see? That's what the Spanish are after; trying to undermine confidence, shake and weaken new foundations."

And this is why I am a cardinal and you are my secretary, he added silently to himself.

"So, if an ordinary Dutchman buys one of these plants then sells it and makes a profit, and he puts that money into a bank, but the bank uses it to finance the war - then if everyone wants their money back at the same time and it's not there -"

"The Dutch economy *could* falter and Spain's Flanders army *could* march straight back into the United Provinces. Except," the young cardinal placed the crucifix back on his desk, "that is not exactly what our Holy Father wants. He's not convinced Spain should regain The Netherlands. Of course he can't say that, and nor must you."

"But if we act against the plan we alienate the King of Spain and the Emperor in Vienna."

"Yes. Rather more than 'ridiculous', isn't it?" The cardinal looked at his older cousin. "*I* shall have to handle it carefully and use the right people."

"Who are?"

"Well to start with we need someone that won't be missed to deliver messages. Then we need someone that doesn't miss anything as our overseer: preferably someone with undercover experience. Father Rogelio would suit. He's been involved in the Black Order for years; runs agents in most European cities and no one has any idea who or what he is. Naturally we cannot be involved."

"And who will bring about the desired outcome? Or are you going to let the Spanish arrange that?"

"Oh, no; our desired outcome is not quite theirs remember."

"Ah. Well in that case you need someone that travels between Italy and the Low Countries, who already deals in tulips so he knows what's what, and someone completely unethical. He'll demand a high price for his silence afterwards I should think."

"Rogelio will arrange his silence. First we need to choose the right man."

"Our family in Florence uses a Genoese silk merchant. He has something of a reputation and not just for dealing in exotic goods."

"Genoese? Convenient. The Genoese virtually run Spain; they

certainly fight her wars."

"I say Genoese, he's actually from Portovenere, which means -"

"He's as good as a pirate. Mm - that also means his loyalty goes where the booty lies. He could be in anybody's pay."

"Or nobody's. I understood pirates only looked out for themselves."

"Precisely the point I'm making."

The older cousin tried to avoid looking confused and said, "Pirates are not known for loyalty or scruples. I doubt anyone will come looking for him later."

"Is he dashing?"

"Dashing?"

"Good-looking, well-favoured."

"Ah, yes. My sisters met him once, don't know how, they tittered about him for days – weeks afterwards. If that's what you mean?"

"That's what I mean." The Pope's younger nephew weighed the priceless object in his hands. Without looking up, he said, "Find him."

Visit our website to download free historical fiction, historical romance and fantasy short stories by your favourite authors. While there, purchase our titles direct and earn loyalty points. Sign up for our newsletter and our free titles giveaway. Join our community to discuss history, romance and fantasy with fans of each genre. We also encourage you to submit your stories anonymously and let your peers review your writing.

www.knoxrobinsonpublishing.com